LAST SUMMER *at* MAINE CHANCE

A Novel

JESSICA EVERETT

Published by Sourcebooks Landmark, an imprint of Sourcebooks
1935 Brookdale RD, Naperville, IL 60563-2773
(630) 961-3900
sourcebooks.com

Cataloging-in-Publication Data is on file with the Library of Congress.

Printed and bound in the United States of America.
VP 10 9 8 7 6 5 4 3 2 1

PRAISE FOR

LAST SUMMER AT MAINE CHANCE

"Sparkling, smart, and big-hearted, *Last Summer at Maine Chance* transports readers to Elizabeth Arden's legendary Maine spa in the 1950s. A scholarship student hiding a staff job, a housekeeper guarding family secrets, and a widowed artist searching for renewal find their lives unexpectedly intertwined over one transformative summer. Jessica Everett has written a captivating story of ambition, reinvention, and the bonds that change us."

—Christina Baker Kline,
#1 *New York Times* bestselling author

"I loved this charming, witty, and heartwarming story of ambition, self-discovery, and the courage to break societal expectations. Jessica Everett's novel, set in an iconic place and time, is funny and full of surprises—and it delivers a powerful message that sometimes the best investment is in yourself. A must-read for anyone who believes in rewriting the rules."

—Susan Wiggs, #1 *New York Times* bestselling author

"A charming and spirited tale brimming with wit, heart, and romance. Jessica Everett brings 1950s Maine to vivid life with grace and insight. *Last Summer at Maine Chance* introduces us to a plucky heroine navigating the fault lines of class, gender, and ambition. Even the legendary Elizabeth Arden comes to life on the page, and the setting, equal parts glamorous and revealing, is as luxurious as the story itself. Cynthia Proctor's journey is as enlightening as it is engaging—a story of self-discovery and transformation."

—Patti Callahan Henry, *New York Times* bestselling author

"*Last Summer at Maine Chance* by Jessica Everett is the perfect summer read. This fun, fascinating novel, set in 1954, is as relevant and significant to women today as it was back then. Book clubs will love it!"

—Nancy Thayer, *New York Times* bestselling author

"Set at a rural spa in Maine and told through the voices of three women, young and old, rich and poor, this book gives a great feel for the 1950s. You will cheer the young heroine who battles the snobbery and prejudices of the time to come out on top. It's also a perfect vacation read with an escape to Maine."

—Rhys Bowen, *New York Times* bestselling author

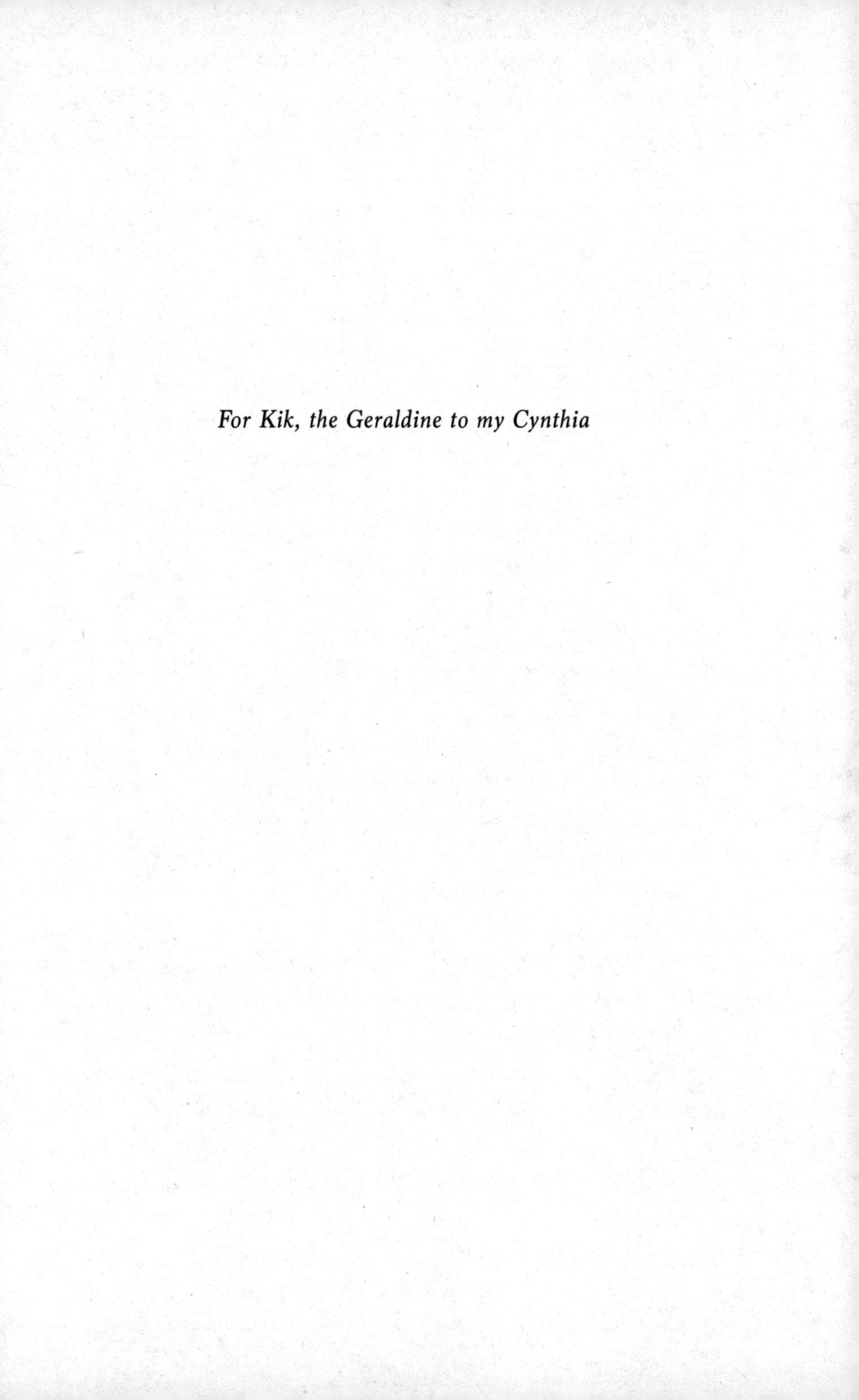

For Kik, the Geraldine to my Cynthia

CHAPTER 1

Cynthia

Late May 1954

IT BEGGARED BELIEF THAT THE ordinary-looking man in front of her held her future in his hands. Nothing in the slope of his slim shoulders or the tilt of his head, only thinly covered in graying hair, suggested the outsize influence he wielded in his chosen field. But one way or another, she needed an answer. Cynthia raised her fist and rapped on the sturdy wooden doorframe.

Professor Avery glanced up from a stack of papers on his large oak desk and waved her in. Even from the doorway, she could see bright-red ink scrawled across the uppermost sheet on the pile. An enormous D+ was circled at the top of the page. Her heart thudded as she stepped closer, silently assuring herself that the grade surely could not belong to her.

"Close the door, please, Miss Proctor," he said as he gestured to the chair opposite his desk before riffling through the stacks in front of him.

Cynthia smoothed her skirt and lowered herself into the chair.

"You must be wondering why I wanted to see you," he said, leaning back heavily in his seat.

She had thought of little else since she discovered a note from the professor in her mailbox at the women's dormitory, requesting she appear at his office the next day.

"Considering you were somewhat involved in the research, I thought it only right to let you to know before you head off for the summer that the article has been accepted for publication by the *American Economic Review*."

Researching and writing the article had been a great deal of extra work over the past two semesters, but she had enjoyed every minute of it. When the professor had asked for a volunteer to assist with his paper on the projected economic impact of the planned Maine Turnpike expansion on tourism, she had been both surprised and delighted to have been chosen for the role. What had started out as a way to prove that she could hold her own in a major dominated by male students had turned into a passion project. During the spring semester, she had skipped out on dances, sporting events, and even an occasional lucrative babysitting job in order to devote herself to the research.

She found herself engrossed in the details, like the bold decision to fund the nation's second superhighway project through bonds instead of public funds, and the innovative and controversial use of asphalt instead of concrete as the paving material. While such things might not make every girl's imagination soar, Cynthia had found the information provided fertile ground for her own theories of how promising Maine's economic future could be. Boot factories, textile mills, and even commercial fishing might someday fail, but she could not imagine a day would come when the beauty of her home state would not draw throngs of visitors, at least in the warm months.

Professor Avery had encouraged her to do the grunt work of reading studies and interpreting the data as well as to write the majority of the actual article. She hadn't minded, though. Not only was the project engrossing, but she was also betting that her work would put her in the running for a paid job as a research assistant to Professor Avery. It was a prestigious post, and one that she needed, financially, if she was to continue her studies. She was all the more pleased that she had a subscription to the magazine and would be able to see the fruits of her labor, and her own name in print.

"That's wonderful news. I'm delighted to have been involved in something so successful. I hope to be able to assist you in your upcoming projects," she said.

"Duly noted," he said, looking pointedly at the pile of papers still requiring his attention. He flicked his glance back to her face. "Is there something else?"

Cynthia pressed her hands against her thighs, damp wicking through the light cotton of her skirt. It was now or never. After all, she was due to leave campus the following day.

"I wondered if you have come to a decision about the research-assistant job?"

He looked up as if surprised by the question. "The paid position for next year?"

"Yes. I applied for it when the job first posted several weeks ago, and I hoped to hear something before I left for the summer."

"The position has been filled," he said, picking up his red pen and tapping it on the desk between them.

Her stomach clenched. "May I ask by whom?"

"I don't suppose he will mind if I share his name. I am told on good authority that being selected to assist me is something students are proud to claim, as I am sure you can attest." He smiled at her. "Ronald Dryden was given the job."

She had no firsthand knowledge of Ronald's bank balance, but if his wardrobe, late-model car, and the trips he reported taking with his family were anything to go by, the stipend from a researcher job would have little impact upon it. What she did know firsthand, from attending several economics classes with him, was that he was a lackluster scholar at best. He often arrived late for class, contributed little of value to discussions, and was ready with excuses when it came to his responsibilities on group assignments.

"I must admit that I am surprised to hear this. I had thought that my work on the article would put me ahead in the running," she said.

He dropped his pen back onto the desk and leaned forward, propping his elbows on its cluttered surface.

"Surprised? Come, come, now. You're much too bright to think an opportunity like that would be wasted on a coed when there are young men like Ronald, who will actually be able to make use of the experience in a career."

"Are you saying that you don't believe I will be able to make a career in this field myself?" Didn't the publication of an article she had researched and written prove she had promise?

Professor Avery's gray eyebrows lifted. "I hardly think it likely. You are a woman, after all. Given your commendable grasp of economic theory, you must admit that women are a poor investment."

Cynthia stiffened as though she had been slapped. An unwelcome lump formed in her throat. How foolish she had been to think that she would be the exception to the rule. Sadly, no female student at Barlow College had ever been awarded a paid position as a researcher. Heck, they had only begun to allow female-student admittance to the college during the early years of the Depression. Still, she had held out hope that somehow there would be a solution to her predicament. It had been vanishingly unlikely that she would receive a scholarship to attend in the first place. She had buried herself in her studies, forcing the notion that she might not be in a position to complete her degree from her mind, telling herself she had beaten the odds so far. The expression on her professor's face told her that her luck had run out. Still, she couldn't risk confronting him or complaining. Careers had been launched by a recommendation from Professor Avery, although she was pretty sure, so far, he'd only recommended men. As a woman in the field of economics, she needed every advantage she could get.

"Are there any other sources of funding that you know of?" she asked. "Is there a paid post for another professor, or even in a different department?"

He removed his glasses and buffed the lenses with a clean handkerchief. Cynthia recognized the gesture as one that preceded an announcement that the majority of the class had performed poorly on an exam. Slowly, he slipped the glasses back on his face and shook his head again.

"Anything of that sort has been assigned months ago. And again, any positions would have been awarded to male students rather than coeds, regardless of their qualifications."

"So there is nothing available that could help me fund the next two years of my studies?" she asked. "If I don't find something, I'll be forced to withdraw from Barlow."

"Nothing comes to mind. But I have every confidence that a clever girl like you will figure something out." His gaze moved over her shoulder towards the door.

She glanced behind her and spotted a student from her microeconomics class hovering in the hallway. Her financial woes were not something she wished to discuss with anyone other than her intimates. Most of her fellow students would not have any idea what it was like to rely on financial aid to pay for their college experience. Barlow had a few scholarship students, to be sure, but the vast majority of her classmates came from wealthy families who had never had to wonder how their bills would be paid.

She nodded as if she agreed with his assessment of her resourcefulness and slipped out the door without another word. She didn't trust herself to speak. A tirade of angry words jostled on the tip of her tongue. Nothing in the study of economics had taught her that women were a poor investment. Her legs wobbled with rage as she moved down the hallway. Her gaze ran over posters and flyers announcing trips to Europe, seaside cottage rentals, and language lessons. Everything listed involved spending money, and lots of it. Nothing whatsoever mentioned a way to earn any.

Cynthia hadn't arrived at college with an intention to study economics. In fact, she had thought she might study English, with an eye towards a career in journalism. The romantic notion of being a star reporter at a bustling newspaper appealed to her. But when a scheduling challenge led her adviser to suggest she register for Introduction to Economics in her freshman year, her plans took an entirely new tack.

To her surprise, the study of economics provided her with an unexpected lens on the world. So much of life had always felt so tumultuous. No one who had spent much of their childhood witnessing the chaos of a World War would discount the value of predictability. But her studies had shown her that it just might be possible to explain human behavior, and even the way people made decisions that led to their actions. She found that economics provided a practical way to combine her aptitude for mathematics with her interest in history, politics, and psychology. Before that introductory class had ended, she was utterly smitten. Now the chance to make a career of it seemed to be slipping out of her reach.

The lump returned to her throat as she meandered past the stately brick library where she had spent so many hours lost in her studies over the past two years. The weather had turned exceptionally fine after a bitterly cold, snowy Maine winter, and students sat in small groups scattered about the velvety lawn surrounding the building. As she passed by, their easy laughter left her feeling even more isolated.

A surge of determination filled her chest. After all the work she had done to be admitted to Barlow in the first place, she was not going to concede defeat so easily. As the professor had said, a girl like her could surely think of something, couldn't she? She picked up the pace as she turned in the direction of the women's dormitory.

CHAPTER 2

Cynthia

THE ROOM SHE SHARED WITH three other girls had been mostly cleared out. Sharon and Carol had each left earlier in the week for a European vacation and a shopping trip to New York City, respectively. Only Pauline's bed remained, spread with linens, and her desk, covered with papers, a box of dusting powder, and several half-wilted bouquets from her many admirers. Pauline lay stretched out on her unmade bed, her eyes turned towards the ceiling. She rolled over and propped her face in her hand as Cynthia stepped into the room.

"You look like someone just ran over your dog," she said, swinging her feet towards the floor and sitting on the edge of the bed. "Does that mean you didn't get the job?"

If only that were the sole problem. She hadn't wanted to mention the full extent of her financial troubles to anyone until she was sure how dire they might prove to be. Even though she considered Pauline to be her closest friend at Barlow, she had not yet revealed the precarious nature of her situation. But after the meeting with Professor Avery, she craved Pauline's support.

Cynthia crossed the room and opened a drawer in her desk. She pulled a sheet of official Barlow letterhead from underneath a pile of notebooks and extended it to her friend. Pauline took it with the same enthusiasm Cynthia's mother showed for occupied mousetraps. Cynthia watched as Pauline's eyes moved back and forth over the brief lines of text.

"Although we have decided to offer our financial support to another deserving student, we wish you well with all of your future endeavors," she read aloud as she reached the end.

"If they really cared one whit about my future, they would have extended my scholarship," Cynthia said. She tried to keep the bitter note from her voice but needn't have worried. Pauline was on her feet, pacing the floor, her manicured hands on her slim hips.

"So, you don't have a scholarship and you didn't get the researcher job. Now what?" Pauline asked.

"I don't know yet. I asked Professor Avery about any other opportunities, but he said they've all been filled by male students."

"But I thought Professor Avery valued your work on that article. How could he not find a spot for you?" Pauline asked.

"Apparently, the problem is my gender, not my ability."

Pauline's eyes widened. "What about your parents? Won't they help if you ask?"

As much as Cynthia valued her friendship with Pauline, it

could be painful to be reminded of how different their situations truly were. If her friend weren't so good-natured, it would have been easy to resent her for her lack of understanding about how the world worked for so many. Pauline's mother had descended from a Maine lumber baron, and as far as Cynthia could tell, penny-pinching was not within living memory of any of her close relations.

"My parents don't have the means to assist me. Asking them would just make them feel bad, and it still wouldn't be of any use."

"How about if I ask my parents for the money? I know they have it." Pauline waved a slim hand in the air as if able to brush away the problem with the flick of her wrist. If only it were that easy. Even if Pauline's parents were so eager to part with large sums of money, her own would die of shame if she was to even consider accepting any kind of a handout. It was simply not the way things were done. Convincing them to allow her to attend college, especially one with a reputation for exclusivity, had been difficult enough. If they were to suspect she had become high-and-mighty and forgotten herself as a result of it, they would order her home even if she could find a way to pay for the rest of her education.

"I appreciate the offer, but I couldn't possibly ask your parents for money."

"How would that be any different from asking for a scholarship?" Pauline said.

"It isn't the same at all. I didn't ask for a scholarship; I applied for one. There was a lengthy process that wasn't based on personal connections."

Pauline shook her head, sending her glossy blond hair spilling about her shoulders. "Mother says that everything is about personal connections. If you won't allow me to ask them for help, what are you going to do?"

"Even though my parents are going to pitch a fit at the idea of me working, I suppose I shall have to take a job as soon as I can find one and hope that I can earn enough over the summer to pay for at least the next semester."

"You know, Mount Vernon is a tourist town. I am sure there must be all sorts of jobs available in a place like that. You could still come for the summer like we planned and use some of your time to look for a job. That way your parents won't even need to know what you're up to."

Pauline had a point. Maine had been a tourist destination for decades, and places on the coast or at the lakes were among the most popular. There was a better chance of her finding something in a resort town than there was back home in South Berwick, where the mills were closing down and outsiders rarely ventured unless they had lost their way. And if she was honest, she was not looking forward to heading home in the least. Her breaks from college had become increasingly tedious. Both of her parents had strong opinions about how a woman her age should behave and made sure to remind her at every opportunity. Her father would not approve of her taking a job to earn tuition money any more than he did of her mother working after he'd returned from overseas. She doubted either of her parents would allow her to work at anything other than babysitting, and even if she worked round the clock all summer, there was no way she could earn enough from that.

While her parents were more than willing to inform her and her brother that they did not have much money left over for extras, they had no intention of allowing the outside world to share that knowledge. They lived in dread of the neighbors knowing their business. If she found a job in Mount Vernon, she could simply tell her parents she had been invited to extend her stay for the entire summer with Pauline's family. It would be the perfect solution to her problem, even if she hated the idea of lying to her parents.

Besides, she enjoyed spending time with Pauline. And, she had to admit, she was more than curious about her friend's life away from Barlow. The things she shared about her family and their lifestyle were entirely different from what Cynthia had experienced. An even darker thought crossed her mind: If she couldn't earn enough money to return to school in the fall, it was likely the last time she would get to spend with her friend. She doubted their paths would overlap in the future if she was forced to drop out.

"Are you sure you won't feel used if I go with you just so I can look for a job?"

"Of course not." Pauline held up a finger. "But I have no intention of letting you spend all of your time working. There are at least as many eligible young men from good families as there are jobs to be had."

"If I manage to find a job, I'm not sure I'll have much time left over for dates."

Cynthia's lack of a social life had been a sore trial to Pauline ever since they met. She had done her darnedest to fix her up time and time again, but to no avail. Cynthia had come to college for more than an "MRS degree," regardless of how hard her friend tried to pair her off.

"Those are my terms. If you want my help in finding a job, you have to accept it for finding a boyfriend as well. And think of how pleased your mother will be if you wind up getting engaged before the summer is up."

Pauline had a point. Her mother had asked about potential suitors in each and every one of her letters. She prodded her mercilessly during school breaks as to why she had not attracted a boyfriend, given how many young men were enrolled. It was all very tedious. Cynthia wasn't opposed to falling in love, but she was not at all interested in following in her mother's footsteps. Still, it would be nice to send letters home that put her mother's mind a bit more at ease, at least as far as her efforts were concerned. There was no reason not to acquiesce.

"It's a deal."

"There's just one other thing." A flicker of discomfort crossed

Pauline's face. "I think it would be best if you don't mention to my parents that you are looking for a job. They won't approve of it any more than yours will."

Cynthia's stomach squeezed. Maybe she ought not accompany Pauline to Mount Vernon after all.

"Are you sure it's a good idea for me to visit? I have to find a job."

"Of course you should still come. My parents won't have any idea about what you are up to so long as you don't come right out and tell them."

The idea of deceiving her hosts didn't match with Cynthia's notion of what being a good guest entailed. Her stomach pulled into a tight knot.

"I feel uncomfortable doing something behind your parents' backs."

"It isn't your fault that they're snobs. Besides, you don't plan to mention your job search to yours, either, do you?"

That settled it. "How soon do we leave?"

CHAPTER 3

Cynthia

"YOU'RE ABSOLUTELY CERTAIN YOUR PARENTS won't mind me bringing so much stuff with me? It looks like I plan to move in," Cynthia said as she wrestled with the zipper on her baby-blue suitcase, willing it to shut. Halfway closed, it juddered to a stop, a bit of clothing trapped in its metal teeth. She reminded herself of all the examples she had seen while at Barlow of how differently the very wealthy lived. On occasion, Pauline had mentioned the parties that her parents threw. They never sounded in the least like the bridge nights with nibbles that her mother hosted on the last Friday evening of each month. Pauline had never spoken of snack dishes shaped like playing-card suits, or tiny sandwiches cut into diamonds and hearts. Rather, she remarked on valet parking and ice sculptures commissioned to keep the shrimp cocktail chilled long into the night. From the offhand way Pauline described it all, her surname might as well have been Gatsby instead of Mayhew.

Pauline gently pushed Cynthia's hand aside and deftly coaxed the material from the zipper's teeth, closing the suitcase effortlessly.

"I'm sure my mother is delighted for me to have a companion from Barlow staying with us. She worries that I'll spend too much time with the locals," Pauline said.

"Why would she worry about a thing like that?"

Pauline dropped her gaze and, for the first time since Cynthia had known her, hesitated before answering a question about her family. Then she smoothed an imaginary wrinkle from her shell-pink cashmere cardigan and flashed one of her confident smiles.

"Doesn't your mother worry about the most unlikely things, too, sometimes?" she asked as she tugged on a pair of gloves in the same pale shade as her sweater. She fiddled with the tiny pearl buttons at the wrists before reaching for a straw hat.

Cynthia's mother did worry about the most unexpected things. She had the usual concerns about polio and more ordinary childhood diseases like measles and mumps, but her imagination tended to run wild when it came to the safety of her family. When Cynthia and her brother were small, she had persistent fears that they would be killed by falling down the attic stairs, by running out in front of a speeding car, or by malnutrition. She never allowed them to play on the third floor, among the old cedar chests and toys from her parents' childhoods, lest they take a tumble. She had insisted on holding their hands with bone-crushing intensity when approaching the street, and she obsessed over feeding them sufficient protein at every meal.

Strangely, she had been far less besieged by such preoccupations during the war years, when so many other women were beset with worry. If anything, Cynthia's mother had bloomed during those tumultuous times. War work and the sense of independence it had brought along with it appeared to agree with her far more than the role of housewife had. Cynthia remembered her mother singing as she readied herself for her shifts at the textile mill. She hummed as she swiped on Victory Red lipstick and tucked her long hair up into a turban to keep it safe from the machinery. Not only did the work seem to agree with her, so did the ability to choose how to spend any extra money she had earned, often on treats or toys for Cynthia and her brother.

It wasn't until Cynthia's father returned from serving overseas and announced that he didn't hold with any wife of his going out to work that she once again began obsessing over the danger everyday life surely posed to her children. With little success, she tried to appear engrossed in their idle prattle and take pride in other diversions. She devoted herself to starching and pressing the family's clothing into crisp perfection, mastering molded gelatin salads, and bottoming out the house twice a year like clockwork.

But everyone who had seen her during those fleeting war

years noticed the change, and the most astute of them pulled Cynthia aside to ask if her mother was quite herself. It was clear to everyone but her own husband that she was not. By the time Cynthia was thirteen, she had decided she would do whatever it took to create a career for herself that could not be so easily set aside by someone else's whim.

If heading to Mount Vernon—even if she wasn't entirely sure of her welcome—was what it would take to reach her goal, then that was what she would do. She reached for her own gloves, a navy pair that were woefully practical compared with Pauline's. "The one thing she doesn't seem to be worried about is my visit to your lake house."

"Perhaps that's because I phoned her and mentioned all the eligible boys I plan to introduce you to during your visit."

Cynthia's stomach squeezed. "You didn't."

"Of course I didn't. I wish to keep the pleasure of meddling in your love life all to myself." With that, she tucked her hand under Cynthia's arm and tugged her towards the door. "Now, let's go before we miss our train. Mother will be in a snit if we do."

Cynthia looked back over her shoulder, casting what she hoped wouldn't be her last peek at the inside of a Barlow dorm room. Then she heard Professor Avery's voice echoing in her ear. She lifted her chin. Surely a clever girl like herself would figure out a way to make it back.

Cynthia followed Pauline as she descended from the train onto the platform. In less than two hours' time, she had made the journey from Barlow College near the coast to the inland Belgrade Lakes region in central Maine. Men in pale suits and straw hats milled about as the train whistled and chugged, pulling away from the station. At the far end of the platform, a newsboy waved a paper over his head and added his hawking cries to the clamor. Pauline lifted a gloved hand to shield her eyes from the sun and looked out at the cars parked nearby. Suddenly, she raised her other hand in a wave.

A middle-aged man strode up the short set of steps, a broad smile on his face. Pauline moved towards him and wrapped him in an embrace. With his golden-blond hair and large blue eyes, no one would fail to recognize him as Pauline's father.

As Cynthia noticed the expression of joy on Mr. Mayhew's face, she felt a pang of envy. Not only was Pauline wealthier when it came to money, but from the looks of it, she was also richer in love. Cynthia's father was not the sort to tolerate public displays of affection. He wasn't one to either appreciate or offer them in private either. Never before had she felt the disparity in their backgrounds so acutely. She hung back, hesitant to interrupt. Pauline gave her father a peck on the cheek, then released him.

"Mother said she was sending Parker to collect us. She mentioned you would be too busy at the newspaper to get away," she said.

"I told him not to bother. You know I'm never too busy

for my favorite girl." He turned to Cynthia. "You must be the impressive roommate I've heard so much about."

Cynthia had no idea that her friend had ever mentioned her to her family other than to ask if she might visit. She felt her cheeks pinking at his compliment.

"And now you are lucky enough to meet Cynthia for yourself," Pauline said.

Mr. Mayhew took a step forward and stretched out a hand. "It's a pleasure to put a face to the name. And what a pretty face it is," he said. Before she had to construct a response, he let go of her hand and turned back to his daughter. "This cannot be all of your luggage."

He gestured to the train cases each of the girls had carried in the compartment with them.

"Of course not. It's a good thing you brought the station wagon instead of your convertible," Pauline said.

Just then, a porter appeared, pushing a luggage rack piled high with Pauline's set of oyster-gray leather suitcases. A second porter followed on his heels, guiding Cynthia's own blue ones. Mr. Mayhew waved them over and spent the next few moments ensuring that the luggage was properly stowed in or on his wood-paneled station wagon. Cynthia slid into the back seat, leaving Pauline to sit beside her father.

He pulled the car out onto the main street and soon turned off onto a road that swiftly left the small shops and eateries of Mount Vernon behind. He pointed out the window of the station wagon as a sliver of sparkling water appeared through a gap in the tree line. Billowing white clouds drifted overhead, draping shadows over the treetops and across the small islands dotting the lake. The road bent away from the shoreline, and once again the lake disappeared from view.

"Is that Long Pond?" Cynthia asked.

"It sure is. Our camp is farther along the lake, but it's the same body of water."

Cynthia leaned out the window, feeling the wind blow her long hair away from her face. She felt a surge of excitement, the first in what seemed like ages, as she caught a broader view of Long Pond. She spied several boats, one pulling a water skier behind it, crisscrossing the lake. A surge of pride in her home state filled her chest. Long Pond was but one example of Maine's enduring beauty. Of lakes, there were aplenty, but then, too, there was the section of the Appalachian Mountains that terminated at Mount Katahdin. The Great North Woods, with its vast acreage of towering trees and thunderous rivers, offered vistas bold and untamed. And who could forget the coastline, with its rock-strewn beaches, reeling gulls, and quaint villages? Truly, Maine in summer left one spoilt for choice.

Pauline had told her that her mother's family had owned the camp for decades, and that she had spent summers there throughout her entire life. Most Mainers who had a second home of any sort called it a "camp," that term covering anything from tar-paper shacks used for hunting weekends to palatial estates designed to host high-society guests. For Cynthia, though, the word conjured up visions of a wooden structure with an outhouse and an old-fashioned cast-iron cookstove. She tried to picture her friend inviting her to any place that could be considered the least bit rustic.

Mr. Mayhew turned off Castle Island Road and onto what amounted to barely more than a dirt track wending its way through the pines and descending steadily, tantalizingly, towards the glinting blue of the lake. Tiny cabins—some of them could charitably be called shacks—lurked in the shadows, well back from the road. All about them, weathered hammocks sagged between the trees, and loose dogs and overall-clad children tumbled about in piles in the pine needle–strewn dooryards. Did the Mayhews really enjoy spending the summers in the Rusticator tradition that was so popular with the exorbitantly rich at the end of the last century?

Mr. Mayhew slowed the jouncing car to a funereal pace and leaned over the steering wheel.

"It's just up ahead, Cynthia," he said, a lilt of excitement tinging his voice.

He maneuvered the car around another sharp bend, and she felt her breath catch in her throat. The trees gave way to open lots that ran straight down to the wide expanse of shimmering blue water. Enormous houses with wide covered porches and private docks with boats tethered to them sat at respectful distances from one another, nary a shack in sight. Pauline turned in her seat and smiled at Cynthia.

"Beautiful, isn't it?" she asked as her father turned into a graveled driveway flanked by fieldstone pillars.

Cynthia nodded. The house sat nestled beneath a towering cathedral of pines. As soon as the car eased to a stop, she reached for the door handle. She pushed it open and stepped out onto the wide front yard. She lifted a hand to shield her eyes from the slanting sun and spotted a dock floating a hundred yards or so from the shore. A half dozen tanned bodies were stretched out on the dock, and even from such a distance, Cynthia could tell that they were about her own age. Almost as a confirmation, one of the shirtless figures shoved another from the dock in a youthful demonstration of horseplay.

Pauline hurried past her and stopped at the top of the steps leading down to the shore below. She raised both arms above her head and waved them back and forth. The figure who had shoved his companion into the water raised his own hand and vigorously gestured for her to join the group on the dock. Pauline nodded before turning back towards Cynthia. She glanced at her father, who was lifting luggage from the car, and lowered her voice.

"What did I tell you about eligible young men? I'll bet I can find you a boyfriend before you can find a job."

Cynthia looked towards the floating dock and fervently hoped that her friend was wrong. If luck was on her side, she'd be gainfully employed by the same time tomorrow.

CHAPTER 4

Geraldine

Late May 1954

IF THERE WAS ONE THING Geraldine knew about herself, it was that she had always been considered outrageous. Her mother had said it, her grandmother had said it, and on occasion, even her dead husband, Anselm, had mentioned it. Geraldine could not see what all the fuss was about. Why was it perfectly acceptable for the men of the world to run around saying exactly what they thought and what they wanted without recrimination, but it wasn't remotely the done thing for women? No, she had decided early on that she would live as she saw fit, regardless of the consequences.

Fortunately for her, such leanings and inclinations led her straight into the life artistic. Not only were such thoughts acceptable in the artistic world, but they were also often encouraged. Opera singers, actresses, and artists were all known for their temperamental behavior, which suited Geraldine just fine. Her father hadn't even batted an eyelash when she announced her intention to travel as a young woman to Paris and study at the École des Beaux-Arts for a year.

He had given his permission wholeheartedly, with one condition: Geraldine could have her year abroad, but when she returned, she would be required to fulfill her duty as a daughter of the household and marry the man her father had chosen for her, the son of another wealthy family in their social set, and one she had never seriously considered as a match. Her father explained that a union between the families was highly desirable to him, and if travel to Paris was important to her, she would do as he required. She readily agreed, telling herself that perhaps her father would change his mind before the year was up. She should have known better. Her father was famous for never changing his mind once it was made.

When she had returned home with a portfolio full of avant-garde paintings and a wardrobe that raised eyebrows in her rural Maine community, she knew she would never quite fit in again. Fortunately for Geraldine, her husband had found her behavior endearing. He had enjoyed his bride's boldness and benefited from her willingness to tell things as she saw them. Their marriage had not been one blessed with children, but it had been blessedly without difficulties. There had been more than enough money to indulge both their joint and separate passions. Anselm's love of fine houses and water views had led them to purchase the house on Long Pond. Geraldine's skill as an artist had brought her fame throughout the country as a landscape painter. Together, they had rubbed along quite comfortably, until his demise two years earlier. She had done absolutely nothing outrageous since.

She still found herself depleted by grief over his passing. It happened one evening, as a newly acquired housemaid entered the dining room with a soup tureen held aloft, a look of terror on her face as though she might drop it should the least little thing startle her. Just as the poor girl had placed it in front of Anselm and whisked off the bone-china lid, Geraldine's husband let out a groan and grasped both arms of his ornately carved dining room chair with his large hands. The maid dropped the soup tureen lid and let out a gasp of her own when it shattered as soon as it struck the floor.

It was funny how one's mind tried to make sense of incomprehensible things. Geraldine quite distinctly remembered feeling far more annoyed at the loss of the serving dish than worried about the state of her husband. At the time, it had seemed as though he had deliberately provoked the poor girl. It took her far longer to realize something had been wrong with him than that property had been damaged. She had started to chide him—after all, servants were not necessarily the easiest thing to acquire in the modern world—when she realized his eyes were bulging and his face was turning purple.

Before she could rise from her chair to investigate matters further, he had slithered underneath the table and banged his head upon the floor. It was a spectacularly undignified end to a decorous life. When Geraldine thought of the scene even two years on, the thing she most remembered was the fact that he was wearing mismatched socks beneath his carpet slippers at the moment of his death. In fact, sketches of his feet had been the only works of art she had managed to produce since that evening.

Still, she had not struck such a very bad bargain in the end. Anselm had been kind to her in his way and had demanded very little that she did not wish to give. He had turned a blind eye to any indiscretions she might have indulged in with far more interesting men of their acquaintance, and she had done the same whenever his attentions wandered. And her year in Paris had set her up with sufficient skills to launch her on a lifetime of artistic success. Shortly after they had returned from their honeymoon—another trip to Europe—she informed her husband that she would require a room of her own to be set up as an art studio. Not one to miss the chance to indulge his new bride, he had readily acquiesced, offering her the opportunity to take her pick of the rooms their new house included. She had settled on one on the third floor looking out over the lake, its wide windows offering just the right sort of light throughout most of the year.

During the many years of their marriage, she had thrown herself into painting after painting, capturing the lake at all times of the year and almost every hour of the day. She had luck with her reputation too. Anselm had been most willing to entertain lavishly, and they cultivated friendships with gallery owners and art critics who made it a point to indulge in the current fashion for travel to Maine during the summer months. Before long, her works were hanging in galleries and museums throughout the country. She had been stunned when the realization came over her that Anselm, with his predictable conversation and stolid dependability, had been—if not her muse, exactly—the presence that made it possible for works of great beauty to flow from her brush and onto the canvas. Every day since his death, she had sat in her studio, looking out over the lake and feeling limp with emptiness.

Months had passed, and she'd produced nothing new. A hum of panic had rumbled through her mind almost constantly. The week before Anselm died, her agent had booked a gallery exhibit, promising never-before-seen works. At the time, she had been delighted. After Anselm died, she had to ask for the show to be rescheduled again and again. Producing any new work without her husband's steady presence had proved impossible. The show was now scheduled for November, which still felt too soon.

But finally, time and the warming weather seemed to be working their magic on her. The fog of her grief was ebbing away, slowly but noticeably. As she lay in bed listening to a jay calling out the latest gossip to its neighbors, she pictured the blue of its feathers and how they would compare to the color of the lake beyond. She could almost smell the familiar scent of linseed oil and mineral spirits as she remembered the joy of squeezing bright blobs of pigment onto her well-worn wooden palette. She felt a slight stirring in her heart that she had almost forgotten could be there. Could it be that she was ready to return to her work?

She swung her legs from her bed and hurriedly pulled on a pair of dungarees and a cotton blouse that had seen better days. Arriving in the breakfast room, she astonished and delighted Mrs. Burns, her long-suffering cook/housekeeper, by asking for an omelet instead of waving away any suggestion of food. She managed several forkfuls before the housemaid placed a stack of mail at her elbow. Her stomach soured as she spotted Louise's elegant script on the topmost letter. Geraldine slit the envelope with her butter knife and plucked out a thick sheet of stationery. She should have known better than to read correspondence at the table, especially when it came from her in-laws. Both her appetite and improved mood abandoned her as she skimmed the missive: Louise cheerily announced that the whole lot of them planned to arrive that very afternoon.

The sprawling estate on the lake had been part and parcel of her large inheritance from her husband. Unfortunately, so had his extended family, who had taken to visiting just as soon as the Maine spring had given way to summer. Since her title had changed from wife to widow, the whole troupe of them had generally confined their unwelcome presence to frequent letters and occasional telephone calls. But come the mildest months, they seemingly could not resist the lure of the motto on the state's license plates: *Vacationland.*

Despite the fact that she had never proffered anything remotely resembling an invitation, she'd made an effort to be the sort of hostess everyone expected her to be each time they appeared on her doorstep. Without a word of recrimination, she had put up with innumerable toddlers grasping every surface of her immaculate house with their sticky little hands. She had graciously endured condescending inquiries after her health by members of the younger generation as their predatory gazes roamed over her home, silently toting up the value of the art hanging on the walls and the antique rugs spread across the gleaming hardwood floors. She had smiled at his ne'er-do-well younger brothers when they pressed her for loans or offered to relieve her of the burden of managing her own finances.

But of all of them, Louise was the most repellant. Not only had she made a habit of treating Geraldine's house as her own, but she was also an indefatigable social climber. Geraldine wondered how the woman managed not to bloody her own nose with the lofty social heights she seemed determined to scale. Incredibly, Louise had proved remarkably adept at making friends with prominent families all around the lake. Geraldine suspected it was the younger woman's habit of dropping the Putnam name into conversation early and often.

Just as a dark mood threatened to envelop her once again, she remembered that she was considered outrageous. *Chin up,* she chided herself. A change was as good as a rest. Geraldine Putnam was not the sort to allow herself to be bested, even by her own dark thoughts and certainly not by other people.

She pushed back her chair and crossed the room, passing through the wide hallway and into the morning room. Settling into the seat of the telephone table, she opened a small drawer and removed her address book. Within a few moments' time, her outlook had brightened once more, and she returned to the breakfast table.

She reached for the bell placed conveniently at hand, and the housemaid appeared so swiftly Geraldine wondered if she had been hovering just outside the door.

"Yes, madame?" she asked.

"I have decided to go away for a bit and shall need you to pack enough items for at least a month. I will need several formal gowns, in addition to day dresses and painting clothes. You know the sort of things I mean. Please be sure to include my jewel case with suitable items as well. I will have Mrs. Burns deposit the rest of my jewelry in the safety-deposit box at the bank. I'll be leaving shortly."

The girl's eyes widened before she bobbed her head and hurried out the door. Geraldine nodded to herself. The maid had been the very same one who had dropped the soup tureen, but she had turned out to be a remarkably good hire in the end. She might still be a bit skittish, but she knew her place and how to hold her tongue.

Geraldine hummed to herself as she polished off the rest of the omelet and drained her bracingly bitter cup of coffee before mounting the stairs to the studio. She strode to one of the cupboards tucked in under the eaves and wrenched open the door. Bending over, while reminding herself not to twitch in any direction too suddenly and risk throwing out her back, she extracted a wooden case by its handle. Her heart lifted as she was transformed almost instantly back to the young girl who had bought that same French easel on her first trip to Paris. It would be the perfect thing to take with her.

As she glanced around the room, she realized she was almost looking forward to a change of scenery. While she had no intention of giving up a view of the lake, especially not once the weather had become so heartbreakingly delicious, she could not say that she was unhappy to enjoy a slightly different angle on it. She hoisted the strap on the easel to her shoulder. After one last glance around the studio, she walked out the door.

CHAPTER 5

Cynthia

SHE SHOULD HAVE KNOWN THAT Pauline's family's camp would not tend towards "rustic"; the Mayhews were no hunters. Cynthia silently chided herself for not using her savings on more new clothing than just a daring two-piece bathing suit. She wished she had purchased at least one summer frock that was worthy of the house that rose before her.

The sprawling structure, clad in brown shingles and festooned with porches, stood on a slight rise offering a commanding view of Long Pond. Towering pines and lush rhododendrons shielded it from view of nearby houses. Window boxes spilling over with brightly colored blooms gave the place a European sensibility. A breeze wafted up from the lake, bringing with it a hint of woodsmoke and decaying leaves.

Cynthia hoped she had kept her astonishment to herself. While she had been made decidedly aware of the disparity between her family's wealth and Pauline's, sometimes reality still surprised her. Her time at Barlow had been a learning experience beyond the traditional coursework. Until she had arrived on campus, she had no idea of how much luxury truly existed in the world. And here she was, about to be surrounded by it for the summer due to her roommate's generous hospitality.

Pauline reached for Cynthia's hand and tugged her towards the wide stone steps leading up to a deep porch that wrapped around the entire front of the lake house. "Let's get you settled in your room, and then we'll head for the lake. I'll introduce you to the gang."

Cynthia's heart pounded faster in her chest. Pauline had introduced her to members of her crowd on campus too. Her friends had been pleasant, to be sure, but it had been painfully obvious that they did not feel she was quite their sort. Besides, Cynthia wasn't one for parties and the like, no matter the circumstances. Her reticence to mingle had been one of the reasons why Pauline claimed she had not secured herself a steady boyfriend in the two years they had known each other. Despite Pauline's best efforts at introducing her to every eligible young man to cross their path, Cynthia had not found herself paired off, as had so many of her fellow coeds. Perhaps it was her reserved and studious nature. It also might have been because she spent most of her spare time either studying or working on that blasted article for Professor Avery. She willed a smile to her face, determined to be a good sport and not ruin Pauline's fun at matchmaking.

The house was as breathtaking on the inside as it was from

the outside. With eleven bedrooms, six bathrooms, a gaming room, and a library—not to mention the expected dining room, living room, and enormous kitchen—Cynthia felt she needed a map to find her way around. But the most intimidating thing of all was Pauline's mother.

As Pauline wound down the tour, she finished up in a small sitting room overlooking the lake. A dark-haired woman dressed in a linen shift and pearls sat at a desk tucked into the bay window. She turned as Pauline pushed open the door to the room, and Cynthia immediately marked less warmth between her roommate and the older woman than had been on display with her father. Pauline turned towards Cynthia and beckoned her forward.

"This must be your guest," the woman said, nodding towards Cynthia.

"Mother, meet Cynthia," Pauline said.

"Thank you so much for inviting me, Mrs. Mayhew," Cynthia said. "I appreciate your hospitality."

The older woman looked her up and down as if calculating her suitability as one of her daughter's intimates. Once again, Cynthia wished she had spent some money on higher-quality clothing. She did not feel poorly dressed in her pale-yellow sundress and low-heeled sandals, but she knew that her wardrobe would never measure up to Pauline's. Still, she must have passed muster to some extent, as the older woman nodded and gave her a brief smile.

"It's lovely that you could join us." Mrs. Mayhew turned towards her daughter once again. "I've invited the Harringtons for bridge and cocktails this evening. It's a bit of a welcome party for you as well as them."

"We'll still have time enough to go to the beach for a bit before it starts, won't we?" Pauline asked.

"As long as you're quick about it. But be sure to return with enough time to make yourselves presentable before they arrive. You know how important it is to make a good impression on them." She looked Cynthia up and down once more. "I've decided to put your friend in the Lilac Room."

Pauline nodded, then grabbed Cynthia by the hand once more and pulled her from the room. As they raced up a wide central staircase to the second floor, Cynthia couldn't shake the feeling that she had failed some sort of unspoken test.

"Who are the Harringtons?" she asked when they'd reached the second-floor landing.

"They're another old-money family with a place on the next cove. Everyone thought my mother would marry their eldest son, but she married Daddy instead."

Cynthia tried to picture her own mother inviting a former flame to a card party where her husband would be in attendance. It was impossible to imagine. The rich really did do things differently.

Pauline strode towards the door at the end of the hallway and flung it open. "This will be your room. It's right next door to mine. I'm sorry it doesn't have a view of the lake. I can't imagine what Mother was thinking, putting you in here on your first visit."

It had been all too clear to Cynthia what Mrs. Mayhew had been thinking: She had taken her measure and found her wanting. Her chilly reception gave Cynthia even more incentive to find a job as quickly as possible. She was certain she wouldn't be encouraged to stay for very long.

CHAPTER 6

Iris

Late May 1954

NEW-JOB JITTERS, THAT'S ALL, IRIS told herself as she smoothed her hand along the satin coverlet adorning the carved wooden bed. Plump pillows enclosed in crisp white cases were piled high at the headboard. Flocked wallpaper patterned the walls, while velvety cream carpet lay across the floor, muffling her footfalls. The sun streamed through the long windows overlooking the pond. By this time tomorrow, there would be a paying guest ensconced in the bed, ready to begin at least a week of rest and rejuvenation that time spent at the exclusive Maine Chance resort promised to provide. She should think it had better, considering what those women from away were paying for the privilege of lakeside calisthenics sessions and meals prepared with so little food that she couldn't really see the point in bothering to dirty up the bone-china plates. Not that she would say such a thing out loud.

No, if a bunch of pampered, demanding women wanted to

traipse into the middle of nowhere and pay through the nose to be slathered with beauty creams and half-starved for weeks on end, it was no concern of hers. Her business was to see to it that the guests wanted for nothing—at least not as far as the facilities were concerned. With a ratio of two staff members to every guest, it ought to be easy enough to meet any demand. But somehow it never seemed to work out that way.

Satisfied that the room would meet even the highest of standards, she moved into the hallway and down the back stairs. As she ran a dustcloth down the gleaming banister, she told herself she was ready for the day. And why shouldn't she be? She had worked as the head maid at the Maine Chance for enough summers to prepare her for the opportunity to move up once it presented itself. Still, she couldn't help but feel like a vulture, flapping and feasting on Alice Merrick's corpse.

But when she'd heard about her friend and predecessor Alice's fatal car accident, her first thought had not been about her loss of life. No, Lord forgive her, it had been to wonder whether or not the resort would be forced to close for the rest of the season.

It wasn't that she had no feelings of sorrow for Alice. She was heartily ashamed of herself for such selfish considerations, especially in light of their long friendship, but the fact remained that she, along with so many other year-round residents of Mount Vernon, relied on summer wages earned at the resort to make ends meet. There were very few decent-paying jobs available during the off-season, and she had no idea what she would do if the resort shuttered its doors for even a week of the already too-short season. She envied the employees of the second Maine Chance, located in Arizona. Their employment season was nowhere near as fleeting. It opened as soon as the brief Maine summer ended and offered guests the same level of service and luxury in a warm locale, from autumn through spring. Miss Arden saved money and time by shuttling the spa technicians between the two facilities as the seasons changed. Iris quelled a feeling of unproductive envy and turned her thoughts to the heavy workload at hand.

She reached the bottom of the staircase, then strode down a long hallway and through the wide arched doorway into a room covered in fawn-colored wallpaper printed with bold golden leaves. Small tables covered with snowy linens, gleaming silver candlesticks, and sparkling crystal vases brimming with freshly cut flowers dotted the dining room. She nodded with satisfaction at an enormous urn filled with sprays of delphiniums and roses filling the marble-tiled fireplace. Even in the Belgrade Lakes region of Maine, there would be no need to light a fire in mid-June—at least, not if one had the good sense to pack a sweater in among all the sleeveless gowns and bathing suits.

She glanced up at the crystal chandelier, its brass arms dangling at the center of the spacious room, and inspected it for stray flecks of dust on the faceted pendants, or cobwebs clinging where they ought not above the diners' heads. Finding nothing untoward, she continued to the main drawing room, as Miss Arden called it. The room's generous windows provided sweeping views of Long Pond, and Iris paused for a moment, as she always did when alone in the space, even after a lifetime of living in a lake town, to soak in the serene beauty.

Long Pond was a lake, really, but for some reason, the many lakes in the area were all called ponds. Perhaps it was the almost pathological desire not to make too much of oneself or one's surroundings, which was part and parcel of Maine culture. But whatever it was called, she had to admit a certain pride in the beauty of the building and of the property surrounding it. She nodded with satisfaction at the tasteful arrangements of flowers filling vases on the occasional tables placed strategically around the room. A glittering crystal clock on the mantel chimed seven o'clock and reminded her there was no time for dawdling.

She glanced about the entryway, where the tasteful and understated reception desk stood with its guest register, pigeonholes to sort guest mail, and a shallow tray of brass room keys. Pulling a dust rag from the waistband of her starched apron once again, Iris ran it, more from habit than necessity, across the surface of the reception desk before opening the reservation ledger.

She ran her finger down the names printed neatly on the page. Several congressmen's wives, a famous opera singer, and a half dozen society ladies whose names made the rounds in the newspapers as chairwomen of charity committees and hostesses of debutante balls were par for the course. But one name on the list did give her pause. Iris's finger hovered over it: Geraldine Putnam.

Guests came to stay at the Maine Chance from almost everywhere, with one exception: They did not come from Mount Vernon. Mrs. Putnam was a local fixture, and an important one at that. She owned an enormous elegant home on the lake. What possible reason could she have to book an indefinite stay?

And how was Iris to treat this unexpected guest? She had often found herself in Mrs. Putnam's presence at church functions, town meetings, and in the lobby of the post office. It was one thing to bow and scrape for people she would never see outside of her work—and even then, only ever during the season. It was quite another to think she would need to do so for someone she would see again and again throughout the year. They regularly ran into each other at the grocer's, for heaven's sake.

It was difficult to imagine her interesting herself in what, to Iris's mind, could be considered frivolous—albeit luxurious—pursuits like the ones offered at the Maine Chance. Could a woman with as much restless energy as Mrs. Putnam be contented with endless sessions at the spa being slathered with new-fangled hormone cremes, or sitting for precious moments of each day having her hair styled and set like so many resort guests?

She had always admired the older woman, with her outspoken ways and independent spirit.

She was generous too. It was well known that her staff was more than happy with the pay they received, and it was rumored that an anonymously funded scholarship awarded to a high school senior heading off to college was thanks to her. She even opened her lovely grounds for a veterans' fundraiser every year.

That said, she could be terrifying. Mrs. Putnam was forthright to a fault and was quick to point out when she felt a thing ought to be done differently. Iris knew for a fact she was a woman of high standards and did not mince words when those standards were not met. More than once, she and her mother had been hired as extra help when Geraldine and her late husband had thrown a large party at their lakefront home. She had always proved exacting on such occasions.

As she thought of her mother and her increasingly worrying lapses of memory, a cold lump filled Iris's stomach. What if she did not measure up to Mrs. Putnam's expectations? Would she complain directly to Miss Arden? After all, Miss Arden's and Mrs. Putnam's names were often linked in the society columns of the local newspaper for attending the same charity functions and sophisticated parties. What would she do if she lost her job before she had even gotten used to having it?

CHAPTER 7

Iris

THE WICKER BASKET WAS HEAVY, and Iris's shoulders ached as she carried it to the laundry house. It was located some way from the main building, as one would only expect. Nevertheless, it would not do for the high-class guests to be confronted with something as vulgar as dirty linens. Since the estate comprised over 750 acres, there was plenty of space to separate the working areas of the property from those devoted to leisure.

Up ahead, a low-slung building sat nestled in among rosebushes and neatly trimmed rows of privet hedge. On the side of the building announcing it to be the laundry, flower boxes were mounted at each of the windows and filled with vibrant plants heavy with lush blooms. It was as though Miss Arden did not wish for any part of the estate to appear utilitarian regardless of its purpose.

It was all carefully cultivated to court the notion of a

rural paradise. From the deftly pruned fruit orchard to the overflowing containers of blossoming plants, evidence of Miss Arden's standards was everywhere to be seen. In addition to her housekeeping expectations that all bed and table linens be perfectly pressed, only the freshest flowers appear in the rooms, all crystal—from the glassware to the chandeliers—ceaselessly sparkle, and the floors remain polished to a satiny gleam, the grounds were required to be impeccably kept as well.

The lawns were rolled and clipped just so. The fruit trees' limbs had been pruned to create pleasing symmetry in the orchard. Flowers in the garden beds were deadheaded as soon as blossoms began to show the least sign of fading. Outbuildings were repainted every three years, a fact that baffled the locals since no one could ever justify the exorbitant outlay of hard-earned cash on something that could be put off for a decade. In fact, many folks left the back of their house alone until the harsh winters took a toll on the clapboards, since no one saw the rear of the home except for family and their intimates.

Iris admired how much effort had gone into creating the illusion of perfection, but she could not shake the feeling that it was somehow disingenuous. She knew from long experience that *rural* was not synonymous with anything close to *Eden.* She could think of more long stretches of derelict barns and dispirited dairy cows than fancy houses, even in the lakes region.

As she reached for the laundry-house door handle, the sound of shouting floated across the warm summer breeze. It was so out of place at the tranquil resort that, for a second, she froze. She dropped the wicker basket and sprinted around the side of the building. Across the field, near the tree line, she noticed a pair of women. Iris recognized one of the women as Marjorie Billings, a resort guest. To her horror, she also recognized the other. Her mother, Orla, stood beside Mrs. Billings, shouting and flapping her hands back and forth as if to ward her off.

Orla, in her sensible house dress, was bareheaded, without a handbag. Nor did she wear gloves. Mrs. Billings took a step back, but Orla grabbed her by the arm and held fast.

“I don’t know who you think you are, wandering around on private property, but you’d best get yourself gone before I call the police,” Orla said, her voice raising to a thunderous shout. “I know your type, missy. You’re all trying to sneak in to steal from my strawberry patch, but I’m not having it.”

“I assure you, I had no intention of stealing strawberries or anything else from you. I had no idea I had left the Maine Chance Farm,” Iris heard Mrs. Billings say. “I do apologize for invading your privacy.”

The woman scowled at her and shook her finger harder. Iris broke into a run.

“There’s no such thing as a Maine Chance Farm. I don’t know what kind of nonsense you want me to believe, but we don’t hold with that kind of uppity talk here,” Orla said as Iris reached her side. Seeing her daughter, she released her grip on

Mrs. Billings and crossed her arms over her ample bosom. “Iris, tell this woman she’s trespassing.”

“I’ll take care of it,” Iris said, placing herself between her mother and the paying guest. “Mrs. Billings, will you please come with me?”

Mrs. Billings looked at Iris, then nodded and followed her to a distance far enough away to not be overheard.

“Who is that poor dear?” Mrs. Billings asked as they stopped next to an apple tree covered in small green fruit.

Iris hesitated. In her experience, guests at the Maine Chance rarely wanted to hear unpleasant truths. If they did, they would not spend so much money on starvation diets or skin creams. Besides, Iris had never subscribed to the notion that a burden shared was a burden halved. She was more inclined to believe that the least said, the soonest mended. A carefully edited story would be best.

“I’m so sorry that she bothered you. She’s a local woman who lived on the estate twenty years ago. She’s become a bit forgetful of late and has trouble remembering that she sold her farm to Miss Arden long ago.”

“How sad. Doesn’t she have family who could see about getting her some help before she ends up hurting herself or someone else?” Mrs. Billings rubbed a red patch on her arm where Orla had squeezed it.

“She has a daughter who is doing the best that she can,” Iris said.

Marjorie glanced over her shoulder at the older woman standing near the tree line.

"I hate to say it, but her best might not be good enough."

Iris breathed in slowly and bit back a reply unworthy of her position as housekeeper.

"From what I understand, she's clearheaded more often than not," she said, wishing that were entirely true.

Mrs. Billings shook her head. "I volunteered at a VA hospital during the war, and I can promise that problems of the mind rarely sort themselves out without help. If she were my mother, I wouldn't leave her on her own."

Mrs. Billings turned and walked back towards the beach. As soon as she was out of sight, Iris returned to her mother's side. With everything else she needed to do, she had no time to take Orla home, but she couldn't let her stay at the resort, threatening the guests, either.

If they took the path through the woods, she'd be back in less than an hour. If Iris was very lucky, her neighbor Frances would be able to stay with her until she took a break at suppertime. But even if she was, Mrs. Billings's warning rang in her ears. No matter how much she hated to admit it, there was something very wrong with her mother.

CHAPTER 8

Cynthia

"IS THAT WHAT YOU'RE GOING to wear?" Pauline asked, looking her up and down as Cynthia joined her on the porch. "I want you to make a good impression on Glenn, if he's arrived in town yet."

Cynthia smoothed her hands down along the front of her beach cover-up, noticing her nails could do with a manicure. "Aren't we just going swimming? How much more dressed up do I need to be?"

Pauline put her hands on her hips and tipped her head to one side. "I suppose if you just add a little bit of lipstick, you'll do. You're pretty enough not to need to worry too much about what you wear." She opened a drawer in her dressing table and pulled out a swivel tube. "Here, try this one on. It'll go great with your coloring." Pauline winked at her and held out the lipstick.

Even though it seemed silly to put on makeup before going

for a swim, Cynthia took the tube from Pauline's outstretched hands and rolled up the color. It was a bit more daring than her usual shade of pale pink, but she supposed that Pauline knew more about what was acceptable in her crowd than she did. Besides, it was the perfect time to try something new. After all, she was out from under the watchful eye of both her mother and the college matron who scowled at girls wearing skirts that were too short or too much makeup. The matron even complained if a girl wore more than three pieces of jewelry at once, including a wristwatch.

Pauline pulled a compact from her bag and opened it. Cynthia leaned towards the mirror and touched the tip of the lipstick to her slightly parted lips. Pauline had been right, of course. The berry-colored hue went surprisingly well with her complexion. She had gotten a bit of sun since the weather had warmed, and a smattering of freckles had begun to show across the bridge of her nose. She thought of her mother once again, who did not hold with such things. Not the lipstick, nor the freckles.

"Tell me more about Glenn. Why are you so eager for the two of us to meet?" Cynthia asked.

Pauline held up one of her slim hands, her nails perfectly manicured. She raised her index finger. "One, his mother is hell-bent on marrying him off. She's at least as determined as my own. Two, he's quite decent looking." Pauline held up a third finger. "Three, his family is richer than mine. And that's saying something."

"If he's such a catch, why aren't *you* interested in him?" Cynthia asked. It was a good question. Pauline had mentioned Glenn off and on in the two years they'd been roommates, but never in a romantic way. Cynthia hoped there was nothing worrisome about him.

"I think it's because my mother has always hoped the two of us would end up together. Not that Mother is a bad sort, but it's not my intention to let her make every decision about my life. Besides, I have my eye on Kenneth Harrington." Pauline took back the lipstick and placed it in her vanity drawer. "Let's be off, then, shall we? We've got a husband to find for you."

CHAPTER 9

Geraldine

SHE PUSHED AGAINST THE WIDE floorboards with her toes, setting the wooden rocker into motion and filling the air around her with cracks and creaks as its joints—as old and clamorous as her own—chided her. That particular spot where the gap in the pines at the shoreline afforded an expansive view of the lake was her favorite. At least, it was when it failed to include members of her deceased husband's extended family. But there they were, just as the weather had finally turned heartbreakingly beautiful. Long Pond sparkled, as if to mock her with its very cheerfulness. Geraldine tightened her grip on her highball glass as a speedboat streaked towards the dock anchored to the edge of her private beach. A depressingly large contingent of her in-laws heaved themselves up out of the boat and clattered towards her along the dock's weathered wooden decking.

She braced herself for the clamor that accompanied them

whenever they appeared. The young man shoved open the screen door and raced past her with the merest bob of his head. Remembering the way he had behaved on previous visits, she guessed that he was headed straight for the kitchen. His parents arrived at a more decorous pace. Louise's glance landed on the empty glass, and her thin nose twitched as if she were sniffing out mischief. If there was one thing Geraldine could not abide after years of enduring the privations of Prohibition, it was recriminations concerning her right to imbibe whenever she saw fit. If only Louise had not raised her over-plucked eyebrows at her, she might have lost her nerve. Thankfully, Louise did. Her even more judgmental husband, Dickie, was captivated by the set of matching leather suitcases stacked neatly by the porch door.

"Have other members of the family arrived ahead of us?" he asked.

Geraldine shook her head. "The suitcases are mine." Before he could reply, she spotted yet another boat cutting swiftly through the water in the direction of her dock. "It seems that my taxi has arrived."

"Where are you going?" Louise asked.

"I have booked an indefinite stay at the Maine Chance Farm. Be so good as to leave word with Mrs. Burns when you have concluded your vacation in my home."

"But you cannot possibly leave," Louise said.

"Who's Mrs. Burns?" Dickie asked. Typical. The man didn't

even have the decency to remember the name of the long-suffering housekeeper who put up with his family's locust-like descent on her domain year after year. Geraldine ignored him.

"I can see no reason why I am not as entitled as all of you to enjoy a pleasant summer, and for a change I have determined to do so."

"But you've given us no notice of your intentions. You did not consult us about how that might affect our plans," Louise said, an uncharacteristic flood of color rising to her alabaster cheeks.

"Come, come, my dear. Considering the ease with which you descend upon me with a similar lack of warning, I had understood that such niceties were entirely unnecessary," Geraldine said.

"But what will people think?" Louise asked, lifting a slim hand to the base of her throat.

"I have no idea, and even less interest." With that, Geraldine grasped the handle of the smallest of the suitcases and strode out onto the lawn.

Bernard Eames, the owner of the seasonal water-taxi service, hustled up the slope between the house and dock to lend her his arm. She would have preferred to drive herself, but if she did, she would run the risk of communications from Louise et al. concerning the use of her car. Besides, it was a lovely afternoon for a boat ride. The towering pines surrounding the lake cast cooling shadows onto the surface of the water. Birds swooped low, skimming the water in the hope of scooping fish or swarms of aquatic insects into their hungry bills.

Bernard glanced over to assure himself that she was safely settled before returning to the porch for the rest of her luggage. Geraldine pointedly refrained from glancing towards the house until he had clambered aboard the boat, cast off, and revved the engine. Just as they moved out of earshot, Geraldine turned back for a final look. She had no idea how long it would be before she laid eyes on it again. She spotted Louise standing on the dock, waving furiously at her. She turned her face towards the opposite shore and felt her spirits lift for the first time since she had received Louise's letter announcing their arrival date with her unquestioning expectation of welcome.

CHAPTER 10

Cynthia

As she moved quietly along the hall, the muffled sounds of youthful voices could be heard through the room assigned to Pauline's cousins, Freddie and Patsy. A shaft of sunlight fell across the polished oak floorboards creaking gently under her feet. The door to Pauline's room remained firmly shut as she paused in front of it. No sound emerged from within. Cynthia considered turning around to return to her own room. Perhaps it was not the done thing to rise early in the Mayhew household.

She moved forward once more. No matter where she found herself, she had always been a morning person. Besides, Mr. Mayhew had lent her his copy of *Fahrenheit 451*. It had been out since the previous year, but with her course load, she had not yet found time to read it. She clutched it to her chest like armor as she descended the wide staircase.

At the base of the stairs, she paused, torn between the

hammock she knew lay just beyond the front door and the quiet clink of cutlery against china somewhere in the opposite direction. The bracing scent of coffee floated towards her. That decided it. She turned to the interior of the house, hoping that Mr. Mayhew could be found at the head of the dining room table. He had been so welcoming at the train station.

As she came in sight of the dining room threshold, Mrs. Mayhew's slim frame sat facing the doorway. She lowered her coffee cup and gestured towards the table. No other seat was occupied, and Cynthia hesitated as to which to choose. Somehow she had the sense that Mrs. Mayhew was not particularly pleased to see her. Leaving a protective space between them seemed the thing to do.

"Good morning, Cynthia. I trust the room was adequate to your needs?" Mrs. Mayhew said, placing her coffee cup in its matching saucer. A wafer-thin slice of toast and a wedge of cantaloupe sat untouched on a plate before her. Placed at her right hand lay a pad of paper and a slim gold pen. As Cynthia drew closer, she could read the words *evening frock*, *bathing suit*, and *sundresses* written in an elegant, spiky script. She lowered herself into a chair two removed from her hostess and nodded as Mrs. Mayhew lifted a porcelain coffee pot, her eyebrows raised in question.

"The room is lovely. Everything about your home is simply beautiful."

Mrs. Mayhew shrugged, her slim shoulders moving elegantly

beneath a pale-yellow twinset. Even at such an early hour, she was dressed for the day—every hair in place; lipstick, perfume, and powder all flawlessly applied. A string of creamy pearls adorned her neck, matching drops dangling from her small earlobes.

"Aren't you sweet?" She lifted her cup once more and leveled her dark gaze over its rim. After taking a sip, she lowered it again. "So, tell me, Cynthia, what is it that your father does?"

It was a simple enough question, but there was something in Mrs. Mayhew's tone that made it feel like a test. For a moment she was tempted to embellish her family background, but the impulse faded as quickly as it came upon her. Surely her hostess would discover any untruths, and that would be far more embarrassing than it would be to simply own up to her family's middle-class status. She sat up as straight as possible. Posture was power, after all.

"He's an insurance agent."

Mrs. Mayhew's eyes widened in her face before she recovered herself. "Really? I believe you are the first of our guests to be able to make such a claim."

What could she possibly say to that? It was likely a statement of fact, but one with barbed hooks. She had endured similar comments during her time at college. She had yet to come up with a response that did not sound defensive. It felt even more awkward coming from her hostess rather than a classmate.

"I shall be sure to let him know of his singularity," she said, hoping that would not give offense.

"How is it that the daughter of an insurance agent came to be at Barlow?" Her tone was one of incredulity, and Cynthia fought down another wave of defensiveness.

"One of my neighbors attended Barlow and spoke of her time there so fondly I decided to apply."

"And just like that, they admitted you?" She raised one thin eyebrow and looked Cynthia up and down.

"I believe my academic record had something to do with it. Since I was the valedictorian of my high school class, I decided to apply to schools with rigorous expectations."

"How very ambitious of you." Mrs. Mayhew allowed a brief smile to flit across her face. Fortunately, she spoke again before Cynthia was forced to think of a reply to what could only be considered an insult. "I wonder if you might do me the most enormous favor."

Cynthia nodded reflexively. Despite Mrs. Mayhew's barbed remarks, she would be pleased to help. It was the least she could do to thank her generous hostess.

"It would be my pleasure." Cynthia hoped her voice did not betray her nerves. Mrs. Mayhew was an intimidating woman.

"How kind. In a typical display of self-centeredness, my brother-in-law and his wife have telephoned to say that their arrival has been delayed for another day or two and that they will not be available to watch their children. The result of their poor planning is that my shopping trip with Pauline today is endangered." Her gaze lingered on Cynthia once more, and her smile tightened. "I shouldn't think that a girl like you would wish to tag along, now, would you?"

Cynthia hesitated to respond. Did Mrs. Mayhew mean to imply that she didn't care about her appearance, or that, for someone of her station, shopping could not make much difference? Her spirits sank. She had seen that same look on the faces of the mothers of her other roommates, Carol and Sharon, as well. Their messages had all telegraphed that she was not good enough to be an intimate of their daughters'.

Before she could come to a decision, Mrs. Mayhew narrowed her eyes and looked Cynthia up and down. "Could I count on you to babysit for me today? Pauline is in dire need of a freshening to her wardrobe, and I had scheduled a trip to Portland to take her to the shops for a few desperately needed items. She is hardly fit to be seen in last year's summer clothes."

Cynthia had long admired Pauline's vast wardrobe. She had never known her roommate to be less than beautifully turned out, but perhaps Mrs. Mayhew's standards were higher than her own. Be that as it may, she liked Freddie and Patsy. They reminded her of the kids she babysat during the school year to pick up some spending money. As generous as her scholarship had been in covering tuition, room, and board, there were still many costs that were unmet. Every time she needed toiletries, hygiene products, or an occasional trip to the university soda fountain, she needed to find a way to pay for them on her own.

"No, Mrs. Mayhew. I'd be happy to watch the children."

Mrs. Mayhew smiled triumphantly. "I knew that you would be agreeable. I already instructed the cook to prepare a picnic for the three of you. You will take them to the beach for the day as soon as you have had your breakfast." Mrs. Mayhew carefully placed her napkin on the table in front of her. She pushed back her chair and rose to her feet. "Be sure to have them back, bathed, and ready to greet our guests by the time I return with Pauline for the cocktail party this evening."

Cynthia watched as her hostess glided out of the dining room. Had she just been relegated to the role of unpaid nanny? Part of her wished to be offended, but mostly she was relieved to be freed of Mrs. Mayhew's presence.

CHAPTER 11

Geraldine

IT WASN'T HOME, THAT HAD to be said. But it was a remarkably fine substitute. Geraldine had had a bit of a qualm once the water taxi was halfway across the lake. Had she been too hasty in her decision to cede possession of her house to the invaders? The thought had plagued her like a dance tune she couldn't get out of her head, until Bernard cut the boat's engine and drifted to a stop alongside the dock at the Maine Chance Farm.

Despite its name, it hardly looked like a farm. The dock anchored to a wide strip of recently raked sandy beach. Bernard handed her out onto the dock and into the care of a trim young man with broad shoulders and an easy smile. Something about him struck her as familiar. She searched her memory for a moment, trying to recall where she had seen him. In a moment's time, all of Geraldine's luggage sat neatly on the dock and the water taxi had eased away from the shoreline.

"Welcome to the Maine Chance, Mrs. Putnam. My name is Calvin. If you will follow me, it would be my pleasure to escort you to the Arden House." With that, the young man tucked a suitcase beneath each arm and grasped two more by the handles. While she considered herself far too old to seriously entertain any amorous notions, she still found herself admiring his graceful movements as he led the way up a path that wended between two stands of mature pines and maples.

Even weighed down by her luggage, he strode swiftly along, his back straight. That did it. She was able to place him. He had been one of the many handsome young men in uniform who had marched so smartly in the Memorial Day parade earlier that season. Even out of uniform, he cut quite a dash. Age had not dimmed her eyesight, nor her appreciation for attractive youths.

Although she had been to the property during the offseason as a dinner guest of Elizabeth's, she had never before arrived by boat. The path led across a rolling manicured lawn; past triangular garden beds luxuriantly filled with marigolds, dusty millers, and salvias; and up to the Arden House. With its generous proportions and twin wings on either side of the main building, it made for a pleasing sight.

The door to the building swung open, and a familiar woman of middle height and age appeared on the threshold. In her navy cotton dress, with its starched white collar and cuffs, and her neat bun, she was exactly the sort of servant of which Geraldine heartily approved. The woman bent towards the young man's ear as she stepped slightly aside to allow Calvin to pass into the building. He nodded without comment and disappeared from sight.

"Good afternoon, Mrs. Putnam. It is my pleasure to welcome you to the Maine Chance Farm."

"Hello, Iris. I haven't seen you since sometime before ice-out. How have you and your mother been keeping?"

The day the last bit of ice had finally melted on Long Pond was a much-welcomed event in the community, rather like the spotting of the first spring robin or the last frost. Mentioning it shouldn't have brought a flicker of discomfort to Iris's face. It must have been caused by the question about her mother, although Geraldine could not imagine why that might be. Orla Hubbard was a respected member of the community and not the sort to stir up worry. In fact, she and Iris both helped out when Mrs. Burns needed extra staff for the large dinner parties or fundraising events she hosted from time to time.

"Things are much the same as usual. She is sure to be pleased to hear that you asked after her."

Geraldine took the hint; the subject of Orla was not one Iris cared to entertain. She rarely cared to discuss her family either. The least she could do was respect that same preference in another.

"Allow me to congratulate you on your new position. Housekeeper must be quite a responsibility at a place like this."

Iris bobbed her head. “I wished that such an opportunity could have come in some other way, but I hope that I am doing Alice proud.”

Geraldine was sure Iris meant what she said. Alice had given her a chance and taken her under her wing during the resort’s first season twenty years earlier. She would have been desperate for a job, as was everyone else, given how hard-hit Maine had been by the Depression. Alice could have given the position to any number of more experienced young women, but for some reason she had chosen Iris. As far as Geraldine could tell, Iris had spent all summers since making sure to live up to Alice’s faith in her.

“Miss Arden hasn’t built her successful business by setting low standards. I am certain you are up to the challenge.”

Geraldine had long been aware of those standards. She’d first encountered Elizabeth Arden when she visited her friend and mentor Elisabeth “Bessie” Marbury at her home in Mount Vernon back in the late twenties. Elizabeth had become so smitten with Long Pond and its environs that she purchased parcel after parcel of the land adjoining Bessie’s and set about building a lavish home. No detail was too small for her attention. She’d hired the best builders, decorators, and landscape designers to bring her vision of a perfect country estate to life. When Bessie died just a year later, Elizabeth bought her property as well and joined it to her own. Not long after that, the Maine Chance Farm resort was born. Even though she spent most of the year elsewhere, somehow her enthusiastic and exacting presence could be seen and felt throughout the estate.

A small smile lifted the corners of Iris's mouth. Geraldine could not remember the last time she had seen the younger woman smile. Even at town meetings or whenever she encountered her at shops in town, she appeared to have something weighing her down.

"Shall I show you to your room, or would you prefer to have a tour around the resort?" Iris asked.

"If it is all the same to you, I shall just roam about on my own for a bit and look things over. I have need of an outbuilding to use as a studio while I am here, and the sooner I find the right spot, the better."

Iris appeared taken aback by the suggestion but recovered her composure quickly, as a woman with as much experience as she possessed in catering to the whims of others might be expected to do. Geraldine hadn't meant it as a slight. She simply preferred to take things at her own pace and poke her nose in wherever she felt inclined. Besides, she imagined that Iris had far too much to do to indulge in a leisurely stroll about the property.

"If that is your wish, you are most welcome to do so. I've had Calvin take your luggage up to the Mille Fleurs Suite. With your keen interest in gardening, I thought you would find it appealing."

"I am sure that it will more than suffice." Geraldine thought it best to smooth any ruffled feathers. "Even though I don't wish to monopolize your time with a private tour, perhaps you could provide me with an overview of the schedule. I've heard that it's surprisingly regimented."

"Miss Arden does believe in structure for her guests, especially those who are here to slim down. They only have so much time with us, and we strive to help them achieve the maximum results through a variety of activities."

That all sounded ominous. Not for the first time, Geraldine was grateful for her own effortlessly slender build. "What sort of activities?"

"Swimming, badminton, reducing baths, horseback rides. For those guests with more than just a few pounds to shed, a three-mile daily walk is strictly enforced."

Geraldine snorted. "'Enforced'? How would anyone know if one of the slimming guests simply sat under a shady tree for an hour or two before heading back, claiming to have followed the recommendation?"

Iris leaned forward and lowered her voice. "I wondered the same thing the first time I heard of it. Miss Arden insists on the use of pedometers."

"Pedometers?"

"Yes, they're tamper-proof devices that measure the number of steps one of our slimmers takes in a day. They are tied about the guests' waists in order to accurately track their movements."

Having come of age in the era of the corset, Geraldine found the notion of anything restrictive cinched about a woman's waist, especially something whose sole purpose was to ensure that her body dwindled in a slavish adherence to fashion, to be repulsive.

"How astonishing. Is there anything else I ought to know before I strike off on my own?"

"Dinner is at seven o'clock in the dining room, and I would mention that it is a formal affair. Guests are encouraged to retire by nine p.m., so there is little ever scheduled after the evening meal."

"But it is still light out at nine. Are we paying through the nose to be treated like children?"

Again, a small smile softened Iris's face. "Perhaps that is the secret to the youthful glow our guests acquire by the end of their time here."

"Somehow I doubt that. Are there any other outrageous practices of which I should be aware?"

"While I understand from your reservation forms that you are not here for slimming, there is one dietary restriction that applies to all of our guests."

Geraldine braced herself. As a child, she had been dosed daily with spoonfuls of cod-liver oil and made to drink tonics of one sort or another that her mother had sent away for by post. Surely it could not be as bad as all that at a luxury resort.

"Which is...?"

"This is a strictly no-alcohol facility."

She stiffened. How on earth could a place consider itself civilized, let alone opulent, if it ascribed to such barbarous austerity?

"No wine with dinner? No nightcaps?"

"No, nothing of that sort, I am sorry to say. We do serve iced vegetable juices at cocktail hour before dinner is served, if that is any consolation. I understand from the guests that the chef has come up with some delicious options."

"Vegetable juice instead of cocktails?" Geraldine gripped the reception desk in alarm. "Is nothing sacred?"

"I'm sorry, Mrs. Putnam. Do you wish to cancel your reservation?"

Geraldine considered it. While she was never one to say no to a cocktail—not after the shenanigans of Prohibition—she could not imagine heading back home to endure Anselm's family. No, if the price of being well shot of them was abstinence, then that was cheap enough. Besides, she had never been all that interested in following rules. She was confident there was a way around that one.

"I shan't let a little thing like that bother me. Now, where would you suggest I start my perusal of the property?"

"Well, considering how beautiful the weather is today, I would recommend that you take a stroll around the grounds. As I am sure you are aware, the property is comprised of hundreds of acres, most of them displaying Miss Arden's deft touch and love of beauty."

"Then that is where I shall begin. And I'll be sure to be back in time to dress for dinner, cocktails or no cocktails."

CHAPTER 12

Geraldine

GERALDINE SKIPPED THE LIVING AND dining rooms, as she had seen them both many times before. For more than two decades, Elizabeth had been a valued part-time resident of Mount Vernon and had often opened her home as a meeting place for various clubs and organizations of which she was a part. Both her political involvement and her agricultural interests had raised her profile with her neighbors. While it had surprised some people when she enthusiastically used her vast acreage for food production during the war years, it had endeared her to others in town. She had also generously supported the town's efforts to raise funds for war bonds.

Of far more interest to Geraldine was the spa wing of the main house and the lush grounds and outbuildings dotted about them. Following Iris's directions, she made her way along a plushly carpeted corridor leading into the treatment area, where a smiling young woman in a gleaming white smock greeted her by name. Geraldine assumed that particular courtesy had more to do with a quick call from Iris than it did with her fame as an artist.

"Would you like to book an appointment, Mrs. Putnam? We have no openings this afternoon, but we can easily fit you in tomorrow morning if you'd like."

"I suppose that would depend on which services you offer." Geraldine had not spent too much time on such pursuits since Anselm died. She might enjoy a bit of pampering.

"If you will just follow me, I'd be happy to show you." The woman slipped out from behind the reception desk and moved towards the spa proper.

Geraldine trailed behind her, taking in the tranquil atmosphere. The walls were papered in a pale-gray moiré. Long windows flanked by deep-blue drapes offered sweeping views of carefully tended flower beds on one side and a large swimming pool ringed by deck chairs on the other. A woman in a pistachio-green bathing suit and matching swim cap dived from the tiled surround and sliced neatly through the clear water.

"We pride ourselves in offering all the same services here as we do at our world-famous Red Door salons." The woman, whose name was Camille—if the name embroidered on the front of her smock was to be believed—gestured a slim hand towards a bank of chairs, most of which were reclined and occupied by women sporting thick white terry-cloth robes.

At one chair, a technician swiped a cotton pad across a guest's forehead. At another, a manicure was underway. Geraldine stopped abruptly at a third.

"What is going on here?" she asked.

A woman leaned back in a treatment chair, her face entirely covered in taut strips of damp gauze. Even from a distance of several feet, a medicinal scent filled the air. To Geraldine, she looked as though she had just been bandaged up after a surgical procedure. The technician leaned over her client and gently placed two rounds of well-moistened cotton wool over her closed eyes.

Camille lowered her voice. "That is our *Tie-Up Treatment.* It contours the face and lifts sagging muscles."

"What on earth is that smell?"

Camille's ferociously plucked eyebrows raised ever so slightly. "I expect you are referring to Miss Arden's world-famous Special Astringent. The mixture of proprietary ingredients produces a signature scent."

"That's one way to describe it, I suppose."

Camille moved along, gesturing to another client. Another smock-clad young thing bent over her, tapping all along her face and throat with something akin to a drumstick tipped by a felt disk.

"Perhaps I could interest you in a facial, designed to invigorate the skin and restore a youthful glow. It is one of our most popular treatments."

"What, pray tell, is she doing with that stick?"

Her guide let out a tinkling laugh. "That's Miss Arden's renowned *Patter.* When used faithfully as a part of her *Muscle-Strapping Skin-Toning Method,* it works wonders on double chins and flaccid facial muscles by increasing blood flow and aiding the removal of toxins from the skin."

Despite herself, Geraldine realized her hand had slipped to the base of her throat as if to check for the effects of gravity. Sadly, they were all too plainly present.

"Perhaps I will book a treatment or two while I am here. Even if they do little good, I cannot imagine there is much harm in them either."

"I am quite sure you will be more than pleased with the results. If you'll follow me, I'll show you the steam room and the hair and makeup salon."

Camille kept up her spiel as they wended their way between billowing clouds of steam, skirted snippings of hair on the gleaming tiled floor of the salon, and hurried past one woman undergoing some sort of hair-removal process best not remarked upon. Geraldine stopped at the reception desk before exiting and made an appointment to have her own face trussed up like a mummy the very next afternoon. Before she could be convinced to submit to anything else, she hurried out to scout the extensive grounds for a building to commandeer as a temporary studio.

CHAPTER 13

Cynthia

CYNTHIA HAD NOT EXPECTED TO spend any of her summer babysitting. Still, she could hardly refuse, and she was here to make money, anyhow. It had been more than generous of the Mayhews to have her to stay. That said, she couldn't help but feel that if she were not an insurance agent's daughter, she would not have been asked to perform such a task. In less time than she would have thought possible, she had managed to wriggle the children into their bathing suits and had collected an old wicker picnic hamper filled to the brim with sandwiches, slabs of cake, and bottles of lemonade from the Mayhews' cook.

After a thorough search of the boathouse, she and the children located a red metal pail and two sand shovels. Mrs. Mayhew handed Cynthia a large plaid blanket that had probably once served as a bedspread and practically pushed them out the door. Cynthia glanced back over her shoulder as they reached the bottom of the porch steps, but Mrs. Mayhew had already retreated into the depths of the house.

Patsy and Freddie raced ahead, and Cynthia hurried to keep up, encumbered as she was by the blanket, bucket, and hamper. She wouldn't like to admit it, but she did not feel entirely comfortable at the water's edge. At least, not comfortable enough to allow the children to get too far ahead of her. Visions of Freddie floating face down in the lake swam before her eyes as she strove to close the gap between them.

The children had no such concerns about their own safety and sprinted pell-mell towards the water. Freddie had stripped off his shirt and waded up to his knees before she could even put down her load. Her heart slowed to a normal speed as Freddie began splashing in the shallows rather than venturing farther out into the lake. Cynthia unfolded the blanket and shook it, watching it flutter and spread as it descended towards the dry sand at her feet. Patsy helped her place small piles of stones on each corner of the blanket before joining her brother.

Cynthia slipped her gaze over the view before her. Speedboats tore up and down the center of the lake, some pulling water-skiers behind them. As far as the eye could see, clusters of sunbathers lay sprawled out on stretches of sand or along the lengths of wooden docks like so many seals basking in the sun. As she straightened, she suddenly became aware that a few of them had focused their gaze upon her.

She turned her attention back to the children, who were

calling for her to join them. Self-consciously, she slipped out of her bathing suit cover-up and folded it neatly, placing it in the center of the blanket before picking her way across the hot sand and stepping into the water. The weight from passing motorboats sent ripples of water cascading up over her ankles. It was still early enough in the season that the water was thrillingly chilled.

It had been only a few weeks since newspapers had announced ice-out in all the lakes throughout the state of Maine. Perhaps that would have been enough time for a small lake to warm up, but it certainly had little effect on a body of water the size of Long Pond. She took a few steps towards the children and felt the unsettling ooze of half-decayed leaves squish between her toes. She winced as Freddie slapped his small hands against the surface of the lake, splashing her with water. A shock ran through her body as droplets landed on her arms and legs.

Much of the next hour was spent teaching each of the children to float on their backs, in turn. Cynthia could remember days at the beach playing with her brother. It seemed forever ago. Finally, Cynthia announced she was too cold to stay in a moment longer. She had been attempting to coax the children out for the last several minutes, citing the fact that each of them had blue lips and goose bumps covering their bodies, but it was not until she reminded them of the picnic hamper—and the promise of chocolate cake covered in a layer of thick white frosting for dessert—that she was able to convince the two to head for the shore to warm up.

As the children sat shivering, their teeth chattering loudly as they hunkered beneath their gaily striped towels, Cynthia knelt on the beach blanket and pulled out a packet of cheese sandwiches. She handed half of one to each of the children before peeling back the paper on one of her own. Taking a bite, she turned back towards the lake once more. She hugged her knees with her arms, convinced that the warmth of the sun would dry her off far more quickly than any towel.

The children downed their food ravenously, making entire sandwiches, pickles, and huge wedges of cake disappear as though they were performing a magic trick. Despite their begging to return to the water, Cynthia insisted they wait at least half an hour and handed them each a shovel. Before long, they were engrossed in the construction of a sandcastle and moat.

Out on the lake, a speedboat filled with young people whizzed past, and a boy with dark curls turned towards her and waved. Cynthia waved back, and she felt a momentary squeeze of loneliness as their boat sped away. She had hardly had time to chide herself before the boat turned back around and headed towards her once more. As they came alongside the Mayhews' picnic blanket, the boat driver cut the engine, and the dark-haired boy beckoned Cynthia towards them. She got to her feet and moved to the water's edge.

"Aren't those some of the Mayhew brood?" the boy asked, cupping his hands around his mouth so that his words could be heard across the yards of windswept lake separating them.

Cynthia nodded. "Yes, they're Freddie and Patsy," she said.

"You must be Cynthia," the boy said. "Pauline's roommate."

"That's right," Cynthia called back, feeling shy and awkward as she stood shivering in her new bathing suit in front of a group of strangers.

The young man reminded her very much of Pauline, who always seemed so self-assured. He appeared to be just as impetuous as her too. Without any warning, he dove off the side of the boat and began swimming towards shore with long, graceful strokes. Cynthia had never quite mastered anything besides the breaststroke, and watching his body slipping through the water, expertly exhibiting the proper form for an Australian crawl, impressed her. The motorboat shot away, passing the dock it had launched from, and made its way well down from the lake before he lowered his feet to the lake bottom and strode onto the shore.

"I'm Glenn Bradford." Glenn looked her up and down appraisingly. Once again, she wished her bathing suit covered more of her figure. "I expect Pauline has mentioned me," he said as he ran his hands through his hair and squeezed out some of the lake water. It splashed down onto the sand, disappearing between the thirsty grains. So, this was the boy Pauline had been so eager for her to meet. Her friend was disappointed when Glenn hadn't been at the lake to greet them on that first day on Long Pond.

Before she could respond, Glenn lowered himself onto the picnic blanket and stretched out as if he had been invited to stay. Cynthia could see that he was one of those boys who took the fact that he was welcome anywhere he chose to turn up for granted. Cynthia felt a wave of discomfort wash over her as she resumed her place on the blanket. She wished she were more like Pauline when it came to situations like this one. Hers was the sort of attitude her mother had always wanted her to cultivate. And Glenn was just the sort of boy she wanted her daughter to marry.

"Will you be here for the whole summer?" Glenn asked, shielding his eyes with his hand and watching the children for a moment before turning his blue-eyed gaze back to Cynthia.

"I hope to be."

"What is there to stop you?" Glenn asked.

Cynthia hesitated and then decided there was no reason not to tell the truth.

"My mother may wish for me to return home. And I wouldn't want to wear out my welcome with the Mayhews."

Glenn leaned back on his elbows and looked her in the eyes. "Where's home?"

"South Berwick."

"Never heard of it. Is it in Maine?"

Cynthia was taken aback. If Glenn's family had a place on

the lake, he ought to have heard of South Berwick. Even if he was unfamiliar with Berwick Academy, surely he should know of Sarah Orne Jewett, the town's most celebrated resident. Perhaps he wasn't much of a reader.

"Yes. It's in the southern part of the state, near Wells and Kittery. Do you live on the lake year-round?"

Glenn arched a neat black eyebrow. "Heaven forbid. It's bad enough that my parents make me visit family here for a few weeks every summer. Our home's in Massachusetts. Luckily for me, I don't spend too much time there either."

"Are you a college student?" Cynthia asked.

"That's right. This fall I'll be a junior."

"We're in the same year," she said.

"Really?" His eyes widened in surprise. "I would have guessed that you were older than me."

Patsy scrambled to her feet and raced closer to the lake, a pail in hand. Cynthia kept her attention on the little girl until she returned to the castle and poured an entire bucketful of water into the moat.

"I must just have one of those faces," Cynthia said. But she didn't believe her own words. Her mother had spent countless hours chiding her for behaving so seriously. She would never attract a husband unless she presented herself in a more carefree way.

Glenn rolled onto his side and smiled. "I expect you just need a bit more fun. I don't suppose those two are the best of company." He tipped his head towards the children. Cynthia was mercifully spared the need for a response. "Do you have a steady boyfriend?"

Cynthia shook her head. "No, I don't."

"Even with all the men available at Barlow?"

"You sound like my mother," she said, hoping her tone was more lighthearted than she felt.

"That was forward of me. Please say that I haven't offended you."

"You haven't. It's just that I haven't had much time for dating while I've been away at school."

"Ahh, I see. You're one of those studious types."

Cynthia felt a sudden urge to be someone—anyone—else. She longed to be the sort of girl who flopped onto other people's beach blankets without any feeling of intrusiveness and knew how to effortlessly encourage attention from the right sort of boy. But the truth was, she knew she was neither of those things. Still, she was loath to admit it to a virtual stranger, no matter how friendly.

"I prefer to think of myself as particular," she said, hoping her tone was self-assured rather than defensive. "In fact, I have a good feeling about the prospect of meeting someone here at the lake."

Glenn winked at her. "Maybe you already have." With that, he stretched out on the blanket and closed his eyes, as if he meant to stay indefinitely.

CHAPTER 14

Geraldine

GERALDINE SLID A FINAL JEWELED hairpin into place, hoping that her hasty toilette would do in the purported sophistication of the dining room. Her self-guided tour of the resort had taken far longer than she had bargained for, and she barely had time to change into a silk evening gown and matching slippers if she had any hope of arriving before the meal commenced. She glanced at the dressing table with a feeling of discomfort. It was not her habit to leave her jewelry case unlatched. It was even less like her to leave various bracelets, rings, and necklaces scattered like fallen flower petals over the surface of the table. She was a tidy woman by nature, and it distressed her to appear to be slovenly, especially before the staff learned such behavior was an exception rather than the rule.

Still, it couldn't be helped. What little time she had once she had found her way back to the main building had been gobbled up by deciding which of her evening gowns to wear and wrestling her unruly abundance of gray hair into submission. The grounds had been lovely to view, but the steady breeze off the lake had whipped her hair into the sort of shape her mother had likened to a rat's nest after she had spent the day playing out of doors as a child.

A wave of weariness washed over her as she pulled the door to her room closed behind her and slipped along the corridor as swiftly as she could manage. She prided herself on her health and stamina—as well she should—but the day had been a long one and, truth be told, a bit draining. However, she was seventy-three rather than the fifty-year-old woman she so often told herself she felt like.

She grasped the banister of the gracious stairway with more gratitude than she would have done had she not spent the day wrestling with irritation at the arrival of Anselm's family. She wasn't at all sure that dinner was a good idea. After all, what would they serve at a place rumored to be in not only the pampering business, but one of weight loss as well?

She held her head high as she descended the stairs and made her way along the wide hallway towards the chatter of feminine voices and the clatter of cutlery. As she paused at the threshold, the dining room was already almost filled with women of all ages and sizes, from elderly ladies dressed in formal taffeta gowns that rustled as they shifted slowly in their seats to middle-aged women wearing tea-length gowns with fitted bodices and full skirts like those made popular by Grace

Kelly. The vast majority of them were chattering away with other women seated next to them.

She swept her gaze across the room, evaluating the possibilities. She recognized a clutch of politicians' wives claiming the table with the most commanding view of the dining room and determinedly avoided eye contact with any of them. She had no interest in spending time with women such as them, considering the way the wind was being gusted about by Senator McCarthy and his cronies.

The seats of other well-positioned tables overlooking the lake were completely filled with women smiling and speaking animatedly with their dining companions. It would feel awkward to horn in on already established groups.

She peered deeper into the room and spotted a plump woman sitting alone at a table set for two. At first glance, she appeared to be suffering from a sort of rhythmic twitch. With a jolt of surprise, she realized the woman was knitting. Intrigued, Geraldine crossed the threshold.

"You won't mind if I join you, will you?" she asked as she stopped next to the table and rested a bejeweled hand on the smooth back of a polished wooden chair.

The woman smiled and shook her head. She bent to the side, and when she straightened, her knitting had vanished. Geraldine looked about for a waiter. She wasn't about to pull out her own chair. In an instant, a handsome youth appeared at her side and eased her into her seat before draping a snowy linen napkin across her lap. She nodded her thanks, then returned her attention to her dining companion.

"I don't believe we've met. I'm Geraldine Putnam," she said.

The other woman let out a slight gasp of recognition and drew harsh glances from two older ladies at the neighboring table.

"Marjorie Billings. It's lovely to make your acquaintance. Are you *the* Geraldine Putnam?"

"I suppose it depends on which of us you refer to. I am not under any illusion that there is no one else by that name in the world." Although, truth be told, Geraldine expected she was *the* Geraldine Putnam in most anyone's book.

"Do say that you are the artist."

"Guilty as charged. Are you familiar with my work?"

"Yours are amongst my favorite paintings. I was an art history major in college and worked at a gallery in Boston for a bit before my marriage. We sold more than a few of your paintings during my time there."

"Are you an artist yourself?" Geraldine asked. Although she was quite certain she knew the answer. If she had felt compelled to keep her hands busy, a fellow artist would have brought a sketchbook to the table rather than a ball of yarn.

"I'm afraid that I am merely an admirer of the work of others. Are you here on a painting retreat?"

"Let's just say that I find a change of scenery is a good way to stay inspired." There was no need to discuss her creative block, or Anselm's relations with anyone else. It was time to move the subject away from herself. "Is this your first time at the Maine Chance?" Geraldine asked.

She took a moment to evaluate her tablemate's appearance. Marjorie appeared to be in her early thirties and had a round face and sparkling brown eyes. The wavy dark hair framing her face added to its full appearance, and in Geraldine's opinion, the ruffles across the bodice of her dress only served to make her ample bust appear larger.

Even the color of her garment was not flattering to her vivid complexion. With her dark features and pale skin, more vivacious tones would have suited her far better than the coral color of her dress. She had applied her makeup with real skill, however. Her artistic taste could be witnessed there, even if it did not extend to her choice of clothing.

Marjorie nodded. "There really was no point until recently," she said. "My husband said I might as well wait until I'd finished packing on the pounds with each of our babies. Now that we aren't planning to have any more, he said it was high time I sorted myself out," she said.

Geraldine felt a hot spurt of outrage, like a bout of heartburn searing her chest. For all his faults, Anselm had never criticized her appearance. He had, for the most part, not bothered to compliment her on it, either, but it had made little difference in their marriage. They had both understood that theirs was a practical arrangement, and neither depended on the other for their sense of self. From the look on Marjorie's face, the same could not be said of her own partnership.

"How many children do you have?" Geraldine asked, hoping that was the right way to steer the conversation. It must have been, as Marjorie's face lit up with another beaming smile.

"Three. The littlest one is four months old now. Donald said I'm overdue to shed the baby fat," she said with a sigh.

Before Geraldine could think of a response, a waitress appeared at their table and placed a mound of shredded lettuce topped with a shimmering dome of tomato aspic in front of each of them. Marjorie reached for her fork and lifted a bite to her lips. Geraldine reached for her cutlery and sliced off a bit of the quivering red mass. Just the sight of it made her feel vaguely nauseated; she had always been a picky eater. She pushed it about her plate in an effort to make it appear as though she had consumed at least a part of it. Marjorie was not so easily fooled.

"No wonder you're so slim. Aren't you just about famished?" she asked after swallowing the last bite of her aspic.

"Not for something like that, I'm not. Besides, I've never been particularly interested in food," Geraldine said with a shrug. And it was the truth. She had always been the child whose mother tried to force additional servings of potatoes or pieces of bread on her. She had been made to stay at the table until she cleared her plate, night after night, and it was always a sore trial to her to do so.

"I wish that I were less interested. Being slim is a requirement in my life, but I don't seem to be as naturally inclined to do so as you. Some women have all the luck," Marjorie said without rancor.

"Why is it a requirement?" Geraldine asked, her interest piqued.

"I'm the wife of a wealthy man who gives to charity organizations and attends high-profile society events. He cannot be seen with an unattractive wife on his arm when the newspaper flashbulbs go off, as both he and his mother are quick to point out," Marjorie said.

"But you've just had a baby. They don't expect you to have returned to your pre-pregnancy size so quickly, do they?"

"They most certainly do. My mother-in-law told me that if I don't manage to slim down, it will be my own fault when Donald begins seeing other women." Marjorie shrugged again. "Maybe your attitude and habits will rub off on me and my stay here will be a success."

"How long have you been here?" Geraldine asked.

"Two weeks. I don't mind telling you, they've been the longest of my life." Marjorie looked around as if she had said too much.

Mercifully, the diners at the other tables appeared not to have noticed. Somehow Marjorie seemed a bit out of place, as though she were a fresh-faced country girl who had been dropped without warning into the heart of a bustling city. There was something unsophisticated and naive about her, and it prompted a wave of protectiveness from the older woman.

"Has it been difficult because of the diet regimen?" Geraldine asked.

"That hasn't been particularly pleasant, but what has been truly difficult is the nonstop activity." Marjorie lifted her hand and began counting off on her fingers. "The maid brings lemon and water at seven thirty and then a breakfast tray of juice, coffee, and a single poached egg on wheat toast at eight."

Geraldine grimaced. "Barbarous!"

"After that, we're sent off on a three-mile trek."

"Iris, the housekeeper, told me all about the forced marches and their accompanying pedometers. After such a paltry breakfast, I am sure you are quite wrung out."

"That's just the beginning," Marjorie said. "As soon as we are done with the hike, we're directed to the beach for calisthenics or to the tennis court for a match."

"Calisthenics?" A shudder ran up Geraldine's spine as she recalled the days of her youth, when girls in bloomers attempted to improve their posture and the size of their busts by swinging Indian clubs—things that looked remarkably like bowling pins—in complicated patterns, as recommended in magazines for ladies.

"Yes. We all change into unflattering singlets before trooping out to the beach to make arm circles with Hula-Hoops balanced on our biceps."

"Hula-Hoops?"

Marjorie nodded. "They make us do toe touches and jumping jacks too. All of that is followed by sunbathing."

"Sunbathing? I should have thought Elizabeth would know better than that." In Geraldine's day, a girl preserved her looks by keeping out of the sun as best she could. It was the one piece of her mother's advice she had never neglected to follow.

"I'm afraid so. They send you off to a white-canvas-draped cabana, where a spa attendant vigorously slathers you in perfumed tanning oil. Then, at eleven thirty on the dot, they send you off to the lake for a swim. Thirty minutes later, they send you to the spa for a massage. I confess, it usually puts me to sleep after so much fresh air and exercise."

"Do tell me they give you lunch eventually."

"At one o'clock, there is some sort of salad, followed by a fruit dessert like a baked pear drizzled with raspberry juice. After lunch we have free time to rest in our rooms or to lounge about anywhere on the estate until four in the afternoon."

"More exercise?"

"Thankfully, no. They send us to the spa for facials, masques, and to have our hair shampooed." Marjorie sighed. "I rather enjoy the afternoons."

"When I arrived, I was told that cocktail hour consists of iced vegetable juices, followed by dinner, bridge, and an early bedtime."

"That's right. Everyone is worn out enough from the day's

activities that they are more than happy to retreat to their rooms."

"No wonder you feel that it is difficult," Geraldine said. She hadn't endured such a rigid schedule since she outgrew the need for a governess.

"The program isn't the hardest part of it. What I find truly difficult is spending time away from my children. I miss them terribly, especially the baby."

Geraldine could not relate to that sentiment. Children had not been a significant part of her life.

"How long are you booked to stay?" she asked.

"As long as it takes to drop twenty pounds," Marjorie said, her face clouding over at the thought. She laid down her fork, a few bits of lettuce clinging to the tines. "At the rate I'm going, I'll probably be here until they close down for the season."

Geraldine allowed her gaze to wander across the rest of the dining room once more and noted the average age of the guests was probably twenty or more years younger than her own. Maybe she might just have a good time here after all. She always felt more youthful than her age would suggest. And there was nothing she enjoyed more than a new project. She hadn't had one in ages. Helping Marjorie reach her goal was just the sort of thing she loved to throw herself into. At the very least, she could provide Marjorie with some companionship and maybe even a bit of fashion advice. Even if Marjorie didn't lose a pound during the course of her stay, she could go home looking as if she had simply by making better choices with her clothing and hairstyle.

"Well, my dear, it could be far worse. Like me, you could have upwards of four hundred pounds to shed."

Marjorie's dark eyebrows lifted towards the ceiling. "Surely you are joking."

"Not in the least. I am absolutely determined not to check out of the resort until my dreadful in-laws have removed themselves from my home. As a group, I estimate they weigh approximately four hundred pounds."

A wide smile spread across Marjorie's face. Despite her unfashionable plumpness, she was a pretty woman when not overcome with sadness and self-doubt. Geraldine felt herself smiling back. It had been a good long while since she had done so. Perhaps her stay at the resort would be more than just a way to avoid her in-laws.

CHAPTER 15

Iris

IRIS TENSED AS THE DOOR to the kitchen opened and Dr. Jennings entered. He strode across the squeaky-clean linoleum floor and pulled out a chair across the table from Iris. From the way he drummed his elegant fingers, with their well-scrubbed and trimmed fingernails, on the top of the Formica table, she knew she would not like what he had to say. Not that she had expected good news.

"It's never a pleasure to deliver difficult news, but I expect it will not come as a surprise to you if I say that your mother is suffering from a steep mental decline," he said.

"What exactly do you mean by 'steep'?" she asked, hanging onto hope.

The doctor stilled his fingers and directed his gaze at her. "There's no easy way to say this. Considering your mother's level of befuddlement about even ordinary things, like her own mother's name or which year it is, I would say that she is experiencing significant dementia."

"But that's just it, Doctor. She has spells where she has trouble with knowing what day it is or even what year. Occasionally, she seems to forget that I'm a grown woman, although truth be told she's always had some trouble with that concept," Iris said allowing herself a small smile. "But other days she's as she always has been. She's opinionated, up-to-date on all the goings-on around her, and sharp as a tack. How can you say that she is headed for a steep decline?"

The doctor leaned back against the vinyl-wrapped chair, a creaking sound filling the quiet room. "That's one of the cruelest things about this sort of trouble. People who are suffering from senility can have good days and bad. Sometimes physical strain like a cold or hay fever can tax their mental capabilities. Other times it's an emotional upset or change in their routine that leads to bouts of disorientation. But then they'll have another day or two where they seem like their old selves, and it gives their loved ones false hope."

"Are you saying that if she remains physically healthy and does not experience unsettling conditions, she'll be fine?" Iris said.

He shook his head. "No, that's not what I'm saying at all. It's just that those things can cause the underlying condition to be more obvious. Even on those days when she seems the most lucid, if you pay careful attention, you may notice that she's not actually telling you anything that is specific. One of the things about people suffering from this kind of difficulty is that they are often unwilling for anyone else to become aware of it. They can become quite secretive and crafty and use all of their resources to maintain a facade of normalcy no matter the toll it takes on them."

That did sound like Orla, Iris had to admit to herself. Her mother had never been one to display weakness. She had prided herself on her ability to withstand whatever sorts of bugs were laying waste to all the people around her. She had a sister who had died during the flu epidemic at the time of the First World War and had often proudly announced she had never even been in bed for a day during that crisis. She had even bragged about how quickly she had returned to her duties on the farm after Iris was born. No, she certainly would not have wanted to be seen as unwell.

She also had very little patience with anyone's emotional or mental fragility. While Orla was not an unkind person, she had strong opinions about what she thought of as moral weakness. She was quick to point out when she thought that someone was simply unwilling to pull their weight in life as opposed to those rare people who she thought warranted an actual bit of compassion for real illness. She had even appeared to feel a bit disappointed in her husband for having succumbed to heart disease.

Iris thought back to the sorts of conversations she so often had with her mother. Was it possible that she had assumed her mother was following along when they spoke, but in truth, she was simply giving the sorts of responses Iris took for granted throughout the course of her life? Was she really far worse off cognitively than Iris had realized? The thought that she had been such an unobservant daughter dropped a queasy ball into the pit of her stomach.

"Can she be helped? Is there some sort of medication or a type of rest cure that might return her to her normal self?" Iris asked.

"I'm afraid there is nothing to be done as far as any improvement or even a halting of the disease. Such things take the time they take, but there is no stopping them. I would advise you to reconcile yourself to the fact that while she will have some good days sprinkled in amongst the bad ones, she is not going to recover. Even if her body maintains its current vigor, her mind will continue to deteriorate."

All Iris could hear was the hammering of her own heart and the ticking of the clock on the wall. While she and Orla had not always seen eye to eye, nor had they had the closest of relationships, the prospect of losing any part of her mother was grim. Orla was spryer than most women her age. She kept her home ruthlessly clean and did her own errands, including banking. There was nothing frail about her body, and Iris had not been remotely prepared for the fact that she might slip away mentally before she did so physically.

A tear slithered out from the corner of her eye and rolled down her cheek. She tried to tell herself not to allow such a weak display in front of the doctor, but to no avail. The doctor shifted in his seat and pulled a freshly laundered cotton handkerchief from his back pocket, which he slid across the gleaming surface of the table. She plucked it up and dabbed her eyes.

"So, what is to be done?" she asked.

"It has come to my attention that Orla's been out wandering in town without a real sense of where she's going or why she's there. These episodes have become more frequent, and it sounds as though they are quite unsafe. In my opinion, your mother requires more rigorous supervision."

"I don't know how to manage, not with my job. Are you sure that it's come to that?"

"I wouldn't have suggested if I didn't think it was going to be necessary sooner rather than later. Perhaps you'd be able to get away with her being on her own for a few hours at a time, but that won't last. You are either going to need to hire help or you're going to have to place her in a live-in facility," he said. "I know that's hard news, but it's for her own good."

Iris had never considered placing her mother in any kind of an institution. It simply wasn't what the family did. Elderly men who had lost their wives moved in with their children or younger siblings. Grandmothers or aunts who had become too frail to cook their own meals or wash their own clothes were ensconced in spare bedrooms with some family member or another. But no one had struggled mentally.

Perhaps it was because of family loyalty, but it also might have been because of the expense. No one in Iris's family had ever had enough extra to pay for hired help even in the home, let alone for a facility that provided round-the-clock care. A visit from the doctor was considered an extravagance. With the increase in salary offered by Miss Arden, she might be able to afford care for her mother, but it would still be difficult to manage.

"How soon do you think I'll need to come to a decision?" she asked.

"If you have the rest of the summer before something with Orla comes up that you just can't ignore, I'll be surprised. Once families get to the point that they call me, it usually means that the situation is coming to a head. You won't be the first daughter not to want to see something like this, and you won't be the last. But I promise you, if you bury your head in the sand about it, you will be sorry."

The doctor scraped back his chair and stood. As she walked him to the door, she felt the tears begin to well up in her eyes once more. He paused at the screen door to the front porch and turned to face her once more. He patted her on the shoulder kindly.

As she watched him stride across the dooryard and slide into his dark-colored station wagon, the tears began streaming down her cheeks. She dabbed them away with the doctor's handkerchief. There was no time for a fit of crying. There was simply too much to do.

CHAPTER 16

Geraldine

THE STAFF HAD BEEN THOROUGHLY accommodating. The Maine Chance's reputation was not undeserved. Geraldine watched as the young chauffeur—Calvin, she thought his name was—carried a small wooden table into the modest-size outbuilding. It was one of several she had been offered for use as her temporary studio, and she had been surprised at how well-suited it was for the task. Long windows on one end gave a view off towards the lake. Windows on the other three walls allowed plenty of light to flood the room. The mellow hardwood floor could easily be scrubbed should paint spatter and land upon it. A deep windowsill served as a pleasant perch for any number of things, including her aged backside.

Yes, Geraldine thought, this would do nicely. If only she could manage to get herself to justify her request of its use. She unfurled her paintbrush roll and removed the brushes one by one, placing them carefully into a mason jar thoughtfully positioned on a nearby table.

"Will there be anything else, Mrs. Putnam?" the handsome young man asked, his voice filling the airy space.

She tipped her head to one side and crooked her finger for him to come closer. He seemed a smart lad, and one who likely would be capable of discretion. With his military bearing, it was clear the boy had seen something of the world and made it home safely to tell the tale. There was likely nothing wrong with his intelligence.

"As much as I have found the vast majority of things on offer here to be satisfying in the extreme, I have noticed one notable absence of what I consider to be a common, everyday necessity." She arched an eyebrow at him, wondering if he would fill in the blanks for her.

Leaving his face carefully neutral, he leaned slightly closer. "And what might that be, ma'am? We aim to please in every particularity," he said.

She slipped her hand into her painting-smock pocket and withdrew a crumpled packet of cigarettes, along with a five-dollar bill.

"There seems to be an utter dearth of scotch, gin, or anything else worth drinking at this establishment. I will say that the coffee is good, but it's hardly the sort of thing one wishes to drink at cocktail hour."

“The regimen does not include any alcohol whatsoever, Mrs. Putnam. My understanding is that Miss Arden believes abstinence does a world of good.”

“Miss Arden may be a genius when it comes to potions and lotions, but she ought to leave tippling well enough alone.” She held out the money and watched as Calvin’s eyebrows inched ever so slightly upward. Unless she missed her guess, she had him. “Bring me back a bottle of something decent, and keep the change. Once you’ve brought it to me, there is another five in it for you.”

“Anything to keep the guests happy, Mrs. Putnam,” he said, taking the bill and slipping it into his pocket. “Is there anything else?”

“Don’t be greedy. I expect you back before cocktail hour. I’m not likely to be able to face another of those minuscule dinners without some liquid fortification beforehand.”

He nodded and bounded away. She wondered what sort of thing he’d most like to spend any extra money on. Surely he had no great need to pay for groceries or rent, at least not for the summer, since the staff primarily lived in at the resort and took their meals there, from what she had understood from Iris. Perhaps he was saving up to purchase an automobile. That was all the rage with so many young people these days. Not that she could blame them; she happened to appreciate a fine automobile herself.

She turned her attention to setting up her supplies and

equipment just the way she kept them at home. She found it soothing to snap open the latches on her wooden tackle box and reveal her half-empty tubes of paint and palette knives all nestled cheek by jowl in their compartments. Next, she slipped her folding easel out from its canvas bag and busied herself by straightening its legs and tightening the wing nuts until the whole contraption stood ready for business next to one of the large windows on the lake side.

Now to wait for her muse. She carried the folding chair and an oversize pad of foolscap to the window and perched there. She rummaged through her supplies and plucked up a square stick of charcoal. After propping the pad on her lap, she began sketching out the view of the lake. Seeing it from a different angle began tickling her sense of curiosity about the scene before her.

An island that was not visible from her home studio view was clear to see from her current angle. A lone tree rose up from its center like some sort of watchtower. The shoreline curved and cut behind the island, and she found herself absorbed in the task of trying to represent it authentically. Usually, she was much more concerned with the feeling of the place, but whenever a dry spell such as the one she had been experiencing reared its ugly head, she found it best to go back to basics. She could almost still hear the sound of her most fearsome instructor at the Parisian art school as she used minimal strokes to render the image accurately.

Still, something was missing, and it was not just a lack of her own unique style being demonstrated in the sketch. It was as though the tree were not enough to create in her a sense of satisfaction. She found herself startled by the thought. For so many years, landscapes had been her passion. Never before had she considered a lone tree to be insufficient to serve as the protagonist in a painting. She leaned back in the chair, the scene in front of her suddenly feeling lackluster and unnerved. At this rate, no change of scenery would be enough to help her be ready for the rapidly approaching exhibition.

CHAPTER 17

Cynthia

"SO, WHAT DO YOU THINK?" Pauline asked, leaning towards Cynthia and tilting her head at the group of young men jostling and calling out to one another as they raced to the end of the dock and launched themselves into the air. "Husband material, every one of them—wouldn't you say?"

Cynthia raised a hand to shield her eyes and considered the question. There were several good-looking men in the group, but she couldn't say that any one in particular had grabbed her attention, at least not yet. Truth be told, she barely knew them well enough to keep their names straight, let alone imagine heading to the altar with any of them. Besides, from the way they were behaving, they didn't seem like the marrying kind. Not that she would say that to Pauline. Her friend's eyes were glued to the sets of long, tanned limbs scissoring through the water.

Pauline elbowed her gently as if to prompt an answer.

"I couldn't say. I've only just met them," Cynthia said.

She wriggled her toes deep into the coarse sand, noticing the way the tiny flecks of silica gleamed in the sun. She hoped she hadn't sounded prudish. Pauline tended to tease her about sounding like a schoolmarm, especially when it came to men. The reality was that Cynthia found it difficult to flirt like Pauline or play dumb like their mutual friend Sharon. She simply hadn't the knack or the desire. Despite all the advice spouted in popular magazines for young women, she just couldn't seem to behave in ways guaranteed to attract the admiration of eligible men.

Majoring in economics hadn't helped any either. Although men filled most of the other seats in almost all her classes, none of them exhibited a particular interest in her, at least not as a possible romantic partner, especially not after she so often received the highest marks on tests and assignments. She could still see the crumpled look on her mother's face when she explained the wide chasm between home economics and the other sort. Perhaps if she were to have taken her mother's advice to heart and switched her major, she would already have a steady young man rather than being told she was in the market for one.

"So, what do you think about Andrew? He is a good dancer, and his family is more than well off." Pauline leaned back against her elbows, showing off her bathing suit to good effect.

"Which one is he?" Cynthia asked.

"That one there." Pauline pointed at a russet-haired young

man who had pulled ahead of the others and landed gracefully on the dock. It was easy to imagine him making a good impression on the dance floor, with his long limbs and slim build. He cupped his hands around his mouth and called out something indistinguishable to the others, who were still jostling and ducking one another in the choppy water. He wasn't bad looking in the least, but he wasn't the sort that ever caught her eye. Still, she didn't want to insult Pauline, nor did it seem wise to make a snap judgment. After all, she had only just been introduced to him that afternoon.

"Maybe. I would have to get to know him better before I could form an opinion."

"What more do you need to know? He is available and will be well set for life."

Cynthia wasn't at all sure what to say to that. Pauline sounded a lot like Cynthia's mother. Her idea of Prince Charming involved four usable limbs and a robust bank balance. Common interests, or even good character, didn't seem to be a part of the marriage equation as far as she was concerned. It certainly hadn't seemed to be the most prominent aspect of her parents' marriage. She had privately hoped for more from a partnership of her own but worried that might prove too much to ask.

"Do you know what sorts of things he likes to do?"

"Besides horsing around with the other guys?" Pauline asked. Cynthia nodded. "He plays tennis and golf. And he's crazy about fancy cars."

None of those interests aligned with hers. Cynthia loved to read and preferred long, rambling walks to organized sports. As for cars, she knew how to drive but thought of vehicles mostly as a durable good that, fancy or not, inevitably depreciated. At least they had a love of dancing in common. Perhaps a successful marriage could be based on less. Not that she was entirely sure what she thought constituted a successful marriage.

"I don't really know much about cars. Or sports. You know I'm hopeless at small talk."

"The only thing you need to do is smile sweetly and play hard to get. Any one of those boys won't be able to resist that."

"Isn't that kind of underhanded? What if I end up liking one of them?" Cynthia asked. "Won't he lose interest if I don't let him know how I feel?"

"Trust me. The shortest route between two points is not always a straight line, especially when it comes to romance."

Three of the young men, including Andrew, dived off the end of the dock once more, but one with dark hair and a confident stride emerged from the water and made his way to their blanket. He bent over and plucked up Pauline's towel without asking and began rubbing himself dry with it.

"Make yourself at home, why don't you," Pauline said. Her tone was teasing, and Cynthia could tell that despite the words, her voice held no malice.

"Are you suggesting you aren't thrilled to see me?" His eyes widened with mock surprise, and he tossed the damp towel at Pauline, who squealed and batted it away.

"Beast," Pauline said. She turned to Cynthia and winked. "This horrid boy is Glenn. Don't pay him any notice, though. He is far too full of himself to require any additional attention."

Cynthia had told Pauline about meeting Glenn the day it had happened. She must be giving her a lesson in how to attract the interest of someone like him.

Glenn smiled down at her, and she felt her cheeks warm from more than just the sun. His dark-blues eyes crinkled at the edges as he bent down and extended his hand. She reached out and grasped it with one of her own. Glenn wrapped his long fingers firmly around her palm and held it for just a moment longer than customary politeness dictated.

"Cynthia, isn't it? Or are you Cindy to your friends?"

"Everyone calls me Cynthia."

He bent closer, keeping his eyes trained on her face. "Yes, I suppose they do. Somehow you don't seem much like a nickname sort of girl."

Her stomach twisted. She had always wanted to have a group of friends who gave one another meaningful nicknames, but somehow she hadn't made those sorts of friends. Her parents didn't believe in informal forms of address, so she hadn't been given a nickname by her family either.

Pauline turned towards Cynthia. "Have the two of you met already?" Pauline asked, her voice tinged with mock surprise.

"Didn't she tell you? Cynthia and I met on the beach the other day."

"You never said anything to me about it," Pauline said, winking once more.

Cynthia played along. "There wasn't anything to tell really," she said.

"You cut me to the quick," Glenn said, his eyes widened in mock offense.

Cynthia turned to her friend and proceeded to tell her the same thing she'd told her as soon as Pauline returned from her shopping trip. "He introduced himself when he saw me with Freddy and Patsy on the beach while you were away shopping with your mother."

"I see. There was nothing to tell because we were chaperoned by two little cherubs," he said. "Now, about this nickname—what do you think, Pauline?"

Cynthia blushed. Pauline adjusted her sunglasses and shrugged.

"I don't think you should give a nickname to someone you hardly know," Pauline said.

Glenn broke off his glance and turned his attention to Pauline. There was a current running between the two of them that Cynthia didn't quite understand. Pauline had said she wasn't interested in him in the least, but maybe Glenn hadn't noticed.

"You are right, as always." He lowered himself onto the

blanket and stretched out on his side, propping his head on his hand. "What do you say we get to know each other better?" Glenn stared into her eyes with an intensity that knocked the wind from her chest. She felt tongue-tied, until she noticed Pauline giving her a slight nod.

"I suppose that depends," she said.

"On what?" he asked.

"On what Pauline thinks of you." She stood and carefully brushed the sand from her calves. She lifted her hand to Pauline and then started to walk away.

Glenn called after her, "What does Pauline think of me?"

Cynthia turned around. "You should ask her yourself." From the smile on Pauline's face, she thought she was right to walk away.

CHAPTER 18

Geraldine

Late May

GERALDINE RETURNED TO HER ROOM after lunch, which had consisted of a raft of whipped egg whites floating in a small bowl of clear soup, accompanied by three radishes cut into admirably intricate roses. She was certain the chef hoped the creativity of his offerings would distract from the complete inadequacy of the portions or the utter lack of nourishment the so-called meal provided.

It was more than the food that left her feeling cross. She had gone out soon after the maid had brought in her breakfast tray with an idea of sketching one of the gardens she had seen on her wanderings. But try as she might, she wasn't able to even make an attempt at a drawing. Discouraged, she'd set aside her charcoal and sketchbook and instead spent an hour in the treatment room having her face slathered in a noxious variety of ointments and creams. She was heartily ashamed of herself for wasting the best part of a fine day on such frivolous pursuits when she had nothing whatsoever ready for her upcoming show.

However, as she glanced in the mirror above her dressing table after returning to her room, she had to admit that her face looked rosy and the lines around her eyes and lips seemed far less noticeable than they'd been before she subjected herself to the specialist's ministrations. Even her mood had continued to improve. Perhaps this would be the day she managed to produce a sketch of something—anything—worthwhile. She leaned forward on her bony elbows and pulled back the skin around her cheekbones, for a moment seeing the woman she had been twenty years earlier. Feeling foolish, she dropped her palms to the surface of her dressing table and glanced down at the items still spread across its top.

One of the things she had been reasonably confident in when booking a reservation at the Maine Chance was the high level of service rendered by the staff. But there, still scattered over the top of the dressing table, were the pieces of jewelry she had left out so carelessly the night before. Truly, she should have taken care of them herself when she returned the prior evening after dinner and found the items were still out of place. But the truth was, she had felt quite worn out from her long day. Between the confrontation with Anselm's family, all the fresh air from checking about the grounds, and the genteel din of the dining room, she had simply not felt up to anything beyond removing her makeup and tumbling into bed. In fact, she had slept so deeply that it was only the sounds of other footsteps in the hallway and female voices chattering to one another that woke her from her deep sleep in time to be pulled into an upright position when her maid had entered carrying her breakfast tray.

As she looked down, something bothered her that she could not quite put her finger on—that was, until she thought about fingers. One of her rings, a large pearl surrounded by rubies and set in white gold, had been among the many items she had tried on and then discarded the night before in her hasty preparations for dinner. Geraldine pushed back the vanity stool and glanced about on either side of the dressing table. It was the sort of thing that could easily have fallen from the table with a slightly exuberant flick of a maid's feather duster. Finding nothing, she bent down and lifted the ruffled skirt with its many fabric flounces wrapping around the base of the dressing table. There was nothing to be spotted underneath either.

She clicked open the small brass lock on her white leather jewel case and searched it carefully. Her heart sinking in her chest, she had to admit that the ring was nowhere to be seen. And although she was in her seventies, she was certain her memory was not slipping in the least. No, there was no doubt about it—the ring had been moved.

The next ten minutes she spent searching the rest of the space, hoping that perhaps it could have been flung farther from its anticipated location than she would have expected. But to no avail. She even went so far as to inspect every nook and cranny of the bathroom. Cash was missing from a dresser drawer as well. With a heavy heart, she considered what to do next. If she had been in her own home, she certainly would have felt sure of how to proceed, but here, at the resort, things would be handled differently than in a private residence.

Besides, she liked Iris and had no desire to put her in a difficult position. She also had no idea how many different employees might have been involved with the cleaning of her room. As she was so new on the premises, she had no sense of the trustworthiness of any of their employees, besides Iris herself. She knew she could simply lift the white Bakelite telephone receiver and ask for the housekeeper, but somehow she felt it was a matter best handled face-to-face.

Geraldine glanced in the mirror once more and touched up her lipstick. Suddenly, her face no longer looked quite so fresh and well rested. While Geraldine was not the sort to suffer fools gladly or hold back when she felt she was right, this was exactly the sort of unpleasantness she knew could alter someone's life. But if there was one thing she never could stand, it was a thief. She made her way down the stairs swiftly. Once she had made up her mind, there was no sense in putting things off. After determining Iris's whereabouts from the young woman stationed at the reception desk, she assured the girl that she would be happiest to track the housekeeper down in her private room.

Following the receptionist's directions to an outbuilding discreetly tucked behind a large stand of lilacs not so very far from the main building, Geraldine stepped up onto the freshly painted porch and, without bothering to knock, twisted the shiny brass knob on the door. The two-story building had likely once been a single-family home, but now it served the purpose of housing for many of the female staff at the resort. She made her way along the creaking floorboards towards the very back of the hallway. After raising her hand and rapping firmly on the closed door, she waited to be invited in before pressing it open and stepping inside.

Iris was seated with her back to the door, a ledger spread out on a desk in front of her. A shaft of sunlight spilled through the large window and highlighted a few strands of silver hair woven through her neat braid. When the housekeeper turned, her mouth opened slightly with surprise before she remembered herself and shot to her feet.

"Mrs. Putnam, what can I do for you?"

"I don't believe in mincing words, Iris. I'm afraid that what you're going to have to do for me is to relieve one of your staff members of duty."

Iris's sturdy hand clutched the base of her throat, and her mouth opened slightly once more.

"I don't understand. Has someone offended you in some way?"

Geraldine shook her head. "It's rather more serious than

that. I'm very sorry to have to bring this up with you, especially so early in your tenure as a housekeeper, but I'm afraid it cannot be helped. In fact, it could be considered a blessing to root it out before there is any damage to either the resort's reputation or even your own."

Iris's face flushed deeply red, but she did not stammer. "That sounds very serious, indeed. What exactly is the problem?"

"A valuable pearl-and-ruby ring is missing from my room. I've made a tediously thorough search and distinctly remember trying it on last night before dinner. In addition, there is a crisp twenty-dollar bill missing from my dresser. I'm afraid you have a thief on your staff."

All the color drained from Iris's face like a wave pulling back from the shore.

"When did you first notice that the items were missing?" she asked.

Geraldine was pleased to note that Iris did not question her as to whether or not she was correct in her assessment that the item was actually missing. It galled her no end when people assumed that just because she was getting on a bit, her mind was not what it once was.

"It was just now, when I returned to my room. I was gone for most of the morning. To be fair, the last time I noticed the ring was just before I went down to dinner last night. I paid no attention to the items still scattered on top of my dressing table when I prepared to go out this morning. I placed the money in the drawer when I arrived yesterday afternoon. I haven't had any need of a twenty-dollar bill since then."

"Are you saying that not only are you missing a piece of jewelry and money, but also that your dressing table was left littered with items since last evening before dinner?" Iris asked.

A note of suppressed outrage tinged Iris's voice. Geraldine made another mental note as to the younger woman's capability as a housekeeper. It spoke volumes that not only had she accepted a guest's version of events without question, but that she also understood how inept it was for the dressing table not to have been tidied hours earlier.

"I'm afraid so. I would not have bothered you with something so trivial, at least not the first time it occurred, but the missing jewelry and cash is something I simply could not ignore. I count Miss Arden as a very friendly acquaintance through our shared interest in the local garden clubs and charity events. I would hate to see her business damaged by something so distasteful as employing staff known to be thieves."

Iris squared her shoulders. "I truly appreciate you coming to me directly with this. Please rest assured that it will be attended to immediately. Is there anything I can do to make you more comfortable while I am handling this matter?"

"Just see to it that whoever was in my room is dismissed from your service. I cannot abide a thief, nor—if you value your job and the reputation of this establishment—should you." With that, Geraldine turned on her heel and left the room.

CHAPTER 19

Cynthia

Early June

EVEN THOUGH THE DAY WAS waning, the summer sun warmed the paddle in Cynthia's hand, bronzing her skin and leaving her feeling drowsy and languid. The slightly musty smell of the lake water rose to her nostrils as waves created by passing speedboats slapped against the side of the canoe. With a few long strokes, she pulled up to the Mayhews' dock. She tethered the small craft to a metal cleat mounted to the end of the dock and exited the boat with little enthusiasm.

She had spent the better part of the day making the rounds at lakefront campgrounds and hotels looking for work. Everyone she'd encountered was pleasant enough—kind, even—but not a one of them had a job available. In fact, a few of them looked at her as if she were a bit touched in the head when she asked about possible employment. If she didn't find something soon, she would have little choice but to head home and ask her parents to allow her to look for work there.

She had even hinted to Mr. Mayhew that she would be interested in a position at the seasonal newspaper where he worked as the editor every summer. He had lit up at the suggestion and had spent the better part of an hour telling her all about the paper before mentioning that there were no openings. The newspaper was a small one, and the only other positions were highly valued by the local residents who had held them for years. He told her that they depended on the income from their summer jobs and that he could not see depriving them of it for a college girl like herself.

She stood on the splintery dock, lost in thought and lulled by the sound of small waves slapping against its side. A voice called to her from the lake, and she turned to look for the source of the sound. She lifted a hand to shield her eyes from the glare of the lowering sun. Mr. Mayhew pulled a paddle through the water, deftly propelling another canoe across the lake, swiftly closing the gap between them. He lifted the paddle a few feet from the dock and allowed the momentum to gently push the boat up against the dock before tying it off and disembarking.

She had not realized it had grown so late. He used the canoe to make the daily trip to the newspaper office, usually returning in time for the cocktail party his wife was sure to either be throwing or expecting him to accompany her to at one of the many neighbors' equally lavish homes. Cynthia would be expected to have already changed into evening clothes.

In the three weeks she had been in Mount Vernon,

something of a routine had emerged. For the most part, she spent some of each fine day at the beach with Pauline. Searching for a job had taken up much of her time, as well, sadly to little result. Each evening, Mrs. Mayhew expected them back home to socialize with the people she deemed worthy. Parties at the Mayhew home, or at that of one of their neighbors', had been held each day since she and Pauline had arrived. Bridge, whist, cocktails, and even dancing were par for the course. Pauline seemed to look forward to all of it, but Cynthia had had her fill. Still, she could hardly refuse her hostess.

"You have some mail," he said as he pulled a large envelope from the breast pocket of the sports jacket draped over his arm.

Cynthia recognized her mother's rounded hand on the front of the oversize envelope. She accepted it from his extended hand.

"It's from home," Cynthia said.

"I hope it isn't a message insisting that you return. Pauline has been so much easier to have around with you here to keep her company. And I must say, the rest of the family has enjoyed your visit too," he said.

Cynthia felt her cheeks begin to burn. She had never quite learned the art of gracefully accepting a compliment. Besides, she couldn't credit that his wife was pleased to host her. To hide her discomfort, she hurried up the path ahead of him.

"I've enjoyed myself too," she said. "It has been so kind of you to have me."

"Think nothing of it," he said. "The pleasure is all ours."

Mrs. Mayhew appeared in the doorway of the screen porch, a martini glass held aloft in her slim hand. Sunlight glinted off a delicate gold bracelet dangling from her wrist. From the set of her jaw, Cynthia could tell she was not best pleased with her husband. Cynthia stole a glance at her wristwatch and noticed he had arrived at least half an hour later than he had in the time she had been in Mount Vernon. She lifted a hand in greeting to Mrs. Mayhew, waggling her envelope at her hostess.

"I've had a letter from home. I hope you will excuse me from the festivities for long enough to read it," she said. Not that there was any real question. While she was welcome to join the older generation for cocktails, such gatherings were not sit-down affairs and she would not be missed by anyone, likely not even by Pauline, who used the alcohol-fueled gatherings as an opportunity to make an impression on potential in-laws. Besides, she had a sneaking suspicion that Mrs. Mayhew inexplicably regarded her as competition for Pauline.

"Take your time." With that, she turned her gaze on her husband and held the door open to allow him to enter the house. Cynthia noticed she turned her face away just as Mr. Mayhew attempted to kiss her cheek.

Up ahead, strung between two lofty pines, was a hammock that was perfect for reading. She had polished off several books while stretched out on it since she had arrived and thought it would serve just as good a place to read her mother's letter.

She climbed into the hammock with as much grace as she

could manage, then kicked off her shoes and lay back, her head nestled against a folded-up blanket left by the last occupant. She carefully tore open the envelope and slid out the contents.

Her mother had saved up and forwarded all of her mail. Cynthia sorted through it, noting letters from high school friends, an invitation for an open house at a new beauty parlor in her hometown, and even a newsy note from her mother conveying the activities of her bridge club friends and fellow churchgoers. At the bottom of the pile was the latest issue of the *American Economic Review.*

Her heart thumped wildly as she thumbed through the magazine until she reached the article Professor Avery had assured her was to be included. She read the title, one she had agonized over creating, and felt her spirits sink. There, in bold black type, was Professor Avery's name on the byline. Hers was nowhere to be seen.

A wave of cold washed over her despite the warmth of the night. She had consoled herself that a publishing credit in such a prestigious journal might still make it possible to start a career as a stockbroker or even a columnist with a financial publication. She had been counting on the article to convince someone to give her a chance at a job in her field even if she couldn't get back to school. Now even that was impossible. Angry tears welled up, and she brushed them away with the back of her hand.

Lights were blinking on inside the house and in the homes

dotted around the lake. She swung her feet over the side of the hammock and slipped her shoes back on. She wasn't sure how she could manage it, but more than ever she was determined to get back to Barlow and show them what a clever girl like her could do.

Laughter from the cocktail party spilled through the open windows and out into the yard. She slipped in through the back door, hoping she might reach the rear stairs without encountering any of the Mayhews' many boisterous guests. She was in no mood to make small talk with strangers. Not that she ever looked forward to parties all that much, but she doubted she would be able to do a good job of masking her true feelings with such news weighing heavily on her mind.

The kitchen was brightly lit but empty as she moved quietly past a long counter covered in platters filled with canapés and meatballs skewered onto frilled party picks. She gasped as her elbow jostled a large plate placed close to the counter's edge and set the towering molded gelatin salad it held quivering.

"I wondered where you had gotten off to—but I confess, I had hoped you were involved in more mischief than endangering the Jell-O," Pauline said as she stepped out from the darkened breakfast nook, waving a hand in front of her face.

Cynthia smelled cigarette smoke. Despite her own habit, or perhaps because of it, Mrs. Mayhew discouraged her daughter from smoking and made a fuss about it whenever she caught her with a cigarette.

"Sorry, I just wasn't up for a party," Cynthia said. She felt her nose begin to sting and willed herself not to burst into tears.

Pauline cocked her head to the side and scrutinized her face. "What's happened?"

Cynthia considered keeping her bad news to herself. How could someone in Pauline's situation understand her own? But as her friend stepped forward and reached for her hand, she felt her resolve melt away.

"I've had a mail packet from my mother," she said. "It had some bad news in it."

"No one is ill, are they?" Pauline asked.

"No. It was nothing like that."

"Well, what else could leave you looking so glum? She hasn't asked that you return home early, has she?"

"It wasn't anything my mother said. My magazine came, and it seems that Professor Avery took all the credit for the article I wrote myself."

Pauline's eyes widened. "What a crook."

"I had been hoping that even if I couldn't fund the rest of my education, I might be able to get a job in my field anyway if I had a prestigious publishing credit on my résumé."

"You still haven't found anyone hiring here in town?"

Cynthia shrugged and tried to hold back tears. A mixture of humiliation and rage churned in her chest, and her words erupted from her more harshly than she intended.

"Not one nibble."

Pauline squeezed her hand. "Things look bad, but it could all still turn out okay. What if you were to become engaged before the summer's out? I'm determined to receive a proposal from Kenneth, and I bet you could do the same with Glenn."

Cynthia shook her head, and the tears she had been so carefully holding back spilled down her cheeks. "That isn't my idea of turning out okay."

"Still, wouldn't it be far better to marry well rather than to return home without anything to show for all of your hard work over the past two years?" Pauline asked.

Her friend had completely misunderstood her distress. Pauline had not applied herself to her own studies to any greater degree than what permitted her to pass her classes. She would not be likely to understand that even if Cynthia had to leave after only two years, she would not feel the effort had been for naught. A hastily gotten proposal would not take the sting out of the derailment of her education, no matter how wealthy or well-connected the partner.

"We shall have to simply throw you together with Glenn whenever possible until he pops the question," Pauline said.

Footsteps sounded from behind Cynthia's back. She patted her eyes with the backs of her hands, hoping to erase all signs of tears without smearing her mascara. If only someone would come up with a waterproof mascara that wasn't made with turpentine. Pauline smiled and waved her hand at whoever it was standing just out of Cynthia's sight.

"Are you all right?" Glenn asked, crossing the room in a few long strides and coming to a stop at her side.

She nodded, not trusting her voice not to crack with emotion she didn't care to share.

"She will be once we get her paired off seriously with the right sort of young man," Pauline said, elbowing Cynthia gently in the ribs.

Cynthia flinched. She had no intention of discussing something so private with a relative stranger, and a male one at that. How could Glenn possibly understand the position she was in? He surely had no trouble accessing tuition money. Besides, as much as women were reputed to be the romantic sex, she knew that men were at least as eager to marry for love. They could afford to by and large since a wife's income was not to be considered when contemplating a match. She pulled a face at her friend, hoping to silently convey her reluctance to include Glenn in the conversation, but Pauline gave no sign she understood.

"Are you looking to get married?" Glenn asked, arching an eyebrow in surprise.

Before she could answer for herself, Pauline spoke again. "Of course she is, but only to the right sort."

Cynthia felt her face grow flushed. Pauline made her sound so grasping.

"Who did you have in mind?" he asked.

Pauline tapped a long forefinger against her chin as if she needed to give the matter thought.

"Andrew would do nicely, don't you think?" she said.

Glenn crossed his arms over his chest and widened his stance. "You can't possibly want to saddle a girl as charming as Cindy with a square like Andy."

"Andrew is a catch," Pauline said, her smile starting to slip.

"Not for Cindy, he isn't," Glenn said turning towards her.

"Why not?" Pauline asked. "His family is fabulously wealthy; he's a good dancer, and he isn't bad looking."

Glenn shook his head. "He's a stick-in-the-mud. A girl like Cindy needs a guy who knows how to show her a good time." He placed a hand on his chest. "She's particular when it comes to men. She told me so herself."

Cynthia didn't want to say anything one way or the other, but she was inclined to agree with Glenn. Andrew seemed pleasant enough, but he wouldn't distract her from what mattered. The only thing she really wanted was a job.

Pauline's eyes narrowed. "Did you have someone else in mind?" she asked.

"Maybe," Glenn said, leaning slightly towards Cynthia and smiling. Then he turned around and strode out the door without another word.

Pauline giggled. She turned her gaze on Cynthia. "You sly dog. It looks like you've made quite the impression on Glenn. Is there something you haven't been telling me?"

Cynthia shook her head. "I can't imagine what's gotten into

him. I've only spoken with him once or twice when you weren't around."

Pauline placed her hands on her hips. "They must have been memorable conversations."

"Not for me, they weren't," Cynthia said.

"I'd say that if you just put in a bit of effort, you could have a ring on your finger before Labor Day."

"I wish you wouldn't say things like that."

"Why not? Not only do I think it's true, I hope that it is. If he gets engaged to you, my mother will stop pushing me at him."

As if summoned by her daughter's comments, Mrs. Mayhew appeared in the kitchen doorway, another martini glass held aloft.

"Pauline, what are you doing skulking around in the kitchen like the help? Glenn's parents are asking after you." She waved her daughter towards the living room, pointedly ignoring Cynthia.

Pauline turned back as she reached the doorway and winked before gliding towards the din of the party. Cynthia turned in the opposite direction and headed into the hall. There, on the telephone table, was a local directory. She tucked it under her arm and started up the stairs, taking them two at a time. There had to be somewhere on Long Pond where she could find a job.

CHAPTER 20

Iris

Early June

IT HAD TO BE DONE, Iris told herself. The girl simply hadn't been suited for the task. There would surely be fallout from the sacking, of course. There always was, in a town as small as Mount Vernon. But what else could she have done?

Velda had been a problem from the very beginning. More than once, Iris had come upon episodes of canoodling between Velda and one of the farmhands. Not only that, but some of the other girls living in the staff house had complained about catching Velda riffling through their personal possessions. Two of them had mentioned missing money from their coin purses.

Geraldine's complaint had spurred Iris to inspect the girl's room in the staff house. Her breath caught in her throat when she peered into a pocket of a small handbag hanging in the back of Velda's closet. A large ring matching the description Geraldine had given sat at its bottom, hidden beneath a freshly creased twenty-dollar bill. Such a sum had no good explanation for being in the girl's possession. Velda was the sort whose pay packet burnt a hole in her pocket the minute she received it. Iris could not remember her ever returning from a trip into town without some new trinket or bit of frippery she had splurged on at the five-and-dime store. With a heavy heart, she returned the items to Geraldine.

Iris was still shaking slightly from the confrontation with Velda. While she did not think she had betrayed her nerves as she was dismissing the girl from her job at the resort, she had been quaking on the inside, almost to the point of nausea. It was not a part of her new role she thought she would ever entirely make peace with. The longer she stood in Alice Merrick's shoes, the more she respected her former supervisor. Alice had run a tight ship, and Iris couldn't imagine anyone daring to steal from a guest on her watch. She could only hope to create half such a formidable reputation herself.

Velda had seemed surprised at the news her services would no longer be required, which Iris thought spoke volumes about the girl's understanding of what the position involved. She had been in little doubt before confronting her that removing her from the property was the correct thing to do. By the time Velda had flounced off, hurling insults and making a scene, Iris was convinced she had been right to do so.

That still did not leave her in a sunny frame of mind or feeling as though the problem was solved. With so many people in town being either blood relatives or connected through strong bonds of friendship, Velda would have many people in Mount Vernon taking her side of things and thinking Iris had become self-important since she had been promoted to housekeeper.

Not the least of her worries, however, was the fact that she was down one maid. The staff at the Maine Chance numbered two for each guest in order to maintain Miss Arden's high standards. What would Iris do now that she was shorthanded? Any of the help worth having would already have taken jobs elsewhere since the season was well underway. Two weeks might not seem like much time in other industries, but the tourist season in Maine lasted only fourteen on a good year.

It was true that the Maine Chance paid well and had a decent reputation among the townsfolk for the way employees were treated—at least, it did before Iris let Velda go. How quickly could that change? All in all, the entire situation was regrettable. Even if the resort's reputation was not damaged, it was likely that Velda's would be. A thing like that could stay with someone for the rest of their life in a town with under a thousand year-round residents.

Iris sighed and wondered if she would be able to even hang on to her own position under the circumstances. She thought she could ask Frances if she would look in on her mother that afternoon rather than doing so herself. The time saved might be enough for her to catch up on what little work Velda might have performed herself had she been there for the rest of the day. The telephone at the reception desk rang and jolted her from her worries.

"The Maine Chance Farm, Iris Hubbard speaking. May I help you?" she said, hoping her voice sounded calmer than she felt.

"Hello, Iris. Elizabeth Arden speaking. I need to discuss two matters with you."

In the space of two heartbeats, any semblance of calm fled from Iris. The voice of her employer filled her ears. Miss Arden telephoned from time to time, often to say she would be arriving with almost no notice, requesting one of the cars be sent for her in only a few hours' time. Occasionally she even telephoned from the train station, announcing she would require a car immediately. Often Alice had mentioned she wished the train station in Belgrade was just a bit farther away. But this was much different. Iris swallowed twice and hoped her thudding heartbeat could not be heard along the telephone line.

"How may I be of service?"

"I have given my assurance to a high-profile guest that you will have room for her starting tomorrow. That won't be a problem, will it?"

Iris raced through the list of reservations she kept in the back of her mind at all times. Two senators' wives, an internationally renowned opera singer, three socialites, and a Hollywood starlet were all due to arrive that week. Fortunately, one of the many things she had learned from Alice had been the need to always keep at least two rooms available for Miss Arden's last-minute visitors. It would not do to refuse any of her requests, but most importantly not one that caused her to lose face in front of her social set.

"That won't be any trouble at all. The Blue Satin Suite will be ready by the end of today. May I inquire as to the name of the guest?"

"Vivian Shaw. She arrives by train tomorrow morning and will require a car to collect her in Portland."

A movie star. No wonder Miss Arden wanted a car sent instead of having her transfer to a local train upon reaching Portland. Many of the visitors, including Miss Arden herself, took a connecting train out of the state's largest city to one of the smaller stations nearby. With so many people traveling to Maine on vacation, there were several stations to choose from that brought passengers within only a few miles of their final destination.

"Excellent. This brings me to the second reason for my call. I have a proposition for you," Miss Arden said. "The housekeeper of the Maine Chance in Arizona has just informed me that she does not plan to return for the upcoming season. It occurred to me that it might be a good thing for each of us if the same person held the position at both locations. Essentially, since the resorts run at different times of the year, you would become a year-round employee."

Whatever Iris might have expected her employer to say, that was not it. She gripped the edge of the reception desk in an attempt not to lose her balance. The world felt as if it had shifted on its axis. What would it be like to not scrimp and save all summer in order to barely get by in the offseason? What would it be like to travel so far from home? She felt both elated and petrified at the same time. The silence on the other end of the line jostled her back to the task at hand.

"I am very flattered that you would even consider me for the position. I will endeavor to meet all of your expectations," Iris said.

"The offer is, of course, dependent on your performance in Mount Vernon this season, but I expect it would be worth your while to impress me."

"I understand. I will need to discuss the matter with my family before I can agree, however." She hoped that just speaking up that much had not put her out of the running for the job.

"It was my understanding that you are unmarried, or I would not have thought to consider you for such a position. Am I ill-informed?" Miss Arden asked, a note of irritation creeping into her voice.

"You are correct. I'm not married, but I do have an aging mother with whom I live in the offseason. I would wish to discuss it with her before giving you an answer."

Iris could make out a quiet grunt on the other end of the line. Her heart hammered in her chest.

"That's very admirable, I'm sure. Do speak with your mother at the first opportunity. And remember, the offer would be entirely conditional on your performance this summer. There cannot be any reduction in quality of the way that resort is run from the time your predecessor was in charge."

"I understand completely. I won't let you down."

"I should hope not. Otherwise, I will be forced to replace two housekeepers."

A wave of dizziness swept over Iris once more. The idea of losing her position just after it had improved didn't bear thinking about. Her voice caught in her throat, and the pause gave Miss Arden time to name a figure that the year-round salary to take on both jobs earned. Iris's throat went dry. Never in her life had she made such a sum.

"I will speak with my mother as soon as possible," Iris said.

"I suppose that will do. I shall telephone back within a few days and will expect your answer when I do," Miss Arden said before hanging up.

Somehow, despite her trembling hands, Iris managed to replace the receiver in its cradle. Not even in her wildest dreams had she imagined such an opportunity would come her way. The notion that she might earn such an income was at least as impossible to consider as the fact that she had the opportunity to relocate, even if only for part of the year, to a place as far away and exotic as Arizona. But if she was going to make it happen, she'd have to figure out how to take care of her mother in her absence. And even if she solved that, what in the world was she going to do about finding a replacement for Velda?

CHAPTER 21

Cynthia

CYNTHIA STEPPED OUT INTO THE sunlit street. Despite Pauline's insistence that there must be jobs to be had in Mount Vernon, she had not been able to find one. Every restaurant, boardinghouse, cottage rental, and storefront where she had made inquiries politely but firmly assured her that they had filled all openings weeks ago. As she moved to a shady patch beneath a towering maple, she admitted to herself that she might have to head home in defeat.

She couldn't very well impose on the Mayhews' hospitality for much longer, no matter how vigorously Pauline waved away her concerns. Mrs. Mayhew had asked at the breakfast table that very morning if Cynthia's mother wasn't eager for her return. Pauline might not believe there were limits to her parents' generosity, but Cynthia was certain she was mistaken. It had occurred to her that even if by some miracle she managed to get a job, she would likely need to spend some of her hard-earned wages on room and board. The Mayhews could not be expected to offer free housing for the entire season. With each passing day, it seemed the likelihood of earning enough money to return to Barlow before the end of the summer decreased.

She glanced at her wristwatch, a prize from her high school for being the class valedictorian, and realized she was due to meet Pauline at the newspaper office in a few minutes' time. She moved slowly along the sidewalk, dodging a group of young boys clutching drippy ice cream cones, no doubt purchased at the shop that needed no more staff. When she reached the newspaper office and peered through the plate-glass window, she could see Mr. Mayhew seated behind a wooden desk. A lazily turning ceiling fan ruffled the newspaper held in his hands. He looked up as she entered and gave her a warm smile.

"Pauline hasn't arrived yet, so you'll have to make do with me for the time being," he said. Before she could reply, the door opened behind her, and a heavyset woman with gray curly hair topped by a green pillbox hat pushed past her and headed straight for the desk next to Mr. Mayhew's.

"That Iris Hubbard has gotten above herself, and make no mistake," she said, thumping her brown leather handbag down beside an old-fashioned typewriter. She dropped into the desk chair and spun it around to face Mr. Mayhew.

"That doesn't sound like Iris to me," Mr. Mayhew said as he lowered the paper.

"According to my niece Velda, Iris's new job has gone right to her head."

Mr. Mayhew raised his eyebrows. "I thought Velda and Iris got along just fine."

Cynthia wasn't quite sure what to do. She felt as though she were eavesdropping, but the woman must have seen her when she entered the office. After all, she'd practically bumped into her as she made a beeline for her desk. She decided it would be more awkward to leave than to simply stand quietly and wait for Mr. Mayhew to introduce her—or better yet, for Pauline to arrive.

The woman continued as if she didn't care who heard what she had to say. "By all accounts they did, until Iris fired her without warning."

"Are you sure? That doesn't sound like Iris to me," he said again.

"I hardly think Velda would make up stories about being let go. Regardless, where is she going to find another job now that the season is already underway? Everyone already hired any staff that they need weeks ago."

The feeling of discouragement Cynthia had been striving to hold off washed over her. It had not been panicked imagination on her part. There truly were no jobs to be had. She glanced over at Mr. Mayhew, hoping the woman was wrong.

"Iris would know that Velda wouldn't find other work. She must have had a good reason to dismiss her," he said.

The woman crossed her arms over her ample bust and scowled.

"Oh, she gave a reason, all right, but it wasn't what I would call 'good.' I also wouldn't say there's a bit of truth in it either." The woman's voice grew louder and more strident. "Iris accused her of stealing. She said she can't have any untrustworthy staff, but especially not one of the maids."

Mr. Mayhew sucked in a sharp breath. "That sounds serious."

"It will utterly ruin Velda's reputation. Iris's opinion counts for something in town, and if she's going around saying Velda's a thief, then no one else will hire her either. Not now and not in the years to come. I cannot believe she would do a thing like that."

It seemed to Cynthia that her niece's plight wasn't being helped by the woman gossiping about her misfortune in front of a total stranger. If she had been the girl accused of stealing, she would hardly want a family member spreading the story to someone like Mr. Mayhew. Considering his role at the paper, as well as his large social set, he was in the position to pass the story along to any number of others, should he choose to do so.

"I'm sure that Velda is upset, but I cannot imagine that Iris would make such an accusation without some sort of proof. After all, she is new to the housekeeper role, and she won't succeed at it if the service provided to guests at the Maine Chance falls off. Miss Arden isn't known for her tolerance of anything less than the best," Mr. Mayhew said.

"It would be no more than she deserved if Iris got the boot, too, after what she's done to poor Velda." The woman spun back around in her chair and yanked open her purse. She pulled out a cigarette case and, with a trembling hand, flicked her lighter. She leaned back in her chair and closed her eyes as she took a long drag. "Considering the fact that Velda is probably the only person in Mount Vernon who doesn't already have a job, Iris will have a devil of a time finding someone to replace her."

Cynthia's heart pounded faster. Out of the corner of her eye, she spotted Pauline across the street. She raised a hand to Mr. Mayhew and hurried out of the newspaper office and rushed towards her friend.

"Sorry I'm late. I ran into Kenneth, and he invited us to meet him on the beach this afternoon to water-ski," Pauline said as she reached her side. "How goes the job search?"

Cynthia shook her head. "What's the Maine Chance?" she asked as she laid a hand on Pauline's arm to keep her from crossing the street.

"It's a spa and beauty resort. Elizabeth Arden owns it."

Cynthia felt a thrill race through her. She admired the cosmetic mogul and looked up to her as one of the most successful businesswomen of the age. She had no idea that the older woman had a connection to Maine.

"If Elizabeth Arden is involved, it must be exclusive."

"You could say that. I've heard that Eleanor Roosevelt and Rita Hayworth are both frequent visitors."

"A place like that is here in Mount Vernon?" Cynthia asked. She knew that tourists were drawn to Maine in droves, and for good reason. The state was famous for its rocky coast, vast forests, and pristine lakes. Still, even though she didn't take her home's assets for granted, she was startled to think such illustrious names made their way to as quiet a place as Mount Vernon. The town was charming, to be sure, but it wasn't a place Cynthia would have expected to attract the notice of First Ladies and Hollywood starlets.

"Yes. It's on Long Pond. Why do you ask?"

"Because from what that woman in the newspaper office is saying to your father, they have just had an opening for a maid."

Pauline squinted at the window. "That's Daddy's right hand, Bernice. Did she say they were hiring?"

"She said her niece has just been fired from the place. And she said the housekeeper will have trouble finding a replacement." Cynthia tried to keep the glee from her voice. After all, it felt wrong to be so encouraged by another's misfortune.

Pauline tipped her head to one side. "I should have thought of the resort straightaway, but somehow it just slipped my mind. It's one of those places that's so self-contained there isn't much impact on the town because of it, other than seasonal employment for maids and gardeners."

"The guests don't spend money in town?" Cynthia asked. Service jobs in the tourism industry were beneficial to the economy, but the value of tourist dollars at gas stations, restaurants, and shops selling souvenirs, toiletries, and clothing items was considerable too. A business that contributed one without the other was nowhere near as useful to a community as one that offered both.

Pauline snorted. “The types of ladies who spend over five hundred dollars each week to stay at the Maine Chance are not the sort to shop at the five-and-dime. If they need to shop, they have a driver take them to Augusta or Portland to do it.”

At least that meant they were still spending money in the state’s economy. Between the profit on the actual goods, the sales tax, and the toll money spent on the new turnpike, the dollars could add up considerably. Still, Cynthia knew that the most desirable outcome for a town was to keep as much of the lucrative tourist money in their own communities. As much as she felt guilty about it, even if she got a job, she wouldn’t be spending her hard-earned paycheck on anything but the bare necessities either.

“If it isn’t too far, I think I’ll head over there straightaway.”

Pauline’s forehead crinkled. “But what about waterskiing? Kenneth promised that Glenn would be there.”

“You know I have to make the job search my priority. I’m sure there will be other times.”

Pauline nodded. “I guess. I wish I could offer you a ride, but if I do, Daddy will want to know why I need the car, and then your secret will be out.”

Cynthia looked down at her shoes. They weren’t ideal for walking, but they would do if the resort wasn’t too far off.

"Just wish me luck and point me in the right direction. I'm sure I'll get there on my own."

She listened carefully to Pauline's directions, then started down the road, hoping that at last she would have some luck. With a name like the Maine Chance, she felt as though she might just be about to see a change in her fortunes.

CHAPTER 22

Cynthia

JUNE IN MAINE RARELY REACHED temperatures above the midseventies, but the sun was strong and there she was, dressed in a sensible skirt and cotton blouse she worried would stick to her sweat-slicked torso before she even made it halfway to the Maine Chance Farm. Her nerves were jangling. Surely it was worth showing up somewhat worse for wear if it meant she would arrive before another, more qualified candidate.

From somewhere behind her, she heard the sound of a vehicle approaching. She stepped down into the soft shoulder of the road, looking with regret at the way the powdery dust settled on her newly polished shoes. She looked over her shoulder as the car roared into view. It slowed to a crawl and then stopped completely. There was no other traffic, and the driver leaned towards the passenger side and waved.

"Need a ride?" the man asked.

The car was large, late model, and immaculately clean. She

had never seen a more respectable-looking vehicle in all her life. The man behind the wheel, however, had something of a rakish look about him. His dark hair waved as if it refused to bend to the ministrations of Brylcreem and a comb. His dark eyes crinkled in a smile as he leaned a little closer. On the seat next to him sat a cap like one generally worn by a chauffeur in the movies. She glanced into the back seat, where a dark-colored suit jacket was neatly spread across it. Her mother had always cautioned her against taking rides from strangers, but she seemed to be ignoring most things her mother had said lately. Besides, she was likely in far more danger of sweating through her outfit than suffering at the hands of some madman in a fancy car.

"I wouldn't say that I need one, but if you're going in the right direction, I'd appreciate a lift," she said, bending over slightly.

"Where're you headed?" he asked.

"The Maine Chance Farm," she said. "Do you know it?"

He nodded and smiled. "It just so happens that I'm one of the chauffeurs who works there. But I didn't have a pretty young woman like you on my schedule for pickup," he said.

She wasn't sure what to make of his compliment. It suddenly made her feel less sure about accepting a ride. He seemed to realize he had behaved with an overly familiar attitude and rearranged his features into a more serious look.

"I'm not registered as one of the guests. I'm actually headed there to ask about a job," she said.

He raised an eyebrow and looked her up and down. The expression on his face pricked at her small measure of confidence. Then he cracked another wide smile and moved the chauffeur's cap towards him. He patted the seat and grabbed the door handle, pushing the heavy door open with a well-tanned hand. "Hop in. Old Mother Hubbard is my boss. You can pick my brain for tips on the way."

That did it. She slid into the seat and pulled the door firmly shut before she could change her mind. She crossed her ankles and smoothed a few wrinkles out of her skirt with her slightly sweaty palms. He checked the rearview mirror, gave her a reassuring grin, and pulled back onto the roadway. The breeze coming in through the open window quickly cooled the trickle of sweat that was running down the back of her neck, and she was grateful for the ride. Not so assured that she did not leave one hand close to the door handle in case she needed to throw herself from the vehicle, but grateful nonetheless.

"I'm Calvin," he said, turning towards her with a slightly raised dark eyebrow.

"Cynthia. I appreciate the ride. It's farther from town than I expected."

"What's the job that you're applying for?" he asked. "One of the technicians?"

She shook her head, not quite sure what sort of technician he was referring to but certain she wasn't it. "I was told that she was looking for a maid to replace an employee who did not work out."

"You don't look like a maid. You're not local, are you?" he asked. "I'm sure I would've remembered seeing you around."

Once again, her stomach fluttered with nerves. What exactly did a maid look like? Was she overdressed? Could that be why she'd been turned away everywhere she had applied? Calvin's tone had given nothing away on that front. Nor had his frank appraising look. She squirmed slightly in her seat.

"No, I'm not local. I'm here visiting with the Mayhews, who spend summers at their cottage on the lake. Why don't you think I look like a maid?"

He reached over and lifted her left hand. "Your nails are in too good of shape and your skin is too smooth."

"Do you think that the housekeeper will think I'm unqualified based on my appearance?" she asked.

Calvin shrugged and dropped her hand gently into her lap. "Whether she does or whether she doesn't, I happen to know that Iris is in a tizzy about being down by one maid. Even a girl like you just might have a shot. But I wouldn't get my hopes up too much if I were you."

"My hopes are already up. I really need this job."

"What does a girl who spends the summer living with people who have a cottage on the lake need with a job?" Calvin asked.

Even though she was grateful to him for providing her with

a ride, she wasn't quite sure she owed him an explanation about her finances. The fewer people who knew the whole story, the better, as far as she was concerned. She simply wanted to fit in with the others, do a good job, and get paid for it.

"Why does someone like you need a job as a chauffeur?" she asked.

"I was at loose ends when I left the navy, and because I've worked here every summer since I was fifteen, I came back while I consider my future," he said. Cynthia noticed he tightened his hands around the steering wheel as he mentioned his military service. Still, she would rather talk about his situation than her own.

"I would hope that there would be a lot of positions on the coast for a man with military experience," she said.

"There certainly are plenty of those sorts of jobs. Bath Iron Works is hiring, as well as several more local boatyards. But since I served on an aircraft carrier, I've had enough time at sea to last me a lifetime. I don't even like to go out on the lake," he said, thrusting his thumb towards the water that stretched out on the other side of the road.

Any more questions would probably seem rude. And she wouldn't want to get on the bad side of a potential coworker. She decided to change the subject.

"Do you have any suggestions on how to get on the housekeeper's good side? Anything I should avoid?"

He loosened his grip on the wheel and flashed her another

broad smile. "Iris appreciates hard workers. Experience isn't as important as being on time and doing what you're told. If you can do that, I'm sure you two will get along just fine."

Cynthia hadn't been making a habit of doing what she was told very much lately, but then again, she hadn't been getting paid for her compliance. Besides, although she wasn't entirely in lockstep with her parents' worldview, she had been raised to value a good day's work, whatever form it took. Her mother might not have wanted her to grow up to be a maid, but she had been relentless in schooling her daughter on the finer aspects of housekeeping, and as far as Cynthia could see, they were one and the same. One of the reasons her mother was so set on Cynthia marrying into a family wealthier than hers was so that Cynthia could hire help to maintain the same housekeeping standards women were encouraged to aspire to.

Cynthia's mother was up before dawn, scrubbing and polishing and fiddling with every little detail in her home. Nothing was ever the least bit out of place nor likely to invite criticism of her efforts. Not that Cynthia's father seemed to take much notice or even value what it was that she did all day. In fact, he had remarked on that very thing more than once a week throughout Cynthia's childhood. Most days when he arrived home from his job at a local insurance company, he would ask what it was she had spent all day doing while he crunched numbers and made sales calls. Perhaps it was no surprise she wanted something more for her daughter.

"I can be on time, and I do know how to work hard."

Calvin turned right and onto a gently curving gravel drive. He slowed the car, and Cynthia was able to take in the sweeping view before her. Rolling green lawns, their emerald surfaces broken up by lush beds of blooming flowers flanking either side of the driveway. In the middle distance, she could see what appeared to be carefully tended fruit trees. Before long, a large understated yet impressive building came into view. The main building was made up of at least two stories, plus a tall attic, if not a full third floor, as well as a one-story wing on either side, each attached to the main building at an angle. The structure looked rather like a boomerang. Striped awnings and more beds of cheerful flowers brought color to the building's facade. Calvin rolled to a stop and cut the engine. He shifted in his seat and looked her straight in the eye.

"This is where I'll leave you off. I've got to park the car in the garage at the far end of the property. If there's one thing we don't do here, it's make a big show of the practical underbelly of how things run. You might be just what Iris is looking for. If anyone spots you in the wrong place, they'd never guess that you were one of the maids. I'd come round and open the door for you, but I think that might make you look like you were too good for the job."

Cynthia wrapped her smooth fingers around the door handle and tugged. She stepped out onto the gravel driveway, hearing the crunch of it beneath her feet. She closed the door as quietly as she could manage and leaned in through the open window once more. "Thanks for the ride. I really do appreciate it. And for all of the tips."

Calvin reached for his chauffeur's cap and settled it firmly on his head. "Good luck. I'm rooting for you. I'd like to see you around."

With that, he threw the car into reverse and headed back down the driveway. As she turned towards the building, she considered the irony of her situation. For the past two years, she had felt like everyone at the college would discover that she didn't really belong there. Everyone else came from a far wealthier background than she did, and she felt as though she were trying to hide her modest background from them.

Now that she was able to admit that she needed a job, she was told that she looked too wealthy for any such thing. Perhaps the housekeeper would have a far different assessment of her than Calvin had. All she could do was hope so. She squared her shoulders and smoothed her skirt once more. She looked down at her shoes and pulled a handkerchief from her handbag. Crouching down, she gave her shoes a quick buff before tucking the soiled piece of cloth back into the bottom of her bag and removing a pair of gloves. She slid her hands into them, tugging at the wrists. She'd never be more prepared than she was at that moment, she told herself without truly believing it. Before she could change her mind, she stepped towards the large door centered between two long bay windows.

CHAPTER 23

Iris

THE PHONE RANG JUST AS Iris had tucked the third sheet corner under the mattress of the bed she was making up. It was the girl at the reception desk, who had managed to track her down in a guest room on the second floor. Apparently, there was someone there to see her. She asked the name of her visitor, and when told that it was Cynthia Proctor, it rang no alarm bells. Still, she assured the receptionist that she would be down momentarily and hurried as quickly as she could with the rest of the bedding. In two minutes flat, she had plumped all the pillows and was back in the hushed corridor, a bundle of sheets clamped beneath her arm. There was no real reason to change all the sheets every day, especially since the guests spent a great deal of time lounging about in the pool or the oversize bathtubs each room boasted. And it wasn't as if any of the ladies had male companions sharing their beds. No, the only reason for it was Miss Arden's insistence on attention to the smallest of details.

Iris felt a rising panic in her chest as she shoved the sheets into a discreetly placed laundry chute and descended the plushly carpeted front stairs. If Cynthia Proctor was a last-minute guest of Miss Arden's, she wasn't sure she would be able to keep her job. Velda's dismissal had stretched the maids to the limit, and even with Iris pitching in to the best of her ability, it was tough going.

To top it all off, Miss Arden had telephoned to announce she had again decided to honor her guests with an extra-early preview of her fall fashion line. She had sent the manager of her clothing line to the resort earlier in the week, and the woman had insisted that the models for the show be Maine Chance employees. Some of the models were chosen from the spa side of the resort, but the rest were to be picked from the housekeeping staff. She and Dolores, the girl on staff who showed the most promise to take over her own former role of head maid, were unlikely to have a day off for the foreseeable future, even without an additional guest to accommodate.

She paused on the fifth step from the top. It provided a clear view of her caller. Her heart rate slowed to a more sedate pace. The woman standing at the desk was no impatient matron covered in cashmere and pearls. In fact, she could barely be called a woman at all. Unless Miss Arden's skin potions worked as well as she claimed they did, her visitor wasn't a day over twenty. Curiosity piqued, she moved swiftly down the remainder of the staircase.

"Miss Hubbard, at your service. How may I be of assistance?"

she asked as she crossed the wide reception hall and held out a hand. The one that clasped it felt slightly damp despite the white cotton glove covering it. Was the girl overly warm, or was she feeling nervous?

"I was rather hoping that I might be of assistance to you," the girl said. "It has come to my attention that a maid position here at the Maine Chance has recently become available. I would like to apply."

Iris blinked. How on earth had a complete stranger heard the news of Velda's dismissal before she had even had time to phone in a help-wanted advertisement to the newspaper or have one of the chauffeurs hang up a notice at the shops in town?

"I haven't posted any such opening. How is it that you know that there is a job to be had?"

The girl's cheeks tinted ever so slightly, but she answered with a strong, clear voice.

"I was in the newspaper office when a woman who worked there came in and announced that her niece had been asked to leave your employ."

Of course Bernice would be the sort to carry tales even if they were about her own kin. Iris wondered at the need for a newspaper in Mount Vernon with a woman like Bernice in town. All the news could be had for free when she was around.

"Is that so?" Iris said. "Did she say anything else?"

Cynthia paused as if Iris's tone warned her not to proceed. She seemed to think better of it and nodded.

"She implied that you would need to replace the maid as soon as possible in order to maintain the standards your establishment is known for."

"And armed with so little information, you came here hoping to gain what another poor girl has lost?" Iris asked.

"I admit, I felt sorry for her, but since I am in need of a job myself, I saw no reason to hesitate."

"I haven't seen you in town before, and I don't recognize your name. What brings you to Mount Vernon?"

Cynthia met her gaze. "I'm here visiting the Mayhew family. That's how I happened to be at the newspaper office."

"You know the Mayhews?" Iris asked.

"Pauline Mayhew has been my roommate at Barlow College for the past two years."

Any spark of interest Iris felt in hiring her sputtered out. It wasn't that she didn't like the look of the young woman standing in front of her. Truth be told, she seemed like an entirely respectable sort of girl. With her modest skirt and demure blouse, she certainly would do the company credit as far as her appearance was concerned.

Even though her face was flushed with the heat, she looked well groomed, just a bit of powder and a hint of lipstick. There would be no need for an awkward conversation about what could be considered slovenly or tawdry. No, the problem wasn't that she did not appear to be a very respectable sort of girl.

It all came down to a question: How could Pauline Mayhew's

fancy college roommate be willing to lower herself enough to perform the amount of manual labor that the position of a maid at the Maine Chance Farm would involve?

And no matter how desperate she might be to replace Velda, Iris was not at all convinced that any college girl—private school or public—would treat the job with the amount of dedication she truly needed from her employees. Without proper motivation towards doing so, staff members were of little use to her. It was surprising how challenging it was to find people who hit that sweet spot between the need for a job and the ability to perform it.

Certainly this young woman could be seen by guests without causing concern. Iris tipped her head to one side and looked Cynthia up and down once more. If she were to be discovered in one of the guest's rooms tidying things up or carrying in a breakfast tray in the morning, she would know how to politely converse should the need arise. In the few moments Iris had spent with her, it was clear she was a well-spoken person.

But could she spend a day changing sheets, mopping floors, and scrubbing down the bathrooms? Iris simply couldn't see it. As much as she wanted this young woman to be the solution to her problem, she had her doubts. And the fact was, she didn't have the time to waste training someone who most likely would be gone before her first day was out.

"I'm afraid we have no room on staff for a college girl, no matter how much you claim to want the job. Being a maid is far more difficult than those who are used to being served are aware. If you are interested in a bit more pocket money than your parents are willing to spare, I suggest you offer your services as a babysitter to the Mayhews' social set. I'm sure that you would appeal to them."

Before the girl could reply, Erma Bancroft, the fashion manager, bustled into the hall with her lips clamped unbecomingly together.

"Miss Hubbard, I am afraid we have a crisis on our hands." She came to a stop and flapped her hands in front of her. "Janet, the manicurist who is scheduled to be one of the models for tonight's show, has, for reasons she refuses to disclose, developed too great a girth for the clothing collection we plan to present. I'm sure I need not tell you what that means."

Indeed, she did not. Surely the spa would be down one manicurist before the week was out. Erma rushed on.

"Not only that, but it's also come to my attention that you have dismissed that girl, Velda, who was supposed to be in the show too. What could you possibly have been thinking?"

"I assure you, it could not be helped."

Erma sniffed. "If you say so. But that doesn't make the problem any easier. Do you have anyone else on your staff that is a size eight?"

Iris ran the staff list through her mind. Most of her girls were trim, but the clothing for the show was especially small, and most of the maids were too sturdily built to fit into them.

They needed to be to endure the rigors of the job, at least in her opinion.

"I'm afraid not. Velda was the only one."

Erma turned and ran an appraising glance up and down the girl standing at Iris's side.

"You look about the right size," she said to Cynthia.

The girl stepped forward. "I'm exactly a size eight."

"Walk up and down the hall for me," Erma said.

Cynthia did as she was told, neatly turning at the end of the corridor. Iris had to admit, she was far more graceful that Velda had ever been.

"You'll do just fine. Iris, why didn't you suggest her?"

"She isn't a member of staff."

"That is a shame. What are we supposed to tell Miss Arden? She won't want to hear that the show was canceled because we didn't have the staff for it. I won't take the blame for this all on my own."

Iris's heart jumped about in her chest again. She could almost hear Miss Arden's voice telling her to pack her things and go with far less concern than Iris had delivered that same message to Velda. But it was the sound of Cynthia's voice that actually filled her ears.

"Perhaps I can help. Strictly speaking, I don't work here because I was just about to accept the available maid's position when you came through the door with your urgent concern. Isn't that right, Miss Hubbard?" Cynthia beamed at her, but Iris could tell the girl was holding her breath. She hoped she didn't need a job for the very same reason the manicurist was about to lose hers. She narrowed her eyes at the girl, who simply kept smiling, not the least little sign on her face that she had just told Erma a bald-faced lie.

"It is, indeed," Iris said.

"Your timing is exquisite. I'm sure Iris can spare you from your maid duties this evening to participate in the show. I'll expect you in the bowling alley at eight o'clock." Erma hurried off without another word.

"Let's go into my office," Iris said, turning and threading her way through the long corridors that led to the back of the building.

The staff kitchen, the laundry facilities, and her own office were in a separate building from the Arden House. It wouldn't do for rough domestics to encounter the paying guests any more than could be helped. Just because one likes to eat sausage, one doesn't wish to visit the factory was the general attitude towards commingling. With each passing day, Iris had increasing respect for her former supervisor, Alice. She had truly not realized how much went into the selection of staff and how fraught each of the decisions as to who to hire and where to place someone on staff truly were. Her friend had always seemed to handle such difficulties with ease and a minimum of feather-ruffling.

One point in favor of Cynthia was the fact that Iris had to check over her shoulder two or three times during the course of their journey to be sure the girl was still following her. Many of the girls on staff plodded along with such heavy footfalls they weren't allowed on the second floor when guests were in the dining room below. Cynthia, however, could have been a cat burglar, considering the way she moved through the hall. She walked along swiftly as well. No lollygagging for her. Each time Iris checked, Cynthia was noiselessly right on her heels. Perhaps there was more promise in her than first appearances had indicated.

She wasn't chatty either. Some of the girls who came, and many of the men as well, kept up a steady stream of commentary from the moment they stepped into the building until she made her decision about whether or not to add them to the staff. She could understand their reaction, even though she had had an intimacy with the estate for many years. For most people, but especially people living in the town, the level of opulence at the resort was something they would have seen only at the pictures.

From the velvet draperies to the gilded picture frames to the crystal chandeliers, everything about the Maine Chance Farm was luxurious. The guests wanted to feel as though they were nestled in the bosom of an unspoiled Eden, but they wished to do it without any sacrificing of creature comforts. These were women who were used to having interior decorators on retainer and wardrobes on loan from the most revered fashion designers. She had seen many of them wearing real diamonds and pearls with their calisthenics outfits during their morning exercises. It was a far cry from the modest Cape Cod or even colonial-style homes that most of the employees lived in.

This girl, however, seemed to take it all in stride. Perhaps her experience at college had made it so that she was more accustomed to a lifestyle that involved servants and plush surroundings than the average applicant. By the time they had reached Iris's small office and the two of them had seated themselves on opposite sides of her small wooden desk, she was softening her view on the interviewee. Cynthia sat with good posture, her hands neatly folded in her lap.

Despite her reservations, Iris liked the way the girl met her gaze instead of darting her eyes around the room with idle curiosity. Iris pulled a notepad from a drawer in her desk and uncapped her pen.

"I think it only fair to tell you that I don't much like having liars on my staff," she said.

"I hope that since you offered me the job, you won't think of me as one," Cynthia said. She held her head high and sat in the chair opposite Iris's desk without slouching.

The girl hadn't come right out and sassed her, but she had come devilishly close. From the way she fiddled with the truth, Iris guessed she was at her fancy school to study law.

"How old are you?"

"I'll be twenty-one in September," the girl said.

Iris jotted her answer down on the notepad before posing

her next question. "Are you aware of what it is that we do here at the Maine Chance?"

"My understanding is that this is an exclusive spot for women of means. Diet, exercise, and beauty regimens are provided by technicians trained in these areas. I believe that the resort prides itself on providing the highest level of accommodation to women who are willing to pay for it," Cynthia said.

Iris felt a jolt of surprise run through her. That was exactly what they aimed to provide and what the clients demanded. She had not expected someone who had never been there as a guest or as an employee to summarize it so succinctly. In fact, the girl could write an employee handbook based on her evaluation of their goals.

"Precisely. Our expectations for employees here at the Maine Chance are rather different than one might encounter at a motor court or even a luxury hotel that served far more guests at a time than we do here. Our staff-to-guest ratio is two to one, and there's a reason for that. We endeavor to provide the highest level of service with the least amount of intrusion possible."

"Considering the types of guests you cater to, I would expect nothing else," Cynthia said.

Iris tipped her head to one side and squinted slightly. "What do you mean, 'considering the types of guests we cater to'?"

"It's my understanding that many of your guests are people who are famous and/or extremely wealthy. They have staffs that cater to their wishes at their own homes and expect nothing less when they are paying for what is essentially a vacation experience," Cynthia said.

"Yes, that's true. We do cater to the famous and the wealthy. One of the most important factors in providing a good experience for these clients is a sense of discretion. We do not prefer that our staff make any sort of a fuss when encountering movie starlets, for example," Iris said. "Do you think that you would be able to manage not to fawn over someone like that?"

"I expect so. I confess, there are certainly people whom I would be thrilled to have the chance to see in real life as opposed to only on the silver screen, but I do think I could manage not to foist myself upon them asking for an autograph or trying to take their photo, if that's you mean."

It didn't bear considering. She tried to imagine some of the guests they had hosted in the past having autograph books thrust at them along with their breakfast trays. No, this young woman didn't seem the sort to make such an egregious error in judgment.

"I see," Iris said, jotting down Cynthia's response. "It seems as though you might be someone who could navigate the social aspects of the job, but it doesn't look to me as though you would be up for the physical ones. We've never had a college girl working here before, and I am quite concerned that you will find the work beneath you and actually be ill-equipped to complete it."

Iris kept her gaze firmly fixed on Cynthia's face, trying to read how her frank disclosure of concerns had been received. There was just a flicker of fear that rippled across Cynthia's face before she caught it and replaced it with a more neutral expression.

"I can understand why you might be troubled by what you perceive to be my background. I am a student at Barlow, which does make me a college girl. That said, I'm a scholarship student. The funding was only for the first two years. If I want to complete my studies, I need to earn some money," Cynthia said. There was something in the tone of her voice that Iris perceived as strength. Perhaps there was more to Cynthia than first met the eye.

"And you think that working here will make it possible for you to pay your own way?" Iris asked. She was genuinely curious about this young woman. She reminded her a bit of Iris herself when she had been that age. She had chosen a path that did not agree with her own parents when she was only a year younger.

"If you are paying the going rate and I am able to work full-time, I think I just may be able to manage it."

"Have you ever cleaned anything before in your life?" Iris said.

"Although Barlow's an expensive private school, my background is solidly middle-class. My mother employs no help around the house, and since I'm her only daughter, I was expected to pitch in. I can make beds, vacuum, scrub the floors, do the laundry, and even help with the cooking if that is required. If one of your gardeners calls in sick, I'm skilled at weeding and planting. I also have a driver's license, in case you need someone to fill in as a chauffeur," Cynthia said, her voice growing slightly more confident with each item she added to her list.

Iris jotted down the skills she listed and wondered how truthfully she had answered.

"We do not employ women as chauffeurs. Miss Arden does not prefer it, but I will make a note of your other qualifications. You do realize that if I were to hire you, you would be expected to back up your claims?"

Cynthia nodded. "I understand."

Iris looked her up and down once more and laid her pen down on her notepad. Although she didn't appreciate the way Cynthia had wangled her way into the opportunity, she had to take a risk on someone. And she desperately needed the help. Nevertheless, with guests like Geraldine Putnam in residence, there was no way she could allow the standards to fall, especially considering Miss Arden had her under a microscope. Still, she couldn't resist pressing the girl a bit more. Someone ill-suited to the job was worse than no one at all.

"Do you realize that you would be expected to live in the staff quarters here on the property?" Iris asked.

Cynthia's eyes widened slightly before she recomposed her face.

"I didn't know that, but I can see how it would be very sensible to have staff available at a moment's notice. I just need to thank the Mayhews for their hospitality and to let them know I won't be returning. After that, I can be available to move into the staff quarters immediately."

"That won't disrupt your plans to spend the summer at the lake?" Iris asked. "The Mayhews do have a lovely home right there at the water's edge."

"My only plans for the summer are to get back to school in the fall."

Iris drew in a deep breath and then exhaled loudly. "You will be paid every other week, and your housing and meals are included. You'll be expected to wear a uniform, which we will provide, and your employment here will be on a trial basis until I decide otherwise. Is that understood?"

Cynthia nodded. "Absolutely."

Iris pushed back her chair and stood. She might be making a terrible mistake, but she couldn't see doing otherwise. Considering the cultured way in which Cynthia spoke, she might end up being more trouble than she was worth. The guests might find her easy to interact with, but there was every likelihood she would stir up resentment with the other staff members. She didn't appear as though she would fit in all that well with the local girls. And even the guests might find her a bit too well-bred for them to feel entirely comfortable treating her as a servant.

Despite her claims of a middle-class upbringing, she certainly had managed to take on the patina of the upper classes that she would have spent time with at her private college. Still, there was something about her forthrightness and her eagerness to be given the position that made Iris willing to take the risk.

"I'll have Calvin take you back to the Mayhews to say your goodbyes and collect your things." She glanced at her wristwatch. "If you can't be back within ninety minutes, don't bother to return."

CHAPTER 24

Cynthia

CALVIN DROPPED HER OFF A few houses down from the Mayhews' without question. Although it still left her with a bad feeling, she had promised Pauline not to apprise her friend's parents of her job search, and she had no intention of going back on her word. How she would explain her sudden leave-taking was still a worry since she was loath to tell a complete untruth. Besides, what if one of the Mayhews spotted her around town in some way? She mounted the steps to the porch and paused with her hand on the doorknob. A clever girl like her would surely think of something.

The sounds of voices floated down the hall as she slipped quietly into the foyer. She made her way towards the living room, with its expansive view of the lake. Mr. Mayhew stood near the windows, a rocks glass in his hand. He smiled as she stepped into the room. His wife, seated with her back to the door, turned and raised an eyebrow as if to question Cynthia's sudden appearance. Pauline jumped up from a spot on the sofa and moved swiftly to her friend's side.

"My parents have been asking where you've been all afternoon," she said, giving Cynthia's arm a squeeze that felt like a warning.

"We were surprised when you did not return with Pauline this afternoon as expected," Mrs. Mayhew said.

"Cynthia's a guest, not a prisoner, my dear. She is welcome to come and go as she likes," Mr. Mayhew said.

Mrs. Mayhew's eyebrow arched higher. "She may be a guest, but a well-bred girl does not go sneaking off without a word to her hosts."

The Mayhews all turned towards her, awaiting an explanation for her sudden absence. Pauline bit her lip and gave her head a slight shake. Cynthia's stomach clenched as she looked at Mrs. Mayhew. Then she looked over at Mr. Mayhew, who smiled once more. She stood up straighter and smiled back.

"I am so sorry to have worried you," she said, looking directly at her hostess. "I overheard one of the employees at the newspaper office mention the Maine Chance Farm. I had not understood that Elizabeth Arden's famous resort was so close."

"Go on," Mrs. Mayhew said.

"I am not sure if I have mentioned it, but my major is economics. Elizabeth Arden and her innovative business practices have been mentioned in several of my classes. When

I realized her property was so near, I had to take a look for myself."

"But it's several miles away. Why didn't you ask for a ride?" Mr. Mayhew asked.

"I didn't want to put you out. Besides, I love a long walk."

"How quaint," Mrs. Mayhew said, her tone implying that Cynthia's behavior was anything but. "Did you satisfy your curiosity?"

Cynthia glanced at Pauline before continuing. "I must confess, my brief visit only piqued my interest. When I told the housekeeper that I would love to spend time at the resort to do some hands-on research into the economic value such a place could provide, she offered to allow me to stay at the resort."

"Even Eleanor Roosevelt doesn't stay at the exclusive Maine Chance Farm without paying," Mrs. Mayhew said. "Why would such an invitation be extended to someone like you?"

Any compunction Cynthia had had about telling white lies to her hostess dissolved as quickly as the morning mist off the lake. The truth was, it was exactly because she was herself that she was not paying, but rather being paid to stay at the resort. Mrs. Mayhew had reminded Cynthia of her place, but not in the way she had intended. Her words and the tone of them had a galvanizing effect on her spirit, so much so that she permitted herself a further flourish.

"I expect that Mrs. Roosevelt is far too busy to offer to write an article for the *American Economics Review* on Miss Arden's extraordinary enterprise. The housekeeper seemed to think Miss Arden would welcome someone reporting on her business acumen with as much interest as most do about her product lines."

Mrs. Mayhew narrowed her eyes. "You cannot possibly expect us to believe that a young girl like you could be capable of writing an article for a national magazine."

"She already has, Mother. Her economics professor had her working on an article for the same journal all last semester."

Mr. Mayhew's smile broadened. "Good for you. I'll be sorry to see you go, though."

Pauline piped up. "When do you have to leave?"

"I am expected back this afternoon. They have a fashion show scheduled for the evening, and the housekeeper suggested it would be wise for me to attend. It is a highlight of the guest experience each season and something she said I should not miss," Cynthia said.

At the mention of the fashion show, Mrs. Mayhew's eyebrows moved upward once more. "I see. Should we expect you to return once your research is done? I had been counting on you to watch the children tomorrow and the next day."

"As much as I hate to disappoint you, I do not anticipate returning. Between the research and the writing, I doubt there will be much time left over for socializing."

"I see. Shall we send your things to the Maine Chance? Even someone as dedicated to long walks as you won't wish to make the journey back carrying suitcases. You'd look like a hobo."

"I appreciate the offer, but there is no need. I have a chauffeur from the resort waiting to take me back."

"I didn't hear a car," Mrs. Mayhew said.

"I asked him to wait a few doors down where there is a lay-by that would be easier to turn around in. The limousine is a bit large for these narrow lanes around the lake."

Perhaps it did her no credit, but Cynthia's spirits raised as Mrs. Mayhew pressed her lips tightly together at the word *limousine.* The older woman raised an elegant hand as if in surrender. "We shan't dream of delaying you, then," she said.

Mr. Mayhew and Pauline each stepped towards her. "Should your plans change, you are always welcome here," he said. "Pauline, why don't you help her pack so that she can be sure to be back in time for the event."

Pauline nodded and crossed the room. She took Cynthia by the arm and piloted her out the door and up the stairs to the guest room before she spoke.

"Does this mean that you got the job?" she asked.

"I did. I start just as soon as I can get back."

"Thanks for not letting my parents know the real reason you'll be at the resort. My mother would be appalled."

"It was no big deal. Besides, my mother wouldn't approve either." Cynthia opened the closet and pulled dresses from the hangers as quickly as she could. She didn't want to give Iris an excuse to change her mind about hiring her.

Pauline pulled one of Cynthia's suitcases from the bottom

of the closet and zipped it open. Cynthia thought back to their last day at Barlow.

"I won't be seeing much of you, either, will I?" Pauline asked.

"I'm sure I'll have a day off now and again. When I do, we can meet up at the lake, and you can tell me how things are going with Kenneth."

"I guess that will have to do. If he asks about you, what should I tell Glenn?"

Glenn and the rest of Pauline's gang were the least of her concerns. She shoved the last of her belongings into the smaller of the suitcases and zipped it shut. With a final look out the window at the lake, she hoisted the suitcase from the bed.

"Whatever you think is best. The only thing I plan to worry about is doing a good enough job to stay employed for the rest of the summer."

CHAPTER 25

Cynthia

IRIS LED CYNTHIA OUT THROUGH one of the single-story wings of the building angled off from the main structure. The wing contained a large dining room not currently in use, and despite her experience with upscale surroundings at the homes of her college friends, she found herself impressed by the display of luxury. Tables draped in crisp white cloths each held vases filled with the freshest of blooms. A large but tasteful crystal chandelier sparkled from the center of the ceiling. Velvet draperies hung at the sides of the long windows, and the flocked golden wallpaper gleamed even though the chandelier was switched off. Unless her eyes deceived her, all the artwork hanging on the walls was original, one quite possibly a Stubbs. While Cynthia did not share Miss Arden's taste for scenes depicting horses standing in fields or riding to hounds, she admired the quality of the compositions and brushwork.

She barely caught a glimpse of the lake through the long

windows looking out across the sweeping lawn before they had passed on to a smaller anteroom and then exited the building. Iris walked at a pace that could be considered a slow jog, and despite the two decades the older woman must have on her, Cynthia found herself pushing to keep up. While she did not want to entertain the notion that Iris might have a point about her own level of physical fitness for the job she had agreed to, she had to admit it had been a long time since she had hurried so quickly, if she were not almost late for a class. Cynthia wondered whether it was a matter of urgency or whether Iris always walked at such a brisk pace. Did everyone in her employ?

The staff house—as the dormitory for employees in residence was called—was a one-story structure clad in white clapboards and dark-green trim. In this way, it resembled so many of the houses Cynthia had seen all over the state of Maine. The house sat tucked away from view so that it would not be able to be seen by guests at the resort, but close enough at hand that workers could be on the spot for any needs that arose with little time wasted.

Even though it was not designed to be seen by the guests, lush plantings of flowering shrubs and climbing vines softened the front facade and corners of the building. Flower boxes clung to the windows on the front, and a screened porch stretched across the left side. Cynthia wondered if it had been custom-built for staff or rather it had been a home that had been repurposed.

"What a charming building," Cynthia said as they started

up the stone pathway to the front door. "Was it built for the staff as a dormitory? It looks like a year-round home."

"It's one of many buildings that Miss Arden purchased when she set about creating the estate. None of it was built to be what it's been turned into," Iris said, not slowing her pace until she reached out and grasped the screen-door handle and pulled it open.

Cynthia followed her inside before commenting again. "Are there many other buildings on the estate?"

"Over a dozen."

"As many as that? How did Miss Arden find so many people willing to sell to her?" Cynthia asked.

As soon as she asked the question, Cynthia realized she had blundered. No one would have sold their homes if they were not in need of the money.

"The resort was conceived in the early thirties, and I'm sure that a well-educated college girl like you must know something about the Depression. She had a vision for her business, and she made offers to people who were too grateful not to accept them."

There was something in Iris's tone that made Cynthia wonder if she had touched on the housekeeper's nerves. Iris was a local woman, according to Mr. Mayhew, and perhaps knew someone who had been affected by the sales. It seemed best to keep any further questions to herself.

"Miss Arden seems to have lavished a lot of attention to

detail on the estate. The landscaping outside this building is so pretty you would not think it was meant for housing the help," Cynthia said.

"She certainly does have an eye for detail and holds the strictest standards for the entire estate. That said, many of the plantings outside this building predate her acquisition of the property," Iris said.

Again, Cynthia was certain there was a bit of history behind Iris's words. It was clear from what she said that she respected her employer and was not inclined to portray her in any sort of negative light. That didn't mean, however, that there was no complication to the situation.

Cynthia knew full well, from her own upbringing in a small town with one major employer, how resentment could grow towards that company or the family that owned it. Folks did not particularly like being beholden to people who might consider themselves their betters. In a town where there was such a difference between the wealth of the visitors and that of the permanent residents, Cynthia could easily see how, no matter her intentions, Miss Arden might not be an easy favorite with everyone.

Iris led her towards the back of the building and opened a door into a small, bright room, complete with a pair of dressers and a set of bunk beds. Except for the fact that it was missing desks and chairs, the accommodations reminded her to a remarkable degree of the dorm room she shared with Pauline. A wave of nostalgia washed over her as she thought of all the late nights of studying, talking, and sharing secrets she had spent with her college friend. A lump rose in her throat as she considered that if she wasn't able to meet Iris's expectations for her staff, she might not experience any more of them.

It appeared that the bottom bunk had already been claimed. A dressing gown, a Raggedy Ann doll, and a teddy bear lay displayed on the foot of the bed as a stamp of ownership, however temporary it might be.

"It's a good thing you have young legs," Iris said, pointing to the top bunk. "That one is yours. I hope you manage to keep it longer than the last occupant. Fresh linens and pillows are in a cupboard down the hall."

Cynthia nodded and headed for the bunk pressed against the far wall. She always preferred to sleep at a distance from the doorway. "It looks very comfortable," she said, reaching up to give the mattress a bit of a squeeze. While it did not seem particularly thick, it was not unyielding either. It certainly was no worse than the one she was used to at college.

Iris nodded. "We have a room to store the suitcases in the back of the house. Now, let's get you a uniform."

Iris crossed the room and opened a small closet tucked into one wall. A row of freshly laundered and pressed blue cotton dresses, with white piping and full navy-blue aprons with large pockets on the front, hung neatly inside. Iris flipped through them, peering closely, until she found one that seemed to meet with her approval. She held it out to Cynthia.

"I expect this one is just about your size. Why don't you go ahead and try it on? If it doesn't fit, choose a different one from the closet. I'll meet you in the staff kitchen once you're dressed."

Cynthia waited until Iris closed the door softly behind her and pulled the curtains shut on the two large windows. As she tugged them together, she caught a glimpse of two of the gardeners in the near distance. She slipped out of her own blouse and skirt and stepped into the uniform. Iris had a good eye for size, as it fit her as though it had been made with her in mind.

While it was not the sort of thing she generally wore, it was well-made and quite comfortable. She slid her head and arms through the openings in the apron and cinched it firmly around her waist. There was no mirror in the room to check her appearance, but she had every confidence that she was presentable.

There was something about the uniform that gave her a feeling of officialdom, somehow. While she had not worked as a maid before, at least she looked the part. The pockets were enormous, and she could imagine they would be useful for stashing plenty of cleaning rags or dustcloths. Before she exited the room, she located an empty drawer in the dresser and neatly folded her blouse before tucking it inside.

She wondered how long it would be before she would have a reason to wear her own clothing again. She had not thought to ask about time off during the interview; she had been too eager to secure the job to ask such a thing. After all, what kind of impression would she make if the first thing she wanted to know was when she could stop working?

She left the room, leaving the door open behind her, just as they had found it when they arrived. She followed the corridor towards the back of the building and easily located what must have been the staff kitchen. Iris stood next to a short woman of advanced age. The old lady's eyes barely peered over the top of a tall stockpot placed on the large range oven. Her hand was raised above her head to stir the contents of the pot with a long wooden spoon. Both women turned and gave Cynthia an appraising glance as she crossed the threshold and stepped across the well-scrubbed green linoleum.

Iris bobbed her head as if satisfied with Cynthia's appearance. "It fits you, then," she said, pointing towards the uniform.

"Yes, it does."

"Let's get you fed, and then I will put you to work. We are behind since we have been short one maid, and I'm not going to have time to give you the same amount of training the staff usually gets. Most of them start at the beginning of the season, when we host college girls and young working women. I'm afraid you are going to have to jump straight into the fire," Iris said.

"I'll do my best to get up to speed," Cynthia said, hoping she didn't sound cocky. From Iris's comments, she knew she was being evaluated through a slightly tinted lens.

"I suggest that you do," Iris said. "Mrs. Dudley is the staff cook. She'll be in charge of all your meals while you're staying here. The food isn't fancy like the sorts of things our guests are served, but it will keep your energy up without a doubt."

"That's right," the small woman said, letting go of the spoon and wiping her hands on her apron. She gave Cynthia a welcoming smile before opening the oven door and pulling out a plate covered with a metal lid. Mrs. Dudley indicated the table with her head and carried the plate to the table. "Have a seat and tuck into that."

Cynthia pulled out the chair and lifted the lid off the plate, feeling an uncomfortable heat as she touched it. Perhaps Calvin the chauffeur had been right about the state of her hands. Mrs. Dudley had had no trouble lifting the hot plate straight from the oven and carrying it across the room. She was going to need to develop a few calluses before such feats were second nature to her too. The plate was filled with thick slices of roast pork, a mound of mashed potatoes swimming in gravy, and a quantity of peas that looked as though they'd come straight from the garden rather than a can.

"I'll leave you to it. Once you've finished your meal, come find me in the Arden House and I'll set you on your first task," Iris said. "There's no need to gobble your meal, but I'd rather you didn't linger over it too long either. As I said, we have been shorthanded, and there's quite a lot of work to catch up on." With that, she nodded at Mrs. Dudley and hurried out of the kitchen with the same speed she had shown on their walk from the main house.

Mrs. Dudley set a tall glass of milk on the table in front of Cynthia's plate before sliding a cut-glass butter dish towards her.

"You look like a girl who could use a biscuit," she said.

Cynthia's stomach rumbled, and she found herself nodding enthusiastically.

Mrs. Dudley placed a tea towel–lined basket in front of her and turned back towards the stove without another word. Cynthia felt a little uncomfortable being the only one in the room eating, with Mrs. Dudley toiling away behind her, but she couldn't keep Iris waiting. And she was rather hungry. The walk from town until the chauffeur had picked her up must have used up what little breakfast she had eaten that morning.

Plain the food might be, but only in terms of its homey reputation. The roast was tender and savory, and the mashed potatoes and gravy were silky and rich. Cynthia could not remember the last time she had tasted garden-fresh peas. Her mother was a great believer in convenience foods. They were just the sort of modern touch her mother enjoyed displaying in her home. Cynthia, on the other hand, vastly preferred foods prepared from scratch and was delighted to think she might spend the summer enjoying more meals like the one before her. Mrs. Dudley hovered over her shoulder as she reached for a second biscuit to mop up what remained of the gravy. She whipped Cynthia's plate out from under her and replaced it with another filled with the same quantity of food the first had held. Cynthia was about to protest when she heard footsteps coming along the hallway.

Calvin stepped through the door and smiled at Mrs. Dudley before turning his gaze towards Cynthia. "Something smells delicious," he said.

"Sit yourself down and I'll fetch you a plate," Mrs. Dudley said, beaming at him.

"You're the best, Mrs. D," Calvin said, helping himself to a biscuit. "Memories of your cooking got me through some bleak times overseas."

Mrs. Dudley placed a plate even more heaping with food than Cynthia's own in front of him before patting him on the shoulder. "You just say that so I'll feed you extra," she said. He reached out for her hand and gave it a squeeze.

"It's the honest truth. Every time I sat down to a meal and looked at the god-awful mess they served up there, I would just tell myself it was a plate filled with your pork and mashed potatoes. Pretending that's what it was is the only thing that helped me choke it down."

Calvin lifted his knife and cut off a hunk of butter. He slathered it onto his biscuits and then reached for a pitcher like the ones Cynthia had most often seen at breakfast restaurants. He drizzled a generous dollop of molasses onto the tops of his biscuits before biting into one. Cynthia had thought Calvin handsome when sitting behind the wheel of a car, but he was dazzling when his face split into a broad smile.

"So, Iris hasn't scared you off already," he said.

"Not a chance," Cynthia said. "Thanks for the helpful tips earlier."

Calvin waved a biscuit at her. "I'm sure you didn't need any help for me to get the job. I just told you all those things to give you a little boost of confidence. So, you're starting right away, then."

"As soon as I finish eating, Iris wants me to get started."

"I'm sure she does. We've had some A-list guests arrive, and it's put her in quite a tizzy. I'm running around ragged, too, when it comes to that."

"I'm sorry if I added to your duties by having you drive me out to the Mayhewses."

Calvin waved his hand again before reaching for another biscuit. "I run extra errands all the time." He lowered his voice and leaned across the table towards her. "Some of the ladies like to send me out to smuggle in contraband."

Cynthia wondered what kind of contraband one could smuggle into a luxury resort. It wasn't as though it were a children's summer camp, or even a college dormitory. Surely he wasn't referring to illegal drugs. Such things were not unknown on campus, but they were not commonly seen, even at parties put on by fraternities.

"What kind of contraband?" she asked, her voice pitched low to match his own.

"Hooch," he said. "Alcohol is not part of the menu here at the resort, but that doesn't stop some of our guests from asking for it anyway. Since they aren't able to access it through the dining room, they find other ways."

"Are you the other way?" Cynthia asked.

"I am if they tip as generously as they usually do," he said. "Since you're here to earn as much money as possible, I'd suggest you acquiesce to any such request you may receive. I'm sure they will make it worth your while if you do."

"But if it's against the rules, won't I get fired for doing so?" she asked.

Calvin shrugged. "How is anyone going to find out? Besides, it's not illegal; it is simply frowned upon by the dietitians. If these ladies want to sabotage their own weight-loss efforts, it isn't our place to refuse them."

"But if they fail to lose weight, won't they be dissatisfied with their experience and decline to return another time? Won't they tell their friends it isn't a successful program?"

He smiled at her, a wide, slow smile that sent a bit of a shiver from her tailbone to the back of her neck. "As much as most of our guests may say they're here to drop a few pounds, the fact of the matter is, they're really here on a vacation, and one they can brag about to their friends. The only exceptions are those who are here to stop drinking."

"There are women who are here because they want to stop drinking?" Cynthia asked. She didn't know why, but she felt shocked to the marrow. In her nice middle-class world, she had never heard of any women whom she thought of as problem-drinkers. Certainly the ladies in her mother's bridge club indulged in cocktails during afternoon card games, as well as at parties hosted in the neighborhood or at the Rotary club. But excess drinking was something she associated with men, and those in the lower classes at that. The idea that women with as much wealth and fame as the guests at the resort could claim would have any struggles with alcohol seemed incomprehensible.

"Why do you sound so shocked? I would have thought that a college girl like you would insist that women can do most things just the same as men, virtues or vices."

She paused, considering Calvin's point. She supposed that for all her belief that her gender shouldn't hold her back, she did think there were some things she simply didn't consider seemly for a woman. Perhaps she ought to be more open-minded.

"You're right. That is foolish of me." Still, she worried about breaking the resort rules. "But aren't you worried about being caught fetching contraband?"

"I'm only worried about getting fired for leaving any of our guests unsatisfied with their experience here," Calvin said. "I'm not going to give anyone cause for complaint."

"Would Iris really fire you from your job?" she asked.

"Iris would fire me in a heartbeat if the guests were displeased with my service. And if she didn't, Miss Arden would," he said. "I suggest you don't give any of them a reason to complain about you."

Suddenly, the pork and mashed potatoes sat heavily in Cynthia's stomach. Between satisfying both Iris and the guests, was there any way she was going to be able to keep the job long enough to earn her tuition?

CHAPTER 26

Cynthia

DESPITE BEING MUCH YOUNGER THAN her supervisor, Cynthia had to admit that Iris was running rings around her. She took the steps of the servants' stairs two at a time, usually weighted down by a stack of freshly laundered towels. How she managed it, Cynthia simply did not understand. She wondered if she would be half as fast or as strong by the end of the summer. From the way Iris kept scowling back over her shoulder, she didn't think her boss would be willing to give her that long to improve.

Despite her show of conviction during her interview, she was beginning to have doubts as to whether or not she could manage to keep the job. After only a couple of hours, every muscle in her slim body howled from the unaccustomed exertion. She hurried along the second-floor hallway as quickly as her aching muscles would allow, following Iris to a discreetly placed supply closet at its end. Iris yanked open the wooden door, which looked just like the ones separating the guest rooms to the eyes of passersby, and pulled a small rolling cart out from its depths. She shoved it towards Cynthia and nodded wordlessly before striding on ahead, running her fingers along the surface of mahogany tables, checking for dust.

The cart was neatly stacked with all manner of cleaning products, although none of them seemed to be the ones her mother favored. Judith Proctor was as eager to be in the know about modern innovations, and whatever happened to be considered the latest thing, as she was for her daughter to marry a man with excellent financial prospects.

Not for her were boxes of borax or bars of Fels-Naptha soap like what Cynthia had worked into stain after stain, marring the tablecloths and napkins destined to return to the dining room in a pristine state. She squinted between the bottles of concentrated Lysol and the canisters of Ajax cleanser, hoping to spot a pair of rubber gloves. Her hands stung as she gripped the handle of the cart just firmly enough to keep control of it as it rumbled across the plush carpet.

Even over the slight squeak of the cart's wheels, Cynthia could hear Iris cluck her tongue as she came abreast of a table supporting an enormous urn of flowers. Iris stopped dead in her tracks and plucked two yellowing petals from an ivory-colored rose and secreted them away into a pocket of her inky black uniform dress with its severe, old-fashioned collar.

"It is the duty of all staff to notice details like that one. If you see even the slightest little thing that is less than perfect, I expect you to pull your weight by taking care of it. Don't come to me and ask; just fix it before any of the guests should happen to see it. Do you understand?"

Cynthia nodded, and before she could make any other sort of reply, Iris was on the move again, heading for the end of the hall as if the devil himself might be looking for her. Although, remembering the remarks made by Calvin, Cynthia thought that maybe the housekeeper was trying her best to keep ahead of Miss Arden.

Iris stopped in front of a door once again and fitted a key from a ring attached to a sash tied about her waist into its lock. Cynthia was put in mind of a course she had taken on European history, and she was suddenly struck by how much Iris had in common with a medieval chatelaine. She stifled a giggle. It would never do for a peasant girl to get above herself.

Iris flung open the door and stepped across the threshold. Long windows flanked by heavy brocade drapes looked out over a deep-green lawn that ended at a sandy beach hugging the edge of the lake. Between the building and the water's edge, wooden deck chairs with jauntily striped umbrellas placed behind them for shade sat in a tidy row. Cynthia could see women of all shapes, sizes, and ages lounging in them. Gardens overflowing with radiant blooms dotted the lawn and perfumed the breeze that floated in through the open windows.

The view of Long Pond itself from the second story was

breathtaking. Towering spruce trees ringed the shoreline, and several small islands dotted the lake. It was even more beautiful than the aspect afforded by the Mayhews' spacious porch.

She turned her attention to the room as Iris began to move about it. The walls were papered in pale blue printed with golden vines climbing up and down in undulating columns. A high bed with a satin coverlet and a flotilla of plump pillows encased in snowy-white linens lay against one wall. Small bedside tables flanked it on either side, each holding a reading lamp with a pleated shade in soft pink.

The opposite side of the room featured a fireplace surrounded by delicately painted tiles, an overstuffed chair, and an ottoman upholstered to match the draperies, as well as a table supporting another large vase of flowers. But the showpiece of the room, if one did not count the view, was the dressing table—or rather, the myriad of pots, tubes, and brushes placed upon it. Cynthia had never seen anything quite like it in all her life. A tufted stool covered in deep-blue velvet was placed in front of it, and a large gold-framed mirror hung above it, reflecting light from the long windows opposite.

"This room is to be occupied by one of our most important guests and, as you can see, is in need of a rigorous cleaning," Iris said, sweeping her arm out in front of her to indicate the extent of the problem.

Cynthia nodded, her heart hammering in her chest. To her inexperienced eyes, the room looked guest-ready, no matter their importance. The bedspread lay smoothly tucked around the bed. No dust appeared to have spread over any of the dark wooden surfaces. The crystals in the chandelier dangling from the center of the ceiling sparkled with such brilliance it made her eyes water to look at them directly. Still, if Iris wished for her to clean the room again, clean it she would.

"May I ask who is expected to stay in this room?" she asked.

Perhaps she would recognize the name and Iris's insistence on a second round of cleaning would make more sense. After all, she had heard the rumors of all the famous names that were known to visit.

Iris pursed her lips. "Her name is Vivian Shaw, if you must know, and she is expected to arrive this evening. I hope that you can be counted on to be discreet concerning her stay. We do not bandy about our guests' names under any circumstances." Iris pushed past her and opened yet another door at the end of the room opposite the fireplace.

Vivian Shaw! Pauline had mentioned that Rita Hayworth was a frequent visitor, but Cynthia hadn't expected to see her, let alone a starlet who was even more famous. No wonder Iris was so eager to not be caught shorthanded. Cynthia followed her and found herself in the largest bathroom she had ever seen. Another crystal chandelier—albeit a slightly smaller one—hung from the ceiling. An oversize porcelain tub in pale blue with gold-toned taps sat tucked into an alcove. The toilet and sink were constructed of matching porcelain. Fluffy white towels were draped over ornate bars. A set of French doors with frosted panes took up one whole wall.

"Surely you will agree that the bathroom is not fit for use. I will expect you to go over it as though your job depends upon it—which, in fact, it does. Start with the fixtures and finish up with the floor. The bucket and brush are on the cart."

Cynthia nodded again and stepped into the main bedroom to retrieve the cart. That was when she noticed something was missing.

"Will I find a mop in the supply closet?" she asked, returning to the bathroom.

"Mops are vile, filthy things that simply push dirt about and spread germs as they do so," Iris said, one eyebrow cocked in the air, like Cynthia had suggested wiping the floor with a dead raccoon.

"What am I to clean the floor with instead?" she asked.

"If a bucket and brush are the tools trusted by my late predecessor, Alice Merrick, then they are good enough for the likes of you," Iris said. "But you'd best be quick about it. Vivian Shaw will surely not appreciate arriving to discover that her room is not ready and that you are in it."

The telephone in the room rang, and Iris turned away to answer it. Based on Iris's side of the conversation, the call was not an entirely pleasant one. Cynthia stepped as far from her supervisor as the confines of the room would allow in an attempt to provide her with some semblance of privacy. She ran her finger along the top of the chair rail. Just as she suspected, not a speck of dust clung to her finger.

She peered out one of the tall windows once again to take in the view. The lake sparkled in the sun, and boats whizzed by with water-skiers in tow. She noticed once again the women of varying ages and modesty of swimming costumes dotted along the private beach. While most sat at their ease, apparently unoccupied by anything more than chatting with their neighbors, one woman stood out. She was by no means the oldest of the assembled guests, but one would not call her young. That said, she was striking, with her broad-brimmed cobalt hat and a long, flowing set of beach pajamas that looked like they would have been the height of fashion on the French Riviera in the 1930s. She wore an intricately patterned scarf draped over her shoulders and knotted around her neck. But most interesting of all was the sketchbook propped on her knees. She held her hand above the paper, but she did not appear to be holding any sort of drawing implement. She appeared utterly absorbed in the scene in front of her rather than in her fellow guests.

The telephone rattled down into its cradle, and Cynthia felt Iris's gaze boring into her back. She turned away from the window, worried that she appeared to be slacking.

"As soon as you are done here, you are to report to the salon manager, Erma, to prepare for the fashion show," Iris said. "It doesn't start until this evening, but it seems that there is much to be done to prepare the models, so you will need to make quick work of this job."

Without awaiting an answer, Iris swept out of the room, her dark braid streaming out behind her as she sped away.

Cynthia plucked an ancient-looking brush that surely had provided inspiration for Disney's film *Cinderella*. She could not believe that she had been asked to scrub a floor on her hands and knees with a stiff brush. Even her mother, as fussy and house-proud as she was, had the good sense to use a mop and wringer. Still, if Iris insisted that was how it was to be done, then so be it. It would not matter one bit when she was back at Barlow.

CHAPTER 27

Geraldine

GERALDINE DIDN'T PARTICULARLY INTEREST HERSELF in the latest fashions. For one thing, she was old enough to have seen them all before. For another, although she wouldn't say so out loud, she prided herself in her unorthodox appearance. She would be most disappointed in herself if she wished to purchase anything that might appeal to the other guests at the resort.

But Marjorie had looked so eager to attend the fashion show that Geraldine didn't have the heart to refuse to accompany her. The younger woman was so desperately homesick for her children that anything that brought the slightest bit of enthusiasm to the surface was worth encouraging. Besides, Geraldine thought that Marjorie might benefit greatly from some fashion advice. Yet again, she was dressed in an entirely unsuitable ensemble. Her figure would benefit from more severe cuts and tailored details than the flounces and ruffles she seemed to favor.

Geraldine knew a bit about visual sleight of hand from all her years spent at the easel. Anyhow, what was foreshortening if not a bit of trickery? And if there was someone she wished to see tricked, it was Marjorie's odious husband. Besides, she was sure Marjorie had a generous clothing allowance even if she had very few other freedoms. Her husband and mother-in-law would not allow her to appear shabbily clad even if she wore things that were entirely unflattering. Just the notion of Marjorie's husband receiving a bill for the amounts a private collection from Elizabeth Arden would surely command raised Geraldine's spirits.

The fashion show had been announced the evening before, and Marjorie had broached the subject over dinner. But it wasn't until luncheon, and Marjorie's unfortunate choice of outfit, that Geraldine had made up her mind. She had thought that Miss Arden would be there herself to provide the presentation but was somewhat disappointed to discover it was being led by an underling. Not that the woman did not command the room with brisk efficiency and a genuine sense of enthusiasm.

It was somewhat surprising to find that the event was being hosted in the resort's bowling alley. It seemed an odd choice, but upon viewing the space, Geraldine had to admit that it served its purpose well. A runway had been improvised down the length of one of the bowling lanes by unfurling a wool carpet runner along its center. Seats were clustered around the sides and the end of the room, leaving plenty of room for chairs on either side of the improvised catwalk. Marjorie waved to her from a chair positioned front and center and indicated she had saved her a place. Once again Geraldine felt her heart squeeze at Marjorie's childish delight.

It seemed the event was a popular one, as the spaces filled up quickly and the voices swirling all around the room echoed Marjorie's appetite for the occasion. Before long, the presenter clapped her hands together, and from somewhere out of sight, music began to play. A door at the far end of the room flung open, and out onto the carpet strode a line of lithesome young beauties. Three of the girls, she instantly recognized as technicians from the spa. In fact, one of them had been instrumental in helping lower her into the Ardena Wax Bath the day before. Despite how different they looked in Miss Arden's beautiful designs rather than their clinician's white coats, Geraldine would have known them anywhere. With her artist's eyes, she made a practice of noticing her surroundings and their inhabitants to a degree most others did not employ.

But there were women and girls Geraldine did not recognize modeling the fashions too. So many of the staff toiled away out of sight that it was no surprise they should not seem familiar to her. What was surprising was the way her hands itched for a charcoal pencil and her sketchbook. There was something about the way the fabrics rustled and the models moved that reminded her of the year she'd spent at art school. Live models were part of many of her classes, and she had been quite adept at figure drawing. Not that she had continued with it—at least, not professionally, since her career as a landscape artist had taken off.

She snapped open the clasp of her evening bag and extracted a small notebook and pen tucked near the bottom. After bending back the notebook's cover and propping it up on her handbag, she began brief sketches of the models as they strode along the catwalk. As the silks and satins and taffeta gowns swirled past, she worked quickly, filled with a sense of inspiration she had not felt since her husband's death.

Out of the corner of her eye, she noticed Marjorie straining forward, her face aglow with pleasure at the spectacle before her. The younger woman's features were completely transformed by her interest in the spectacle. Geraldine shifted slightly in her seat and made several quick renderings of her new friend without being noticed. By the time the third showing of gowns had been completed and the catwalk portion of the event was over, Geraldine was surprised at how much she had produced. Page after page of the notebook was filled with images that captured the lively spirit of the event. The presenter clapped her hands once more, and the music faded away.

"Ladies, I hope you have enjoyed the evening thus far. We would now like to offer each of you the opportunity to approach the models and the samples of fashions you've seen worn here tonight. We have a variety of colorways and accessories for you to peruse as well. This is an exclusive preview of the collection, never before seen by the public. Miss Arden fervently hopes that you will all be as delighted by it as she is. Please feel free to ask any questions. I am happy to assist."

Marjorie laid a hand on Geraldine's wrist. "I had no idea that you ever turned your hand towards figure drawing." She squinted and leaned over the open page of Geraldine's notebook. "You know, if you ever wanted to populate your landscapes with figures like these, I am sure your audience would be enchanted. These are so lively and compelling."

Geraldine looked down as though seeing the sketches through Marjorie's eyes rather than her own. When she worked, she had no real sense of the effect of the strokes she laid down on the paper. They just felt correct to her somehow, and she never evaluated them in real time. It was only after she'd put down her implement and took several steps back from any work that she had a sense of how it had turned out. She had to agree with Marjorie: There was something inspiring about the images before her.

"I shall have to give your suggestion some thought," she said. She stuffed her notebook into her handbag and snapped it shut.

Marjorie smiled, then turned her gaze to a clothing rail on the opposite side of the room. "Would you mind if I take a few moments to look over the gowns?" she asked Geraldine.

"I would be upset if you didn't," Geraldine said. "Why don't you see what you think of that red cocktail dress with the black-lace overlay?"

Geraldine's mind wandered as soon as Marjorie left her side. In her mind's eye, she could see three figures whirling in gem-colored gowns, the lake glinting in the background. She was eager to get to her easel. But first she had to intervene with Marjorie, who had unfortunately begun running her hand over a butter-yellow dress covered in far too many flounces.

CHAPTER 28

Cynthia

CYNTHIA COULD NOT REMEMBER A time when she had felt so tired. All she wanted to do was peel off her uniform and climb into bed. She didn't think she even had the energy to wash the makeup from the fashion show off her face before sprawling out on her bunk. As she entered the room and glanced up at the bed, her heart sank. She still needed to make it up.

When Iris had shown her to the room she was to share with another employee, she had not been put off in the least by the thought of clambering up into the top bunk. Now the idea of handling even one more set of bed linens left her close to tears. Still, she couldn't imagine flopping down on the bare mattress without even a pillow. Not to mention that even though it was the second week of June, nights at the lake could turn chilly. She didn't relish the idea of waking herself—or her roommate—up in the wee hours with the sound of her chattering teeth.

She turned and headed out into the corridor and began

cautiously opening one door after another until she spotted the linen closet. She grabbed a set of sheets—much more utilitarian than the ones she had seen in the guest rooms—a calico bedspread, and two anemic-looking pillows.

Somehow she found the will to properly make the bed, tucking the ends of the top sheet under the mattress and smoothing the coverlet evenly across. She had just tucked the second pillow under her chin in preparation for slipping it into its case when a young woman of about her same age stepped though the doorway. She wore the same blue maid's uniform that was still clinging stickily to Cynthia's slim frame.

"You must be the new girl," she said. "I'm Dolores."

Cynthia dropped the pillow into place and slid down off the bed. "It's nice to meet you. I'm Cynthia."

Dolores looked her up and down like she was a Christmas goose hanging in the window of a butcher's shop. She reached up and loosened her honey-colored hair from a ponytail and shook it out, leaving soft waves framing her freckled face. She slipped her feet out of her shoes and left them where they lay as she crossed the room and perched on the windowsill. She pulled a pack of cigarettes from the pocket of her skirt and lifted the window screen by several inches. She held out the pack to Cynthia, who shook her head. She had thought about starting to smoke. Many of her classmates did and claimed that it killed their appetites and kept their figures trim, but Cynthia still felt unsure. Even if they weren't terribly expensive, cigarettes cost money, and she had better things to spend hers on than a habit that most people said was hard to break.

The smell of sulfur curled and wafted into Cynthia's nostrils as Dolores struck a match and touched it to the end of a cigarette before slipping it between her wide lips. She took a long drag, then blew the smoke out the window. She held the lit cigarette as far out the window as her arm could reach.

"Miss Arden doesn't allow smoking in the staff quarters, so if you smoke you had better make sure you don't get caught doing it in here," Dolores said.

"I didn't realize that Miss Arden was on the premises," Cynthia said. Her heart raced in her chest. When she had accepted the job, she had hardly dared to hope that she might have the opportunity to meet the famous beauty expert and, indeed that rarest of characters, female business tycoon. Perhaps she would have that chance in the immediate future.

"She's not. But Mother Hubbard has taken to her new position like a woman possessed, and she is hell-bent on enforcing every single one of her boss's rules. She's only been at it for about a month, but it feels like forever. I cannot believe I'm saying it, but I actually miss Old Lady Merrick."

A creak on the floorboards sounded out in the hallway, and Cynthia froze. Would she lose her job for something her roommate was doing? Dolores stubbed out the cigarette and left the windowsill to open the top drawer of one of the dressers.

She pulled out a squat mason jar and, after unscrewing the lid, dropped the butt inside.

A mosquito flitted in through the open screen and hovered nearby as Cynthia waited for the sound of a second creak from the hall floorboards.

"She seems nice enough to me," Cynthia said. "After all, she gave me a chance at a job here."

Dolores crossed to the bed and flopped onto the lower bunk. "You only have that chance because she just fired one of my friends."

Cynthia's heart sank. Maybe she and Dolores would not hit it off. Not that it mattered all that much. Regardless, she was there to make money, not friends.

"I'm sorry that was why the position was available," Cynthia said. Another mosquito whined past her ear. She stepped over to the window and eased the screen closed, hoping Dolores would not take offense. She turned back to face her companion and perched on the edge of the wide windowsill despite her aching desire to stretch out on her own bunk. Her legs felt like lead, and her feet swelled against the insides of her shoes.

Dolores rolled over onto her side and propped her head up on her hand. "It isn't your fault. But you had best be careful not to make the same mistake, or you'll be out on your ear too. And I don't imagine you are busting your hump here for the pleasure of it."

Cynthia smiled. She thought it likely that by the end of the summer, she might well have developed some sort of hump—or at the very least, a hunch—busted or not. Maybe Dolores could give her some advice.

"I definitely am not here for the fun of it. I need to make all the money I can over the next few weeks," she said.

Dolores's eyes widened, and she patted the bed. Cynthia went to sit with her.

Dolores dropped her voice. "You don't need the money to get yourself out of 'the family way,' do you? If Mother Hubbard finds out you're expecting, you'll be fired for sure."

"No, nothing like that," Cynthia said. She blushed just to be asked such a thing. She had heard about a few of the girls she had known at college who dropped out of school and married straightaway, but she had never put herself in the position where that was even possible. Getting her education mattered far too much for that sort of thing.

"Then what are you doing here? You aren't local," Dolores said, fixing her blue-eyed gaze on Cynthia's face.

"I need tuition money if I want to return to college in September."

Dolores snapped her fingers and laughed. "That's it. You look like a coed. What happened? I thought Daddy always paid for girls like you."

Cynthia shrugged. She wasn't sure exactly what to say. It

didn't sit well with her to air her family's dirty laundry to a stranger, but she couldn't think of any reasonable explanation besides the truth.

"I had a scholarship to pay for the first two years. If I want to finish my education, I have to find a way to pay for it myself." Saying it out loud to a girl her age made it feel all the more unlikely. It was one thing to mull it over with Pauline or even Glenn and accept their help and suggestions. It was quite another to mention it to someone who was not associated with the college.

Dolores whistled. "You had better be on your best behavior, then. And you had better make some big tips."

"Are tips a real possibility?" Cynthia asked.

"Sure. Depending on who you meet, you can make more in tips than in your regular wages by the end of the season. Why do you think the regulars return year after year? It sure isn't on account of the working conditions."

"Have you ever made that kind of money yourself?"

"I started to, once I got moved from general duties to being assigned as a maid in the guest rooms. Every time I turned around, someone was handing me a dollar or two. If one of our wealthy ladies takes a shine to you, it could make your summer."

Cynthia thought back to what Calvin had said about receiving tips from the guests for fetching alcohol from town or driving them off the resort for some reason or other. She hadn't expected to make much working as a maid, but if Dolores had

had a similar experience, she might too. Some of her tiredness seemed to shift, and she felt the most lighthearted that she had since arriving in Mount Vernon.

"Do you have any suggestions for me? I really do need the money."

"Be respectful to the old biddies, but don't set your sights on them for any money. Most of them don't seem to ever carry any. You're better off making nice with the jet set. They're younger and like to show off their wealth."

"So far, I haven't met any of the guests."

"I bet you'll get assigned to the guest rooms since you're taking over for Velda. She was a guest-room maid, after all. Not that the position will do you much good if you have the same misfortune she did."

"Is there anything I should be aware of? Are there any particular no-nos?"

Dolores held up her hand and began counting them off on her fingers: "Don't pay too much attention to the guests' belongings, don't slack on the job, don't help yourself to samples from the beauty spa when no one is looking, don't look at one of the guests in a way that offends her..."

"I'll keep all that in mind. Thanks for the advice." Cynthia climbed up onto her own bunk as Dolores fetched her a shower cap from the same drawer where she'd stashed the mason jar. She plucked her dressing gown from the foot of her bed and announced that she planned to take a shower.

As Cynthia stared up at the ceiling, swatting away a mosquito that buzzed next to her ear, all feelings of sleepiness fled. She had no intention of taking things that did not belong to her, money or supplies. That said, how could she be sure not to do something that would offend one of the guests?

CHAPTER 29

Iris

IRIS HAD NOT DREADED A conversation with her mother so much in years. Still, there would be no better time. The guests were all at the fashion show under Erma's watchful eye. She told her feet to hurry as she made her way from her room to the staff house across the fields and along a path worn into the ground by decades of folks cutting through the vast estate and onto points in the neighboring properties. Her heart squeezed in her chest as she noted familiar landmarks at every turn. Although it had been more than twenty years since her parents had reluctantly sold their farm to Miss Arden, a small part of her still felt as though it were hers.

Besides her mother, who remembered every flowering shrub and towering maple as well as she? A raven's rookery swayed in a tall pine above her head, just as it had when she was a small girl, right near the sharp bend that overlooked the lake. The old stone wall where she had hidden childish treasures and then later notes for her sweetheart ran a few yards distant from the path. Even the blackberry thicket near the old farmhouse was familiar and comforting. As she considered being away from them for months at a time, her feet slowed even more.

Her family was not the only one to sell, of course. In the depths of the Depression, when there seemed to be no end in sight, many families had been relieved to take Miss Arden up on her offer of buying them out. Iris's parents had not wished to do so, the farm having been in the family for generations, but in the end, they could see no other way. Miss Arden suggested a price that seemed like one they could not refuse, and her father had been offered a job as a farmhand at a cousin's place in New Hampshire. There was room for Iris and her mother to accompany him, so the matter was easily resolved.

At least, it had seemed that way, until Iris decided to take a job working as a maid at the Maine Chance Farm. When she told her parents, they both looked as though they had been slapped. Her mother had asked how she could shame them by working for pay on their own property. Her father had been rendered speechless and left the room. But Iris was seventeen, old enough to know her own mind. Besides, it was only for the summer, she'd told them, and she would be glad to be able to contribute to the household budget in whatever small way she could manage.

Their leave-taking had been a somber one, and although she knew her parents both loved her, they were not particularly inclined to express such things—at least, not to Iris herself. On occasion, she had overheard one of her parents saying something complimentary about her grades in school or even her looks. But to compliment a child outright was tantamount to spoiling them, something they could never be accused of doing. They were no more inclined to express affection upon leave-taking, especially one that had been so unnecessary in the first place.

As Iris had thought about it in the years that followed, she often chided herself for having made their pain all the more egregious by refusing to accompany them. She knew it had broken both their hearts to leave Mount Vernon behind, and separating from their daughter in addition was a bridge too far. They hadn't even turned around to wave goodbye as a friendly neighbor gave them a ride to the nearest train station.

The time passed and things changed. Iris's parents both found their way back to town only three short years after leaving it. An elderly spinster cousin of her mother's had left them a small but sturdy house that bordered the Arden estate in her will when she died. Relieved of the burden of paying rent, her parents found their feet more quickly than they might have otherwise.

As she approached the house, she wondered what sort of the mood she would find her mother in. Some evenings when she returned home to check on her before Frances arrived for the night, Orla had prepared a large meal and an elaborately set table. Other times, she was still in her pajamas and appeared slightly confused about why Iris was there or, on occasion, even who she was. Having a rational discussion with her about something as important as accepting a job across the country would not have ever proven easy. But under the current circumstances, it would likely be impossible.

She mounted the stairs and pulled open the squeaky screen door and found her mother sitting in her Canadian rocker, nestled next to the fireplace in the parlor, a crochet hook and ball of yarn sitting idly in her lap. The windows were open, and the sounds of birds calling to each other to return to the nest filled the air. A mosquito had slipped into the room and buzzed about. Iris surreptitiously evaluated her mother's appearance. She was wearing one of her favorite housedresses, but her feet were tucked into carpet slippers, as though she had not ventured out at any point during the day. A small blob of something that appeared to have spattered onto her dress suggested she had once again forgotten to don an apron before cooking.

Orla looked up from her lap at the sound of Iris's footfalls.

"You're late tonight," her mother said. "In case you're hungry, there's a casserole in the oven keeping warm."

Iris exhaled, feeling tension ease from her body. Orla's voice sounded faintly chiding and altogether coherent. Perhaps she had not been crocheting because the arthritis in her hands was acting up, not that she couldn't remember how to do so.

Iris crossed the room and sat back on the floral-print sofa.

Her mother had recovered that same piece of furniture at least three times that Iris could recall. Perhaps if things went well with her job, she might be able to afford to replace it entirely. A spring in the seat beneath her worked its way into her backside, as it had done for years.

"Thank you, but I've already eaten," she said.

Orla sniffed. "I suppose my cooking isn't good enough for you now that you're used to the finer things up at the estate."

Iris's shoulders relaxed. Before her mother had started to behave so oddly, she would have found such a comment provoking. Now it was a source of relief. Orla sounded like her usual self—at least, the usual self she had been before the peculiarities started cropping up.

"You know that's not it. It's just that part of my compensation is room and board. It would be like taking a pay cut not to take advantage of it. You know I love your cooking," Iris said.

Orla pursed her lips and began toying with the half-finished granny square in her lap. "You never worked this late before you took over for Alice," she said.

"I'm still learning the ropes, Mother," Iris said. "Besides, there is a lot going on today that I had not expected."

"Is that so? What kind of goings-on?" Orla asked.

Iris would not have called her mother a gossip, exactly, just that she preferred to be well-informed, especially on the day-to-day affairs of her daughter's life. Not that Iris had an awful lot of juicy gossip to share with her. She made a habit of not mentioning anything besides the most glowing praise for things happening at the Maine Chance Farm and, as her mother had pointed out so often over the years, had very little personal life of her own to divulge.

Iris had often thought her mother might have benefited from a career of her own outside the home, but her father would not have stood for it. It was a point of pride that he could provide for his family even under the direst of circumstances. Iris thought there was more to it than just the financial side of things. If she were truly to be honest with herself, the notion of taking on the challenge of year-round work at Miss Arden's exacting standards, and in an entirely new location, lit her up inside. Maybe that was the real reason she dreaded mentioning it: Somehow it seemed selfish.

"Something entirely surprising that I need to discuss with you," Iris said.

There must have been something in Iris's tone that caught Orla's attention. She dropped her needlework back into her lap and clasped her hands together. Even in the lowering light, Iris could see her mother squeezing one hand with the other as if willing herself not to wring them.

"What is it, then? You haven't lost your job, have you?"

She shook her head. "No nothing like that. Quite the opposite, actually. I've been offered a promotion of sorts."

A flicker of uncertainty flashed across Orla's face. Iris's stomach clenched. It was the look of confusion she always wore when she was trying not to show that she did not understand what was going on around her.

"I know about your promotion. Poor Alice, God rest her soul, has been gone for a bit now. You don't think I'd forget a thing like that do you?" Orla jutted her chin out defiantly and glowered as if daring Iris to disagree that all her marbles were quite properly in their jar.

"Of course I would expect you to remember something so important. This is something in addition," Iris said.

Orla let out a braying laugh. "What's above the housekeeper? Has Miss Arden decided to simply give you the place?" she asked. "What a fine thing that would be."

This was not going as well as Iris would have hoped. Although she could not, in any truth, say it was going as badly as she had feared. It was just that she never liked it when her mother spoke disparagingly of the estate, or of Miss Arden personally. Iris felt she owed her employer a great deal, and beyond that she admired her. How many women could claim to have built an empire the size of Miss Arden's? Rumor had it that she was from modest enough means that it was even more remarkable. No, Iris did not like to hear her mother speak of her that way at all. Her irritation forced the difficult words from her lips.

"There is actually one position between mine and hers that has been offered to me. She called this afternoon and proposed that I take over the position of housekeeper in a full-time capacity," Iris said. She searched her mother's face for signs of understanding. Instead, that terrible look of bafflement passed across her features once more.

"But they close down the estate at the end of the summer. Why would she possibly need you to be there year-round?"

"The position would not keep me in Maine year-round, Mother. She's asked me to take over the running of the Maine Chance Farm in Arizona for the upcoming season."

"Arizona? You can't possibly be considering it," Orla said. Her voice had risen an octave, and her eyes had widened.

"I'm afraid I must. We could really use the money."

"We've always managed before. What's changed?" Orla asked, that look of confusion remaining firmly stamped on her face.

"We've always just barely managed to squeak by, and this would give us the chance to have a little breathing room. We can make the necessary repairs to the house, and perhaps even have a few extras we have never been able to afford before," Iris said. There was no need to tell her that the bulk of the extras would most likely be Orla's care.

"I'm sure we can figure out how to put on a new roof and see to the problems with the leach field without needing to go to such an extreme. Something always comes up," Orla said.

"It's not just that. Miss Arden is looking to consolidate the position. If I'm not the one to take it, it's my understanding she will replace me with someone who is willing to work at both properties," Iris said. "Then we really will be facing money troubles."

"I never did like that woman," Orla said. "Why would you ever get tangled up with her?" Orla jabbed her crochet hook through the ball of yarn and flung it into the open work basket on the floor beside her chair. She pushed herself to her feet. "She's trying to take you away from me."

"You must know that isn't true. And it really is a wonderful opportunity," Iris said, standing and offering her mother an arm to lean on. Orla shook her off and stopped at the foot of the stairs.

"It is a wonderful opportunity for you to leave me with no one but Frances to check on me. I'm going up to bed. And I don't need your help getting there. Anyhow, it seems I need to get used to your absence since you're planning to abandon me."

Iris watched in silence as her mother hoisted herself up one stair at a time, leaning heavily on the rail. What in the world was she going to do? Her mother's reaction left her feeling awash with guilt, especially since, even considering the cost to Orla, she'd give almost anything to go.

CHAPTER 30

Geraldine

DESPITE HER BEST EFFORTS, GERALDINE'S stomach's loud complaints could no longer be ignored. Worse still, she suddenly felt lightheaded. How irksome. She glanced at her paint-spattered wristwatch and realized she had worked straight through lunch. Although she had scant interest in food, even she was shocked at how little of it was served to the guests, especially considering how much they paid for the privilege of not eating. Her breakfast tray—consisting of a wafer of cantaloupe and two pieces of melba toast, augmented only by a surprisingly fortifying cup of coffee—had been nowhere near enough sustenance to allow her to skip lunch. She certainly could not manage to keep working away on her painting with her stomach making such a nuisance of itself.

She couldn't be bothered to change her clothes before scouting out something to eat, so she made do by wiping her hands on a clean rag before swishing her brush around in a jar of mineral spirts. She peeled off her smock and hoped her painting clothes would not disgrace her too much. Not that she cared what the other guests thought, but she would not wish to lower her standing to any great extent with the staff. It took far less effort to be formidable when respectably attired, and she wished to save her energy for her painting. Geraldine gave her work in progress one last look before quitting the apple shed and crossing an expanse of lawn that separated her makeshift studio from the Arden House. A side door led straight into an area of the building the guests were not supposed to notice.

There was no possibility that the staff could function on slivers of dry toast and vegetable juices. In a place as self-sufficient as the Maine Chance was rumored to be, she felt certain a staff kitchen had to be somewhere nearby, no matter how determined Miss Arden might be to keep it well hidden. It had to be said that all the functional underbelly of the resort was nearly invisible. From the light-footed staff to the discreet closets for cleaning supplies and laundry chutes, all the work that went into the running of the place took place behind the scenes.

She pushed open the door and smelled the faintest whiff of boiled potatoes. Slipping into the service corridor, she moved swiftly towards what she guessed must be the staff kitchen. Surely nothing so lowly, nor so nourishing, as a potato could possibly sully the guest kitchen. Sure enough, as she moved along, the scent grew stronger. Her stomach growled once more as a puff of warm, fragrant air drifted from an open doorway at the far end of the hall. She stepped into the bright room, flooded with light from long windows facing a field that swept towards a neatly tended apple orchard.

A young woman, somewhere in her late teens or early twenties, sat at a long wooden table centered in the room, a fork in one hand and a copy of the *American Economic Review* in the other. Geraldine paused, not quite sure what to make of the figure before her. With her honey-colored hair and smooth skin, the girl was pretty—or she would have been if not for the scowl on her face. She wore the starched blue-and-white uniform of the Maine Chance maids, which surprised Geraldine, considering her choice of reading material. In her experience, since the recent advent of television, fewer young people seemed to have the patience for reading at all, let alone something as dry as an academic journal. Something about her seemed familiar.

The girl glanced up and laid her fork down quickly. She snapped the magazine shut and sprang to her feet.

“May I help you, ma’am?” she asked, a bit of color appearing—charmingly, it had to be said—on each of her cheeks.

Geraldine moved to the table and pulled out a chair. She dropped into it and leaned forward. “What’s that you’re eating?”

The girl looked down. “Meat loaf, green beans fresh from the garden, mashed potatoes, and bread-and-butter pickles. I was told to help myself to a slice of chocolate cake for dessert, if I liked. May I offer you a plate of your own, Mrs. Putnam?”

So, the staff was trained to know the names of the guests even if they had not been introduced. How like Iris to be so thorough.

"I wouldn't say no to any of it."

The young woman moved from the table to a nearby cupboard. As she reached for a plate, Geraldine realized where she had seen her before. She snapped her fingers at the memory.

"Weren't you the girl who was wearing the pale-blue robe, amongst other things, at the fashion show?"

"That was me." The girl bobbed her head as she scooped a generous helping of mashed potatoes onto a thick china plate. She added meat loaf and green beans but left off the pickles, choosing to carry the jar to the table. After fetching cutlery from a drawer near the table, she placed it all in front of Geraldine and stood to the side as if awaiting further instructions. Geraldine waved a paint-spattered hand at her, signaling the girl should return to her meal.

Geraldine skewered a forkful of green beans and closed her eyes as she chewed. The bright burst of vegetal green in her mouth transported her back to her childhood, when she had often snuck into the kitchen to take meals with the family cook, a jolly woman named Nancy, whose sturdy arms were always dusted with flour and available for a motherly embrace. She swallowed, noticing a lump that had nothing to do with the food as it swelled in her throat. How long had it been since she had thought of Nancy's kindness? Best not to dwell on such things.

She sliced off a bite of meat loaf with the side of her fork and nodded towards the magazine still lying closed on the table.

"I'll wager that you don't have to fend off many requests to borrow your reading material," she said.

The young maid smiled. "It hasn't happened so far."

"I would have imagined that a fashion magazine or one about Hollywood stars would be more popular with most people."

The girl smiled. "There's no accounting for taste, I suppose."

Geraldine leaned back in her chair. The girl intrigued her. Her voice was less deferential than she was used to when it came to servants, but there was nothing in it to reprimand her. It was more like a well-raised young person speaking to an elder without the reservation that frequently shaded interactions with staff. But it was the magazine that piqued her curiosity the most.

"You don't find it a dull subject?"

"Not in the least. Economics touches almost every part of everyday life, whether people realize it or not. I prefer to be informed."

If there was one thing Geraldine admired and respected, it was a person who spoke their minds, especially if that person was a woman. She liked it even more if the opinions were unexpected or controversial.

"And do you do that by reading articles in scholarly journals?"

"I do." The girl reached for the magazine and flipped through the pages, coming to one that, even from across the table, appeared well thumbed. "But I find it even more useful to research the material and contribute an article myself." She tapped a slim finger over the name of the man who was credited in the byline. Geraldine noticed a blister forming on the webbing between the girl's thumb and forefinger.

"You wrote an article for the *American Economic Review?*" She tried to keep the note of incredulity from her voice.

"You wouldn't think it from the byline, but yes, I wrote this article."

Geraldine extended her arm and pulled the magazine towards herself. "Who is Professor Arthur Avery?"

"He's the head of the economics department at Barlow College."

Like everyone else in her social set, Geraldine had heard of Barlow, with its reputation of understated exclusivity. If its crest was on one's degree, doors effortlessly opened in business, medicine, and politics. If the girl in front of her spoke the truth, she was well positioned for a bright future. So what on earth was she doing wearing a maid's uniform at the Maine Chance?

"I don't see a second name listed here." Geraldine gestured towards the professor's name.

"Sadly, neither do I."

"If there was one, what would it be?"

"Cynthia Proctor."

The Proctor family hadn't arrived on the *Mayflower*, but they weren't too far in its wake. Geraldine approved, on general principle, of New Englanders with deep roots. It was undeserved, of course, but she couldn't seem to shake the assumption that they had things in common that mattered to her. It wasn't the sort of thing she would say aloud, but she added it to the positive column in her head.

"I assume you're a student at Barlow."

"That remains to be seen," Cynthia said, glancing at the magazine once more. This was not a response Geraldine expected. The girl continued to surprise her.

Geraldine popped the meat loaf into her mouth as she looked the girl over with an artist's eye. Even in a maid's uniform, instead of the designer gowns she had worn the night before, she was still a charming creature. Pale skin with a warm undertone. A pointed chin and high cheekbones contrasted with the full cheeks of youth. Thick lashes fringing eyes the color of strongly brewed tea. Hair scraped mercilessly into a ponytail. A neck too short to be elegant, but serviceable nonetheless. A strong nose perched above full lips. Dimples, freckles, and dainty earlobes. Geraldine itched to sketch her once more, but her sketchbook and charcoal lay too far off in the apple shed.

She swallowed. The meat loaf was delicious. She ought to ask for the staff cook to send the recipe to her housekeeper.

"You don't look like the sort to be on academic probation."

The girl's eyes widened. "I most certainly am not."

"Why the uncertainty, then?" Geraldine realized she was prying, but she felt it her due. After all, she was a paying guest, and she was old. Who better to indulge in overt nosiness?

Cynthia met her gaze with surprising frankness, given her age and position.

"My family isn't wealthy. The school didn't renew my scholarship, and the paid position I hoped to win by writing this article was given to a boy with better connections than my own. If I earn enough tuition money this summer, I will return. If not, I won't."

It felt like ages since Geraldine had encountered someone so forthright. The country was awash with postwar optimism, and most people she met tended to look for the bright side of everything since the boys who could had come home. She didn't think of herself as a pessimist, but to her, it often felt forced. Cynthia's frank assessment of her situation was refreshing.

"So you found a job here as a maid? Wasn't there something that could have made more use of your skills?"

"I was very lucky to find this job. By the time the semester ended, most of the summer opportunities had already been filled. I tried at more than two dozen places before I heard about a maid leaving here."

Geraldine didn't think she needed to mention that she had been instrumental in the position becoming available. However, an idea was forming, and she preferred for Cynthia to continue to speak openly and personably with her.

“And what exactly is it that you do here?”

“So far, my duties have been to do whatever Iris asks of me.”

“Iris hasn’t assigned you to any particular guest rooms as yet?”

“Not so far. To tell the truth, I’m still in training,” Cynthia said.

Geraldine glanced around the room and spotted a writing tablet on the counter near a wall-mounted telephone and a cup filled with pens.

“Fetch me that pad of paper and a pen,” she said.

Cynthia did as she was asked without hesitation or question. Geraldine quickly dashed off a note and folded the sheet of paper in half, creasing it firmly. She polished off the contents of her plate before sliding the note across the table.

“As soon as you’ve finished up here, take this note to Iris. Mind you, it’s for her eyes only.” With that, she pushed back her chair and got to her feet. Her knees protested ever so slightly, but there was a spring in her step nonetheless as she turned from the table and headed back towards her makeshift studio. Maybe her time at the Maine Chance would be even more interesting than she had imagined it could be.

CHAPTER 31

Cynthia

CYNTHIA'S HEART POUNDED AND HER throat felt dry as she left the staff kitchen in search of Iris. Mrs. Putnam's note crinkled in her pocket with each step she took. Had she given offense in some way? Mrs. Putnam certainly was an unusual woman. Who could possibly know what she might wish to communicate to Iris?

Running was expressly forbidden on the property, as it was considered unseemly and inclined to draw unnecessary attention to the staff, not to mention it caused them to perspire, which was certainly not something the guests would wish to be subjected to. Still, Cynthia saw no reason not to walk just as quickly as she possibly could. If she was going to be fired based on a comment from Mrs. Putnam, she had best know it sooner rather than later if she hoped to secure a different job—if that was even possible. Her stomach roiled with nerves as she slipped along the staff hallway and into the main part of the building.

A quick inspection of the dining room, with its vases of freshly cut flowers and sparkling chandelier, revealed no trace of the housekeeper. Cynthia checked the writing room, with no more luck. But as she was about to cross the wide hallway to inspect the sitting room, she spotted her quarry. Iris, with her silver-streaked dark hair swept severely into a bun, stood behind the reception desk, running her finger down the page of a very large leather-bound volume. From a distance, it looked like an old-fashioned ledger, but as Cynthia drew closer, she realized it was a guest book. Iris glanced up with a slight scowl stamped on her strong features.

"I thought I told you to report to the laundry house after your lunch break," she said, pausing her finger halfway down the page in front of her.

"You did, but Mrs. Putnam asked that I bring this to you immediately," Cynthia said, sliding her hand into her apron pocket and withdrawing the crinkly sheet of paper.

Iris held out her hand, and Cynthia swallowed dryly as she placed the note in it. The housekeeper unfolded the piece of paper and read through the contents quickly, her lips pressing together more tightly with each line her gaze passed over. Cynthia detected the barest bit of a grumble under Iris's breath as she placed the note on the desk in front of her and tapped a long, strong finger on top of it.

"How did you manage a thing like this?" Iris asked. "Not only is this highly unusual, but it couldn't have come at a worse time."

Cynthia was certain she was about to be fired. Whatever the note contained, it was not something that pleased her employer in the least. She hardly knew how to answer, considering she had no knowledge of the note's contents. She forced herself not to allow her gaze to focus sufficiently on the paper between them in order to read the message.

"I'm not sure what it is I'm supposed to have done, but I assure you, it was not my intention to offend Mrs. Putnam in any way."

Iris exhaled sharply through her nose, creating a bit of a whistling sound. It did not indicate pleasure or good cheer.

"Offend her? I should say you didn't do that in the least," Iris said, shoving the note in her direction. "You don't know what this is about?"

Cynthia shook her head. "No, ma'am, I don't. Mrs. Putnam instructed me not to read the note before handing it to you."

"And she didn't tell you what she wanted?"

Cynthia shook her head once more. "No. She simply instructed me to carry it to you as swiftly as possible. I thought she must be displeased with me for some reason."

Iris crossed her arms over her chest. "And you brought the note to me anyway?" Iris asked.

"If Mrs. Putnam is unhappy with me, it would hardly make matters better by flouting her instructions."

"We might just make a decent maid out of you yet. That is, if you don't get too above yourself, on account of Mrs. Putnam's request," Iris said. "She's requesting that you should be the only one assigned to her room. And she asks that you be made available to serve as an artist model whenever you can be spared from your regular duties."

Cynthia's thoughts jumbled and swirled. She knew she was still far too slow at the job she had been hired to do. How would she possibly manage to find time to pose for Mrs. Putnam as well?

"Do guests often request particular maids?" Cynthia asked.

She had so many questions that she didn't ask. What did that mean for her job? Would she still be paid at the same rate if her duties had altered from the ones Iris had expected when she hired her? Mrs. Putnam wasn't the new-money sort that Dolores said was most likely to splash their wealth around, but maybe she would turn out to be generous with tips. No matter what, it was better than being fired for refusing her request.

"Not often, but occasionally we have guests that take a shine to certain members of staff. Although asking for you to serve as an artist's model is a first."

"I'm flattered. I only hope that it won't leave you shorthanded," Cynthia said.

It was a legitimate concern. As much as Cynthia knew she was throwing herself into her work as hard as she possibly could, the fact remained that she was not entirely up to speed. Compared to someone like Dolores, who had been at the job for several years, she felt clumsy and slow. Try as she might, she was still learning the ropes, and those ropes were not easy. Again and again, she had spotted Iris pitching in with jobs that the maids were assigned to tackle. Dolores had mentioned that generally the hotel ran with at least one more female member of staff, but the death of the former housekeeper had thrown a wrench into the usually well-oiled machinery.

"We'll have to make it work. There's no possible way I could refuse a direct request from a guest, especially not one as esteemed as Mrs. Putnam. She happens to be a personal friend of Miss Arden's, and it would never do to disappoint her. And all this happens straight on top of Vivian Shaw's arrival. I'm not quite sure how we'll manage."

Iris looked Cynthia up and down, drumming her fingers on the guest book in front of her before snapping it shut, wedging the note between its covers in her haste. She stepped out from behind the registry desk and inclined her head towards the stairs. "You had best follow me. There's still plenty of work to be done."

CHAPTER 32

Cynthia

THE VIEW OF THE LAKE from the edge of the lawn at the Maine Chance was at least as beautiful as the one at the Mayhews' cottage. Cynthia bent over one of the many lounge chairs placed strategically to best take in the view and retrieved a crumpled towel from its seat. The guests had completed their morning-calisthenics sessions and had returned to the Arden House for what passed as a meal. Cynthia had noticed waiters carrying trays of clear bouillon and cherry tomatoes with chilled shrimp skewered onto ruffled picks. Cheerful bouquets of blooms fresh from the garden valiantly distracted the eye from the paucity of calories. Cynthia had overheard the other staff members joking and laughing about the guests paying such exorbitant fees for what amounted to starvation rations. One of them had gone so far as to remark that they could have saved themselves enough money for a trip to Europe if they had simply fired their cooks and stayed at home.

Iris had come in at that very moment and rebuked the maid who had been making such disparaging comments. She mentioned that they all might be on starvation rations if they lost their jobs, should the wealthy clients decide not to spend their money in Mount Vernon. Cynthia couldn't help but agree. It was none of her business how others wished to spend their money. All she cared about was how she saved hers. Iris had sent her out to the grounds to gather up stray towels wherever she might find them.

Some people might have considered it an unpleasant job, but Cynthia was grateful for the chance to spend some time out of doors. After all, it was a glorious June day, and with the weather in Maine being so changeable, it was always a delight to take advantage of a fair day whenever it occurred. Besides, it passed the time until she was to meet Mrs. Putnam for her first modeling session, the idea of which left her feeling at least as unsure as performing her duties under Iris's watchful eye. What did she know about modeling, other than the one evening parading about in designer gowns? Surely posing for an artist was completely different. And why had Mrs. Putnam chosen her in the first place?

She added the towel to the others already placed in the wicker basket propped on her hip and made her way towards a deck chair several yards down the beach. Out in the middle of the lake, she spotted motorboats whizzing past, creating a wake that sent paddlers in canoes scrambling to steer their crafts into the oncoming waves. For just a moment, she felt ever-so-slightly sorry for herself.

She spared a thought for Pauline, no doubt enjoying time with Glenn and the others out on the lake, or off on a shopping trip with her mother. Then she caught sight of Calvin striding her way, and her thoughts of her roommate and whatever she might be up to evaporated like water droplets on hot asphalt.

"I see they have you on towel detail," Calvin said. He bent over, retrieved the towel on the closest deck chair, and carried it towards her basket. He reached out and took the burden from her, clamping it under his arm with apparent ease.

"I consider myself lucky. It's a beautiful day out, and just look at the view," Cynthia said, sweeping her arm towards the expanse of water. "We have nothing like this back home."

Calvin paused and looked out over the water as if considering the way that Cynthia must be seeing it. "I suppose you get used to such things when you grow up around them. Perhaps the people here are spoiled."

"I think you must be. The closest thing to a lake in my town is the mill pond."

Calvin smiled as he followed her. "Where is it that you're from?"

"South Berwick. It's a lovely place to live, but it isn't exactly a tourist destination."

"That's down on the New Hampshire border, isn't it?" he asked.

"That's right. It is one of the towns along the Salmon Falls River dividing the southernmost border of Maine and New Hampshire."

"I've never been there. Is it a lot different than Mount Vernon?"

She considered the question for a long moment before answering. "I suppose it depends on what you mean by 'different.'"

"For instance, Mount Vernon's population is under seven hundred people. Are there more in South Berwick?"

"We've got about two thousand more."

"That practically makes you a city girl, at least by Maine standards," he said.

"I suppose it does in a way. South Berwick is a mill town, which is different too. There are many rural areas, but the mill buildings give a more industrial feel than you see here in the lakes region." She swept her hand out towards the water in front of them. "We've also got Berwick Academy, which brings students from other places to town during the academic year, while your outsiders tend to come during the summer break."

"But it's still Maine, though, isn't it?"

The notion that they belonged to the same place in that way gave her heart a squeeze. Like most other Mainers, she was proud of her claim to be a native, for reasons impossible to articulate to outsiders. Either you were one of them or you weren't, and that was entirely a matter of birth. It was as if something entered a body at the first breath, and if that was Maine, it was something to cherish. She liked the notion that she and Calvin shared that.

"How did you end up here?" he asked.

"I came north to attend Barlow College," she said. She wasn't sure how much she wanted to reveal about the exact journey that had taken her to the Maine Chance. It embarrassed her that her scholarship hadn't been renewed. Somehow she didn't want Calvin to think ill of her. She wasn't quite sure why it mattered to her, but it did.

"So, you are a coed at a swanky school. And yet somehow you ended up working here as a maid. There's got to be a story there somewhere," he said.

"Not every coed—even ones that attend private colleges—are wealthy," she said, bending over yet another towel.

"I thought you seemed like a different sort of girl that day I spotted you on the side of the road," he said.

"Different how?" Cynthia asked.

"You just didn't look the type to be walking down the road in search of the job. I had to blink a few times to be sure you were real when I first laid eyes on you," he said.

Cynthia felt the back of her neck grow warm, and she didn't think it was because of the bright sun bearing down on them.

"You are a bit different too," she said, hoping to deflect any further comments on her strangeness.

Calvin stopped and shifted the laundry basket to his other

arm. "I suppose I'm not like the college boys you're used to. I bet I'm a bit rough around the edges, and not anywhere near so cultured."

Cynthia tipped her head sideways and looked up at him. He was right about that. He was not much like the parade of young men Pauline always had swarming around her. For one thing, he didn't seem to be all that concerned about making a good impression. Nor did he project the false world-weariness of the young men who attempted to look sophisticated beyond their years. No, he certainly did not remind her of her fellow students in most ways.

She wasn't even quite sure that he was the same age as the average college student. On the one hand, he seemed as though he was still young enough to have not filled out to his final size. On the other, his level of self-assurance made him seem like he might be several years older than herself. She wondered what had caused it, until she remembered that he had mentioned serving in Korea.

"I wouldn't describe you like that at all. You don't remind me of the students I've been in classes with, but that doesn't mean that comparison is unfavorable. For one thing, you seem a great deal more mature than most of them. I can't imagine the most important thing in your life is figuring out what to do on a Saturday night," Cynthia said.

Calvin smiled down at her. "I'll take that as a compliment. I do have a few weightier matters usually preying on my mind."

"Like what?" Cynthia asked, feeling emboldened.

"I'm considering what to do with my future now that I've managed to make it back home unscathed," he said. "I'm only at this job for the summer while I figure out my next move."

"Do you intend to stay in town after the season is over?"

He shrugged. "I suppose it depends on what kind of employment opportunities are available. I have my sights set on something, but it might be a long shot."

Calvin's tone had lost a bit of its confidence. If she had to guess, whatever he was hoping for meant a great deal to him.

"Do you want to tell me about it?" she asked.

He stopped and tipped his head to one side, considering. "Maybe someday."

"What sort of job do you think you might be looking for if your plans fall through?"

"I hope that it won't come to that, but if it does, then I shall have to take whatever there is going. There aren't too many jobs to be had that pay worth a damn here in the offseason, but there's always the need for laborers of some sort or another," he said.

"You mean like people who work on farms, that kind of thing?"

"Farming is one, although there's not the same call for that as there used to be. There are opportunities for lumberjacks and positions for driving log trucks to the mills. And of course, there are the boot factories to consider," he said.

There were boot factories near her hometown too. Enormous brick buildings with streams of workers flowing in and out three shifts during the day. For some people, the work seemed to be agreeable enough, but somehow she couldn't imagine Calvin feeling that way. He came off as too restless. And why wouldn't he be? After all, he had been as far away from home as Asia. Could a small, rural town with few job prospects satisfy him? She knew from her classes as well as her research that the economy in Maine had not quite caught up with the economic boom that much of the rest of the country was experiencing after the war. Small farms were being forced out of business at an alarming rate, and an entire way of life in the rural areas was changing. Many of the young people in the state had left, looking for more opportunities elsewhere. One thing had led to another, and the situation became increasingly dire. She didn't envy Calvin his choices.

"Whatever your plans for the future include, I hope that they work out for you. You don't seem likely to be satisfied by settling for anything less than what you really want."

Calvin shifted the laundry basket to his other side. He stared into her eyes with an intensity that ran through her like an electric shock. "You're right about that. And you know, the list of what I want seems to be getting longer by the minute."

CHAPTER 33

Cynthia

Late June

THE STAFF GATHERED AT IRIS'S request in the employee kitchen. Even Mrs. Dudley stopped stirring a giant stockpot atop the stove in order to give the housekeeper her full attention.

"Quiet down, quiet down, please," Iris said, lifting a broad, work-worn hand in the air. The chattering stopped immediately, and Cynthia had to wonder how often such a meeting was called. It seemed to her that perhaps it was a bit unusual, from the way the other more experienced members of the staff were behaving. "I know that you have all been working very hard throughout the season, and believe you me, I appreciate it. But I'm going to have to ask for you to give a little more today than usual. As most of you have been here in years past, you'll know how much strain extra events can cause. For those of you who are new, brace yourselves. Additionally, I am sorry to say that if you had a day off scheduled for today, it will have to be postponed."

Cynthia's heart sank. She had hardly managed to pull herself out of bed the past three mornings from sheer exhaustion. She had been looking forward to her time away from the resort, more to give her body a rest than for the plans she had made with Pauline to spend the day lounging on the beach and going for a ride with Glenn in his boat.

"*Everyone's* day off?" Dolores asked, shooting a disappointed look in Cynthia's direction.

"Everyone's, I'm afraid. Miss Arden just rang up to let me know that she has been asked by the Maine Federation of Garden Clubs Conference to allow them to tour the property. They were scheduled at a different location, but their plans have fallen through at the last minute due to a fire on the premises."

Calvin raised his hand. "Is it the same crowd we hosted last year?" he asked.

"To my knowledge, yes, it is." Iris looked around the room, her gaze settling on Cynthia for just a beat longer than it did on the other members of the staff. At least, that was the way it felt to Cynthia. "We cannot allow the high standards at the Maine Chance to slip just because we're hosting a garden club in addition to our normal guests. Mrs. Dudley, Maurice may need you to pitch in with the after-tour luncheon Miss Arden has promised to the members of the local garden club. Will you be able to do that?"

Mrs. Dudley snorted and placed her pudgy hands on her hips. "I expect I can manage just fine to help turn out a few dozen small sandwiches and whatever fancy desserts he's got planned. If I'm there giving him a hand, I'll be able to make sure to bring all the leftovers back for the lot of you," she said, winking at the younger maids and chauffeurs.

Cynthia had never been so hungry in all her life as she had since starting her job at the Maine Chance. She had not realized how many calories it must burn to be on one's feet all day, making beds, vacuuming, and scrubbing bathrooms. Even her time with Mrs. Putnam did not seem to slake her constantly rumbling belly. She was pleased to note that however much she ate, she didn't seem to have gained an ounce. If anything, she was slimmer than ever, with her muscles toning up and any available excess paring away like the peel from a potato.

"I knew I could count on you, Mrs. Dudley," Iris said with the briefest of smiles. "Now, as to the rest of you, you need not make yourself expressly available to those guests visiting from the garden club, but if any of them makes a request of you, please do your best to try to honor it. They will certainly make some sort of additional mess, and I have never known them not to try and take advantage of anything that might be on offer here at the resort. For most of them, it's a peek behind a very expensive curtain, and they can't help trying to get the best look they possibly can manage. Are there any questions?"

"How long will they be here?" Calvin asked.

"The tour is scheduled to last between two and four this afternoon, with refreshments to follow immediately afterwards in the West Garden. I will be sure to hurry them along if they haven't all left by five thirty." Iris looked around the room for more questions. Hearing none, she pointed towards the door. "Let's get to it. I appreciate you putting in the extra effort."

Cynthia hurried out of the room with Calvin directly on her heels. She turned towards him once they were out of Iris's earshot.

"Does it really make that much more work for the staff to host a garden party?" she asked.

Calvin nodded. "It changes the atmosphere entirely. The local women who attend don't always confine themselves to the grounds but sneak off into the house and run around looking to spot celebrities or eyeball the house. I can't say that it tends to be the year-round locals. In fact, it almost never is. Those women are above such things. But people who visit the lake seasonally oftentimes have enough money to want to name-drop but not enough to stay here at the farm. They are the worst of all possible combinations."

"Do they just wander around?" Cynthia could understand the temptation. Even though she had been at the Maine Chance for some time herself, she could still not quite believe the opulence of the surroundings. And while the staff had every reason to keep the guests' identities to themselves, if they wanted to keep their jobs, members of the public would have no such compunction.

"For the most part they do."

"If it causes so much trouble, why does Miss Arden allow it?" Cynthia asked.

"Miss Arden is an avid gardener and loves to show off her grounds. Besides, she is deeply committed to the community, even though she doesn't make her home here full-time, and if the garden club wishes to include her property on its tour, she is more than happy to say yes. After all, the garden club sells tickets and raises money for local charities every summer. Any time she allows it, this property sells the most tickets of any of them."

Cynthia could well imagine that it would. As spectacular as the house was, the grounds were at least as beautiful. In the twenty years since the resort had been in Miss Arden's hands, it had been lavished with attention and what surely must have been truckloads of money.

"I shall have to tell Mrs. Putnam I may not be as available. I don't expect she will be any too pleased to hear it," Cynthia said.

Calvin put a hand on her shoulder reassuringly. "I can tell her if you want. Mrs. Putnam does seem to have a soft spot for young men," he said, a broad smile spreading across his face. "Besides, she doesn't want to get on my bad side, not since I'm the one who keeps smuggling in her preferred contraband."

"Which contraband is that?"

He leaned close to her ear and whispered, "She's rather partial to gin."

"I thought she brought the bottle in her studio from home," Cynthia said.

"She may have brought something from home, but she sent me out to procure more since she's been here. And nothing but top shelf for Mrs. Putnam, I can tell you. But it's all hush-hush, so don't you go telling anybody now, you hear? Smugglers like me end up earning most of our summer money with contraband."

"My lips are sealed. Anything that goes on between you and Mrs. Putnam is absolutely not my business." Cynthia winked at him and was gratified to see a faint blush coming to his cheeks. "But I will take you up on your offer of telling her about today. And I'll have to think of a way to thank you when the garden club event is behind us." She wondered whether she was coming off as too forward.

"I've already thought of something. On your next day off, come for a drive with me. There's a place I've been wanting to show you."

Her heart fluttered, and she nodded. Out of the corner of her eye, she caught sight of Iris bearing down on them. It wouldn't do to be seen fraternizing with a male member of the staff—at least, not with so much to do. Calvin seemed to have the same thought, and he gave her a fleeting smile before turning on his heel and heading off for the outbuilding where Mrs. Putnam had set up her studio. Cynthia permitted herself one last glance at him before turning towards the Arden House. Had Calvin asked her on a date, or was it just a ride with a friend?

She gave herself a mental shake and, with difficulty, turned her attention to racking up a list of duties that needed fulfilling before the garden club descended that afternoon. If some of them were going to come snooping, there mustn't be the least bit out of place.

CHAPTER 34

Cynthia

CYNTHIA KNEW BETTER THAN TO take a shortcut through the guest dining room rather than adhere to the protocol routing staff through back corridors and keeping them generally out of sight of the guests. Still, she was in a hurry and deemed it better to risk breaking the rules than to incur Iris's wrath by failing to perform her duties in a timely manner. The housekeeper had been on edge lately, and Cynthia wondered if it had to do with her own newness in the position.

While Cynthia had limited experience being a maid, hers was only a summer job. But Iris relied on her income, and must be feeling the pressure to perform in her new role as housekeeper. Cynthia certainly did not envy her the task. She had no illusion that Iris was more demanding than Miss Arden was herself. And on a day like this one, with additional persons prowling about the premises, Iris must have been feeling enormous strain.

It was the lull between lunch and dinner, and as Cynthia had expected, the dining room proved empty. Sweeping her gaze over the long sideboard and tables covered in snowy-white cloths, she paused to remove scattered petals from vases placed here and there about the room. It would never do for such inattention to detail spoiling the ambience of the resort.

Cynthia knew the dietitian and the chef relied on the presentation of the meals to distract guests from the minute quantities of food they contained. Having carried Mrs. Putnam's breakfast tray to her again and again, she marveled at the meager portions. It boggled her mind to think that women paid such exorbitant sums to be so severely deprived. But she would keep those thoughts to herself, just as she had with so many others since arriving at the resort. What pampered guests wished to do with their own money was their affair and had no bearing on her own life whatsoever.

As she tucked a handful of discarded petals into the pocket of her uniform apron, her thoughts drifted to Calvin. At the far end of the dining room, a small door opened into a staff corridor leading to the guest kitchen. Beside it was a far larger pair of French doors giving an expansive view of the lush grounds.

Unfamiliar women dressed in tea-length frocks, wide straw hats with cotton gloves, strands of pearls around their necks, and straw handbags dangling from their wrists strolled past bedding gardens bursting with red, blue, and white blooms. Now and again, one of them would stop and bend over a rosebush, plunging her nose deep into its fragrant blossoms, just as Cynthia herself so often did.

It seemed the visitors were enjoying themselves immensely if the broad smiles on their faces were any indication. She slipped into the corridor and made her way towards the kitchen, where she collected one of the heavy trays loaded down with tiny tea sandwiches and iced cookies. Even the tray held a small vase filled with colorful blooms, plucked, Cynthia was sure, that very morning from the garden beds just outside the kitchen. Maurice, the guest chef, gave her a warm smile and a nod as she grabbed the tray and headed back down the hallway.

She could not quite believe how much strength she had built up since her arrival. It gave her a new appreciation for all the labor her mother had provided for the family over the years. Cynthia had never been all that pleased with the fact that she was asked to perform household tasks her brother was never expected to help with. Her time at the resort made her all the surer that housework should be more evenly distributed between all members of the family, regardless of gender.

In fact, she often thought how much more sensible it would be if all the chauffeurs were women, and the servants stripping beds and hoisting laundry were the far more muscular men employed as drivers. She turned and placed her back against the door, pressing it open by levering her elbow down against the handle. She spun around, deftly squeezing through the space while managing not to jostle any of Maurice's delicately arranged platters of food. Just looking at the sandwiches made her stomach grumble. It would be at least another hour before she was able to slip away to the staff kitchen for a quick bite to eat, and that was if she was lucky.

A refreshment area had been set up for the garden-club visitors under a pair of towering oak trees. The spot not only offered cooling shade in the summer afternoon, but also a beautiful view of the rolling lawn and carefully tended bedding gardens. Cynthia carried her tray to one of the several trestle tables set up for the occasion. Each of them had been spread with the same snowy-white tablecloths that adorned the dining room. How like Miss Arden it was for there to be such attention to detail, even outdoors. No wonder Iris appeared so tense.

There, hovering at the edge of the table, stood Mrs. Putnam, helping herself to items from the trays and surreptitiously slipping wedges of cake and ham finger sandwiches wrapped in a paper napkin into her work satchel. A smudge of yellow paint marred her cheek, and her well-used canvas brush roll stuck out from the top of the bag.

It looked as though she had been hard at work. She glanced up at Cynthia and raised a finger to her lips. Cynthia smiled, knowing how much of a sweet tooth the older woman had confessed to having. Besides, she was in no way in need of a slimming regimen. In fact, it would have done her more good to partake of the far less popular plumping regimen that was also offered on rare occasions to those women who were markedly underweight.

"So, I see you really are as hard at work as young Calvin claimed you to be. It seems preposterous to me that the paying guests should have to do without your attention in favor of interlopers," Mrs. Putnam said, scowling towards the sounds of feminine chattering wafting their way from the gardens beyond. "Still, at least she's put on a good spread for them; I'll give her that."

Suddenly, from behind, Cynthia heard her name being called out but could not quite place the source of the voice. It was familiar but did not seem to make sense in those surroundings. She turned and felt her heart squeeze with shock.

"Cynthia, I thought your claim about a research project seemed dubious," Mrs. Mayhew said, closing the distance between them at an alarming rate. She stared at Cynthia, her eyes wide and her thinly plucked brows raised high. "Although it pains me to say it of a friend of Pauline's, it makes much more sense that you're here as a maid."

Not one coherent thought came to Cynthia's mind. She felt completely robbed of the power of speech. She opened her mouth to speak, but all she could think of was the fact that Mrs. Mayhew had found her out. All the older woman's suspicions about her not being the right sort of friend for her daughter had been confirmed.

Mrs. Putnam strode around the side of the heavily laden

table and came to a stop right beside her. She threw back her head and let out a ringing laugh.

"Don't be preposterous. Cynthia is my artist model. We simply stopped mid-session to fortify ourselves with some refreshments. Creativity is hard work and requires quite a bit of feeding," she said.

Mrs. Putnam wrapped one of her strong hands around Cynthia's arm as if to help hold her upright. Since her knees felt wobbly, it was a well-timed bit of assistance.

Mrs. Mayhew tipped her head to one side and crossed her arms across her chest. "And who might you be?"

Mrs. Putnam straightened. "My name is Geraldine Putnam, and if I may say so without appearing immodest, I am an artist of some renown. And who are you?"

"June Mayhew. Cynthia was a guest in my home until recently. I feel a certain responsibility for her, considering she's not spending her time as she claimed that she would be," Mrs. Mayhew said. "But now I find her standing here dressed in a maid's uniform. Just what am I to think?"

"I don't suppose you need think anything about it whatsoever, as I can't see how it could possibly be your business. That said, I can see that you're overwhelmed by curiosity. I'm painting Cynthia as a maid because it suits me to do so. The housekeeper here has graciously provided her with the uniform to wear for our sessions." Mrs. Putnam turned towards Cynthia. "In fact, we've been away from the studio for longer than I had intended. Make sure you grab a few of the sandwiches for yourself. I can't have you passing out mid-session because you're famished."

Cynthia nodded. "It was as enjoyable as ever to see you again, Mrs. Mayhew. I hope you will give my best to Pauline." Mrs. Mayhew kept a gimlet eye trained on the pair as Cynthia placed a selection of sandwiches and a slice of cake on a plate before following Mrs. Putnam towards the outbuilding she had requisitioned as a studio.

Once they were out of earshot, Mrs. Putnam bent towards her. "That was a near miss, wasn't it? I suppose we shall have to keep you hidden away in the studio for the rest of the day. How marvelous for me that despite us being descended upon by the garden club, you will have the opportunity to sit for me after all."

CHAPTER 35

Cynthia

FINALLY, A DAY OFF. CYNTHIA still awoke earlier than would have been her habit had she not been employed. Nevertheless, she didn't want to miss breakfast in the staff room. She wasn't working so hard that every muscle in her body ached to spend a penny she'd earned on breakfast at an overpriced restaurant in town. She rolled over onto her side and propped her head on her hand, noticing Dolores had been up even earlier than she was. Her roommate never made her own bed, preferring to leave the rumpled tangle of sheets and light coverlet just as they were when she slipped out and hurried off to work.

She flopped onto her back and stretched, long and luxuriantly. Through the open window, she could hear the sounds of birds and resort guests moving about their business. The calisthenics class held every fine morning on the beach drew the majority of the guests, and she could hear the lilting sound of feminine voices as they made their way towards the water's edge.

Cynthia slid out of bed and crossed to the small closet at the far end of the room. She flipped through the sundresses hanging there next to her spare maid's uniform. Her hand lingered on a blue gingham-checked sundress with a matching bolero jacket, but she found herself disinclined to choose anything blue. Her maid's uniform, with its navy cotton dress and white apron, was the only option during her workweek. After reaching for a pink-and-white-striped sundress, she lifted it over her head, feeling almost defiant. A pair of espadrilles and a broad-brimmed straw hat completed the outfit. She dug in the closet a little deeper and withdrew a raffia handbag, into which she placed her two-piece bathing suit and a towel filched from the supply closet.

Before leaving the room, she could not resist the impulse to make not only her own bed, but Dolores's as well. While Dolores had stated that she made enough beds in the course of the week that she wouldn't include her own among them, Cynthia couldn't stand to leave things so untidy. Besides, who was more deserving of a freshly made bed to slip into at night than a hardworking cleaner?

Calvin was nowhere to be seen in the staff kitchen when she arrived, but Mrs. Dudley was at her usual station, right in front of the stove, extracting a pan from the depths of the oven. She turned and smiled as Cynthia entered the room.

"Don't you look nice," she said.

Cynthia looked down at her dress, feeling her cheeks flush at the compliment. "Thank you for saying so."

"Any plans for the day? You're dolled up enough that I assume you have something special going on."

"Calvin wants to take me out for a drive. He says there's something he wishes to show me, but I have no idea what it is," Cynthia said. She hoped that the warmth she felt in her cheeks was not showing.

"You just be careful with what sort of surprises young men wish to show you," the cook said. "Although I must say that Calvin seems to be a very good sort. You're probably in safe hands with him."

Cynthia's cheeks grew even warmer at the suggestion something untoward might transpire between herself and Calvin, or even that he might consider such a thing. Anyhow, although she liked him perhaps more than she ought to, she wasn't that sort of girl.

"I'm sure he has nothing but friendly intentions," Cynthia said. "I'm not even certain that the drive constitutes a date."

"That's not the way he described it when he was in here asking me for a favor," Mrs. Dudley said, a mischievous smile spreading across her face.

Now she was sure the cook could see her blushing. If Calvin thought it was a date, then perhaps her interest in him was reciprocated. Not that she was sure she wished to be interested in him or that she would like those feelings returned. According to her mother and Pauline, it would be a much better idea for her to set her cap at someone like Glenn, with his money and connections. Still, it was very flattering, and she couldn't deny that she enjoyed his company.

"What sort of favor?" Cynthia asked.

The cook glanced at her wristwatch and then back at Cynthia. "The kind that I wasn't supposed to mention. Now, sit yourself down and eat some breakfast before you end up being late."

Cynthia turned her attention to a hearty breakfast of freshly baked biscuits, scrambled eggs, and bacon. Even though margarine had become a staple on most tables in the last several years, Cynthia was pleased once again to see a crock of real butter placed in the middle of the table, along with a pot of blueberry jam. Under the cook's approving gaze, she slathered her biscuits with both. After refusing a third helping, she thanked Mrs. Dudley and headed off to the converted stable in search of Calvin.

As she stepped out of the bright sunshine and into the gloom of the garage, she could just make out his form bent over the hood of a bottle-green jalopy. There was no way that it was one of Miss Arden's automobiles. Hers were all late-model luxury cars, like the royal-blue-and-black Rolls-Royce Wraith parked at the back of the garage, or the deep-maroon Cadillac Fleetwood 75 limousine positioned near the doors. Calvin had offered to drive her into town on a few occasions, and the interiors of each vehicle, with smooth leather upholstery and exotic wood trim, was as beautifully designed and maintained as the exterior. As her eyes adjusted, she could see he was vigorously buffing the hood of the car with a chamois. He turned his head as one of the floorboards creaked under her foot and flashed her a wide and welcoming smile.

"Hello, sleepyhead," he said. "I thought maybe you had stood me up."

She took a few steps closer as she shook her head. "It's nowhere near as late as you're making it out to be. The biscuits in the kitchen were still fresh out of the oven when I sat down to gobble them up. We weren't all raised on dairy farms, you know."

"I suppose that's a decent enough excuse for laying abed all morning," he said, folding the chamois carefully and placing it on a bench nearby.

"It's still barely eight o'clock," Cynthia said. "Wherever you're taking me can't be about to close anytime soon, if it's even open yet."

"Where I'm taking you has no opening time or closing time either," Calvin said. "At least, not yet it doesn't."

"That sounds intriguing. Won't you give me just a hint of what you have planned?"

"I don't think that I will. But like I told you before, it won't take all of your day off." He inclined his head towards her straw bag. "What's that you got there?"

"I thought I would bring along my bathing suit. Since you

had mentioned it wouldn't take all day, I figured we would have time to stop at a beach for a swim if we were so inclined after we finished up with whatever your plan was."

Calvin smiled broadly enough for a pair of dimples to appear in his cheeks. "I expect I could be persuaded to stop in at the beach. Just give me time to grab a pair of trunks from my room."

He sprinted up the stairs at the back of the garage. The chauffeurs had their own accommodations on the second floor of the converted stable. At least, that was what Dolores had told her. Cynthia would not have been brazen enough to visit male members of the staff in their private quarters. In a flash, Calvin had returned with a towel and bathing trunks tucked under his arm. He walked to the far side of the jalopy and opened the passenger door for Cynthia, waiting for her to be comfortably settled on the seat before closing it. He slid in behind the wheel and flung his arm over the back of the seat as he turned to back out. Cynthia could feel the warmth of his body radiating through her exposed shoulders.

As they slid out of the garage and into the bright sunshine, the cook's warning about being careful what young men might wish to show her screamed through her head. But before she could begin to fret about it, Calvin withdrew his arm and placed both broad hands on the steering wheel. The air suddenly felt cold around her shoulders despite the warmth of the morning. She looked over at him.

"Are you ready?" he asked.

She nodded, but she wasn't entirely sure she was.

Calvin slowed the car to a stop at the edge of a hillocky field beside a For Sale sign from a local real estate brokerage. He leaned over the steering wheel, peering through the windshield. Cynthia shaded her eyes with her hand and gazed out at the field stretching before her. The ground looked nothing like the manicured grounds of the Maine Chance. Then he popped open the driver's-side door and sprang from the vehicle. Never one to forget his manners, he moved to the passenger side and held open the door for Cynthia. Mindful of her skirt, she swung her legs out carefully, her knees clamped tightly together. He offered her his hand and helped her to her feet.

After closing the door behind her, he swept out his arm towards the sprawling acreage in front of them.

"So, what do you think?" he asked.

Cynthia took a few steps forward, watchful of the rocks and roots beneath her feet. Truth be told, the property was not particularly lovely to look at. Evidently, someone had clear-cut it for the lumber. Still, there was a small view of the lake in the distance that provided the property with some small measure of beauty. She in no way wished to be discouraging. Calvin caught her by the hand and tugged her forward, his enthusiasm bubbling up from within him.

"What is this place?" she asked. It wasn't her idea of a beauty spot for a picnic, or even any of the water sports she had come to associate with the lake. She had no idea whatsoever why he would bring her to such a place.

"It's where I have in mind to undertake my big idea," he said.

Cynthia looked about her once more. It was a large parcel, clear-cut for what must have encompassed more than a dozen acres. It appeared as though the only thing going for it would be that it was likely being sold for a bargain-basement price.

"And which idea is that?" she asked, hoping any reservation did not leak into her voice.

A giant smile spread across Calvin's face as he held out his arms wide as if to embrace the property. "You know how there are so many wealthy visitors to the resort and the entire area around the lake?" he asked.

Cynthia nodded.

"Well, they don't all like to come by train."

Calvin had a point. According to her research, automobiles were overtaking trains in popularity by leaps and bounds. The Maine Turnpike had been a tremendous undertaking, one of which the state was justifiably proud. Only recently completed, it was being touted as a major source of convenience for increasing tourism to the state. Both economic forecasters and elected officials held out hope that tourism was the way forward for a state where agriculture was losing market share year over year, and factory work was drying up too. Larger facilities and cheaper labor in the South and Japan had given textile mills and even shoe factories a run for their money. Professor Avery had mentioned in a lecture that both Sanford and Biddeford, Maine, were on a US Department of Labor list of top-priority distress areas.

"Are you planning to open an automobile dealership?" she asked.

She could imagine row upon row of shiny Buicks and Cadillacs stretched out across newly poured asphalt. For such an enterprise the clear-cutting would have served as a benefit. But where would a young man like Calvin find sufficient backing to open a car dealership? She couldn't imagine it would be an inexpensive undertaking.

He shook his head. "No. The very wealthy aren't all that inclined to go on road trips either. What I have in mind is to open an airfield." He gestured towards a flat spot near the road. "That's where I plan to build a multibay hangar and small office."

Cynthia peered around herself with surprise. She'd always imagined airfields requiring far vaster tracts of land than the space she saw before her. And was there really enough call for such a thing in rural Maine? Still, Calvin seemed quite sure of himself.

"Are you familiar with airplanes?" she asked.

"As a matter of fact, I am. I served as an aircraft mechanic in Korea. And I even have my pilot's license."

She was impressed. She'd never met anyone before who had a pilot's license. But still, she had concerns. "Is there enough room here to land an airplane?" Cynthia asked.

"You need less than you think for the size of plane that people coming to the area tend to own or charter. I'm not talking about any sort of commercial aircraft, but rather the little private ones. All I need for a runway is about five acres, and this parcel has fourteen. See over there?" He pointed off in the direction of the lake.

"The lake, you mean?" Cynthia asked.

Calvin nodded. "I was even thinking about putting in a dock for any seaplanes that wanted to land and tie up. Not everyone has a big enough dock at their estate for such a thing, or if they do, the dock is already dedicated to watercraft. I thought I could offer chauffeuring service from here to wherever it was that they were going after they land."

Cynthia tipped her head to one side and squinted. As Calvin had been speaking, an image of his proposed business sprang up in her mind's eye. She could easily picture wealthy people, like Glenn's parents or Pauline's, bragging to their friends about flying to the lake for the weekend. If they had the money, it would certainly make things more convenient. And if they had the money, why shouldn't they pay for something that saved them so much time?

"Would you need to own a plane yourself to do it?" she asked.

Another wide smile broke out across Calvin's face. "No, I wouldn't. Not that I would be disinclined to purchase one as soon as I was able. I do love to fly, and I can imagine there would be money to be made in providing chartered flights myself, but it would be easy enough to launch the business with just the airfield and a hangar."

"Do you plan to offer repairs as well?" she asked.

"Absolutely. There's no place else in the area that specializes in aircraft. I think I found a niche in the market."

The more she thought about it, the more his idea seemed to her to have merit. The research she had done for the article for Professor Avery had convinced her of the connection between transportation and tourism. With the dwindling opportunities in traditional industries over the past several decades, a steady, significant stream of young people left the state for a chance at a better future. Maine's remaining population skewed older than most other states, and the ongoing impact of that affected the entire economy in one way or another. With fewer young people left, the birth rate dropped. The housing sector showed little growth. Schools were hard-pressed to make a case for robust portions of town budgets. Calvin's idea was innovative and inspiring. With any luck, the turnpike would bring sufficient tourists to spark money-making ideas in other young Mainers, and the population would stabilize, or even grow.

"Calvin, I'm truly impressed. This is a bold plan, and not something everyone would think of, let alone dare to attempt. I'll bet you could even use the GI Bill for a business loan with your sort of experience."

A faint blush spread up the back of Calvin's neck. She didn't think it could be attributed to the sun despite the warmth of the day.

"Do you really think so? You don't think I'm some kind of a crazy dreamer?" he asked, turning towards her and taking a step closer.

She looked him straight in the eyes. "No, I don't think you're crazy, even if you are a bit of a dreamer. And what's the world without dreams, anyway? The Maine Chance wouldn't have been built if Miss Arden wasn't a dreamer. Come to think of it, nothing would have ever been invented or built if someone didn't have the vision and the courage to see it through. Besides, I happen to like dreamers."

She surprised herself by looking him straight in the eyes as she spoke.

"You know, I haven't told anybody else about my idea. Somehow I just knew that you would see it the way that I did."

Calvin reached for her hand and pulled her towards him, bending over slightly to close the gap in their height. Then he leaned in close and kissed her.

CHAPTER 36

Cynthia

EVEN THOUGH THEY HAD STOPPED at the property, they were still early enough arriving at the beach to have their pick of spots. Calvin chose a spot just above the damp edge of the sand and flapped open the blanket he had extracted from his trunk, settling it gently onto the ground. Cynthia slipped off her shoes and used them to anchor two corners of the blanket, then placed her straw handbag on a third.

The two sat side by side, looking out over the lake, suddenly slightly shy in each other's presence. Before she could think of anything to say, she heard her name being called out from farther along the sand. Calvin turned his head, and as she followed where his gaze went with her own, her heart thudded to a stop in her chest.

Pauline waved at her, both arms stretched above her head. In her wake, Cynthia could see Glenn, a couple of the other boys he usually palled around with, and a few girls she had seen in passing. The look on Glenn's face left no doubt of his displeasure at seeing her there with someone else. Part of her was flattered that he would be inclined towards jealousy. The rest of her was horrified at what might turn into an ugly scene. Besides, it wasn't as though she had promised to exclusively spend time with either Glenn or Calvin. Neither of them had made any such request of her. She straightened her shoulders and told herself everything would turn out just fine. It had been too perfect a day to be spoiled.

"I didn't expect to see you here," Pauline said as she paused at the edge of the blanket. "Who's your friend?"

"This is Calvin Willard. Calvin, this is my friend and college roommate, Pauline Mayhew," she said, making introductions.

She wasn't sure how to introduce Calvin, since none of the others besides Pauline knew she had taken a job at the Maine Chance. Being a maid certainly wouldn't earn her any respect in their crowd, and she wasn't about to offer up that information. Not that she was embarrassed by it, exactly, but she still wasn't sure what she thought of Glenn.

She was fairly certain what he would think of her if he knew she had need of employment over the summer, especially something as menial as being a chambermaid for people of his social class. She thought she felt Calvin looking at her out of the corner of his eye, and she wondered if he noticed that she eliminated explaining how she knew him. Her stomach turned, and the thought of the cook's picnic basket made her feel slightly nauseated. The rest of the group caught up with them, and Glenn's shadow fell across her outstretched legs, leaving her suddenly chilled.

"Well, this is a surprise. We haven't seen you for ages, and now you've turned up today with some other fellow," Glenn said. "What am I supposed to think of that?"

Calvin got to his feet. "I think you're supposed to think that Cynthia is free to do as she pleases with whomever she pleases," Calvin said. Cynthia scooted backward slightly and scrambled to her feet as gracefully as possible. Her sundress was not designed for feats of athleticism. She smoothed the back of her skirt with her palms, noticing they had become slightly damp.

She couldn't help but notice how evenly matched the two men were. Both were athletically built and of approximately the same height. Calvin's clothing looked like something you might buy off the peg in a Main Street shop or department store, while Glenn's appeared as though it had been tailored specifically for him. Still, she would not have known which one to put money on if it came down to a physical altercation. Surely it wouldn't devolve into something like that, would it?

Glenn relaxed his posture slightly, apparently coming to a decision. He stuck out his hand towards Calvin. "It's nice to meet you. I'm always happy to see Cynthia, no matter whose company she might be keeping."

Calvin grasped Glenn's hand and gave it a firm shake.

Pauline tapped Glenn playfully on the shoulder, and as the men released their grip, she tucked her arm through his.

"Didn't you say you wanted to swim out to Sheep Island today?" she asked. Several of the others in the group chimed in and reminded him of their plan.

"That's right. Calvin, won't you join us? Or don't you swim?" Glenn asked, looking Calvin up and down.

Calvin turned towards Cynthia. "Would you like to come? I wouldn't want to leave you here on your own."

Pauline spoke again. "She won't be alone. I'll stay with her while you boys go for a swim."

"I don't mind. Have fun and I'll see you when you get back," Cynthia said.

"Why don't we make it a race?" Glenn said. Calvin nodded, and all the young men began peeling off their T-shirts and stripping down to their swimming trunks. Glenn's torso was toasted to an even shade of brown. Calvin sported an endearing farmer's tan, with a pale chest and back and bronzed arms starting at the bicep and moving towards his hands. Pauline stood on the water's edge and counted down—three, two, one, go. The boys dashed into the water and dived under as quickly as the depth permitted them to do so. With long scissoring strokes, they sliced through the water towards the island near the middle of the lake.

"That will keep them busy for some time," Pauline said,

sitting down and tugging Cynthia onto the blanket next to her. "Now, who is this Calvin, anyway?"

"Calvin's a chauffeur at the Maine Chance. I met him on the day of my interview." Cynthia brushed a stray bit of sand from the surface of the blanket. "Did your mother mention that she saw me yesterday?"

"Mother was so angry when she returned home. She said she'd seen you and that Geraldine Putnam was incredibly rude to her." Pauline clapped her hand over her mouth and giggled.

"I wouldn't say that Geraldine was rude, but I would say that she did stick up for me when your mother started to get suspicious about why I was at the resort. I don't know what I would've done without her," Cynthia said.

Pauline squinted. "Mother sounded quite convinced that you were there as a model for Mrs. Putnam. Do you think she suspected something else?"

"She saw me in my maid's uniform and instantly assumed that I was working in that capacity. If Geraldine hadn't swooped in and announced that I was wearing it just as a bit of costuming for a modeling session, I would've been entirely found out."

"Well, it's a good thing that Mrs. Putnam was so fast on her feet. If my mother had found out what you were up to, she certainly would have bad-mouthed you to everybody, including people like Glenn's parents. That would've taken you out of the running for snagging him, I can tell you that for sure," Pauline said.

As she considered it, she knew many other girls would be distressed to be considered out of the running. Glenn was everything she was supposed to want in a man. Her mother would think he was the ultimate prize and surely would consider Cynthia's education more than worth it should she come away with such an important attachment. But as she gazed out across the water, Cynthia silently rooted for Calvin as the boys became smaller and smaller specks slicing through the water.

"I certainly was lucky. Mrs. Putnam is an extraordinary woman in most ways."

"I suppose that you were." Pauline turned towards the lake and held her hand over her eyes, shielding them from the sun. "What are you doing here with a chauffeur, anyway?"

"Calvin and I are friends, and we both have the same day off. He wanted to show me something, and then we came for a picnic afterwards." She felt no inclination to mention the kiss.

"I hope you're very careful about the sorts of things you'll let young men show you," Pauline said. "He's good looking, I'll give him that. But believe you me, Cynthia, you don't want to throw away your chances with someone like Glenn for a summer fling with a chauffeur. Boys in my crowd can give you the sort of life where you have a chauffeur of your own instead of being married to one."

CHAPTER 37

Geraldine

GERALDINE LEANED HER HEAD OUT the window of the Buick, feeling the wind trying to work its way underneath the kerchief knotted under her chin. Strands of loose hair slipped their bonds and tickled the sides of her face as they wended their way onto Castle Island Road.

Her heart felt a bit lighter with every yard they rolled along, Calvin's hands wrapped neatly around the steering wheel, deftly piloting the car.

Although the price was exorbitant for time spent at the Maine Chance, Geraldine could not fault the service. When she had inquired of Iris about taking a drive, Calvin and the Buick had been summoned without question. She knew from conversations with Cynthia that many members of the staff lived on the premises, and she supposed that part of the stellar service had to do with their proximity. Still, it did make one feel like a somebody to have such a small request filled so easily.

Marjorie had offered to accompany her, but she craved a bit of quiet. Calvin could easily be drawn into conversation but seemed equally comfortable passing time in silence. She often found that when she got to a sticky spot in her work, a long drive was enough to sort things out.

Calvin piloted them onto the Augusta Road and pointed the vehicle out towards Rome. The Maine Chance Farm property was so vast it fell on both sides of the Mount Vernon–Rome line. Heading east, then north from the property afforded beautiful views of Long Pond.

She leaned back against the headrest and admired the blues and greens of the unfolding landscape. A water bird swooped low and had just skimmed the surface of the lake when she spotted movement at the edge of the road. Geraldine peered out the window and noticed an elderly woman meandering along the shoulder, not wearing any shoes. Unless her eyes deceived her, it was Orla Hubbard.

"Calvin, pull over, please. Let's offer Mrs. Hubbard a ride."

He nodded and slowed the large car to a stop a few yards away from Orla. Calvin hopped out and approached the woman, speaking with her for a moment before he tucked his arm through hers and led her to the vehicle. He opened the back door and helped her inside. Then he rounded back to the driver's-side door and slid behind the wheel once more. He glanced over his shoulder at Geraldine.

She turned to Orla. "Where are you off to this afternoon, Mrs. Hubbard?" she asked.

Orla met her gaze, but her pale-blue eyes showed no sign she recognized Geraldine or that she knew the answer to the question.

"I'm not sure," she said.

"Let's drive Mrs. Hubbard home," Geraldine said.

She made small talk about the homes they passed and the beauty of the landscape as they made the five-minute drive to Orla's wooden-frame house with a small entry porch. It was a modest home surrounded by close neighbors. Geraldine was relieved to note that Orla appeared to recognize it as she pressed open the rear door and stepped out of the vehicle just as soon as they pulled to a stop.

She bolted up the front steps of the porch and into the building with more speed than Geraldine would have expected. Despite the difference in their ages, it was easy to see that she was closely related to Iris. She was slim and spry and matter of fact, even when she appeared somewhat befuddled.

"I don't think she ought to be left on her own," Geraldine said.

"Should I go fetch Iris?" he asked.

"Iris is far too busy with her work to take off in the middle of the day. Since all I have booked for the afternoon is a facial and a long nap, I could stay until someone she knows better can take over."

"I know that her neighbor Frances is one of Orla's friends. Shall I see if I can track her down and ask if she or someone else is available?"

"Please do. I'll wait here with her for you to return with my replacement," she said as she reached for her oversize handbag.

Calvin waited to drive off until she walked up the porch steps and pulled open the screen door. She could hear the sound of humming from the depths of the building. She followed the sound and arrived in a bright and sunny kitchen papered with yellow roses and sprigs of ivy. A teakettle stood on the large enamel woodstove, and a cake dome filled with what looked like homemade doughnuts sat in the center of a Formica-top table. She cleared her throat gently, so as not to startle the other woman.

Orla glanced over her shoulder with an expression of surprise.

"Don't I know you?" she asked.

"I'm a friend of your daughter's. I was feeling a bit lonesome, so she suggested that I might pay you a call. I hope that's all right," Geraldine said.

Orla wiped her hands on the tea towel hanging from the knob of a cupboard to the right of the sink and nodded. She bustled over to the drainboard on the side of the sink and lifted out two thick mugs, like the ones found in a diner.

"I'm always happy to meet friends of my daughter. What did you say your name was?" she asked.

"You can call me Geraldine."

"What if you have a seat right there at the kitchen table while I fix some coffee to go with a doughnut. You look like you could use a little meat on your bones," she said, squinting at her. "So many women these days want to go about looking like twigs. You will never catch a husband that way; that's what I tell my Iris. Men like a little bit of comfort, if you know what I mean." Orla went so far as to wink as she placed china plates and cloth napkins on the table.

Geraldine pulled out a vinyl-covered chair and sat down. She placed her bag at the far end of the table and surreptitiously observed her hostess. Orla seemed to not have any idea that they had known each other for years. That said, now that she was in familiar surroundings, she had lost her air of befuddlement. She looked like nothing so much as a pleasant, homey hostess bent on kindly welcoming a stranger into her home.

The percolator on the stove began to bubble, and the smell of freshly brewed coffee filled the room. Orla pulled it off the stove before it scorched and poured them each a cup. She lifted the glass dome and gestured for her guest to help herself to a doughnut before she did the same.

"Let's take these to the living room. I always think food tastes best when eaten sitting in a comfortable chair," Orla said.

Geraldine nodded and followed her hostess into the living

room. Orla pointed towards the sofa as she settled herself in an upholstered rocking chair. A large basket filled with yarn sat on the floor beside it. Orla plucked a partially completed blanket made of a dizzying array of colors from its depths and placed it in her lap. She reached for a crochet hook and began darting it back and forth, barely glancing down at the work as she did so. Whatever else she may have forgotten, Orla still seemed to be an accomplished needlewoman.

Geraldine lowered herself onto the sofa, feeling her knees creak as she did. It was funny how aging affected people differently. She and Orla were both in their seventies. Her own mind was as sharp as ever—at least, she believed it to be. Still, she would have bet on Orla to win if they were to participate in a foot race.

She reached for the doughnut. After all the deprivations in the Maine Chance dining room, it slid down with ease. Geraldine had not realized how ravenous she was until she took her first bite. The homey texture and flecks of spicy nutmeg reminded her sharply of eagerly awaiting doughnuts just like these to be fished out of a cast-iron skillet by her family's cook when she was a girl.

They sat in silence as Orla added row upon row to her vibrant blanket, rocking in the chair. Geraldine swallowed the last bite of doughnut, then slid her sketchbook and tin of pencils out of her bag. She wanted to capture Orla's hands, her knobby knuckles flexing as her flashing hook moved back and forth.

She made several sketches before the rocking slowed and Orla's hands stilled. Geraldine glanced up at her face and noticed her eyes had closed. The worry in her face disappeared with sleep and revealed how much her daughter resembled her. Geraldine sketched her portrait from her place on the sofa, and then again and again from various spots throughout the room.

Time passed quickly, and before long the sun was slanting through the window at a different angle when she heard the crunch of gravel under vehicle tires. The sound of the car door closing startled Orla awake. Geraldine snapped the sketchbook shut, as confusion filled Orla's eyes once more, sorry to lose the chance to continue capturing her so deeply at rest.

"Who are you?" Orla asked.

Before Geraldine could reply, a woman she recognized as Frances, the neighbor, bustled into the room.

"I'm sorry it took Calvin so long to find me. I thought she would be fine to leave long enough to have my hair washed and set," she said to Geraldine before turning to Orla. "I hope that you've got an appetite. I plan to make a batch of corn chowder for supper."

Orla rocked forward and tucked the blanket back into the basket by her feet. "That sounds lovely, Frances." She turned to Geraldine. "Do you know my daughter, Iris?"

CHAPTER 38

Cynthia

Mid-July

CYNTHIA RETRIEVED A NOTEBOOK, ALONG with two pencils and an eraser, from one of her suitcases stored in the staff-house storage room and hurried to the staff-house common room. Calvin stood near a window, a shaft of sunlight glinting off his dark, shiny hair. He turned and smiled as she stepped into the room.

"Are you sure that you don't mind spending your afternoon off helping me with this?" he asked.

"I don't mind at all. This sort of thing is right up my alley."

Perhaps that was not strictly true. Economics differed from business in some important ways. Her areas of study had been focused on theory, patterns, and trends. Businesses relied on those components but concerned itself with their practical applications. Still, there was enough overlap between the two disciplines that she thought she could give Calvin some useful feedback on his plans. Just to be sure, she had made her way to the local library on her last day off to look up the terms of the GI Bill and what it had to offer him.

She crossed the room and sat on the sofa in the center. She placed the notebook and pencils on the coffee table in front of her. Calvin lowered onto the seat beside her, and she felt the sofa springs jounce as he shifted slightly closer. She leaned slightly towards him, noticing a slight nick on his jawline where he had cut himself shaving.

"Still, I appreciate your willingness to give me a hand. I have a vision for the airfield, but the details on the way to the goal are a bit fuzzy."

He flashed her another smile, but this one was accompanied by raised eyebrows and shrugged shoulders. His vulnerability was endearing, and she reached out and gave his broad, tanned hand a squeeze before reaching for a notebook and pencil.

"If you are going to apply for a GI business loan, you will need some sense of your total costs, not just that of the land," she said. "Do you have an idea of what you'll need to get the business off the ground?"

"Maybe I should name it Off the Ground Enterprises," he said. "But seriously, I have been calculating the cost of equipment and materials." He rocked forward and pulled a folded piece of paper from the back pocket of his dungarees.

She took it from his outstretched hand and read through the list. Despite his concern about the details, Calvin had been remarkably thorough. He had accounted for the cost of the land, materials to build a hangar and a floatplane base, tools, signage, advertising, fuel, and maintenance costs to keep the unpaved runway in trim. The total came in well under the ten-thousand-dollar maximum the GI Bill offered for rural business loans. Out of the corner of her eye, she noticed his leg jiggling furiously up and down.

Cynthia turned towards him. "If your figures are accurate, you should be able to get this underway."

His leg abruptly stilled. "Are you sure?"

"I am. In fact, you could even apply for a larger loan." She drummed her fingers on the notebook. "I conducted extensive research for a paper on transportation and tourism, and it seems to me that if the cost weren't prohibitive, you might do well to consider adding the price of a small plane to the loan application."

Calvin's eyes widened. "The loan could run to a plane too?"

"Aren't there reasonable uses for one, since you're already planning an airfield?"

"I hadn't given it any thought since the total cost of the venture already seemed so high."

"If you're going to dream big, you might as well go all the way. Besides, it seems to me that the plane might prove a moneymaker that would more than justify the cost," she said. "Aren't there services you could offer, if you had one that might start recouping the investment right away?"

Calvin tipped his head to one side. "I expect there are folks who would be more than happy to splurge on chartering a private plane to fly them to the area even if they don't own one themselves."

Cynthia thought of the people she had met both through the Mayhews and also at the Maine Chance. She felt certain that many of them would enjoy casually mentioning to their friends and rivals that they had arrived by airplane. She could easily imagine Mrs. Mayhew enjoying the option of flying without having to go to the trouble of maintaining one. Still, such indulgences wouldn't take up all of Calvin's time.

"I'm sure you're right about that, but what could you use it for when not flying charters?"

"Parcel delivery would be an option," he said. "Or I could try to win an airmail contract with the postal service."

"Is that a possibility?"

"Absolutely. The USPS relies on private contracts to provide airmail service. In fact, considering our location, I could look into international airmail deliveries to Canada."

Cynthia made a note of potential government contracts. Anything that strengthened Calvin's bottom line would help with the loan application.

"What about sightseeing tours of the lakes, the coast, and even the White Mountains? Or offering to pull advertising banners behind your plane during the busy season? Local businesses might love the chance to get their name out there in a novel way. It seems to me that a plane would be an important source of revenue for your business." She recalled Professor Avery mentioning once that an enterprising individual had added just such a feature to his airmail business twenty years prior. He made a practice of charting a course over the crowded beaches during the summer months, advertising restaurants, hotels, and excursions like whale watches and deep-sea fishing trips.

"I know of a guy over in Auburn who's selling a used Cessna for a bargain price. In fact, I have enough put aside—between my earnings here and what I've saved from my time in the service—to pay cash for it, if that makes good business sense."

Given his work ethic and overall common sense, she wasn't surprised in the least to hear he had accumulated a sizable nest egg. It impressed her far more than the nonchalant mentions of trust funds and vast estates she had heard so often from boys at Barlow and the Mayhews' social set. She couldn't help but hope that his loan would be approved and that he would make a success of all his plans. It would feel wonderful to know she had played some small part in his future.

"Investing in a plane would show a loan officer that you are serious about your business. If you think you can come up with enough to cover the cost, I think you would be smart to go ahead and do so."

"You really don't think I'm crazy to give this a try?" he asked.

"Not in the least. Tourism is growing far faster than many

industries in Maine. If you told me you want to open a boot factory or go into the logging business, then I would've thought you were crazy. But not this. Besides, if you won't bet on yourself, who will?"

A confident grin spread across Calvin's face. "You really are a crackerjack, aren't you?" He reached for her hand and enclosed it in his own.

A flash of heat bloomed over her cheeks. She wasn't accustomed to such glowing praise about her ideas, especially from a man. Her father had discouraged her from demonstrating her facility with mathematics, even though she had inherited the ability from him. In group projects, her fellow students had been quick to dismiss her suggestions, even if they had no better ones to offer. And Professor Avery had shown how little regard he had for her contributions when he failed to consider her for the researcher post.

His response to her suggestions was as welcome as it was rare. She angled her fingers, aware of her still-new calluses as she interlaced them between his. As he squeezed her hand, she felt more committed than ever to her decision to pursue economics and find a way to finish her degree. She could think of no better use of her education than to help someone else plan a path to their own dreams, especially someone she thought of as much as she did Calvin.

"So, you don't think I'm crazy either? Not everyone believes women have any business studying economics." She stared down at their clasped hands, not sure she wanted to see the truth in his eyes.

He slid his hand away, and her heart caught in her chest. She felt his index finger below her chin raising her gaze to meet his.

"I think the only kind of crazy here is how I feel about you." He leaned in close and kissed her.

CHAPTER 39

Iris

IRIS COULDN'T SHAKE THE FEELING that she was crossing the invisible line that existed between staff and guests, but she simply couldn't let the matter drop. She promised herself she would find Geraldine on her own to thank her for her help with Orla.

Most of the guests were creatures of habit, Iris had found over the years. There were the ladies who routinely could be found lounging beside the lake every afternoon. There were others who spent their free time receiving beauty treatments in the spa wing of the resort. Still others spent the majority of their time engaged in one of the recreational activities like badminton or boating. Only a very few kept to themselves more often than not.

According to Cynthia, when she wasn't busy painting, Geraldine could be seen wandering the property, a book in hand, looking for a place to sit and read. It was the only thing

Iris envied about the other woman. She couldn't remember the last time she had spent a fair summer day leaning against the sun-warmed trunk of a shade tree, absorbed in a novel. The very notion of it produced an almost physical pain in her chest.

The winters provided more opportunity to borrow books from the lending library and to justify whiling away a stolen hour here or there indulging in stories that took her far from home—places like Arizona. But every summer, like a dutiful little ant, she busied herself gathering up what income she could before the cool evenings and shortened days drove the summer people back to wherever it was they came from and the taps snapped off on a steady stream of income.

But envy couldn't be on her mind as she offered words of appreciation to a guest. It was a mortifyingly awkward position to find herself in, and when she had heard from Calvin that Geraldine had been in her home, keeping an eye on Orla, she was aghast. She prided herself on her professionalism and knowing her place in the grand scheme of things at the resort.

"No fraternizing with the guests" had always been Alice Morrow's policy, one she had adhered to for all the years she had served as housekeeper. Iris had seen no reason to change it when Alice was no longer there to remind her. Truthfully, there had never been any temptation to do so. But here she was all those years later, needing to find the words to cross that divide. She stepped out of the back door of the staff house and looked towards the wide-open field leading to the orchard and the apple shed, where Geraldine was likely to be found.

That was a thing they had in common, Iris supposed. She herself couldn't see the point of spending a beautiful summer's day being scrubbed down with muddy muck or having yet another thing done to one's hair.

She paused at a large spreading maple tree right near the footpath that led off into the woods. It was one that turned the most gorgeous shade of pumpkin in the autumn, and Iris herself liked to sit beneath it before the guests arrived in the spring and after they'd gone in the fall. The spot provided a glimpse of the lake, and Iris had spent stolen moments there as often as she could, enjoying the view.

The apple shed sat within a stone's throw of the maple. She could see that the door to Geraldine's temporary studio was open, and she rapped her knuckles against the crisp white doorframe. The older woman looked up from where she stood behind a wooden easel and smiled at her.

Her welcome wrong-footed her somehow, and Iris felt her discomfort grow. It only increased as Geraldine raised a hand and waved her in. Iris shook off the worry that Miss Arden would suddenly appear right behind her.

"What brings you all the way out here?" Geraldine asked as she lowered a long-handled paintbrush and stepped out from behind the easel. "Has something happened to Orla?"

Iris stepped into the room and glanced around, surprised

at the transformation. It barely resembled its usual purpose as a storage shed. Someone—likely Cynthia—had polished the windows until they gleamed. Tubes of paint, a coffee can stuffed with more brushes, and piles of rags sat on a card table close at hand. Sketches of hands, trees, and models from the fashion show papered two walls. With a jolt, Iris recognized that several of the sketches were of her mother.

"Orla is why I'm here, but nothing has happened since you last saw her," Iris said.

She stood before Geraldine, smoothing imaginary wrinkles from the front of her dark-blue uniform skirt, gathering her courage to speak.

"I wanted to thank you for keeping an eye on my mother. It was more than kind of you, and a terrible imposition," she said.

"It was no trouble at all," Geraldine said. "There's no need to thank me."

"I think there's rather more to it than that. I know how trying she can be. Besides, it was extremely generous of you to take time away from the resort."

"Do you know what is difficult about being wealthy?" Geraldine asked.

Iris shook her head. From where she stood, it seemed unlikely there was anything difficult. "I have no idea."

"You discover that it's surprisingly difficult to know if someone is eager to spend time with you because they want something from you or because they genuinely like you. It was a refreshing change to be with someone who didn't recognize me," Geraldine said. "I enjoyed every minute of it,"

Iris felt her jaw start to go slack in surprise before clenching it tightly. She wouldn't have expected any such thing. It was hard for her to imagine someone with as many leisure options as Geraldine must have purposely seeking out time with her mother.

"I'm glad to hear you weren't insulted that she didn't recognize you," Iris said. "And it doesn't make your help any less appreciated that you didn't find her company too taxing."

"The pleasure really was all mine. But I do wonder how you all will fare. It must be very difficult for you to be away from her all day."

"It's never been a problem until this summer. But she's getting worse, and now my new job requires more hours, including staying here overnight instead of going home. To be honest, I'm not quite sure what we're going to do."

"Have you considered finding a facility to place her in?"

Iris paused. On the one hand, it could be seen as unprofessional to divulge details of her personal life to a guest. On the other, Mrs. Putnam was no ordinary guest. They had known each other for years, although not at all well. It would be worse to make up an untruth that would likely be revealed for what it was.

"Her doctor suggested it may come to that, but rest homes cost a great deal, and we simply don't have the funds. Miss Arden mentioned that if all goes well with me as the housekeeper this season, she's prepared to have me take over the same position in Arizona too."

Mrs. Putnam arched an eyebrow. "That sounds like a tremendous opportunity. Travel would suit you, I expect."

Iris couldn't agree more, but the chance might just slip through her fingers.

"I'd love the chance to go, but I can't if I need to keep an eye on my mother full-time. And if I can't take the Arizona position, I might lose this one too. If I don't work, I can't pay our bills," Iris said. "So far we've only managed because my mother's friend Frances has offered to stay with her overnight and pop in to check on her throughout the day, but I can't impose on her permanently."

Mrs. Putnam couldn't possibly understand where she was coming from. She probably could have afforded to buy an entire old-folks' home if she wanted to, let alone pay the fees for just one resident. Or she could hire a fleet of in-home help to watch an old lady, which of course would be better than warehousing her somewhere away from home. No, it was hard to imagine a woman like Mrs. Putnam being forced to make difficult choices like the ones that seemed to crop up in Iris's life with discouraging regularity.

"It sounds like you feel stuck between the devil and the deep blue sea."

Iris tried to keep any tone of bitterness from her voice. "Lately I do."

"You may not believe it, but I rather envy you your situation. I haven't any family of my own left to worry about."

Iris felt put in her place. There were lots of ways of being wealthy, and she had always considered herself to be rich when it came to the people she cared about. Orla wasn't easy, but she had proven again and again how much she cared for her family, and Iris wasn't about to do less than her best for her.

"I'm sorry to hear you're so on your own."

Geraldine shrugged and pointed at the canvas on the easel. "What do you think?"

Iris stepped forward to view Mrs. Putnam's work in progress. To her surprise, rather than the typical landscape Mrs. Putnam was known for, the painting depicted Orla sitting on a deck chair in the middle of Loon Island, a mere speck of land visible from the resort's private beach. Her mother's face appeared serene as she sat with a crochet hook in her gnarled hand and a brightly colored blanket growing in her lap. Two other figures flanked her: one plucking balls of yarn from a tree arching above them, the other waving a Jolly Roger at a passing boat. It was as whimsical as it was beautiful. She leaned closer to the canvas and breathed in the strong scent of linseed oil.

"It's lovely but a bit unexpected. I thought your paintings never included people."

"They haven't thus far, but my new friend Marjorie mentioned that I might consider adding figures to my work after she saw some sketches I made at the fashion show." Mrs. Putnam pointed to a half dozen sketches pinned to the wall on her right. "The sketches I made of Orla while I was with her yesterday were just the thing I needed to give her suggestion a try."

"I'm glad to hear that you were able to make good use of your time."

"Orla inspired me. I feel as though she did me more of a favor than I did for you." Mrs. Putnam dabbed a bit of blue paint from the back of her hand with a rag. "I don't mean to tell you your business, but have you had her evaluated by a doctor?"

Iris nodded. "He says she is on a downward path and there is nothing to be done about it."

The memory of Dr. Jennings sitting in Orla's own kitchen, delivering the awful news, washed over her. A lump rose in her throat, and her eyes stung as if she were chopping piles of yellow onions for a beef stew. Her mother had always sworn by plenty of onions. She gave her head a shake, as if that would clear the image of the doctor's kindly expression from her mind's eye, but it only sent a trickle of tears rolling down her cheeks. She reached for a cleaning rag from the pocket of her apron and dabbed her eyes. How could she have been so foolish as to break down in front of a guest, especially one as esteemed by Miss Arden as Mrs. Putnam? She considered it likely that Alice was leaning over the pearly gates and gasping at her lack of professionalism. The thought of her friend unleashed a fresh cascade of tears down her face.

Mrs. Putnam stepped forward and took her by the arm,

steering her towards a wooden folding chair placed near the easel. She propped her backside on one of the windowsills and looked Iris over.

"It's a wonder that the resort is running so smoothly, with all that you've had to shoulder. That said, I can't see how you will be able to keep it up if you're worried sick about your mother every moment you're away from her."

Iris drew in a deep breath and considered how to respond. She knew she ought not confide in a guest, but Mrs. Putnam gazed at her with such encouragement, leaning slightly forward and gently nodding her head.

"It has been a bit much, but I mustn't lose this job. If my mother is going to become as addled as the doctor predicts, I'll need to have put aside some money for help with her care."

Mrs. Putnam slapped her thighs with her broad palms. "Then I have just the solution—at least, for the rest of the season. I shall send Mrs. Burns to stay at Orla's and keep an eye on her."

"Mrs. Burns, your cook/housekeeper?"

"The very one. I have no need of her services while I am at the Maine Chance."

"I couldn't possibly afford to pay Mrs. Burns." Iris's heart began to thud at the very notion of coming up with such an amount.

Mrs. Putnam snorted. "That won't be necessary. I'm already paying her."

"But I would never ask you to do that."

"Of course you wouldn't, which is why I am going to do it." Mrs. Putnam smiled. "Even though the presence of my in-laws drove me from my own home, I'm paying Mrs. Burns her regular wage to make them more comfortable than they have any right to be. They never ask me for favors either; they simply appear and expect I will offer them."

"But won't they be offended?" Iris asked.

"I certainly hope so. They have offended me with their shameless presumption for years. It has only grown more egregious since my husband died." The older woman got to her feet. "With any luck, they will be so offended that they will leave."

"What about Mrs. Burns? Won't she mind being uprooted? I would hate to put her out."

"I can promise you that relocating to Orla's will come as a relief for long-suffering Mrs. Burns. My plague of in-laws is a sore trial to the poor woman. I'm lucky she hasn't left my service on account of them."

It was a novel suggestion, and one that would solve her problem. And she did like the notion of doing Mrs. Burns a good turn. Still, she couldn't help but feel it was some sort of charity on Mrs. Putnam's part. And what if Miss Arden found out that she had taken advantage of one of the guests?

"I just don't think it would be right to accept," she said.

As if she had read Iris's mind, Mrs. Putnam waggled

a paint-stained finger in her direction. "What would your employer think if she heard that you had refused to accommodate one of her guests?" she asked.

Iris felt the knot that had become a permanent fixture in her stomach over the past few weeks begin to loosen.

"Well, since you put it that way, it wouldn't do for her to hear that I have provided anything less than extraordinary service."

"That's settled, then." Mrs. Putnam picked up a rag from a nearby table and wiped her hands on it. "I'll walk over to the Arden House and telephone Mrs. Burns. I'll ask her to head to Orla's straightaway."

CHAPTER 40

Cynthia

Last week of July

CYNTHIA CARRIED HER PLATE TO the sink and stacked it with the other dirty dishes as Mrs. Dudley had indicated she should. The meal might not have resembled those she had seen being carried into the dining room for the guests, but it was delicious nonetheless. Although the dishes served were as different as could be, the produce, eggs, and milk were from the same source; the farm itself and the freshness of the ingredients made even the simplest of recipes taste divine.

Although Cynthia was definitely hungrier than usual on account of all the physical labor the job involved, she didn't think that was all there was as to why the food tasted so good. Mrs. Dudley was a whiz at cooking, especially desserts, and she had outdone herself that day with a blueberry cobbler. Cynthia had spotted a pair of gardeners plucking the ripe, dusky berries from rows of tall bushes at the edges of the enormous vegetable garden early that morning. A metal pail, still half-filled with berries, sat on the end of the table, waiting to be turned into something delicious. As Cynthia turned back towards the center of the room to thank Mrs. Dudley for the meal, Iris appeared in the doorway.

"At your interview, you mentioned that you know how to drive, didn't you?" Iris asked.

Whatever she had expected her boss to say, that was not it.

She nodded. "I got my license when I was still in high school."

Iris thrust out a set of keys. "Since Calvin is otherwise engaged, I need you to head into town to collect an order from the pharmacy for one of the guests. We have an account there, so you can ask them to send me the bill."

"Is there anything else you need while I am in town?"

"The guests' chef told me this morning he could use a couple of boxes of rennet tablets to make junket for tomorrow," Mrs. Dudley said.

Junket, a wobbly mass of milk, was not one of Cynthia's favorite foods. She couldn't imagine how it rated as dessert, but she knew that it was something her mother had served with pride on more than one occasion to members of her bridge club when they held their meeting at the Proctors' home. No, the guests could keep their so-called fancy meals. She was content with Mrs. Dudley's home cooking.

"You should be able to pick up the rennet tablets at the pharmacy right along with the rest of the order. Please don't dawdle, but there's no need to take any risks behind the wheel. Miss Arden is very particular about her automobiles, and it would not do for it to be damaged through recklessness. Do I make myself clear?" Iris asked.

"Absolutely. Where will I find the car?"

"It's out in the stable with the rest of the vehicles." With that, Iris hurried off to attend to the long roster of duties Cynthia was sure she must keep running in her head at all times. Cynthia had always known her mother to keep a similar list of tasks in order to be considered a successful and house-proud woman. How much more onerous would such a list be for a place the size of the resort?

She waved goodbye to Mrs. Dudley after thanking her for the meal and slipped out the back door of the kitchen and off to the garage. As she entered one of the wide doors leading into the building, she noticed a set of stairs at the back. She fought down an urge to slip up the stairs to suss out any additional information about Calvin. She held up the ring of keys Iris had given her and noticed a paper tag serving as a label. *Buick Skylark*, it said in block printing. She squinted into the gloom of the stables, with their small windows and the faint smell of horses still rising up from the floorboards.

The convertible sat in the farthest bay of the building, its top firmly latched into the open position. She had not expected to enjoy the drive, but the idea of tooling along the road skirting the lake, with the wind in her hair and the sun beating down on her shoulders, promised to be an unexpected pleasure. She paused to admire the pale-blue car, with its elegant fins and sleek, prowling look, before sliding behind the wheel and turning the key.

She was a good driver, and a confident one, and in only a moment, she was down the driveway and out onto the open road. She arrived in town far more quickly than she would have preferred, considering how much she had enjoyed feeling the powerful thrum of the engine as she pressed on the gas. She eased the nose of the car into a spot along Main Street, directly in front of the pharmacy.

She glanced through the store's plate-glass window and spotted the gleaming taps and long counter of a soda fountain. Several young men, whom she recognized as part of the group Pauline ran around with, sat on a row of stools at the counter, toying with straws tucked into tall glasses filled with a mixture of soda water, syrups, and ice cream. Glenn, sitting at the center of the group, spun his stool slightly towards the door as she entered, but she ducked behind a display of glossy magazines and hoped he had not spotted her. She felt reluctant for him to see her in her work uniform. She wasn't embarrassed by her job, but she wasn't eager to discuss it with him either.

She made her way along the row of stools and headed for the back wall, where a man in a white jacket stood grinding something in a mortar and pestle. He looked up as she approached and nodded in greeting. In a low voice, pitched with the expertise of someone who was used to discussing confidential matters with a steady stream of customers, he addressed her.

"Are you the young woman from the Maine Chance?" he asked.

"That's right. Miss Hubbard sent me to collect an order for one of our guests," she said. He nodded and reached out for a white paper bag. It was stapled shut, and Cynthia had the sudden urge to peek inside it.

"Will that be all?" he asked as he slid the sack towards her across the polished wooden counter.

"Do you carry rennet tablets as well?" she asked.

"Aisle three, about halfway down. I'll put them on the resort's account," he said.

She thanked him and made her way along the far side of the store, keeping her distance from the young people assembled at the soda fountain. There was no way she wanted to spend any of her hard-earned money on a beverage. Nor did she want to be obligated to anyone else for having treated her. Besides, Iris would expect her to return to work without delay.

But try as she might to be invisible, as she bent over a low shelf looking for the rennet tablets, a hand brushed across her neck before resting heavily on her shoulder. She straightened and turned.

"Fancy meeting you here," Glenn said. He was taller than her by several inches, and she felt as though he were standing ever-so-slightly too close. His hand had lingered on her shoulder even after she straightened up as well. Still, he had been very nice to her from the moment she met him, and she could see no reason not to be friendly in return.

"I guess this explains why I haven't seen you around lately. Pauline has been pretty cagey every time I asked about you." He nodded towards her uniform.

Cynthia wasn't quite sure how to answer. It wasn't the sort of thing Glenn would be likely to understand, considering he didn't need to earn money himself. In the short time she had known him, she had heard him mention several times that neither his father nor his grandfather had needed to work either. They simply spent their time managing the family's investments and serving on the board of directors for a variety of companies. Telling someone like him that she had to work to earn tuition money for college would sound as though she were speaking a foreign language. Still, she had told Pauline she could tell him whatever she thought best. It was probably more surprising it had taken her friend so long.

"There was a last-minute opening at the Maine Chance, and I was lucky enough to be hired," Cynthia said. "That looks like a bit of a sunburn," she said, pointing at the bridge of Glenn's nose.

"I've been out on the lake every day, enjoying the sights. Although the beach hasn't been anywhere near as beautiful without you and your bathing suit perched on it."

Cynthia's face flamed. The memory of her discomfort at

sitting on a beach blanket while strangers roamed past and looked her up and down left her vaguely queasy. Everything about Glenn left her unsettled. From his forthright manner to his suggestive comments, she felt both flattered and wary.

"I'm sure that you've found plenty to keep yourself occupied in my absence," she said, not sure if she would be sorrier for him to admit that he had or happier if he protested.

"I can see that you've made far more of an impression on me than I have on you. I insist that you give me the opportunity to correct that," Glenn said. "Say you'll come to the party I'm throwing tomorrow night. You're not too busy for that, are you?"

With his big blue eyes and cajoling tone, he reminded her of a professor's son for whom she had babysat during the school year. She had never found it easy to resist him.

"Where's it being held?" she asked.

"At my family's place," Glenn said.

"Will Pauline be there?" she asked.

"She's agreed to come, so I can't imagine why she wouldn't be there. The whole gang is invited. It wouldn't be the same without you," he said. "Pauline was saying just yesterday how much she's missed you. You can even bring that guy you were with the last time I saw you, if you like."

"What time?"

"Any time after six. Be sure to bring your bathing suit." He winked at her, and Cynthia felt her cheeks grow even hotter.

It had been too long since she had seen Pauline. And she

missed her friend too. Dolores was good company and had gone out of her way to make Cynthia feel welcome, but it wasn't the same sort of friendship. She and Pauline had shared so many experiences, hopes, and secrets during their time as roommates and friends. It had been strange to see so little of her over the past two months.

"I'll be sure to be there," Cynthia said.

CHAPTER 41

Geraldine

Last week of July

ONE OF THE MOST TOUTED offerings at the Maine Chance Farm was the Ardena Wax Bath. While Geraldine could hardly credit all the claims made about the procedure, she did note that there was something undeniably pleasant about the notion of settling into a tub filled with eight pounds of melted wax.

A cheerful young woman with a dazzling smile and expertly applied makeup greeted her as she entered the treatment room. Geraldine was led to a private changing area, where she slipped into a bathing suit. After a technician helped her pin up her hair and cover it in a cap meant for keeping it clean no matter what was being done to the rest of her, she carefully lowered herself into one of the baths. The tub was lined with waxed paper, and managing to lie down without disarranging all of it was a bit of a trick, especially since both of her knees were playing up.

As soon as she had gotten herself settled, one of the

technicians slowly poured warm liquid paraffin over her body, from her neck all the way down to her toes. Once she was entirely encased, the technician stepped away, leaving her to her thoughts. Little by little, she could feel the wax hardening and a flush of perspiration beginning to spring from her skin. Even her knees had ceased to ache. Her face felt warm, and a sense of relaxation overtook her.

She closed her eyes and soon found herself nodding off, the gentle murmur of the staff and guests lulling her to sleep. As the brochures claimed, the heat from the treatment was designed "*to reach down into the very roots of her nerves to free her from tenseness and fatigue.*" And free her, it did. She barely registered a presence in the neighboring tub until she heard a voice addressing her directly.

Reluctantly, she pried open her eyes and turned to face the new arrival. Marjorie beamed at her, her mop of unruly curls creeping out from under the edges of her cap. She looked anything but relaxed. It could not be said that bathing caps were flattering for most women, but Marjorie seemed even less attractive in hers than most. Still, few women could boast such a genuinely beautiful smile. As much as Geraldine was not delighted to be awakened, she could not find it in her heart to be irritated with her friend.

"I thought that must be you. There's no one else here quite so regal looking, even in such an outrageous getup as this is," Marjorie said, squirming slightly.

"How kind of you to say. What do you think of the Ardena Bath?" Geraldine asked. Perhaps she could do with the distraction of idle conversation. Worrying over her work for hours on end was getting her nowhere. Besides, she was interested in Marjorie's thoughts on the resort.

"It's all very sticky, isn't it?" Marjorie said, wriggling about a bit. "Do you think it does any good?"

"I'm not sure if it does or if it doesn't, but I have decided that I enjoy it."

"They say it's supposed to help you shed weight. If it weren't for that, I don't think I could force myself to put up with it." Marjorie blew at a stray curl.

"I think it will be more effective if you try to remain still. If you crack the wax, it won't work anywhere near as well," Geraldine said. For an aching instant, Marjorie reminded her of Anselm, someone else who tended to fidget.

"I'm trying my best, but I have a terrible itch on my nose," Marjorie said.

Geraldine stifled a giggle. Her companion's face was flushed to a rosy hue. Before long, Marjorie's curls were damp with perspiration and had stuck unbecomingly to her forehead. "You just need to focus on something else. How might I distract you?" Geraldine asked.

"You could tell me how your work is coming along."

A flicker of concern ran through Geraldine's mind. She rarely discussed her work before it was ready to be exhibited.

Anselm had been her only early confidant over the many long years of their marriage. Had the absence of his encouragement at the first tentative steps of any project been one of the reasons for her inability to work?

She closed her eyes and considered refusing to comment, but there was something so beguiling about Marjorie's smile that she couldn't bring herself to swat away her question. Before she had to answer, Marjorie spoke again, but this time in a hushed tone.

"Look who's here." She nodded vigorously towards a woman approaching their tubs. A bead of sweat rolled down her nose and landed on the hardened wax encasing her ample bosom.

Geraldine followed her gaze and noticed a strikingly beautiful woman. She suspected she had met her before, but she could not quite place her.

"Who is she? I feel that I know her from somewhere."

Marjorie's eyes widened in her round face, and her eyebrows, drenched in perspiration, shot upward.

"Of course you do. That's Vivian Shaw," Marjorie said.

"That's who she is. We both attended a dinner party hosted by Miss Arden a few years ago."

"I just love her films," Marjorie said. "I've seen her a few times here in the treatment rooms or at dinnertime, but I haven't gotten up the nerve to speak with her myself. Imagine her coming all the way out here from Hollywood when she could have gone to the Maine Chance in Arizona instead."

If memory served, Vivian had over-imbibed and become merrier than was considered polite at one of Miss Arden's dinner parties. She had caused something of a scene, even going so far as to flirt outrageously with Anselm. He had been mortified, but Geraldine found it entirely amusing. Perhaps Vivian was there to dry out.

"I would be happy to introduce you to her if you'd like," Geraldine said.

"Would you really?"

"Certainly. It would be a pleasure," Geraldine said. "I'm sure that Vivian would be delighted to make your acquaintance."

"It looks like she is heading this way," Marjorie said, shifting in her tub.

A large crack appeared across Marjorie's plump shoulders as she turned. From behind her, Geraldine could hear the tapping of high-heeled shoes.

"Mrs. Putnam, I thought that was you." Vivian leaned over her tub and flashed one of her justifiably famous smiles. "How is your charming husband?"

"He passed away some time ago, I'm sorry to say," Geraldine said.

"My condolences," Vivian said, frowning.

"Thank you. Allow me to introduce my friend Marjorie

Billings." Geraldine gestured with her nose towards the neighboring tub, where Marjorie seemed to be holding her breath.

"Hello, Marjorie. Are you enjoying yourself?" she asked, sweeping a slim hand above the wax-filled tub.

"It's rather sticky and hot, but it is supposed to do a world of good."

"I think I'll pass. My idea of a good time is decidedly different. Which reminds me why I headed over here." She lowered her voice slightly and turned back towards Geraldine. "I've convinced one of the chauffeurs to drive me to a nightclub in Augusta for a bit of dancing. Would you care to come along?"

Geraldine heard a quiet squeak emanate from Marjorie. She turned slightly to check her expression. It was one of longing, perhaps stemming from her memories of that long-ago dance where she'd met her future husband. Geraldine did not particularly care for nightclubs herself and had not expected to have to attend any at her age. Nightclubs had not crossed her mind since Prohibition. That said, she was ever-so-slightly flattered that Vivian would invite her, considering she was old enough to be the starlet's mother. Not to mention, if there was one thing Marjorie could use, it was a bit of fun.

"We'd love to," Geraldine said.

Vivian appeared taken aback and looked from Geraldine to Marjorie, then back again, one eyebrow cocked in question.

Geraldine ignored it and plowed on ahead. "Marjorie and I will be ready whenever you say."

After a pause, Vivian shrugged her elegant shoulders. It wouldn't hurt her to include another.

"Once I settle with the chauffeur about exactly when, I'll let you both know. Enjoy your tubs," she said with a smile before walking away.

"Are we really allowed to go to nightclubs while we are here?" Marjorie asked.

"We aren't prisoners," Geraldine said. "Besides, I would guess that you're dying to go out dancing." Even though her friend was a mother three times over, Geraldine did not think she could be over thirty. It only made sense that she would be eager to partake in an activity that was livelier than a few rubbers of bridge, or a sedate trail ride through the grounds on one of the estate's many fine horses.

Marjorie giggled and then turned to her with a worried expression. "I have no idea what to wear."

Geraldine thought it likely that Marjorie had absolutely nothing in her wardrobe that would flatter her and be appropriate for such an occasion. Fortunately, not only was the resort stocked with every imaginable lotion and oil for beautification, but it also offered an impressive array of garments for purchase. With a little bit of coaching, Geraldine was quite certain Marjorie could vastly improve her appearance and feel much more confident in one fell swoop.

"You just leave that to me," Geraldine said.

CHAPTER 42

Cynthia

THE INVITATION FROM GLENN WAS still on her mind as she bent over the taps in Geraldine's tub, a buffing cloth clutched in her fist. Without warning, a shadow fell across the gleaming white floor tiles. Out of the corner of her eye, she caught sight of Iris's sensible brown Oxford shoes and sturdy ankles encased in thick stockings. Cynthia jumped to her feet.

"Do you need me for something?" she asked.

"You have a visitor waiting for you in the staff house sitting room," Iris said. "I expect you back to work in fifteen minutes."

"A visitor? For me?" Cynthia's stomach clenched. She was not expecting anyone. "Do you know who it is?"

"She claims to be your mother. She seemed none too pleased when she asked for your whereabouts."

With that, Iris turned on her heel and strode out of the room, swiping her finger along the top of a table near the bathroom door as she passed to check for dust.

The staff house seemed both dreadfully far away and much too close as Cynthia made her way between the second floor of the Arden House and the sitting room, where her mother lay in wait. Even the sounds of the birds singing sweetly in the trees could not bolster her mood as she considered what she would say. All she could imagine was that Mrs. Mayhew must have informed her of her whereabouts. How else would her mother know where to find her? When Mrs. Putnam had been so dismissive of Mrs. Mayhew, Cynthia had suspected something would go awry. Pauline's mother was not a woman to take being put in her place lightly. She seemed to think she was the sort of woman whose place was wherever she decided it would be.

She pulled open the screen door of the staff house, holding her breath and hoping it would not squeak on its hinges. Once again, Miss Arden's extreme attention to detail was something to be grateful for. The door swung silently, and Cynthia entered on tiptoe. Moving quictly along thc short hallway, she was able to catch a glimpse of her mother seated at the very edge of an overstuffed wingback chair. Her legs were crossed neatly at the ankles, and she clutched her small handbag tightly in her gloved hands. Cynthia could see that her mother was wearing her best hat and that her shoes had been freshly shined.

She took a breath and crossed the threshold into the room. Her mother shot to her feet and took a step towards her. She scrutinized her daughter's appearance, her eyes lingering on the feather duster tucked into Cynthia's uniform apron. Cynthia was appalled to see that tears shone in her mother's eyes, threatening to spill over. They were not a family given to displays of emotion, neither positive nor negative, and seeing her mother struggling not to cry caused a tight knot to gather in Cynthia's stomach.

"I came here because I heard from Mrs. Mayhew the unbelievable and disturbing story that you have been spending the summer functioning as an artist model. I worried being involved with an artsy set would give you bohemian notions. It would kill your father if you turned into some sort of a beatnik." Her mother paused to take a breath. "But now I see things are far, far worse. Do you have any idea how humiliating it is to hear from a stranger what your own daughter is up to? And now to find that you lied to me again and again simply compounds that embarrassment."

Cynthia fought back the urge to let out a deep sigh. She doubted very much that anything would kill her father. As far as she'd been able to ascertain, the man was entirely bulletproof. And she doubted very much he had even heard the term *beatnik*. If he did, he probably would assume it was some sort of root-vegetable soup favored by the Communists.

"I never meant to upset you, Mother," Cynthia said, taking a step towards her. Her mother held up a gloved hand like a crossing guard, stopping Cynthia in her tracks.

"Meant to or not, you've done a great deal more than upset

me. You've disgraced me. But what upsets me most is that you have lied to me about where you've been all this time."

"I didn't mean for this to hurt you. I never meant for you to find out."

"Is that supposed to make it better?"

"I suppose I thought that what you didn't know wouldn't cause you pain," Cynthia said.

"But whatever possessed you to hire yourself out as a common servant? Did you go off to that hoity-toity college so that you could end up working as a maid?" she asked, her voice becoming tighter with each syllable that passed between her lips.

"No, of course not. But that college is why I'm here. The college didn't renew my scholarship."

"That's just as well. We expected you to be married by this summer, not planning on returning for a third year of an education no woman needs," her mother said. Gone were the shimmer of tears, replaced by two bright spots of high color on her cheeks.

Cynthia felt anger bubbling up in her chest. Why was it that her own mother felt that she, along with every other woman, did not need an education?

"I'm sorry you feel I've failed. I was trying to get things back on track. I don't want to have to leave school, and I thought if I earned the tuition money myself, I'd be able to return in the fall," she said.

"The only place you're returning is home with me today,"

her mother said. "I suggest you toddle off to wherever you stowed your possessions and gather them up. You are returning with me by the afternoon train, or you need not return at all. But you had best hurry. I need to be back before your father gets home. He'll expect his dinner on the table by five thirty come hell or high water. And you are not to mention a word of this escapade to him, mind you. I can't begin to think what he would say if he knew what you'd been up to."

The knot in Cynthia's stomach grew tighter. Not only did she have no desire to return home and give up her dream of earning the money for the fall tuition, but she also couldn't imagine leaving Iris in the lurch or Mrs. Putnam without her muse. She had made commitments, and she had no intention of dishonoring them. And besides, there was Calvin to consider. She had to convince her mother to allow her to stay. She reached out and took her mother's hands in her own.

"Do you remember the job you had while Father was in the service?" she asked.

The tension in her mother's face softened ever so slightly "Of course I do. What does that have to do with anything?"

"It has everything to do with my desire to get my degree." She squeezed her mother's hands. "I remember that job, too, and how energized you were every day when you headed off to work. I can recall you mentioning funny stories about your coworkers, things you had accomplished that day, and even the pride you took in bringing home a pay packet."

"I suppose you were old enough to remember all that."

"I was also old enough to remember how sad you were when Father made you give it up when he got home."

Her mother shrugged. "It wasn't just because of him. The factory let most of the women go once the men returned. They needed the jobs, and we didn't."

"Which women did they keep on?"

"The bookkeepers and secretaries."

"So, the ones with specialized education?"

"Yes, that's right." Her mother let out a small sigh.

"That's why I want to complete my education. I don't want to give anyone a reason to easily dismiss me from anything, let alone a position that brings me as much joy as yours did before it was snatched away."

"Are you saying that you don't want to be a wife and mother like me?"

"I'm not saying that at all. You've always been a wonderful mother. You just weren't any less good at it when you had a job you enjoyed. Having watched you over the years, I know that, for me, the probability of happiness depends on having a career I love as well as a family if I wish."

Her mother tugged her hands away and crossed her arms over her chest and looked her in the face. Cynthia willed herself not to flinch under her scrutiny.

"You're absolutely determined to do this, aren't you?"

"I am."

Her mother pulled her tightly to her chest.

"So, may I stay?" Cynthia asked.

She kissed her cheek before releasing her. "For now. But not a word of this to your father or anyone else back home. Do you understand?"

"Absolutely, I do. And thank you, Mother. I won't let you down."

CHAPTER 43

Cynthia

WAS IT ONLY YESTERDAY WHEN had she agreed to go to Glenn's party? She never liked parties, not even ones held on the college campus with people she knew. What had possessed her to agree to attend one with strangers? It wasn't as though she had turned into a completely new person just by heading to Mount Vernon for the summer and actually managing to get a job.

She had to admit, the work at the resort had been harder than she would have anticipated when she'd applied for the job. She looked down at the palms of her hands, which certainly did not look as though she were the sort of young lady who would attend parties with the social elite of the summer community. Her knuckles appeared red and raw as she turned her palms towards the floor and evaluated the backs of her hands. Not to mention the state of her fingernails.

As a student, she had occasionally felt a bit embarrassed

by the number of ink stains coloring her fingertips, but she had never seen her hands look quite as rough and unattractive as they appeared at that particular moment. She even smelled faintly of Lysol and lemon furniture polish.

A sudden surge of shyness welled up within her, and she wished she had a friend there beside her who would know just what to do when it came to attending a party. She wished she knew someone who would have all sorts of ideas on how she ought to dress her hair, how to do her makeup, and how to make flirtatious small talk with strangers.

Cynthia had never been an easygoing or flirtatious life of the party. She wished more than anything that she could back out of attending, but that seemed rude beyond bearing. If she happened to come across Glenn on a day off, as she knew that she might, she would not be able to look him in the eye. It would be far easier to simply show up for an hour and then slip out with some sort of excuse.

As she stood staring at the contents of her wardrobe, the door creaked open behind her. When she looked over her shoulder, Dolores stood smiling at her.

"What are you doing in here? Shouldn't you be off tending to your artist?" she asked.

"We finished early so I could get ready for a party." She flipped through the paltry number of garments.

Dolores's eyebrows arched upward. "What kind of party? I haven't heard about a staff party."

Cynthia shook her head. "No, it's not a staff party. I got invited to one by a boy whose family owns a house on the lake."

"Are you sure that's a good idea? Staff at the resort don't mix with the summer people. It's just one of those things," she said. She shrugged her slim shoulders and stared at a spot on the floor near Cynthia's feet. Then she raised her gaze. Cynthia thought she saw a flicker of resignation and embarrassment in Dolores's eyes.

From what little she had said about her life away from the Maine Chance, Cynthia guessed that her family was about as economically removed from Glenn's as she herself was from Miss Arden. Because of their easy camaraderie, she had given no credence to the notion that Dolores was not in the same social position as Pauline. She wished her new friend wouldn't give that sort of thing a thought either.

In her opinion, Dolores was worth any number of people like Glenn. The fact that her father worked in a nearby sawmill and her mother picked berries to sell to the tourists made no difference to Cynthia. She knew that Dolores handed over most of her pay packet to her parents to help make ends meet, and that only raised her opinion of her further. On payday, she felt a twinge of guilt that her biggest concern about her money was whether or not she would earn her tuition. Dolores had confessed one night, after the staff house had grown still and it was just the two of them alone in their room, that her wages made it possible to keep her family in their home.

"Is that some sort of rule that Iris has?" Cynthia asked. She couldn't remember Iris saying anything about not fraternizing with people in town. She had been very clear about keeping the line between staff and guests at the Maine Chance blurred, but she had not said any such protocol extended to the community outside of the resort. She certainly didn't want to lose her job over accepting an invitation she didn't want in the first place.

"No, it's not a rule, exactly—at least, not one like wear your uniform and don't use the front staircase. It's more of a cultural rule. Locals don't tend to like to mix with the summer folk."

Dolores crossed the room and perched on the windowsill. She stuck her hand into the pocket of her work apron and pulled out a fresh packet of cigarettes. Once again, she slid open the screen and leaned slightly out of the room.

"Why don't locals like to mix with the summer people?" Cynthia asked.

"Where do I start? We don't have a whole lot in common with them, and no one particularly likes it when people look down on them," Dolores said. "The guests here at the resort aren't the only ones who think they're better than the year-round residents."

Cynthia had not grown up in a resort community. However, she could see how there might be some tension between the people who earned the better part of their year's salary from the tourist industry and those who spent more than they earned on motorboats and meals out at local restaurants over the course of only a few weeks' time every year. Yes, she could see how perhaps they would not have a great deal in common.

"What about someone like me, who isn't a local?" she asked.

Dolores took a drag on her cigarette, then waved the smoke out the window. "Well, I'm not sure about someone like you. You don't fit in all that well with the locals, but since you needed a job, you may not quite meet the summer-people standards either. Does the person who invited you know that you're working here as a maid?" she asked.

"He does."

Dolores arched her eyebrow up once more. "Did you come right out and tell the guy that asked you?"

Guilt sat in Cynthia's stomach like a lead sinker. She didn't want Dolores to think she was ashamed of her job. If anything, she was desperately proud of herself. But she wasn't sure the other girl would believe her.

"No, I didn't mention it, but a mutual acquaintance went ahead and told him. He let me know that he knew when I saw him at the pharmacy when I was picking up a prescription for one of the guests."

"Were you planning to tell him yourself, if someone hadn't beaten you to it?" Dolores asked.

"I suppose I would not have made any great effort to bring it up."

Dolores crossed her slim arms over her chest, keeping the cigarette tipped carefully towards the open window. "So, you are aware that there is a difference between those who serve and those who are served."

As much as Cynthia didn't wish to seem like a snob, Dolores did have a good point. She was not likely to be able to hide her background even if she wanted to. Dolores had an accent that marked her as someone from Mount Vernon, and she certainly had a wardrobe to match. Cynthia enjoyed her company and the time she had spent with her after hours talking and laughing about shared experiences on the job, but she could not quite imagine her discussing homecoming dances or volatility in the stock market and how that impacted trust funds. No, Dolores would laugh in their faces about such silly things and point out that she preferred men who knew how to field dress a deer or split a cord of wood with a dull axe.

"I suppose there are some differences," Cynthia said. "I would rather stay here with you, but I already agreed."

"If you didn't want to go, why did you say yes when he asked you?"

"I guess I was just so surprised I didn't have a good excuse ready. Besides, I didn't want to hurt his feelings."

"You be careful how you go, then. It never does to be too nice." Dolores crossed the room, retrieved her mason jar lid from her dresser drawer, and stubbed out her cigarette.

She turned back towards Cynthia with a sparkle in her eyes. "You should ask Calvin to go with you. I'm sure he wouldn't mind."

Cynthia's heart quickened like it did every time his name was mentioned. If she were being honest, Calvin was the real reason she wasn't interested in attending a party thrown by Glenn—or any other boy, for that matter.

"I already asked him, but he's driving Mrs. Putnam and a couple of other guests to a nightclub in Augusta this evening."

"That's all right. It won't hurt for Calvin to know that you have options. So, what are you going to wear?"

"I have a sundress that I thought might work. And I have a matching sweater in case the temperature dips, as it is so inclined to do in the evening, especially with the wind coming off the lake."

"What about makeup?"

"I have a powder compact and a lipstick, but I'm not sure either is right for a party. They seem more like daywear."

Dolores pulled open the top drawer and pulled out several boxes, pots, and bottles all bearing the Elizabeth Arden logo. "It's a good thing I have all of this, then, isn't it?"

Cynthia's eyes widened. There was a fortune in products spread across the top of the dresser. How could a girl working as a maid possibly afford all that? Knowing what had happened to Velda, she couldn't imagine Dolores helping herself to anything from the guests' rooms. Maybe the staff was given some sort of deep discount she hadn't heard about. Even if the makeup hadn't cost as much as the guests were charged, it couldn't have been cheap.

"You're too generous. I couldn't use your expensive things," she said.

Dolores waved her hand. "At the end of every season, the staff is allowed to take whatever is left by the guests. Otherwise, it would all be thrown away."

"Are you sure you don't mind?"

"Of course I don't. I'll even help you to put it on properly."

"You don't need to do that," Cynthia said. A shiver of trepidation ran through her. She really wasn't much for wearing a lot of makeup. On the rare occasion she had gone to a dance or a special event on campus, Pauline had always helped her with her face. Besides, Dolores would likely have a better idea of what to do with all the products than she would. "But if you really want to, I'd be very grateful."

"I'd love to. What I wouldn't give to work in the spa side of the resort instead of as a maid," she said as she twisted the lid off a jar of Feather-light Foundation and began dabbing it over Cynthia's face. The cream was cool on her skin and not as unpleasant as she had anticipated.

"Why can't you?" Cynthia asked.

Dolores lowered her hand. "The girls who work in the spa are brought in from Red Door salons or from Miss Arden's other resort out in Arizona. She doesn't hire local girls for skilled work like facials and wax treatments."

Even though makeup was not Cynthia's strong suit, even she was aware of the prestige associated with the Red Door salons. Found in cities like Paris, Milan, Melbourne, London, Hong Kong, and even Honolulu, the salons were synonymous with luxury and sophistication. In large part because of the fame of the Red Door salons, it was said that Miss Arden's was one of the three most well-known American brands around the world, along with Singer sewing machines and Coca-Cola.

After the weeks she had spent learning the ropes and still feeling a bit behind all the other staff, Cynthia had learned maid work was anything but unskilled. It didn't sound like Dolores would agree, though.

"The women who work in the spa may not be from here, but they are local somewhere."

Delores shrugged. "So?"

"It seems to me there is nothing inherently good or bad about being a local. The spa employees have specialized skills, but not because they are from somewhere else. They must have gone to school for it or worked as an apprentice at a beauty salon."

Dolores expertly smoothed another cool blob of foundation across her cheeks and across her nose. "The nearest beauty school is in Augusta. That's at least half an hour from home."

"That's not that far—at least, not for something you would love to do. My college is over three hours from my parents' house."

"That's easy enough for a girl like you." Dolores returned the pot of foundation to the dresser and selected a palette filled with pale-colored eyeshadows. "Close your eyes."

Cynthia exhaled slowly, attempting not to wriggle as Dolores swiped layer after layer of color over her eyelids. “We aren’t really all that different,” she said. “I love economics. You love cosmetics. Working in either requires education.”

“It can’t be as simple as that. I wouldn’t know where to start.”

Dolores reached under her chin, and tilting her head upwards with her free hand, she swiped mascara across Cynthia’s eyelashes. The wand felt damp and feathery. She remembered how overwhelmed she had felt when she had first toyed with the idea of going to college. If it hadn’t been for the influence of an older girl down the street who had graduated from Wellesley, she might have given up on the idea even before she had started. Sometimes all it took was an example and a bit of encouragement.

“Why don’t you knock on the door of one of the spa worker’s rooms and ask how they got their job? If anyone would know where to start, it would be one of them.”

“They wouldn’t want to talk to someone like me. Anyhow, I don’t know anywhere near as much as they all do about Miss Arden’s exclusive treatments.”

“Like which ones?” Cynthia thought it likely Dolores knew a lot more than she gave herself credit for.

Dolores selected a tube of lipstick from atop her vanity table and removed the lid. She swiveled it upward and held the color close to Cynthia’s face. She returned it to the table and chose another, repeating the sequence. This one she seemed to think the best and commanded Cynthia to open her mouth slightly.

"Well, there's the Firmo-Lift Treatment for tightening facial slackness, the Velva Cream Masque for dryness, the Muscle Strapping Treatment to reduce jowls, and of course, the Anti-Brown Treatment to remove fading tan lines. That's just a tiny bit of what they all know."

"It sounds like you are already more than familiar with many of the techniques the spa employees use. How did you learn so much?"

Dolores lowered her voice. "Promise you won't tell?"

"Of course I won't."

Dolores glanced at the door as if to assure herself there was no one in the hallway eavesdropping. She crossed the room to her dresser and opened the top drawer. She pulled out a thick well-thumbed booklet from beneath a pile of stockings and girdles and handed it to Cynthia. "I found this at the reception desk last summer. One of the spa girls must have left it. I've been studying it ever since."

Cynthia read aloud: "*How I Sell My Preparations* by Elizabeth Arden." She leafed through it quickly. Page after page listed recommendations for different treatments based on the complaints or symptoms expressed by potential clients. From the way Dolores had reeled off some of them, Cynthia could tell she had made herself quite an expert. "If you've been reading this, it seems to me you could hold your own in a conversation with the girls who work at the spa."

"Even if I do know what I am talking about, they might snub me for being just a maid."

"If getting the cold shoulder could actually hurt someone, I'd be dead by now," Cynthia said. "Most of my classmates—and even my professors—don't think a woman has any business studying economics. Even the ones who pretend otherwise show their true feelings eventually. At least beauty school is a place where women are welcome."

A crinkle appeared between Dolores's eyebrows. "Then why are you working so hard to earn your tuition if no one wants you there?"

"Because *I* want me there, and my opinion matters more to me than theirs."

Dolores lifted a pad from a compact of Invisible Veil pressed powder and began patting it carefully over Cynthia's face.

"There, have a look in the mirror," she said as she passed the compact with its mirror to Cynthia to view her work. "What's your opinion on that?"

Cynthia couldn't quite believe her eyes. While she certainly appeared more sophisticated than her day-to-day self, she was in no way overly made up. She doubted even her father would complain at her appearance. Somehow Dolores had managed to bring out the green flecks in her eyes, and her lips looked dewy like a summer-morning rose rather than the scarlet-red siren look that Dolores wore. It was remarkable and yet not overdone. She couldn't imagine how her friend had pulled it off.

"I'd say that if you are this good already, any salon would be clamoring to have you once you've completed beauty school."

Two bright spots of color appeared on Dolores's cheeks that had nothing to do with Miss Arden's Pink Perfection Rouge.

"Do you really think so?"

"I do. As soon as I change my clothes, why don't I go with you to find one of those spa girls, and we can show off your handiwork? That should break the ice."

CHAPTER 44

Cynthia

CYNTHIA WALKED DOWN THE ROAD in the direction of town, thinking of all the people she might meet at the party. She expected they would be like some of the wealthier students she had met at college. Her nerves increased as she recalled how often she had felt out of place whenever Pauline convinced her to attend an event at Barlow. Still, her friend would be there to ease her way, just as she had been on other occasions. She increased her speed, eager to spend the evening with Pauline.

She reached the gap in the stone wall that ran along the road, the one that connected to a path through the pines that provided a shorter route to the part of the lake where the party was to be held. The sun had already sunk below the tops of the trees, and the evening was fading into night. Her heart clutched in her chest a bit as she debated whether or not to take the shortcut through the woods.

The light had faded enough that it was not all that easy to

see where she was going. But the skies were clear, and the moon was almost full. It would surely provide enough light to see by for long enough to make the journey. Besides, the path through the woods would make it appear as though she could have been arriving from any number of lakeside homes and would further support the illusion that she had not walked from somewhere away from the shoreline. Not everyone at the party needed to know about her summer job.

She had recognized which house the party was being held at when Glenn had described it to her at the pharmacy. It was one she had seen many times over while riding in the Mayhew speedboat or paddling a canoe with the children at a more leisurely pace. When she popped out from the woods and onto the hard-packed dirt road that led towards one of the coves that hugged the shoreline of the lake, she recognized where she was at once. A car passed her, crawling along in order to save the passengers a good jangling from the uneven surface.

She glanced down and wished she had thought to wear a different pair of shoes as her ankle buckled beneath her. The road was riddled with tree roots and craters, and she needed to keep her attention fixed upon it if she wanted to avoid injury. She was so focused on the roadway in front of her that she almost passed the house where the party was being held. It was only the sound of her name being called out from somewhere nearby that caused her to look up.

Glenn stood on the wide front porch of the three-story house, waving at her. She turned into the driveway, feeling suddenly overwhelmed by shyness. Almost as though he sensed her discomfort, he pushed open the screen door to the porch and hurried down the steps. He held a bottle of beer in one hand and, as he came to a stop beside her, reached for her arm with his other.

"I was worried you were going to change your mind and not show up," he said.

Cynthia was not sure how to respond. He seemed so pleased to see her that she felt a little guilty.

"I don't generally change my mind after I make a commitment," Cynthia said.

"I'm glad to hear it. Come on in and I'll introduce you to everyone, although I think you may have met some of them before," he said, squiring her up the stairs and onto the porch.

Standing around with beers of their own were the two other young men she recognized from the pharmacy, as well as several girls she did not recognize at all. She was relieved to notice that she seemed to be appropriately dressed, given what the other girls were wearing. Each one of them wore some version of a summer frock in a color that would not look amiss as a shade of ice cream. None of them wore gloves, but they all had artfully arranged hairdos and jewelry to finish off their outfits. Cynthia was grateful for Dolores's attention to her appearance.

"Has Pauline arrived yet?"

"No, but I'm sure she'll be here soon. Come on." He grabbed her by the hand and pulled her into the house.

As they made the rounds, he introduced her to each of the many other guests in turn. She offered them all a bright smile that she did not quite feel. Cynthia expected to be presented to the homeowners, but despite making their way through the first floor of the house and out the back door and down onto the lawn leading to the lake, she had seen no one who appeared old enough to own any property, let alone something as expensive as that particular home.

"So, is this your house?" Cynthia asked as Glenn walked her towards a large table set up as a makeshift bar. He popped the lid open on a metal cooler much like the one the Mayhews owned and fished out two bottles of beer. Condensation streamed down the sides of them as he pried off the caps with an opener before handing one to Cynthia.

She had drunk the occasional beer at the parties at college, but she had never really acquired a liking for it. She did her best not to pull a face as she took her first sip and felt its bitter taste fill her mouth and run down her throat. At least holding onto it gave her something to do with her hands. Nerves were getting the best of her, and she hoped that the drink would go a long way in bolstering her courage.

She had never been to a party without at least one friend there before. Glenn seemed eager to see her, but something about him made her feel shy and awkward. She wasn't sure that she would be inclined to think of the event as one of the highlights of the summer.

"It's my family's estate."

"Would you introduce me to your parents? I really should tell them that I appreciate the invitation," Cynthia said.

Glenn raised an eyebrow at her, then threw his head back and began to laugh. "You are a perfect example of middle-class charm, aren't you?"

"Is that not how things are done in your crowd?" Cynthia asked.

She knew from conversations with Pauline that oftentimes her mother's definition of "good manners" did not apply to their social set. They seemed to live by a completely different rule book, one that would have left her own parents aghast. It always left her feeling like she had put a foot wrong when she made inquiries about common courtesy, at least in her way of thinking.

"No, not really. And even if it were, my folks aren't here tonight. They are at one of their other houses on the coast, which is why I decided to throw a party in the first place. It's no fun to try and have a good time with someone's parents around, is it?"

Glenn took a step towards her and ran his thumb along her jawline. She felt a shiver run up the back of her neck and could not decide if it was one of anticipation or trepidation.

There was something almost predatory in the way Glenn eyed her, though, and her stomach suddenly clenched at the idea that no real adults were keeping an eye on the goings-on.

Nonsense, she chided herself. That was just one more of her parents' middle-class attitudes floating to the surface. Sophisticated people like Pauline and Glenn thought nothing of being left in charge of an expensive home. They must be considered responsible enough to take care of things, or surely his parents would not allow it. She took another sip of her beer, this time a larger one, and tried to convince herself that it wasn't bitter. It was bracing!

"No, I'm sure you're right. I wonder what's keeping Pauline," she said, gesticulating at the rowdy assembly of young people clustered near the water's edge.

"I expect she'll show up soon enough, but I'm equally sure she won't look as pretty as you," Glenn said, placing his free hand on the small of her back and lowering his voice conspiratorially. "You seem like the sort of girl who might enjoy something a little different than standing around making small talk and sipping beer."

She nodded. Her heart thrummed in her chest as Glenn smiled at her. She wasn't the sort of girl who enjoyed things like small talk. She had never mastered the art of it at all, and a house full of strangers laughing and carrying on was not her idea of a good time. As soon as Glenn had introduced her to the first group of other guests, she wished that she hadn't come. But perhaps Glenn understood her better than she would have thought. After all, it wasn't every guy who would recognize her discomfort and not chide her for it.

“You’re right about that. A large group of strangers isn’t my thing,” she said.

Glenn reached for her hand and pulled her towards the makeshift bar once more. He let go for a moment and lifted a bottle of gin from the cooler’s icy depths. With his free hand, he plucked a pair of glasses off the end of the table and inclined his head towards the back door out to the yard once more.

She followed him down the stairs and across the lawn, its spongy tufts of patchy grass unstable beneath her dress shoe-shod feet. The moon had risen above the tops of the pines on the opposite shore, and its beams pointed a path towards a low building situated alongside the shoreline.

He pulled open the door to the building and held it for her. As she passed through, she heard the familiar slapping sound of wooden boats tied out to a dock. As her eyes adjusted to the gloom, she realized they were standing inside a spacious and well-appointed boathouse. A canoe, a kayak, and a wide, flat-bottomed rowboat sat tethered cheek by jowl to the short wooden dock.

Glenn stooped next to a trunk beside the door and pulled out a navy-and-green-plaid blanket. He moved in long strides towards the rowboat and hopped down into it, landing as gracefully as a ballet dancer. He unfurled the blanket and draped it over one of the seats before extending a hand to help her down into the boat.

“There’s no better way to view the moon than from out on

the water. It'll give us a chance to talk away from all this noise," he said.

He gestured towards the seat covered in the blanket and waited until she had settled herself there before turning and stashing the bottle of gin between them. He took his place near the oarlocks and asked her if she could untie the boat. After a moment's fumbling, she managed to loosen the knot, and with a few strong strokes, he had thrust them out of the boathouse and onto the open lake.

The silvery beams from the moon continued to snake out across the water, and despite the rapidly cooling air, Cynthia leaned over the side of the boat and trailed her fingers in the silky water. A cloud scudded across the sky and blotted out the light for just a moment, and a chill crept up her spine. The noise of the party faded away with each stroke of the oars. In less time than Cynthia could have imagined, she found they were bobbing like a small island out of earshot of all the others.

Glenn reached down and lifted the gin bottle. He retrieved the glasses and poured them each a measure of the clear liquid, carefully passing one to her.

She shook her head. "I think I've already had enough with the beer."

"It'll keep you warm. Just sip it slowly," he said, lifting his own glass to his lips and downing it in one go. He filled it up once more and smiled at her.

"I'm not much of a drinker."

"There's that middle-class sensibility again," he said. She wasn't quite sure she liked his tone, but she couldn't deny that her mother's friends were not known for over-imbibing. Whenever she had seen them at one of her parents' parties, they all limited themselves to no more than a couple of cocktails, and those were spaced out over several hours. "Well, if you don't want anything to drink, then I suppose it's a good thing I brought that blanket along for the ride."

Glenn moved towards her, the boat rocking with each step he took. She felt her heart begin to hammer in her chest as she could hear the sloshing against the sides of the boat. Before it could capsize, he stopped and reached past her to lift the end of the blanket up and around her shoulders. As he crossed the corners in front of her chest, he pulled her towards him and brought his face right up against her own. Before she realized it was happening, his lips pressed against hers with an urgency she did not expect.

The gin and beer on his breath left her feeling faintly sickened. But that was nothing compared to the roiling in her stomach as she felt as his hands move lower. With practiced ease, he slid one palm over her left breast and the other wrapped around her waist, pulling her closer to him as he knelt in front of her.

Before she could comprehend exactly what was happening, he had slid her off the seat and onto the floor of the boat. Between the way his mouth kept covering her own and the weight of his body pressing down on her from above, she could not breathe. She tried to press him away with her hands, but he simply bore down upon her harder. A rising panic filled her chest as one of his knees wriggled between her legs. As he pinned her in place, he traced one of his hands along her leg and slid her dress up her thighs before fumbling with the waistband of her underwear.

All she could think was how far away from everyone else she was and that no one who cared about her knew where to find her. A sob worked its way up her throat, but the sound of it was cut off by Glenn's mouth pressed against hers once more.

She began to thrash about as hard as she could and thrust her hands out, trying to get purchase on anything that could help to pull herself away. Her hand made contact with something slick and slender. With a flicker of hope, she wrapped her fingers around the neck of the gin bottle and quelled her own movement for just long enough to ascertain exactly where he was in relation to her own body.

He lifted his face away from hers, and the moonlight lit up his features as he stared down at her.

"Don't pretend you didn't know what you were getting into when you accepted the invitation. You know you want it. Girls like you always do."

He smiled at her, and she took her chance. She cracked the gin bottle down on the side of his head as hard as she could and felt him sag to the side. Without hesitation, she squirmed out from beneath him. She heard him groan as she dove over the side of the boat and began swimming for the shoreline as quickly as she possibly could.

Glenn shouted at her from the rowboat, but his words were indistinguishable as the splashing of the water and the pounding of her own blood filled her ears. The only goal she had was to reach the shore before he could catch up with her. She lifted her face just long enough to spot the closest spit of land. Shrouded in darkness, the nearest curve of the shoreline was almost invisible except for a tree growing up from the edge of it, leaning at an angle over the lake itself. She course-corrected as quickly as she could and dived beneath the surface of the water, swimming along underneath, hoping he would not be able to see her if she remained beneath the surface until she reached the shadows.

Out of breath and exhausted from her efforts, she glanced behind her and realized the boat continued to bob somewhere near where it had been when she leaped over the side. Her heart still pounding, she reached the tree and hauled herself up onto the bank by grasping its gnarled roots. As much as she wanted to collapse on the bank, she forced herself to her feet. Her dress and shoes were completely sodden, and lake water ran from her hair in rivulets.

The cooling night air struck her wet skin, and she began to shiver. She looked back along the shore to where the lights of the party lit the small beach and gave her a sense of where she was along the road. She made her way into the yard of the nearest house and felt emboldened to pause long enough to wring some of the lake water from her skirt. It splashed out over her feet, leaving them even chillier than before.

As she made her way along the rutted road that went past the house where the party was still in full swing, no one paid her any mind. She kept to the shadows and did her best not to make a sound as she kept a wary watch on a few partygoers who had spilled out onto the front lawn. She held her breath until she was several houses beyond and within sight of the path that led off through the woods. She bent over and slipped off her shoes. All she could think of was running for the safety of the staff house on the resort. Somehow it felt so much farther than a mile and a half away. She glanced over her shoulder to assure herself she was completely alone and then broke off into a run.

CHAPTER 45

Geraldine

CALVIN HAD OFFERED TO PULL up directly in front of the club to save them from a longer walk in their high-heel shoes, but Geraldine insisted that they park in the parking lot at the rear of the building. They were taking enough of a risk of being recognized just by appearing at the club. There was even less chance of remaining anonymous if a chauffeur stopped at the front door and handed them out of the vehicle, as his training demanded.

Vivian grumbled something about skulking about like criminals, but Geraldine simply ignored her and tucked her arm through Marjorie's after assuring Calvin that they would not prefer he wait in the car. Vivian took his arm with one of the predatory smiles that had made her a famous femme fatale, and in only a few moments' time, the four of them were seated at a dimly lit table near the back of the club.

While it didn't hold a candle—not even a match—to the

clubs she had frequented in Boston or even Portland, there was something undeniably charming about the large room. Tables for two, four, or even six were clustered closely together, their faux-marble tops ringed by vinyl upholstered chairs. Small cut-crystal vases filled with fresh flowers adorned the center of each table, and the chairs were comfortably padded.

Crystal ashtrays that matched the vases sat at the ready, emptied of all signs of previous occupants. Vivian snapped open her evening bag and withdrew a cigarette case from within almost as soon as her backside touched her seat. She had chain-smoked throughout the entire journey, and even with the windows left open to the cooling evening air, Geraldine's throat still burned from the scent of them.

Calvin flicked open a lighter and held it out for her. Geraldine wasn't sure whether to be amused or embarrassed at Vivian's overtly flirtatious behavior. She grasped Calvin's hand as she leaned in to press the tip of her cigarette into the waiting flame and held his gaze long enough that even with the low light, Geraldine thought she detected a blush rising to Calvin's smoothly shaved cheeks.

Perhaps she should have accepted his offer to remain in the car. Maybe it was a plea for help proffered as a servant knowing his place. She had found herself in a similar situation on many occasions as a young, and even not-so-young, woman. She would have been grateful to have had anyone step in on her behalf whenever she had been subjected to unwanted interest.

She could not bring herself to leave Calvin to manage it all on his own.

She glanced over at Marjorie, wondering if she had noticed Calvin's discomfort too. Her friend swiveled her head this way and that, enthusiastically taking in the surroundings. Below the table, she could feel the floor bouncing in time to the music. Marjorie's whole frame jiggled as she wriggled to the beat of the band, which was positioned on a slightly elevated stage at the front of the room. Between the stage and the clusters of tables sat a highly polished wooden dance floor.

"Calvin, wouldn't you love to take Marjorie out for a turn round the floor? From the way her foot is tapping, I am sure she would be a fantastic partner," Geraldine said.

Calvin withdrew his hand from Vivian's clasp and scraped back his chair before Marjorie found her voice.

"I'm not sure that my husband would approve of me dancing with another man," she said, her chin wobbling ever so slightly.

"Then we shan't tell him," Geraldine said, giving Calvin a nod.

Marjorie shrugged her plump shoulders and got to her feet. As Calvin led her away, Vivian watched them through the haze of smoke rising from her cigarette end. She raised her free hand to signal for a waiter. One arrived like a genie from a bottle, his red cropped jacket and tuxedo pants marking him out as a member of staff.

"I'll have an old-fashioned. We'll also need a beer. What do you think your sidekick will want?" Vivian asked, waving her cigarette towards Marjorie's empty seat.

"How about a French 75 for each of us," Geraldine said with a smile for the waiter. He squinted at her, and she wondered if he had recognized either of them.

Vivian kept her eyes fixed on the dance floor as the band struck up another tune, and Geraldine was glad of the reprieve from conversation. She didn't want to talk about the Maine Chance, and she couldn't think of anything else she and the other woman had in common. Calvin and Marjorie made a good-looking pair as they swirled and twirled across the floor.

Vivian downed her first drink and was well into a second before the couple made their way back to the table. Marjorie bounced into her seat with all the enthusiasm of a primary school child on a field trip to the zoo. Calvin raised his beer bottle in a semblance of a toast, and Marjorie squealed as soon as she spotted her drink.

"What is this?" she asked after lifting the glass to her lips and taking a tiny sip.

"A French 75. I thought you might like something sparkly," Geraldine said. "Did I guess correctly?"

"I love it," Marjorie said. "Is yours the same thing?" Marjorie gestured to Geraldine's still-untouched glass.

"Yes, it is. I was simply so diverted by the pleasure of watching the dancers that I forgot all about it."

Marjorie leaned towards her and spoke directly into her ear.

"I don't think much would distract Vivian from her drinks. Do you?" she asked as the waiter arrived once more at the other woman's signal.

"Perhaps not. It is just as well that Calvin is here to help get her back to the car when the time comes," Geraldine said.

The waiter quickly returned, this time with two drinks instead of one. Vivian indicated he should leave one in front of Calvin, but no sooner had the waiter stepped away from the table than she downed first her own drink and then the one meant for him. As soon as she had done so, she wobbled to her feet and grabbed Calvin by the hand.

She propelled them both out onto the dance floor, weaving as she did. Calvin flinched as she pressed herself against him. Geraldine watched as every eye in the room turned towards the pair. From what she had read in the newspapers, stars came in two varieties: those who craved the spotlight not only in front of the camera but also away from it, and those who preferred to remain in the shadows when not on set or engaged in promotional activities for their careers. Vivian was obviously one from the first camp.

Something about the way Calvin moved reminded her of Anselm, and a lump rose in her throat. He had been a moderately skilled dance partner but had still never missed the opportunity to accompany her on the dance floor even into their senior years.

A man in a dark suit threaded his way between the tables

and stopped at Marjorie's side. "I don't suppose you would do me the honor of accompanying me for a dance, would you?" he asked.

Marjorie turned towards Geraldine, her eyes wide with disbelief. She nodded at her encouragingly.

"Go on. I'll be fine here on my own," she said.

"Are you sure?" Marjorie asked.

"Completely," Geraldine said. She watched as the man led her companion away from the table and to a spot right in front of the stage. A shaft of light beamed down on Marjorie, highlighting her shiny hair and dewy skin. Marjorie did not give herself enough credit.

The man was a far more adept dancer than Calvin, but Marjorie had no trouble whatsoever keeping up with him. As he confidently piloted her around the floor, Geraldine took the opportunity to add most of the contents of Vivian's glass into Marjorie's. She thought it best to slow down the starlet's guzzling, if possible.

To her dismay, it seemed Vivian had no intention of slowing down. She leaned towards an unoccupied table at the edge of the dance floor and snatched a partially empty glass from it. She downed the contents as Calvin struggled not to careen into another couple. He turned his head towards Geraldine, a look of humiliation on his face. Other dancers, as well as diners, were pointing and laughing.

Vivian was not done calling attention to herself. She stepped back entirely from Calvin and into the path of an approaching waiter bearing a tray holding an order. She reached out and plucked two tall glasses from the tray and downed first one and then the other in rapid succession. Calvin attempted to take her by the arm to steer her towards their table, out of sight of the other guests, but she shrugged him off with such vehemence that one of the glasses slipped from her grasp and smashed to the floor just as the band wrapped up a number.

A hush fell over the room, and Geraldine could feel heat rising to her cheeks. Marjorie took a step back from her dance partner as if to shield him from association with them all. Vivian raised her hands in the air and spun around.

"Quiet on the set. Take two," she called out. She waved at a nearby waiter. "What I meant is that I'll take two. Two more drinks, that is."

An older man in a black jacket left his post near the door and crossed the room. "I think you have had enough for one evening, madame," he said.

"Do you have any idea who I am?" Vivian asked.

"It doesn't matter your name or your position. I would be remiss to allow you to be served more. If you continue to cause a disruption, I shall have to ask you to leave."

Vivian threw her hands up in the air once more. "Are you implying that I cannot hold my liquor?" she asked.

"I am afraid that is not the point. Regardless of your level of intoxication, you are spoiling the atmosphere for our other guests." The man pushed out his chest and widened his stance.

"I'll have you know that I have been thrown out of places all over Hollywood far classier than this."

"If you say so, madame." The man gestured to several waiters hovering nearby. They advanced slowly, as if Vivian were a wild animal who might behave unpredictably if cornered.

"You can't throw me out. I'm Vivian Shaw."

She placed her hands on her hips and twirled around, losing her balance. Calvin grasped her by the arm before she fell to the floor. A pop of flashbulbs erupted around the room. So many people didn't go anywhere anymore without their Kodak Brownies.

Marjorie moved across the room and came to stand beside her. "Are you ready to go?"

"We had best get her out of here before the police are called."

Marjorie's hand flew to her throat. "I don't know what my husband will do if I am involved with the police."

"You head out now and meet us at the car. Calvin and I will deal with Vivian."

"Are you sure?"

"Completely."

Marjorie did as she was told. Before Geraldine had time to catch a waiter's eye and wave him to her side, Marjorie had disappeared from view.

"How may I assist you, madame?" he asked, barely managing to stammer out the question as his gaze slid past her, not sure he was seeing the real Vivian Shaw in the flesh.

"Could I count on you to make sure that my friend Vivian makes it out to our car in the back parking lot as quickly and painlessly as possible?"

The waiter glanced over at Vivian, who had sunk to the center of the dance floor, her lean legs stretched out in front of her despite Calvin's efforts. The poor boy stood nearby, waiting for some sort of direction.

Geraldine reached into her evening bag and held out two twenties and a ten. "Distribute this to your colleagues as you see fit in order to get the job done. The young man standing beside Vivian looking mortified will show you which car is ours."

"She won't be getting behind the wheel, will she?" he asked.

"Certainly not, but it is very kind of you to be concerned."

She thrust the bills at him before gathering up her evening wrap and strolling towards the door with her head held high. More flashes flicked in her peripheral vision as she made her way across the still-quiet room. She turned and pointed a slim finger at the band leader. He took the hint and struck up a rousing tune. It would be a miracle if they hadn't all made the gossip columns within forty-eight hours.

CHAPTER 46

Geraldine

THE EVENING WAS NOT A success—it had to be said. The moon was bright and almost full overhead as the vehicle purred along under Calvin's expert guidance. They had placed an inebriated Vivian in the back seat with the help of a pair of waiters from the club. As soon as the vehicle had gotten underway, she had promptly fallen into a deep sleep, the distinctly unladylike snores emanating from her completely obliterating the sound of road noise as the tires ground against the pavement.

Marjorie had heroically offered to sit in the back and keep an eye on her should she awaken. No one spoke, for there was not much to say. The more Geraldine thought of it, the more she kicked herself for having agreed to the outing. Marjorie certainly had not had the experience she had hoped to have; she just kept repeating over and over her concern that her husband would hear of it. As for Calvin, he had taken the whole thing stoically. While Geraldine was quite certain he had found the situation embarrassing in the extreme, Calvin had continued to perform like a champion servant, stiff upper lip and all.

She was certain the incident would end up in at least the local newspaper. She had no idea how long it would take to come to the public's attention, but she was certain it would happen soon. Vivian Shaw was known for creating drama on movie sets, and there should have been no reason to expect her to do otherwise in her personal life.

Rumors had abounded for ages about Vivian's drinking, but Geraldine preferred not to pay attention to common gossip. After all, some of the things said about her both in the press and behind closed doors were not things she would want others to believe either. Although, considering the way things had turned out, she had to give a lot more credence to the rumors than she would have before that evening. She wondered once again if Vivian had been at the resort in an attempt to dry out. From the way that Vivian had been knocking back drinks like someone thirsting to death who had happened upon a desert oasis, Geraldine suspected that was indeed the truth of the matter.

If only she had known, she never would have agreed to put Marjorie in such jeopardy. She had simply thought it would be a lark to accompany Marjorie on a bit of an adventure. The poor thing had gone entirely pale as she tried to hold her head high and exit the building with the cheers of the other patrons ringing in her ears. The band striking up a popular drinking number hadn't helped matters either.

She was lost in her thoughts, her eyes slightly unfocused, when she felt Calvin stomp heavily on the brakes. She glanced through the windshield and could not quite comprehend what she was seeing. Before she could make sense of any of it, Calvin had leaped from behind the wheel and run out into the road. There, in the beam of the car headlights, she could see him removing his jacket and draping it over the shoulders of a bedraggled-looking young woman. To her shock, she realized that she was looking at Cynthia. She pushed open her door and hurtled out of the vehicle despite her protesting knees.

"What on earth has happened to you?" she asked as she came alongside the pair.

Cynthia's hair was almost entirely released from its bobby pins and, like the rest of her, was soaking wet. She smelled of lake water and was not wearing any shoes. From the look on her face, she was suffering from shock.

"Will you just take me home?" Cynthia said softly between the chattering of her teeth.

Calvin hugged her to his side, then bent and scooped her into his arms.

"Do you mean back to the Maine Chance?" Geraldine asked.

Cynthia nodded, but it looked as though it took enormous effort to do so. "I just want to go to bed."

Geraldine could hear Calvin murmuring to the poor girl as he carried her to the car and placed her in the front seat. Somehow Cynthia managed to slide into the center, and

Calvin and Geraldine returned to their positions, flanking her. Geraldine wrapped an arm over Cynthia's shoulders and pulled her in close. She could feel the girl shivering, but whether it was from cold or from strong emotion, she could not say.

Calvin glanced over again and again as he barreled along the road, eager to get back to the resort without delay. The swampy smell of the lake filled the vehicle, and Geraldine was certain something deeply troubling had occurred. Cynthia was not the sort to simply jump into the lake in a pretty frock on a whim. From what she had said about her family, she had not been raised with such wealth that the cost of a dress would be of no consequence to her.

Calvin slowed to a stop along the access road near where he had picked them up several hours before. Once again, he peered over the top of Cynthia's head as if asking Geraldine what should be done. She had no idea other than to be certain Cynthia should not be left alone. She widened her eyes as if to say she had no notion of how to proceed. Calvin bobbed his head and exited the vehicle, indicating Geraldine should join him.

Cynthia remained in the front seat as if she could not quite summon the energy to exit it without assistance. Geraldine glanced to the back seat, where Marjorie looked stricken. She reached forward and patted Cynthia on the shoulder, causing the girl to jump.

"I think the best thing to do would be to take her to Iris," Calvin said in a low voice.

"That seems an entirely sensible idea. You don't think it will cost her job, though, do you?" Geraldine asked.

"Of course not. None of this is Cynthia's fault." He looked back at the car, fury clouding his usually genial face. "I had better not hear otherwise."

Geraldine was not sure about that. In her experience, women were held to an entirely different standard than men about the way they comported themselves even on their own time. That said, it was obvious that she needed tending to, and her employer was surely functioning as a mother figure during Cynthia's time at the farm.

"You go ahead and take her to Iris. Marjorie and I will get Vivian settled in her own room," Geraldine said.

Calvin darted a glance at the back seat of the car and then looked back at her. "Are you sure you can manage her? It took two waiters to wrestle her out of the club."

"If we can't manage her, we'll leave her in the car. She should be safe enough there as she sleeps it off. The back seat is spacious, and it's a mild evening," Geraldine said.

She decided leaving her would be the best idea of all. If they tried to lead her inside, she might rouse the whole household. Geraldine could just imagine the glowering glances they would all end up receiving from the upright society matrons who thought little enough of Hollywood types to begin with. She certainly wouldn't want to put Marjorie in a bad position with them. The poor woman didn't need her husband to have any more cause to criticize her.

Calvin nodded and leaned into the car, offering his hands to Cynthia. She moved slowly, the sound of her wet clothing squeaking across the leather seat. Geraldine wondered fleetingly if it would leave a watermark that could not be removed from the handsome leather upholstery. She hoped that Calvin would not end up suffering for their outing. Once again, she kicked herself for having agreed to attend such an event.

She watched as Calvin wrapped an arm around Cynthia once more and helped propel her towards the staff house. She waited until they were out of sight before motioning for Marjorie to join her outside of the vehicle. She closed the door quietly behind her like someone who was used to shutting a nursery door in such a way as to not wake a sleeping child.

"Calvin has taken Cynthia off to be tended to by the housekeeper."

"What do you think happened to that poor girl?" Marjorie asked.

"I think she was out for the evening and it went very badly."

"'Badly' how? The poor creature was sopping wet and so scared she jumped when I touched her shoulder," Marjorie said.

Geraldine looked her friend over. Could she really be so unsophisticated and unworldly as to have no idea what kind of "badly" she was implying? She had fended off advances from a wide variety of boys her own age and men by far her senior from the time she was eleven or twelve years old. Could things really be so very different now?

Somehow Geraldine doubted it. Still, if Marjorie was one of the lucky few who had no concept of such abuses, she wasn't eager to disillusion her.

"Perhaps it was a boating accident," she said.

A look of understanding passed over Marjorie's bewildered face. "Yes, I suppose that does explain it. I am always very careful with the children whenever we're near the water."

"That's very sensible, I'm sure. Now, I think you and I ought to leave Vivian to sleep it off in the back seat. There can come no good in dragging her kicking and screaming through the resort. She'll get as good a night's rest there as she will in her own bed."

Geraldine glanced back towards the vehicle. The sounds of Vivian's snores could be heard through the closed windows.

CHAPTER 47

Iris

IRIS SAT ON THE EDGE of the bed, wrapped in a cotton bathrobe, rhythmically pulling a brush through her hair. Through the window of her room in the staff house, she watched the blink of fireflies in the dark night sky. She would usually be in bed before it had grown so late, but her mind felt battered by the waves of thought assailing it ever since Orla's diagnosis by the doctor. The notion of lying abed with nothing to distract her from them held no appeal. And so she puttered, busying herself with tasks usually saved for the offseason, well past the hour she routinely stopped work for the day.

She crossed the room to return her brush to the top of the dresser and heard a rap on her door. Almost relieved at the excuse not to be alone with her thoughts, she clutched the gap at the top of her robe closed.

"Come in," she said.

The door creaked open, and Calvin's head appeared in the gap.

"Are you busy?"

"You know that I always have time for staff. That said, it is a bit late."

"I wouldn't have bothered you, except I wasn't sure what else to do," he said, pushing the door fully open to reveal Cynthia standing—albeit limply—beside him. Iris took one look at her and gave him a curt nod.

"You'd best be off to bed. Leave Cynthia to me."

With that, she stepped forward and drew the girl inside the room, shooing Calvin out with her free hand. She pressed the door firmly into place and locked it behind him.

Cynthia looked up at her like a dog expecting to be spanked for leaving a puddle on the carpet.

"You look like you had an eventful evening."

Cynthia opened her mouth as if to speak but instead doubled over and began to sob, clutching her arms around her waist as if her body might fly into bits if she loosened her grip. Iris bent over her and stroked her back as Cynthia shook and cried. When she quieted down and straightened, Iris pushed straggling strands of honey-colored hair away from her face.

"Should I call for the doctor?" Iris asked.

Cynthia shook her head and began to sob once more. She sagged to the floor as if all the life were seeping out of her.

"I won't if you would rather I didn't."

Cynthia peered up through wet lashes and shook her head. Iris knelt beside her and pulled a handkerchief from the pocket of her robe.

Cynthia reached out with a trembling hand and took it, dabbed her eyes before delicately blowing her nose. Iris felt a long-ignored gnawing on her own heart as she observed the miserable girl in front of her. She would have liked to have been a mother.

"There's no need for the doctor. I'm fine," Cynthia said.

"We had better get you out of these wet clothes and into a hot bath," Iris said.

She got to her feet and offered Cynthia her hand, pulling the girl to stand. They crept down the hallway as quietly as possible. It was not the sort of situation that Iris thought best discussed with the rest of the staff.

She pulled the cord dangling from the bathroom ceiling, and the small room sprang into light. Iris bent over the tub and pushed the rubber plug into the open drain hole. She wrenched on the taps and checked the temperature, hoping there would be enough hot water at that time of night for a proper soak. She added a measure of bath salts and swished it around.

Like Alice before her, she made a point to set aside any half-empty containers of beauty products to pass along to staff members. Not only were the items luxurious and expensive, but like most New Englanders, she abhorred waste. Iris made sure to save a few bottles of bath salts, dusting powders, body lotions, and hand creams for the women's bathroom stockpiles. Most of the girls who worked there would never have been able to try such things otherwise.

She turned back around to face Cynthia. "You wait here while I fetch your pajamas. I assume they're in the dresser in your room?"

"I tuck them under my pillow. Dolores might be asleep, though, so I wouldn't turn on the light," Cynthia said.

Iris was surprised at Cynthia's thoughtfulness, given the state of her. She wasn't sure that everyone would have bothered to consider how her actions might affect her roommate under the circumstances.

"Believe it or not, I've been creeping around the staff house for more than twenty years. I even know which floorboards to avoid to keep them from squeaking. I'll be back in a tick."

She returned a moment later with Cynthia's pajamas and a pair of warm socks she had fetched from her own room. Outsiders never did think to bring warm socks when they traveled to Maine in the summer. They simply could not be convinced that it could get cool enough to want them. But if one spent enough time at the lake, eventually a chill would set in. Fortunately, Orla knitted a steady stream of garments of all sorts, including pairs of cozy socks.

At least, she had thus far. Iris didn't know if the disease would eventually rob her of those skills just as thoroughly as it seemed to be robbing her of her memories. She shook that thought away as she stepped into the warm bathroom filling with billowing steam.

Cynthia had already removed her clothing and left it in a heap on the floor. The shower curtain had been pulled around the freestanding claw-foot tub, but the back of Cynthia's hair hung down over the lip of the tub, disclosing her presence.

Iris lowered the toilet lid and sat upon it. She suddenly wished she had not given up smoking. Her nerves felt jangled, and the nicotine would have been soothing.

"It's only me. I thought we ought to talk about what happened before I get you tucked up in bed," Iris said.

She held her breath, waiting for a response. She wasn't entirely sure one would be forthcoming. It wasn't as though the girl knew her well, and if Iris were to be completely honest, she had not been enthusiastic about fostering a closeness with a young woman so different from herself. She had judged her harshly based on her expectations of how a girl from her background would perform in her role as a maid, rather than any actual understanding of her as a person.

She heard Cynthia let out a tremendous sigh, audible even over the splashing from the taps. She wondered if the girl was going to begin to cry again, but instead, she spoke in a remarkably clear voice.

"I was invited to a party at the house on the lake. The boy who asked me is an acquaintance of the Mayhews. He decided to try to become far more acquainted with me than I had any intention of allowing, and it all ended rather badly," Cynthia said.

"'Rather badly' how?" Iris asked.

"I was foolish enough to believe he just wanted to talk when he offered to take me out for a moonlit boat ride. When he got me out far enough not be heard, he tried to force himself on me," Cynthia said.

Iris considered what she should say next. If Cynthia had indeed been pushed into something against her will, there were any number of difficulties that lay ahead. Not only would she have a heartache that went with such violence, but she also ran the risk of being labeled as a hussy should the news get out. If she became pregnant, it would be difficult to keep the secret.

"Was he successful in his attempt?" Iris asked, trying to keep her voice steady. She heard the water shift and slap the sides of the tub before Cynthia answered.

"He put his hands all over me in places that still make me feel like I might vomit, but I managed to hit him over the head and jump over the side of the boat before he could get any further than that," Cynthia said. "I swam for the shore and ran back here before he could come after me."

Iris sagged against the toilet tank, limp with relief. She had not realized exactly how tightly strung her body felt from the moment Calvin popped his head through her bedroom door.

"What did you hit him with?" Iris asked.

A giggle rose up from Cynthia. "A bottle of gin. He brought it with him hoping to get me well and truly plastered, I suppose thinking that would make it easier to do whatever he wanted. He had me pinned down onto the bottom of the boat, when I managed to feel it rolling around near my hand. I think I might have stunned him with it."

"It would serve him right if you killed him," Iris said. Her hand reached around the shower curtain and pulled it away from Cynthia's face.

"You don't think I badly injured him, do you?" Cynthia asked.

"No, I very much doubt it. In my experience, men who behave like that have the devil's own luck. You're very lucky yourself, you know. It could have ended much differently."

"I suppose I was lucky, although it doesn't much feel like it just now."

"Trust me, you got off lightly. What were you thinking, going off to a party all on your own?" Iris could hear the chiding note in her voice, but she couldn't restrain herself.

"I didn't think I would be on my own. My friend from college was supposed to be there too. Given how little I've seen her recently, I didn't feel I could refuse the invitation even though Calvin couldn't go with me."

The girl was full of surprises. Iris thought of Calvin as worthy of any young woman he chose, but she had not necessarily thought a college girl would feel the same. If Dolores had confessed an interest in him, she would have expected it. But surely Cynthia had a boyfriend back at college she was eager to get back to. Wasn't that the reason she was so eager to earn money for tuition?

Could it be that she really was only interested in her education? Between her confession and her successful wielding of a gin bottle, Iris had to look at her with new eyes. She had surprised her with the quality of her work too. Iris had expected her to scrape by doing the bare minimum, but she had performed almost as well as girls who had worked at the resort for years. Admittedly, she was still not as fast as many of them at some of the tasks, but she did have an eye for detail and took the initiative when it came to things that she noticed needed doing.

Iris had also worried there would be envy on the part of Dolores when Cynthia had been asked to serve as Mrs. Putnam's maid, but there seemed to be no trouble there either. She had turned out to be a surprisingly good hire. Iris didn't know what she would have done without her. The idea that she might have been put out of commission by some spoilt good-for-nothing didn't bear thinking about.

She heard the water in the tub move again, and Cynthia's hair began to slide away from the lip and down into the water. As the girl emerged, she wiped her face with her palms and opened her eyes.

"Do you happen to have any shampoo?"

If her hair was what was on the top of her mind, it seemed to Iris that Cynthia was going to be just fine.

CHAPTER 48

Geraldine

SHE MADE SURE THAT MARJORIE found her way safely back to her room before setting out for her makeshift studio. Aided by the light of the moon overhead, she picked her way across the dew-covered grass, hardly aware of the dampness seeping in through her satin shoes. She had to get the image down on paper before it was lost forever.

She pushed open the door to the building and flipped the light switch. The glare overheard was at odds with her task, but it couldn't be helped. She was so eager to re-create the image in her mind's eye that she didn't bother to pull on her painting smock. A gessoed canvas stood at the ready on the easel in front of her, and she rushed towards it, impatient to begin.

Using a bit of vine charcoal, she sketched with light, feathery strokes directly onto the canvas. Once the blocking was done, she turned to her tackle box for tubes of paint and squirted them out one by one onto her battered wooden palette.

Phthalo blue, alizarin crimson, cadmium yellow, and titanium white blobs of pigment gleamed up at her like the smiles of lifelong friends. She grasped a palette knife from a vase filled with tools, sliced off wedges of color, and began mixing them into the perfect shades.

Her heart raced as she reached for a blunt-tipped brush and swiped a broad sweep of color across the canvas. Stroke after stroke followed, and in front of her eyes, the image she had imagined, inspired by the one she had seen, steadily came into being. A path like a ribbon snaked through the painting, leading between a dense copse of trees and an expanse of lake beyond. A shaft of moonlight penetrated a cloud-covered sky and illuminated the figure of a young woman, racing after a stag, her bow raised.

Shafts of sunlight filtered through the eastern-facing windows as she finally stepped back to evaluate what she had created. It was only the beginning, but she could see that the work was good—perhaps better than good. There was much more work to be done, of course. The figure was still faceless, and that would never do. It was the look on Cynthia's face as she burst out onto the road, the moon lighting her expression, that had inspired the image in the first place. Geraldine closed her eyes and imagined her once more: furious, determined, victorious.

She dropped into the wooden chair and stretched out her legs. Her hands and shoulders ached from the frenzy of work. A smear of yellow ochre had marred the front of her gown, but no matter. It felt so good to be back at work that she laughed out loud. Perhaps she would cut the stain out of her dress and frame it alongside the painting. It was just the outrageous sort of thing she had always been known for.

The sun reached farther into the makeshift studio, and the warmth of it left her drowsy. It had been years since she had spent a sleepless night painting an image she could not forget. She closed her eyes, imagining the other paintings that would accompany the one before her. Maybe one of Calvin striding across a lush field, a girl in his arms and a look of rage—or perhaps tenderness—stamped on his handsome face. After all, it would take more than one of these to make a show.

CHAPTER 49

Cynthia

THE RECEPTIONIST STATIONED AT THE desk in the foyer lifted a hand to get her attention; nothing so gauche as a raised voice would be acceptable at a place like the Maine Chance. Cynthia approached the desk, aware that the staff brought in from the resort in Arizona or from the Red Door salons around the country looked down on the local workers, who were seen as essentially unskilled labor.

She waited while the receptionist retrieved a stack of messages from a set of wooden mail cubbies mounted on the wall behind the desk. She pressed them into Cynthia's outstretched hand with the admonishment to take them to Vivian's room straightaway.

"See that she gets them. The same caller has been ringing the phone off the hook trying to reach her. There has even been a telegram. I think it must be some sort of emergency," the receptionist said, a crinkle of concern appearing between her perfectly plucked eyebrows. "Also, Dolores is held up with something at the laundry house, so you'll need to take breakfast to Vivian Shaw along with the messages."

Cynthia slipped the messages into the pocket of her apron and headed to the guest kitchen to pick up the tray for Vivian. After what had happened the night before, Cynthia had overslept a bit, but there had been no recriminations from Iris. Just knowing that her boss would allow her such consideration put the spring back into her step, despite the bruises she had felt as soon as she rolled over in bed that morning. She winced as she hoisted the tray covered with grapefruit segments, fresh blueberries, a thin slice of dry toast, and a pot of coffee.

Calvin appeared in the hall just outside the kitchen door. Perhaps the pain in her shoulder blades showed on her face. He took one look at her and took the tray from her hands.

"Where are you headed?" he asked.

"Vivian's room on the second floor. I don't think you're allowed up there."

"You're not in any fit state to carry this all that way. If anyone asks, we'll tell them it was Iris's idea." He strode off towards the servants' stairs, pausing at the base for her to take the lead.

She eased past him, careful not to brush against him in the narrow space. She told herself that she was just being careful with the tray, but she suspected that she was fibbing. For just a moment, the memory of Glenn's face rose up in her mind's eye. She stifled a flash of panic and grasped the banister.

"Speaking of Iris, I didn't thank you last night for taking me to her. She was a great deal of help."

"Iris has always been good in a pinch. I was sure she would know just what to do." As they reached the top of the stairs and stepped onto the second-floor landing, Calvin cleared his throat. It was an oddly masculine sound in a space meant exclusively for women. "I shouldn't have let you go to that party alone. I feel like what happened was my fault."

She stopped and turned to face him. "The only one to blame is the guy who thought he could take something from me that I wasn't willing to give. You had nothing to do with it."

Calvin's cheeks flushed—either from anger or embarrassment, she didn't know which.

"Did he manage to steal from you?" He stared down at the tray as if it held the answers to life's hard questions.

She thought about it for a long moment. Perhaps Glenn had robbed her, but she had gained something as well.

"He took a slice off my trusting nature and maybe scared a year off my life, but he didn't get what he was after if that is what you're asking." She paused and he nodded.

"I'm relieved to hear it. I am not sure I could look myself in the mirror if he had interfered with you." He looked up at her again and met her eyes with his own warm brown ones, the color of strong tea.

"I'm a little more wary than I was when I left here last night, but I'm also more aware of how resourceful I can be when I need to."

"You got a couple of good licks in, then?" Calvin asked.

"I most assuredly did," Cynthia said. She could almost feel the cool glass neck of the gin bottle against her palm. She doubted she would ever enjoy a martini again. Or maybe she would make them her signature drink as a reminder of how she'd managed to save herself from harm. Still, she needn't decide straightaway.

"I still regret not going with you, and not just because of what happened to you or at the nightclub."

Cynthia's ears pricked up. "Did something upsetting happen to you too?"

"You can say that again. I already felt bad about turning you down and sneaking the ladies away from the resort. But then when we arrived, Vivian insisted that I accompany them all inside the club. That sort of place isn't my idea of a good time."

Cynthia could imagine that. He seemed more the kind to enjoy a ball game or even a day spent helping friends on a home-remodeling project or tinkering with a car engine. Still, most men would put up with a lot to be seen with a woman as gorgeous as Vivian Shaw.

"It couldn't have been all that terrible, considering how beautiful the company."

Calvin shook his head. "Her looks weren't the problem."

He lowered his voice. “You weren’t in any fit state to notice last night, but Vivian was completely blotto when we found you. She was so drunk that she got us kicked out. The other customers actually clapped and cheered when management asked us to leave.”

Cynthia was glad she wasn’t holding the tray; she might have dropped it in surprise.

“Vivian got you kicked out of the club? It must have been quite a scene.”

“Let’s put it this way: It took three waiters as well as myself to pull her down off a table and wrangle her back to the car.”

Before he could reply, she turned and faced Vivian’s door. She knocked before slipping her key into the lock.

“I’d better take it from here. It is one thing for you to be on the second floor, but I don’t think we could make up any excuse that would explain you being in Vivian’s room.”

Calvin handed her the tray and held her gaze for a moment. “After last night, I wouldn’t dream of causing you trouble.” He leaned towards her. “I hope that you know the scene at the club wasn’t the only reason I regretted turning you down for the party.”

“It wasn’t?”

“No, it wasn’t. I spent the night wishing that I had been anywhere else with you.”

“You spent the evening with a Hollywood starlet, and you expect me to believe you would have rather been with me?”

"That's exactly what I am saying."

Calvin leaned a little closer, a question in his eyes. For a moment, her stomach roiled, and her heart pounded. But as she smiled at him, her panic eased. Glenn hadn't stolen what Calvin had so carefully asked about. She wasn't about to let him steal how she felt about the man standing before her. She eased forward, despite the ache between her shoulder blades, and gave the slightest nod. He brushed his fingertips across her cheek, then gently kissed her before turning towards the servants' stairs without another word.

CHAPTER 50

Cynthia

SOMETHING HAD CHANGED SINCE CYNTHIA had left Iris's room the night before. She seemed to have gone out of her way to find Cynthia alone. She had stopped and started to speak to her several times that day but had cut it short when another maid or a guest appeared in the area. It had taken until lunchtime before Iris spotted her in the second-floor corridor and waved her into an empty room that needed cleaning for a new guest. She pushed the door firmly into place behind them and, alarmingly, turned the lock. Even more worryingly, she gestured that Cynthia should take a seat on one of the sitting-area chairs. With its creamy silk moiré upholstery, there was no way Iris would be inclined for the staff to risk soiling it with their well-worn uniforms if she did not fear that Cynthia might lose her legs out from underneath her.

Iris paced up and down, a small coffee table between them. Cynthia fixed her attention on the vase of withering flowers on the table's center, remembering Iris's admonishment to attend to flowers as soon as she noticed any lack of freshness. The housekeeper abruptly stopped her pacing and dropped into the chair opposite her.

"I received a phone call from Miss Arden this morning," she said.

That explained it. Iris was always keyed up when she had any contact with Miss Arden. Maids passed along the news that the resort's owner had gotten in touch whenever they were made aware of such a thing. It was far better to give Iris a wide berth on those days.

"Is there another important guest headed our way? Someone even more important than Vivian Shaw? Not that I can imagine who that might be," Cynthia said.

"That wasn't the reason for her call. She telephoned to insist that I dismiss you from your post, effective immediately."

The edges of the room faded and blurred. Iris had been right to suggest that she sit. Her legs began to rattle back and forth without her permission.

"Fired? But what for?" Cynthia asked.

"She says that she has it on good authority that your character is questionable and that your presence reflects poorly on the entire resort."

There was only one thing that came to mind to explain such a turn of events. "My character? Do you think someone has been saying something about what happened at the party?"

There had been a risk in running from the party. There had been one in refusing Glenn at all. Girls were never the wronged party when things got so far out of hand, especially not if the man was wealthy. Had Pauline told someone what had happened? Had Glenn? Surely Mrs. Putnam, Vivian Shaw, and Iris could not have done such a thing, could they?

Iris's eyes grew wide in her face. "I truly have no idea. I would expect that was what she was referring to, but she would only say that she was told you were not the right sort of girl to have on staff. I tried to change her mind, but it was no use. She told me that you had to go, and if I did not see to it, she would be looking for a new housekeeper as well as a maid."

Cynthia sank back against the firm back of the chair, grateful that it at least was supporting her. The look of misery on Iris's face was pitiable, and despite her own worry, she couldn't help but feel sorry for her.

"As much as I want the job, I don't need it to put food on my table. I hope that speaking up for me hasn't jeopardized your chances at the year-round position." Cynthia felt the sincerity of her words as they passed her lips. She honestly could not imagine making things difficult for Iris. In fact, she would make them as easy as she could. "You needn't fire me. I'll quit."

Cynthia wasn't sure, but she thought she saw Iris's lower lip wobble.

"What will you do now?" she asked.

It was a good question, and one that depended on what

she hoped to salvage. Not that she was sure there would be any chance of that. She doubted there was enough time left in the season to find another job in Mount Vernon or to attract and secure the attentions of another young man as wealthy as Glenn. Not that she wanted that anyway. It was Calvin she would be sorry to part from.

Cynthia stood. "I'll go to my friend Pauline's place to say goodbye, and then I suppose I will head home."

"I am so very sorry, Cynthia," Iris said, her voice muffled as if a lump dampened the sound.

"I'll be fine. I hope that you will be all right, considering you'll be down a maid again." She stood and extended her hand. Iris heaved herself to her feet and rounded the table. She pushed her hand away and wrapped her arms around her instead. Cynthia could smell the starch in her uniform and the faint scent of lemon oil from a polishing rag tucked in Iris's pocket. Willing herself not to cry, she gave Iris a tight squeeze before breaking off the embrace.

"If it is all the same to you, I'll just collect my things and head out. I couldn't stand to say any goodbyes."

Iris nodded. Cynthia could feel her gaze upon her as she held her head up and strode out the door.

CHAPTER 51

Geraldine

GERALDINE ROLLED ONTO HER SIDE and noticed, as she did each morning since arriving, the satisfyingly crisp feeling of the snowy sheets against her bare legs. Her hip bones felt sore, as if she had lain on them for too long even though she had spent the hours of the night hard at work. She stretched her arms above her head before propping up on one elbow and casting a glance towards the windows opposite the bed. Despite the heaviness of the drapes, narrow blades of sunlight sliced around the edges of the window frames—and not the milky sunlight of predawn that had accompanied her back to her room, but the scouring brightness of late morning.

She reached for her travel alarm clock and snapped open its small alligator case. Half past ten. Why ever had Cynthia let her lie abed for so long? If she were to complete enough paintings for the upcoming show, every moment counted. Then the events of the previous night flooded back to her. The poor girl might have had a lie-in of her own after her harrowing encounter at the party. She pushed herself upright and threw back the light coverlet. She slid her bony feet into her carpet slippers and reached for her robe.

She lifted the telephone receiver and instructed the front desk attendant to send her breakfast tray to her room without delay. Even if Cynthia was not up for a session in the studio, there was no reason that she couldn't go ahead and get started on her own. Anyway, she had the memory of Cynthia fleeing across the road, a look of determined fury stamped on her features, to use should she feel stuck. And once she was sure of where she was headed with a project, she rarely found herself held back. After her painting session the night before, she felt too inspired to be the least bit blocked.

There had been something inspiring about Cynthia from the moment she'd spotted her in the staff kitchen, but the sight of her pelting across the asphalt, no shoes on her feet and ringing wet, evoked some kind of ancient water goddess. The girl was pretty, there was no quibbling on that score, but that wasn't what made her an intriguing subject. Rather, it was the way she gave off an impression of intelligence and observation. It did Geraldine a world of good to see a young woman less interested in simpering and tamping her fire down to appear docile to a potential beau. It made her feel more hopeful for the future than she had in some time. Cynthia's desire to complete her education had lifted her spirits to no end and had made her aware of how much she missed her own work.

A discreet knock landed on the door to the suite. She called out a welcome, and the door swung open, her breakfast tray appearing in the gap. A silver coffeepot, a single pink china cup, a plate scantily clad in a wedge of melon and a sliver of dry toast, as well as the expected fresh rose, offered no surprises. The maid, however, did.

"You're not Cynthia," Geraldine said, striving and failing to keep the indignation from her voice.

"No, ma'am. I'm Dolores."

"Is Cynthia unwell this morning?" she asked, hoping her tone had softened. Come to think of it, Cynthia likely had been up at least as late as she had.

"Miss Hubbard said I should direct any questions you have to her personally," Dolores said. She carried the tray to the low table placed between the pair of upholstered chairs at the far end of the room. Dolores capably slid the drapes open before crossing to the bed to retrieve Geraldine's robe, which had slithered to the floor. "Will there be anything else?"

Geraldine's brain began to fizz. What on earth could have happened to Cynthia?

"Indeed, there will. Please ask Miss Hubbard to attend to me immediately. And take away the tray. I have entirely lost my appetite."

Geraldine watched as the girl darted like a rabbit to the table once more. As she hoisted the tray aloft, the teacup chattered wildly in its saucer, and the coffeepot lid rattled like dice in a cup. The poor girl would not have lasted a day as her maid. Where, oh where, was Cynthia?

CHAPTER 52

Iris

DOLORES WAS A CAPABLE GIRL and not one to be easily intimidated. She had three older brothers and a mother who might as well have vinegar flowing through her veins, if her lack of sweetness was any indication. Geraldine Putnam could be a handful, but she was rarely rude to the staff. Iris would not have expected her to accept the services of a different maid without complaint, but she had not anticipated that it would prod her to fury. She sent Dolores to the staff house for a fifteen-minute break to recover from her ordeal and forced herself to head up the stairs to the second floor where the older woman awaited her.

Mrs. Putnam opened the door to her room before Iris could land a second knock on the sturdy wooden surface. She flung the door wide and stepped back, sweeping her arm out from her side as if to hurry Iris into the room. She had barely closed it before she spoke.

"She hasn't done something dreadful to herself, has she?" Mrs. Putnam asked.

Iris had not even considered that Mrs. Putnam might be worried for Cynthia's state of mind because of the attack the previous evening. She had been so caught up worrying about what she knew to be true that she had not even considered the sorts of things someone else might imagine. Particularly someone as imaginative as Mrs. Putnam. She shook her head emphatically.

"No, it's nothing like that."

Mrs. Putnam threw a hand up towards her throat and patted the base of it as if to calm herself. Truly, the woman did look wild. While Iris had understood that Mrs. Putnam valued Cynthia as a maid, she had not expected that she would take news of her dismissal quite so much to heart. Artists were peculiar, to be sure, and Mrs. Putnam, with her remarkable level of success, certainly fit into that mold. Even now she was dressed nothing like the other ladies who frequented the Maine Chance. With her worn cotton skirt and oversize men's button-down shirt, she looked more like someone who had come to do a bit of wallpapering than an honored guest.

Mrs. Putnam pointed at the pair of chairs at the far end of the room and strode across, taking one of them for herself. "Well, what is it like, then? I woke up this morning, as I'm sure you can see," she said, pointing towards her outfit, "prepared for a day spent in the studio, and I am informed that Cynthia is nowhere to be had. How will I finish my paintings now?"

Even Iris, with her limited understanding of the art world, knew that a model or a muse was difficult to replace. Still, there was nothing to be done.

"I'm afraid that Cynthia has been dismissed from her post," Iris said. She noticed her mouth drying out as the phrase slid past her lips.

Mrs. Putnam shook her head as if to rid herself of ringing in her ears. "Dismissed from her post? Preposterous. I did not dismiss her."

"Still, she has been removed."

"Why on earth would you do such a thing? You know how happy I was with Cynthia. Does this have anything to do with last night? I wouldn't have thought so ill of you, Iris."

She was relieved to know that Mrs. Putnam would not naturally have suspected her of being so shallow as to dismiss a girl because of some spoiled rich boy's behavior. Still, she felt torn between her loyalty to Miss Arden and her desire to set the record straight. But Miss Arden was not seated there in the fuming presence of Mrs. Putnam. Besides, she did not agree with the dismissal herself.

"It wasn't my decision. Cynthia has turned out to be a surprisingly good employee, and one who will be sorely missed," she said. "Miss Arden asked me to fire her."

"Elizabeth requested her dismissal? Whatever for?"

It was a moment Iris had been dreading. This type of accusation leveled at Cynthia could only harm the girl when seeking employment elsewhere. If she were to have any hope of earning her tuition, it would be quashed by the reason for her dismissal. She hadn't even told Cynthia the whole truth. But she couldn't very well lie to Mrs. Putnam. She would be sure to ferret out the details one way or another, and then it would have all been for naught. Besides, after everything Mrs. Putnam had done to help with Orla, she owed her more than vague excuses.

"Miss Arden received a telephone call informing her that Cynthia had been caught stealing. She was also accused of assaulting a young man, although I happen to know that she was only defending herself."

"I thought it was something like that. She wasn't interfered with, was she?"

"No, but only because she hit the man over the head with a gin bottle before diving into the lake to escape him."

"And someone called Elizabeth to blame her for being attacked?"

"The concerned party wished to do her the favor of warning her that she had a staff member who could not be trusted."

Mrs. Putnam sat back against her chair, her mouth fallen open slightly.

"Cynthia, stealing? What utter nonsense. The girl has been in and out of my rooms and painting studio ceaselessly since she became my maid. I can attest to the fact that not a single bobby pin has been filched, let alone anything of value." She lurched forward and propped her bony elbows on her knees. "Who, may I ask, made this spurious telephone call to Miss Arden?"

"I am not sure it would do any good to say. I can tell you that I don't know her personally, but she is someone who held enough sway with Miss Arden that I had no choice but to dismiss the girl. I was extraordinarily sorry to do so. Miss Arden said that if I did not fire her, I would lose not only my chance at the job in Arizona, but my position here as well."

Mrs. Putnam made a harrumphing noise deep in her throat. "Preposterous. Elizabeth is lucky to have the pair of you. Your job, here or there, won't be in jeopardy if I have anything to say about it." She straightened and drummed her paint-stained fingers on the arms of her chair. "What is the name of the person who leveled the accusation?"

Mrs. Putnam raised an eyebrow and pursed her lips. Even maintaining a thunderous silence, the woman was persuasive.

"Louise Bradford," Iris said.

Mrs. Putnam began to sputter. She launched up and out of her chair and headed straight for the telephone. "Louise. You're sure it was Louise?"

"Yes. I distinctly remember Miss Arden telling me the rumor had come straight from Louise Bradford, and so she felt it must be true. Anyhow, what reason would the woman have to make up such a story?"

"What reason, indeed? I shall set Elizabeth straight immediately." Mrs. Putnam lifted the receiver on the telephone and pointed at the door. “You had best not be here for this. I wouldn’t want to put you in the middle of something that likely will turn a bit ugly.”

CHAPTER 53

Cynthia

CYNTHIA COULDN'T BRING HERSELF TO ask Calvin for a ride to the Mayhews' house, so she had begged Iris to have the other chauffeur drive her. He had dropped her off at the far end of the driveway, eager to get back to the resort, where he could depend on receiving a fat tip from one of the guests rather than an effusive but impoverished thank-you from a disgraced maid. He had done her the courtesy of hoisting her suitcases from the trunk before hurrying off back to the resort.

The suitcases felt far lighter than they had when she first appeared at the Mayhews' summer home a few weeks earlier. She had become much stronger since her arrival in Mount Vernon. It seemed so long ago. The view of the lake was just as breathtaking, but her joy at seeing it had diminished. She adjusted her grip on the suitcase handles and headed for the wide steps leading to the sweeping and gracious porch. Before she could reach the top step, the door swung open, and Mrs.

Mayhew stepped out dressed to the nines in a full skirt and gossamer-thin twinset that appeared to be made of cashmere. She wrapped her arms tightly over her chest.

Cynthia placed her suitcases on the wooden floorboards and wiped her palms on her skirt.

"What are you doing here?" Mrs. Mayhew asked.

"I've left the Maine Chance."

"I am well aware of that. But what are you doing here?"

Cynthia felt as though she'd been punched in the stomach. Ever since Iris had told her about Miss Arden's call, she had hoped that Mrs. Mayhew had not been a party to her losing her job. But even if she weren't, she didn't sound as though she were happy to have Cynthia show up out of the blue.

"I wanted to say goodbye to Pauline before I leave town," Cynthia said, hoping she did not sound as pathetic as she felt.

Mrs. Mayhew's eyes widened. "Surely you must realize there's no way I could allow you to set foot in this house after what you have done. I don't even feel comfortable with you standing on the porch."

"Have I done something to upset you?" How quickly had the accusation against her traveled?

"Don't play dumb with me. You can't expect that, after the incident with Glenn, you'll be welcome into the home of any of his family friends, can you?"

So that was it. Cynthia's stomach roiled. "What is it that you think happened between Glenn and me?"

"You know very well that you were caught pilfering, and when he confronted you about it, you hit him."

"Is that what you think happened?" Cynthia asked, overwhelmed with the feeling of disbelief. How could Mrs. Mayhew believe her to be a thief? It wasn't as though her daughter didn't have plenty of things another girl might wish to take for herself. Pauline had never been the victim of any thefts in the time they'd lived together. Why would she believe something like that just because Glenn said so?

"Whether I believe it or whether I don't, it's what's being bandied about in all the best families on the lake," she said. "We wouldn't be able to go to another cocktail party or host a bridge game if we were seen to be harboring you."

The notion that people who considered themselves to be the best sort of families would make such accusations without hearing both sides of the story sparked a flicker of anger in her chest. Who did they think they were? Did the families who considered themselves to be superior to others believe it was right for wealthy young men to do as they pleased, regardless of how it might hurt others?

"How pitiable for you that would be."

"There's no need to take that tone. I am well within my rights to turn you away."

"You don't want to know what I say happened?"

Mrs. Mayhew rolled her eyes and shrugged. "If you feel you must tell me, I won't attempt to stop you."

"I did hit Glenn. I hit him with a gin bottle, but not in the house, as he has apparently claimed. We were out in a rowboat, supposedly to see the moon rise over the lake, when he shoved me down in the bottom of it and tried to force himself on me. If I hadn't hit him, he would've managed it too."

Mrs. Mayhew arched an eyebrow. "Are you actually trying to convince me that Glenn had to try to force himself on you? He has girls lined up around the block vying for his attention."

"Are you saying that you think I'm making this up?"

Mrs. Mayhew shrugged again. "I'm saying I don't think what you claim is very likely. Besides, even if what you said was true, you must have done something to encourage him; otherwise, I'm sure he wouldn't have acted like that."

Cynthia's mouth flew open, and it felt as though someone had punched her in the gut. All the air went out of her body in a rush. When she finally managed to catch her breath, she could not decide if she was more hurt or angry.

"If by 'encouraged him,' you mean I accepted his invitation to watch the moon rise over the lake, then I suppose I must be guilty. I assure you, I didn't indicate I was interested in anything more than that, and certainly not what he decided was the reason for being out in the boat."

Cynthia thought she saw a curtain twitch in a window overlooking the porch. She wondered whether Pauline had been ordered to remain in the house should she appear at their door.

"Any girl in our social set wouldn't have had any trouble with Glenn."

While she did not think of herself as a violent person, for the second time in less than twenty-four hours, Cynthia was tempted to hit someone.

"Are you saying that my background is why Glenn thought he could take liberties with me?"

Mrs. Mayhew let out a sigh and shook her head. "You know, I've tried to understand what my daughter sees in you. Really, I have. The fact that you even have to ask that question just goes to show that you will never quite be one of us. Pauline should never have encouraged you to believe otherwise." And there it was. She was never going to be one of them. A sense of calm washed over her. Mrs. Mayhew spoke again. "This is for the best, really. Glenn got whatever he thought that you were out of his system and can now turn his attention back to where it belongs."

The smug smile tugging at her lips made her feelings clear. Of course she was happy to see Cynthia sent away in disgrace. With a flash of clarity, she felt sorry for Pauline. She only hoped that she would be able to stand up to her mother and follow her own heart when it came to choosing a husband. She bent down and grasped the handles of her suitcases once more.

"I couldn't agree more. I expect that Glenn will end up with just the sort of woman he deserves. I hope that you realize Pauline is far too good for him."

She turned and began descending the stairs once more. She half expected Mrs. Mayhew to call after her, not content to not get in the last word, but was relieved when she did not. The million-dollar view of the lake from the pine needle–strewn lawn suddenly seemed like it would never be worth it. Her suitcases felt even lighter than they had before as she strode down the driveway towards the road, the sound of the gravel crunching beneath her feet as if clapping for her.

CHAPTER 54

Cynthia

PERSPIRATION ROLLED DOWN THE BACK of Cynthia's neck as the hot sun beat down on her head and shoulders. Even the cooling breeze coming off the lake did little to give her ease. Up ahead, a cloud of dust rose up, and in a moment's time a familiar car pulled into view. An even more familiar figure sat behind the wheel.

"Cynthia, I've been looking for you everywhere," Pauline called through the rolled-down window. "Glenn's mother called this morning with a crazy story about you that sent mine into fits. Are you all right?"

Cynthia shook her head. "Not really."

Pauline leaned across the long bench seat and pushed open the passenger door. "Hop in and tell me what really happened."

Cynthia loaded her suitcases into the back seat before sliding in next to her friend.

"Are you sure that you want to hear my version of events?

I don't want to cause you any trouble with your mother or your gang."

Pauline tipped her head to one side and laid a hand on her shoulder. "I doubt that you were the one causing trouble. Tell me what happened."

"Glenn isn't the person you think he is. At the party, he got me to go out in a boat with him, He seemed to think that meant he could do whatever he wanted since there weren't any witnesses."

Pauline's hand flew to the base of her throat. "Did he hurt you?" she asked.

Tears welled up in Cynthia's eyes. Her friend believed her even if Mrs. Mayhew and Miss Arden didn't.

"I'm a bit bruised from where he pushed me down, but I hit him with a bottle that was rolling around in the bottom of the boat before he could assault me the way he intended to." She restlessly tugged at the wrists of her gloves as the memory of Glenn's sudden, unwanted weight upon her body sent her stomach churning.

"I feel like this is all my fault. I thought that if I didn't show up at the party until late, you and Glenn would have a chance to get to know each other better. I had no idea he would try something like that."

"You couldn't have known. I hope you won't allow yourself to be alone with him, though."

"Not a chance."

"You might want to let your mother know that you aren't interested. She as good as told me that now that I am out of the running, there's nothing keeping you from securing Glenn's attentions."

Pauline leaned back against the leather seat and shook her head.

"Thanks for the warning. As sorry as I am about what happened, I am glad it wasn't worse."

Cynthia shifted in her seat. "I'm sorry to say, there is something worse. I've lost my job because of it."

Pauline let out a small cry. "Why would you lose your job?"

"Someone telephoned Miss Arden and told her that I was a girl of questionable character. She told the housekeeper to fire me, but I quit to save her the trouble."

"But that's not fair," Pauline said. She sounded as outraged as Cynthia felt.

"Not in the least, but there isn't anything I can do about it."

"What are you going to do now?"

"Head home, I suppose." Cynthia peered out the window at the glittering lake and remembered how hopeful she had been when she had first caught sight of it. How could all her efforts at school and over the weeks in Mount Vernon have come to so little?

"Do you really have to go? Can't you find another job in Mount Vernon?" Pauline asked.

"You know no one will hire me here now. Whoever called

Miss Arden made sure of that. If you wouldn't mind, I could use a lift to the train station."

Her stomach squeezed at the thought of leaving Iris in the lurch. Would she lose her job because she didn't have enough help? And what about Mrs. Putnam? It couldn't be helped, though, could it? After all, Mrs. Putnam had enough sketches that surely she could finish the work without needing a live model. The security of Iris's job was far more at risk than the completion of the painting was. Besides, as important as her career was to Mrs. Putnam, it could not be compared with Iris's day-to-day need for a steady income. No, she had done the right thing in leaving, and she would just have to live with it, whatever that meant.

"Does this mean you've given up the idea of returning to school in the fall?"

Pauline's tone was so incredulous that it was as if her voice had reached out and given her a vigorous shake. Did a false accusation mean that she had to give up her dreams? A swell of determination rose in her breast. She turned in her seat to face her.

"No. It just means that things have to be altered. In fact, I've changed my mind about the train station. Would you drop me off at the library instead?"

CHAPTER 55

Geraldine

CALVIN MERCIFULLY ASKED NO QUESTIONS as they hurtled down the road. He glanced at her through the rearview mirror from time to time but, for the most part, kept any comments he might have had to himself. And she couldn't have blamed him for having any. He had appeared promptly when called, his uniform neatly pressed and his hair slicked back. He held the door for her and handed her into the sumptuous interior without so much as a raised eyebrow. But the boy would've had to have been a fool not to notice her barely contained fury.

"Need I tell you how to get there?" she asked.

"No, Mrs. Putnam. Miss Arden expects us to have an excellent working knowledge of all the addresses in the area. Yours is no exception," he said.

Geraldine leaned back against the tufted leather seat and closed her eyes in order to stop seeing red. It had been bad enough that Louise and her ill-mannered brood had descended upon her home without an invitation. But for her to have deprived her of Cynthia just as she had hit her stride with the painting was unforgivable. She could feel her heart hammering in her chest so loudly that it was a wonder Calvin didn't pull the car to the side of the road and lift the hood, wondering what the noise was about.

She could just hear her mother reminding her of how she had always been unreasonable. It wasn't the done thing to get so worked up about a mere servant—and a temporary one, at that. Still, she had made a life out of doing as she saw fit, and she had no inclination to stop now that she had finally gotten old enough for it to be one of the most useful weapons left in her arsenal. After all, her beauty had faded, and her stamina was not what it had once been. But the tolerance most people showed towards eccentric old ladies was still available to her. In fact, for an artist such as herself, it was almost expected. So, unreasonable she would be.

Calvin turned into the circular drive and pulled to a stop at the curve closest to the wide porch. He made to open his door, but she stopped him.

"You wait right here and don't move a muscle. I wouldn't want you to have to see what is about to transpire," she said.

The door swung open with ease, and as she felt the gravel crunch beneath her paint-spattered loafers, her fury returned with even greater force. Feeling Calvin's gaze on her back as she mounted the steps, she squared her shoulders and reached for the front door handle. She stepped inside and sniffed. Unfamiliar cooking smells filled the air, and Geraldine felt all the angrier at the invasion of her space. It felt as though they had completely taken over. Her vigilant housemaid appeared almost at once, her small ears ever trained for the sounds of arrival.

"Mrs. Putnam, we weren't expecting you home so soon," she said, not able to disguise a look of relief. "Shall I prepare you something to eat?"

"No, my dear. But what you can do for me is to tell me where to find Louise," she said, trying to keep the frightening tone from her voice. The girl was quite a proper servant, but one who was inclined to be skittish. She had no appetite for training someone new should the poor girl decide to leave her post.

Her eyes widened, but she bobbed her head and turned on her heel. Geraldine followed her down the hallway until she stopped in front of the breakfast room. She gestured with her hand, and Geraldine stepped through the door to discover Louise seated in Geraldine's own chair at the head of the table, holding aloft a slice of toast slathered in some of Mrs. Burns's famous blueberry preserves. And to think she had been on slim rations this whole time while Louise had made herself free with the pantry. Louise lowered the toast and dabbed at the corners of her mouth with a linen napkin.

"Well, this is a surprise," Louise said, without bothering to get up.

"It's a surprise that I should come to my own home?" Geraldine asked. "Had you received word of my demise?"

Louise let out of nervous twitter. "Of course not, Auntie Geraldine. It's just you were so adamant about your intention on remaining at the Maine Chance until we had departed that I did not expect to see you."

"Nor would you have done so had you not made my presence necessary."

"I can't imagine what I might have done to cause you to return," Louise said, her brow lowering unattractively into a scowl.

"Can you not? You didn't think that telephoning Miss Arden and demanding that she dismiss one of her employees would provoke a response?" Geraldine pulled up the chair at the opposite end of the table and reached for the bell. The maid arrived so swiftly she must have been hovering in the hallway just outside. "Please bring me a cup and another pot of coffee."

"I cannot see how that has anything to do with you," Louise said.

"It's my business because I requested that Cynthia be exclusively dedicated to attending me for the duration of my stay. If I have no complaints about her, I cannot imagine why you have any to voice."

The maid hustled in with a pot of coffee and a china cup on a silver tray. She busied herself pouring out the steaming liquid and placing it close to Geraldine's right hand. Louise waited until the maid left before replying. For all her faults, she at least had the good sense not to argue with Geraldine in front of the staff.

"I had no idea that you had any connection with the girl. I just thought that Elizabeth would appreciate hearing that she had a thief on staff before any rumors started to swirl."

"I expect I would have noticed something missing from my rooms if Cynthia were inclined to be light-fingered," Geraldine said. "I already had one maid dismissed for theft since I arrived there, and I didn't need to involve Elizabeth to do it."

"But that's where you're wrong." Louise allowed one of her condescending smiles to flit across her face as she reached for another slice of toast from the silver rack. "The theft did not occur at the Maine Chance."

"Louise, you have entirely lost me. Where is Cynthia supposed to have been taking things from if not rooms at the Maine Chance?"

"Why, here, of course," Louise said, spooning out another great mound of Mrs. Burns's blueberry preserves.

"What led you to believe that Cynthia was ever here?" Geraldine asked.

Louise had the good grace to give a slight cough of discomfort as if one of the toast crumbs had gone down the wrong pipe. Surely something was afoot.

"Your home is so lovely, and it clearly is such a waste not to make use of it for entertaining. A party seemed like such a good idea," she said. "We were sure you wouldn't mind in the least."

"You hosted a party in my home without asking me?"

"Actually, it was Glenn. He has quite a number of friends here at the lake, and he wanted to get together with them. Considering how lavishly you and my uncle always entertained, we were certain you wouldn't mind."

"You allowed your child to throw a party in my home? Without consulting me? Were you at least here?"

"That wouldn't have done at all. Children these days don't like the old folks to hang around when they're spending time with their friends. No, we went up the coast while the kids were having fun here."

"How does any of this have to do with Cynthia?" Geraldine asked.

"She was at the party. Didn't you know?" Louise gave her another condescending smile. "She tried to steal from me when she thought no one was looking."

"According to whom?"

"My son. If you don't believe me, you can ask him yourself," Louise said. She reached for the bell on her end of the table and rang for the maid once more, ordering the girl to bring him to the table.

Geraldine sat staring at Louise while they waited for the boy to arrive. His mother glanced up and called past Geraldine's shoulder to the young man as he crossed the threshold. He came alongside the table dressed in sportswear and looking as though he had not yet run a comb through his hair.

"There you are, Glenn. I was just telling Aunt Geraldine about the attempted theft last night," Louise said.

"I don't think there is any need to make such a fuss about it, Mother," he said. As he stepped closer to the table, he ran his fingers through his hair to smooth it from his eyes, and Geraldine spotted a bruise darkening one of his eyes and his cheekbone.

"Not make a fuss? The girl assaulted you," Louise said. She pointed at her son and then stared at Geraldine, two spots of high color appearing on her cheeks. "The girl was helping herself to the large amount of cash I had withdrawn from the bank for our visit here, when Glenn caught her in the act."

"I suppose he claims that is what explains his injuries," Geraldine said.

"Tell her, son," Louise said.

Glenn turned towards Geraldine and cleared his throat. "I didn't know Cynthia very well, but as she was a friend of Pauline Mayhew's, I felt compelled to invite her to the party even though she wasn't really one of our sort, if you know what I mean." He glanced at his mother, who nodded encouragingly.

"Go on," Geraldine said.

"I saw Cynthia arrive but quickly forgot about her. That is, until a few minutes later, when I went to the second floor to grab a sweater. You know how chilly it can be after the sun goes down." He turned to Louise, who bobbed her head in agreement.

"It was a good thing too. The girl was in our bedroom rooting round in my train case," Louise said.

Geraldine bristled at Louise's proprietary attitude towards any part of her home, but she ignored the presumption. She had more important things to discuss than that.

"Where do you keep this train case after you settle yourself in for an extended stay?" Geraldine asked.

"I always tuck it out of sight in the back of the closet behind all of our suits and gowns for safekeeping." A crinkle formed between Louise's heavily plucked eyebrows.

"Why would you need to keep an empty suitcase safe?" Geraldine asked.

"That's where Mother keeps the bulk of her money," Glenn said.

"That's right. I move only as much as I think I'll need on a given day into my wallet and leave the rest in the closet. You obviously can't be too careful." Louise let out an exaggerated sigh.

"As soon as she noticed me, Cynthia slipped something into her pocket and slammed the lid of the case shut. When I tried to stop her, she grabbed one of the perfume bottles from the top of the dressing table and hit me across the face with it."

"And she escaped with some of the cash, I suppose?" Geraldine said.

"I'm afraid that she did. I'm embarrassed to say that I was stunned long enough for her to run off before I could catch her," he said.

"How much are you missing?" Geraldine asked, turning her gaze on Anselm's niece.

Louise lifted an elegant hand and placed it at the base of her throat. "Three hundred dollars. I shall telephone the police as soon as I've finished with breakfast."

"Have you ever invited Cynthia to my home before?" Geraldine asked.

"No, never," Glenn said.

"Then it seems to me very strange that, according to your own words, in only a few minutes' time she was able to happen upon the one place in the entire building where a quantity of cash had been hidden away."

"What are you suggesting?" Louise asked.

"I'm suggesting that if your well-hidden money is missing, it seems far more likely that your son, who admits freely that he knew that you had it and where you kept it, is to blame for its absence than a stranger to the house, especially given how little time he reports Cynthia was on her own before he caught her. If you want the police to investigate, I would advise that they begin by having your son turn out his pockets."

Geraldine noted a flush of color flooding Glenn's cheeks.

"Preposterous. If she wasn't doing anything wrong, why would the girl assault my son?" Louise said. "Glenn was seriously injured. Which is why I had to telephone Elizabeth and report her."

"Glenn, are you sure that you wish to stick with the story about how you received your injury?" Geraldine said, turning towards him once more.

The blush on his cheeks spread all the way to his blackened eye. "I'm sure I don't know what you mean," he said, darting a glance at his mother.

"I happen to know there is a completely different reason for your injuries, and they are no more than you deserve," Geraldine said.

"What on earth are you talking about?" Louise asked. "I've been telling my husband how concerned I am about your faculties, but now I'm convinced."

"Cynthia was here last night; of that, I am certain. But she wasn't helping herself to your money. And as to hitting your son with something, it was in order to fend off his violent, unwanted advances."

Louise let out another nervous laugh. "You must be joking. Is that what the girl has been telling you?"

"I haven't spoken with Cynthia since last night, when I found her running down thc road, dripping wet without any shoes on. I learned of the attack on her person but not the name of the boy who had done it. Imagine my shame in finding out it was a member of my husband's own family."

Louise shoved back her chair and shot to her feet. "Do you mean to say you would take some girl employed as a maid at her word before that of your own family? What proof do you have of any of this?" The color in her own cheeks had grown bright, and her voice had raised an octave.

"I'm not implying anything. I am flat-out stating that your son is a liar. He not only held a party in my home without asking my permission, nor even under your supervision, but he also tried to force himself on a young woman he had lured here. His character is blighted, and I cannot stand the sight of him."

"How dare you say something like that. I should have you evaluated for competency," Louise said.

Geraldine pushed back her own chair and pulled herself up to her full height.

"I have put up with the lot of you sizing up my possessions and tallying their value in your greedy little minds, just waiting for me to shuffle off. I can tell you, I've had more than enough of it. I have only tolerated your presence out of respect for my husband, but he would have no tolerance for this sort of behavior if he were alive to see it. I want all of you out of here this instant, and I don't expect you to return. If you do not remove yourself immediately, I shall call the police myself."

"We haven't had time to make any arrangements for departure," Louise said.

"You have just about as much time to prepare to depart as I had to prepare for your arrival. I'll telephone for a taxi and have it waiting to take you to the train station. I expect you to be out of here within fifteen minutes."

She waited impatiently, glancing repeatedly at her Cartier

wristwatch, until Louise and her odious family had removed themselves from her home. As they backed out of the driveway in a huff, she joined Calvin in the driveway.

"Let's go get our girl," she said.

CHAPTER 56

Cynthia

THE SUN BEAT DOWN ON the bench. It should have warmed her, but Cynthia could not seem to feel anything but cold. The sound of an approaching train made her reach for her luggage. She glanced at her wristwatch. It had to be the one that would take her south. A shadow fell across her, and she looked up. Calvin stood there in his chauffeur's uniform, his cap tucked under his arm. Over his shoulder, she spotted Glenn and his family, quarreling and tugging suitcases along the platform. Even from a distance, she could see an ugly bruise clouding the side of Glenn's face.

"What are you doing here?" Calvin asked as she got to her feet.

"Catching a train," Cynthia said. "I believe that's mine now." She gestured towards the locomotive slowly pulling into the station.

"You're not leaving, are you?" Calvin asked.

"I can't stay."

"There isn't anything—or anyone—to keep you here?" he asked, stepping closer and reaching for her hand.

Her throat tightened. There were so many reasons she wished to remain, including the one standing before her. "I'm only leaving because I lost my job." She squeezed his hand, feeling the warmth of his through her cotton glove.

"I think you'll find that Mrs. Putnam has taken care of all of that," Calvin said. "In fact, she sent me here to fetch you."

Cynthia's eyes widened. Could it be true? Was it possible that she needn't board the train?

"You know how forceful she is. Mrs. Putnam won't take too kindly to you leaving before she's done with you. She's right over there." Calvin gestured to one of the Maine Chance's cars, the same Cadillac limousine he'd been driving when he stopped to pick her up on the day she interviewed for the job.

Mrs. Putnam rolled down the window and waved Cynthia over. She descended the platform, Calvin following closely, carrying her suitcases.

"What do you think you're doing, running off before I've finished my painting? Or my stay at the Maine Chance, for that matter?" she said.

"It wasn't my intention to leave you in the lurch."

"Well, you've managed to nonetheless. Get in." She patted the seat beside her.

Calvin stowed her suitcases in the trunk while she slid in

next to Mrs. Putnam. She collapsed against the warm leather seat. Mrs. Putnam stuck her hand into her purse and extracted a billfold. She withdrew a five-dollar bill and waggled it at Calvin over the driver's seat.

"Be a dear boy and fetch me a bag of potato chips and some bottles of cola. You can stash them in the apple shed for me when we get back." He touched his chauffeur's cap as he reached for the money. "And don't feel you should hurry. I wish to speak to Cynthia on my own."

"Thank you," Cynthia said as Calvin closed the door and moved away from the car.

"This is the sort of thing best handled by women. Now, I've spoken to Iris and also to Elizabeth. Your job is not in any jeopardy."

"You spoke to Elizabeth Arden about me?" Cynthia's heart pounded, and her palms grew damp. Iris had always made her sound so formidable. Surely it couldn't be a good thing to come to her attention.

"Of course I did. How else was I to have you reinstated?"

"What about Iris? She mustn't lose her job because of me."

Geraldine snorted. "If either of you had lost your job, it would be because of my husband's fool of a niece and her wretched son. I gave them both an earful and sent the lot of them packing as soon as Iris told me what happened."

"Glenn is related to you?" Cynthia couldn't quite believe her ears.

"Not by blood, thank heavens. After the stunt he and his mother pulled, they might as well not be related to me by marriage either. Anselm left his entire estate to me, and they've just given me more than enough reason to make sure they don't get their hands on any of it."

Geraldine smiled and drummed her fingers on the car seat between them.

"So, Iris won't get in any trouble over this, even if she gives me my job back?"

"Once I explained to Elizabeth what had actually happened, she was more than happy to forget the whole incident. She is a strong, independent woman herself, and when she heard about your quick thinking and decisive action with the gin bottle, she enthusiastically took your side in the matter. In fact, she praised Iris for hiring someone like you in the first place. Iris's position is no more at risk than yours."

"I don't know how to thank you," Cynthia said. It was suddenly hard to swallow. Having women like Iris, Geraldine, and even Miss Arden believe and support her brought tears to her eyes.

"You'll thank me by staying for the rest of the season. I need a maid I can count on, and I still have several paintings left to complete if I am to have enough for the show in November. I expect you'd best tell Calvin that you aren't about to leave."

Cynthia reached across the seat and gave Mrs. Putnam's

hand a squeeze before pushing open the door. Her heart lifted as the gap between her and Calvin closed. He shifted the paper grocery sack to his hip and freed up one hand as he stopped in front of her.

"Does the smile on your face mean you've worked things out with Mrs. Putnam?" he asked.

"It does. It looks like my job is secure for the rest of the season, at least. I'm not going anywhere."

"That's good. If you had headed home, she would have sent me down after you. She was cursing a blue streak in the car on the way to her house. She was adamant that you were needed here."

"Is Mrs. Putnam the only one who wants me to stay?" Cynthia asked.

"No, she isn't. There are several of us who cannot do without you. At least, not until you head back to Barlow in the fall."

"I won't be going back to Barlow."

He tipped his head slightly to the side. "But Mrs. Putnam has arranged it so that you will be able to earn the rest of your tuition money."

"I'll still need the money. I've just decided to transfer to the University of Maine."

"Are you sure about that?" His eyes crinkled.

"I'm sure. It turns out that Barlow is not my sort of place after all. Besides, I checked into it at the library, and the cost of tuition and room and board at U Maine is affordable enough that I can almost cover the costs with what I've already earned this summer."

"Isn't U Maine all the way up in Orono?" he asked.

She stepped forward and reached for his warm, broad hand. "All the way up there. It's a good thing that a certain young man I like will soon have his own plane so that he can easily visit me."

CHAPTER 57

Cynthia

Seven springs later

SHE PULLED THE CAR TO a stop in front of the hangar and reached across the leather seat for a large brown envelope. As she pressed the car door shut behind her, Calvin appeared in the open hangar doorway, a small girl balanced on his hip. Several planes filled the large building, just as Calvin had predicted they would. Cynthia closed the distance between them and exchanged the envelope for the child.

"How was your visit? Did it put your mind at ease?" he asked.

"Indeed, it did. It felt good to be in the same room with them both."

At the end of Cynthia's first summer at the Maine Chance, Miss Arden had been so impressed by Iris's performance that she had offered her the year-round housekeeper position. Despite a dedicated exchange of letters between them throughout the year, every spring, she, Geraldine, and Iris got together at the earliest opportunity after Iris had returned from Arizona. It had been more important that spring than ever.

Orla had passed away just after the turn of the new year, and Iris had taken it hard. Geraldine had been concerned enough about her that a week or two after the funeral, she flew out to Arizona to get her eyes on Iris. She ended up staying most of the rest of the winter, enjoying the climate, the change of scenery, and the creative spark that travel brought about. In fact, Marjorie Billings, who despite her husband's objections had eagerly agreed to represent Geraldine after her agent retired, had booked a new show in July to exhibit the flurry of paintings her trip had inspired. But her news of her friends was not the only thing she wished to share.

"Look at what I picked up at the post office on my way to lunch," she said. "Page three."

Calvin lifted the flap on the envelope and slid out the latest issue of the *American Economics Review.* She tried to interpret his expression as he read through the article. Their daughter squirmed to be put down before he reached the end. Cynthia bent and patted her small shoulder before she darted off in the direction of a robin pecking at a patch of fresh green grass pressed up against the white clapboards of the hangar.

He snapped the magazine open, the smile she loved so much spreading across his face.

"How does it feel to be interviewed in such an esteemed publication about your career?" he asked.

"It feels even better than seeing my byline in the magazine for the articles I've written."

"What did Iris and Geraldine have to say?"

"Iris was, of course, thrilled that I mentioned getting my start at the Maine Chance. Geraldine, for obvious reasons, was delighted by the paragraph referencing U Maine."

Calvin read aloud. "*After being assured by a respected professor at Barlow College that women were a poor investment, Cynthia Proctor Willard, newly appointed economist for the Maine Commission on Tourism and Transportation, transferred to the University of Maine at Orono to complete her degree. This reporter wonders if her choice to transfer explains the generous, anonymous donation the university received to fund an endowment to support women pursuing a degree in economics.*"

"Speaking of Professor Avery, I contacted the magazine and asked that they send him a copy. I wanted to be sure that he had one."

"Did you send it anonymously?" Calvin asked, wrapping an arm across her shoulders.

"I had them add a card."

"What did it say?" Calvin asked.

"*Thanks for giving me the push I needed.*

Sincerely,

A Clever Girl."

AUTHOR'S NOTE

While this novel is a work of fiction, the setting is based in reality. In 1934, Elizabeth Arden opened the Maine Chance, the first destination spa in America. Her choice of location appealed to world-weary city dwellers looking to retreat to bucolic Maine. The lavish estate, with its sumptuous accommodations, exceptional staff, and exquisite landscaping, attracted wealthy guests from Hollywood starlets Ava Gardner and Rita Hayworth to First Ladies Eleanor Roosevelt and Mamie Eisenhower. Renowned writer Edna Ferber spent time at the resort just after this story takes place, in September of 1954.

The novel also took inspiration from treatments and events available on the property. The Arden Bath featuring pounds of melted wax was a real treatment touted by spa technicians as a balm for frazzled nerves as well as a remedy for excess body weight. A pre-preseason fashion show was held in the resort bowling alley to allow guests the earliest possible peek at

Elizabeth Arden's fashion line. The staff house where Cynthia, Iris, and Dolores lived was also a real part of the property, although it burned down in the summer of 1955. The estate contained orchards, a private beach, a fleet of chauffeur-driven cars available to guests, and separate kitchens to feed staff and guests. The property was opened to visiting garden clubs on occasion, as Elizabeth Arden enjoyed sharing her love of horticulture with other enthusiasts.

Not only was the Maine Chance Farm home to ornamental gardens, but it also provided the majority of the produce consumed by the guests as well as the staff. The portions were minuscule, a fact disguised by artful presentation. Although it was not advertised, the retreat did offer assistance for women seeking help with excess drinking by dint of its no-alcohol policy. The Maine Turnpike project, the *American Economics Review*, and the proliferation of small, local airfields were all pulled into the story from reality, as was the availability of business loans for GIs who served in Korea. The resort did provide two weeks at the beginning of the season for college girls and young working women to learn deportment, social skills, and makeup application at a rate far lower than the society matrons paid during the rest of the season. A clever sort herself, Elizabeth Arden used those weeks to train her staff and iron out any wrinkles before the important guests arrived.

Some parts of the novel, however, sprang mostly from my imagination. While Maine is home to several prestigious private colleges, Barlow is not among them. Elizabeth Arden opened a second Maine Chance in Arizona, but to my knowledge, there was never a housekeeper who oversaw them both. The imagined path from the resort to the part of Long Pond where I have placed the Mayhews' property as well as Geraldine's is not on any map. I also took liberties with the location of the train station and created the entirely fictional Maine Commission on Tourism and Transportation.

And while the resort did indeed have a staff ratio of two for every guest, none were the basis for characters populating these pages, although I would like to think that such a beautiful place would have provided the perfect setting for young people like Cynthia and Calvin to meet and fall in love.

READING GROUP GUIDE

1. How is Cynthia treated in the field of economics because of her gender? How might women in that field still face difficulties today, and where have we improved?
2. When Cynthia loses her scholarship, she faces the discontinuation of her education. How does the cost of higher education impact prospective students today? Are there ways we could make it easier for more students to go to college?
3. Is the Maine Chance a resort you would wish to spend time at? Why or why not?
4. Geraldine, an artist, no longer feels the same love for the art she once created and craves new inspiration. Have you ever found yourself in a similar situation where what you used to love has grown a bit stale? How did you work through that?
5. What do you look for in a potential life partner? What is important to you? Looks? Shared interests?

6. Iris finds herself in the tough position of firing the maid who stole from Geraldine. Have you ever needed to be the person giving the bad news? How did you deal with it?
7. Cynthia finds the work at the Maine Chance more difficult than she imagined but thinks it's worth it for the chance to stay in school. What would you be willing to do or put up with to get what you wanted?
8. Are there differences between those who serve and those who are served? If so, what are they? If not, why not?
9. How does Cynthia react to her sexual assault? How does everyone else react? Is Cynthia "lucky," since Glenn didn't achieve his goal?
10. Are sexually promiscuous men treated differently from sexually promiscuous women? How so?
11. In the end, is the path Cynthia follows what she'd envisioned for herself at the beginning of the novel? How did she adapt to changes in her life plan? Have you ever had your set-in-stone plans or goals change? Was it for the better?

A CONVERSATION WITH THE AUTHOR

Where did the inspiration for this book come from?

I came across an article in a newspaper archive about the Maine Chance Farm and Elizabeth Arden's connection to it. I adore research, and that first article sent me on a fun and fruitful hunt through back issues of newspapers, historical society websites, and even a series of audio interviews with former employees of the resort. Before long, several characters for a novel set there sprang to mind, and the idea for the story was off and running.

What was it like to write from three different perspectives? What did you have to keep in mind for each perspective?

I love to write from multiple perspectives. For me, it is great fun to hop from person to person and share things with the readers that other characters might not know. Because each of the characters has a distinct voice inside my head, it is easy to keep them straight. All of them sound different, and while I am writing, it seems as if they are speaking right in front of me.

Did you enjoy writing in this particular time period? What did you find were the major differences between life then and life now?

I love writing about times when major societal disruptions have just taken place and the world is figuring out what the new normal will be. The 1950s fit in with that preference perfectly. After WWII, nothing was ever quite the same again, especially for women. It gave me the opportunity to explore how the return of men impacted women like Cynthia and her opportunities for the future. Writing in that period also allowed me to think in new ways about the life my maternal grandmother would have been living in 1954 Maine as a woman almost exactly Cynthia's age. So much has changed in terms of formality of dress, rigidity of societal rules, and overt sexism. That said, women are still facing sexual assault, pressure to prioritize our physical appearance, workplace discrimination, and the majority of the decisions about caretaking of elderly family members.

Do you have a favorite character?

Geraldine is my favorite. Except for the fact that she loses her husband, I want to be her when I grow up!

What would you like readers to take away from your story?

I hope that readers will feel the transformational power of friendships between women and that they will be uplifted by it. And I hope they will feel inspired to reach out to a friend of their own for a chat, a lunch date, or even a disastrous visit to a nightclub!

ACKNOWLEDGMENTS

This novel would not have been possible without the generous help of several people. Firstly, I want to thank my agents, Meg Ruley and Christina Hogrebe, for their enthusiasm for this story from the very beginning. Without their support and encouragement, I am not sure it would have come into being. I especially could not have finished this novel without the gentle, requested nagging by author assistant extraordinaire, Jen McKee.

Betsy Baker commiserated with me when things moved slowly and showed much appreciated interest in all the drafts of the story. Julia Spencer Fleming provided a sounding board for ideas as well as delightful company on writing retreats throughout the process. Tatjana Kruse checked in weekly and knew just what to say no matter the circumstances. Kathy Chatt steadfastly encouraged me during our visits. My very own Diamond Dogs, Randi Johnson and Michelle Beaver, patiently and kindly asked all the right questions at all the right times. I am also so grateful for the Calling Hours ladies who cheered me on along the way and helped me to celebrate the wins both big and small.

Kik, one of the greatest influences on my life, served as the inspiration for Geraldine, at least as far as her virtues but never her vices. Creative, witty, and wise, she has opened my eyes to so many things and has profoundly shaped the person I've become. She's also outrageous fun.

Additionally, I want to thank my family for all the ways they have supported me while I was writing this novel and throughout my entire career. My sister, Larissa, seemed to know just when to ask about my progress and when not to. My sons cheered at all stages of the journey. My beloved dog, Sam, patiently kept me company as I wrote every single word and considerately nudged me for walks whenever I had been at the desk far too long. And last, I wish to thank my husband, Elias, who has always wholeheartedly championed my goals and dreams and provides the inspiration for all my heroes, including Calvin.

ABOUT THE AUTHOR

Jessica Everett loves research, throwing parties, and walking barefoot along her favorite New England beach, especially in winter. She obsessively knits wool socks and enthusiastically speaks Portuguese with a shocking disregard for the rules of grammar. Jessica splits her time between New Hampshire and Maine, where her family has lived since the 1600s.